Hot Blood

Also by Stephen Leather

Pay Off

The Fireman

Hungry Ghost

The Chinaman

The Vets

The Long Shot

The Birthday Girl

The Double Tap

The Solitary Man

The Tunnel Rats

The Bombmaker

The Stretch

Tango One

The Eyewitness

Hard Landing

Soft Target

Cold Kill

STEPHEN LEATHER

Hot Blood

HODDER &
STOUGHTON

Copyright © 2007 by Stephen Leather

First published in Great Britain in 2007 by Hodder & Stoughton
A division of Hodder Headline

A Hodder & Stoughton Book

1

A CIP catalogue record for this title is available from the British Library

Hardback ISBN 978 0 340 92167 8
Hardback ISBN 0 340 92167 6
Trade Paperback ISBN 978 0 340 92168 5
Trade Paperback ISBN 0 340 92168 4

Typeset in Plantin by Hewer Text UK Ltd, Edinburgh
Printed and bound by Mackays of Chatham Ltd, Chatham, Kent

Hodder Headline's policy is to use papers that are natural, renewable
and recyclable products and made from wood grown in sustainable forests.
The logging and manufacturing processes are expected to conform
to the environmental regulations of the country of origin.

Hodder & Stoughton Ltd
A division of Hodder Headline
338 Euston Road
London NW1 3BH

For Katy

ACKNOWLEDGEMENTS

I am indebted to James (Jesse) Kibbee, Jr, for his insights into life in Baghdad, and for allowing me access to his journal which he wrote while he was working in Iraq. Linda Park and John Deykin were generous with their time showing me around Dubai. Alistair Cumming and David Southern helped me on police matters and on the mechanics of electronic tracking. Any errors of fact are mine and not theirs.

Denis O'Donoghue, Barbara Schmeling, Andrew Yates, Alex Bonham and Hazel Orme helped me get the manuscript into shape and Carolyn Mays was, as always, the best editor that a writer could wish for.

Johnny Lake pulled his legs up against his chest and slowly banged the back of his head against the wall. It was the fourteenth day, and on the fourteenth day they had said he would die. There were six men holding him hostage, but he only knew one of them by name. Kamil. Kamil was the leader of the group. His name meant 'perfect'. He was the one who spoke to the video camera, in accented English. It was Kamil who waved a Kalashnikov and said that the Americans must leave Iraq and that if they didn't Johnny would be killed. When he was in front of the camera, Kamil wore black-leather gloves and a black-wool ski mask with holes for his eyes and mouth. His companions wore masks, too, or had scarves tied round their faces. They said nothing whenever the camera was on, other than to chant '*Allahu Akbar.*' God is great.

His captors weren't aware that he knew what they planned to do with him. Johnny hadn't let on that he spoke Arabic. He had studied the language for two years in Chicago and had spent a year in Dubai, then six months in Kuwait City before moving to Baghdad. He was fluent and could read and write the language, but from the moment he'd been forced into the back of a van at gunpoint he hadn't said a word of Arabic. At first he figured that being able to eavesdrop on their conversations would give him an edge, but all it had done was to fill him with despair. Fourteen days was the deadline they'd set. Two weeks. Three hundred and thirty-six hours.

Johnny knew that there was no chance of Kamil's demands being met. The coalition forces would stay in Iraq until the Iraqis were capable of governing themselves, and that day was a long way off. Kamil wasn't stupid, and he'd know that, too. The posturing in front of the camera was for effect, nothing more. It was part of a process – a process that would lead to just one thing: Johnny's death.

Johnny shivered. He wanted to bang on the door and beg Kamil for his life, but he had begged for the first two days and he knew there was nothing he could say that would change what was going to happen. Johnny had pleaded with Kamil. He'd told him that the stories he filed were always sympathetic to the people of Iraq and that the last two he'd written before his abduction had been about local politicians calling for the early withdrawal of the American troops and their replacement with United Nations peacekeepers.

Kamil had smiled sympathetically and had assured Johnny that nothing would happen to him and that in due course he'd be released. That was what he had said the first time he'd met Johnny. It had been five days after the abduction, and Johnny had been held at a different location each night, always hooded and always trussed up like a chicken. Kamil had been the first person to talk to him, the first person to treat him like a human being and not a piece of meat. But everything Kamil said to him was a lie.

Johnny had heard Kamil talking to his colleagues, and he'd understood every word that Kamil had said to the video-camera. Fourteen days. If the coalition forces did not start to withdraw from Iraq by the fourteenth day, it was the will of Allah that Johnny be killed. Fourteen days. And today was the fourteenth day.

Johnny had asked for a radio and newspapers but Kamil had said that that wasn't possible. Johnny knew why. The media would report his capture, and the demands of his captors. Kamil had provided him with a paperback book, though. *The Da Vinci Code*. Johnny had always meant to read it, but had never had the time. Now he had nothing else to do in the basement, but try as he might he couldn't concentrate on it. Kamil had brought in a travel chess set and they had played several games. Johnny was a reasonable player but he lost every time. All he could think about was the deadline, the deadline that would end with his death. It was impossible to concentrate on anything else.

Johnny knew that Kamil's demands would not be met, but there was another option: money. Cold, hard cash. Johnny's father had money. A lot of money. J. J. Lake was a property developer in Chicago and Johnny was sure his father would pay whatever ransom was necessary to get him released. It was all about money, Johnny knew. What had happened in Iraq was everything to do with money and virtually nothing to do with religion. If his captors were offered enough money they would release him. J. J. Lake knew people. He'd met Oprah Winfrey, Donald Trump and politicians right across the country. He'd be calling in favours left, right and centre and pulling whatever strings needed pulling. That was the hope Johnny clung to. If anyone could save him, it was his father.

The newspapers he worked for would be doing their bit, too. So would the rest of the media. Johnny was a journalist and journalists looked after their own. They would put pressure on the government to act. Editorials would be written, questions would be asked, everything the authorities did or didn't do would be scrutinised. They'd speak to sympathetic Muslims and get them to put pressure on the fundamentalists. Kamil wasn't stupid. He'd realise there was nothing to be gained by killing Johnny. But if he released him, they'd show the world they could be merciful.

There were three loud bangs on the door. There was no handle on it, and no lock, just a peephole through which his captors could watch him. 'Stand by the wall, please, Johnny,' shouted Kamil.

Johnny got to his feet and did as he was told. Every time the door was opened, he had to stand by the far wall with his hands outstretched. Johnny knew it was so that he couldn't catch them by surprise, but he didn't know why they bothered. His captors had guns and Johnny wasn't a fighter. They knew that. He was a journalist and hadn't been in a fight since he'd left elementary school.

The visit was unexpected. It was early afternoon and he'd been fed two hours earlier. Kamil had brought him a paper plate filled with *kubbat burghul,* doughy shells of bulgar wheat wrapped round lightly spiced minced meat and onion. He'd shared the meal with Johnny and they'd talked about baseball. Kamil never discussed politics or what was happening in Iraq. Sport, movies and music were pretty much all he talked about. Small-talk. Idle chit-chat to wile away the time until they killed him.

The door opened. Kamil stood in the doorway with an orange jumpsuit. 'We need another video,' said Kamil, walking over to him. 'We need to show that you are still alive.' He held out the jumpsuit.

'Okay,' said Johnny, hesitantly. He lowered his arms but made no attempt to take the jumpsuit.

'Do not worry, Johnny,' said Kamil. 'It is a video, nothing more.'

'Has my father been in touch yet?' asked Johnny.

Kamil shrugged. 'I wouldn't know if he had,' he said. 'We don't talk to anybody.'

'But if he's trying to pay a ransom, how will they tell you?'

'We'll be told,' said Kamil. He gestured at the jumpsuit. 'Put it on, please.'

'I don't understand why I have to wear it.'

'It shows we're serious,' said Kamil, patiently. 'It's theatre, Johnny. If they see you playing chess and smiling at the camera, no one is going to think you are really in danger.' He pushed the jumpsuit gently against Johnny's chest.

'Am I?' asked Johnny, quietly. 'Am I in danger?' He took the jumpsuit. It was the third time he'd been given it to wear. It was for effect, Kamil had said. He only had to put it on when they were making a video. The rest of the time he was free to wear his own clothes, although they had taken away his belt and shoes.

Kamil smiled. A big, easy smile. 'You are a journalist. There's no value in killing a journalist.'

'Kamil, please, don't kill me.'

'Johnny, we're not going to kill you. I swear. Now put on the jumpsuit.'

Johnny knew that Kamil was lying. He'd interviewed enough politicians and journalists to know when he was being lied to. And Kamil was lying.

'Please, Kamil,' said Johnny. 'You don't have to do this.'

'It's a video,' said Kamil, avoiding Johnny's eye. 'Just a video.' He turned away and spoke to his two companions. They nodded and pulled ski masks over their faces so that only their eyes were uncovered.

Johnny felt as if all the strength had drained from his limbs. He looked at the door. The only way out. But there were three of them and it was only in the movies that one man could outfight three. He felt tears sting his eyes and blinked them away. He took deep breaths, trying to quell the panic that was threatening to overwhelm him. He wanted to cry, to scream, to beg, to do whatever it took to save his life, but he knew there was nothing he could do.

He held the shoulders of the jumpsuit and put in his right leg, then the left. He straightened and pulled the overalls up to his waist. He didn't want to die in the basement. It had been days since he'd smelled fresh air, or seen the sky, or heard birdsong. He wanted to see his parents, his brother, his friends.

He felt as if he was going to pass out and sat down on the wooden chair. Kamil appeared in front of him, holding a plastic bottle of water. 'Here,' he said.

'Thank you,' said Johnny. He unscrewed the blue plastic cap and raised the bottle to his lips. He drank slowly, wanting to extend the moment into infinity. So long as he was drinking, he was alive. He swallowed, and continued to drink.

Kamil held out his hand for the bottle. Johnny gave it to him, then wiped his mouth on the back of his hand. He wriggled his arms into the jumpsuit and pulled up the zipper.

'Good,' said Kamil. He patted Johnny's shoulder. 'Stand up, please, and move in front of the banner.'

Johnny did as he was told. He knew the significance of the jumpsuit. It was identical to those the Americans forced the detainees to wear in Guantánamo Bay. It was a statement. That the hostages in Iraq were retribution for what was going on in Cuba. He stood in front of the banner. The two men with ski masks had taken position at either side of it, arms folded across their chests.

'Hands behind your back, please, Johnny,' said Kamil.

Johnny did as he was told. They had bound his hands behind his back the last time they had videoed him, but he knew that this time was different. He swallowed and almost gagged. His mouth had dried again.

Kamil used a plastic tie to bind his wrists. It cut into his flesh but Johnny didn't protest.

Kamil helped Johnny into a kneeling position, then patted his shoulder again. He walked over to the video-camera and checked the fitting that attached it to the tripod. Then he bent down and peered through the viewfinder. The door opened and four men filed in, wearing khaki jumpsuits and ski masks. Two were carrying AK-47s. The last to walk into the room closed the door and stood with his back to it.

Kamil straightened up. He smiled and nodded at Johnny. Johnny tried to smile back but knew he looked terrified. His knees were hurting and the plastic tie bit into his wrists.

Kamil walked round the tripod, pulling a ski mask out of his pocket.

Johnny closed his eyes and took a deep breath. He began reciting the Lord's Prayer in his head, not wanting to offend the men in the room by speaking it aloud: *Our Father, who art in heaven . . .*

Johnny opened his eyes. Kamil pulled on the ski mask. He motioned for the men to gather in front of the banner.

Hallowed be thy name . . . Johnny bit down on his lower lip. Maybe they really were just making another video outlining their demands. Maybe there'd just be threats and gestures and then they'd switch off the camera, he'd take off the jumpsuit and go back to reading *The Da Vinci Code* and playing chess with Kamil. Part of him desperately wanted to believe it, but it was the fourteenth day and on the fourteenth day they'd said he would die.

Thy kingdom come, thy will be done . . .

Kamil began to speak to the camera in Arabic, waving his hand. In all the time they'd spent in the basement, he had been soft-spoken and polite, but he became a different person with the ski mask on and the camera running. His voice had a hard edge, and every now and again spittle would spray from his lips. He pointed at the banner, and at the men behind him, and then he pointed at Johnny. He screamed in Arabic that it was Bush's fault that Johnny was going to die, his voice loaded with venom and hatred.

The Lord's Prayer continued to loop through Johnny's mind, faster and faster. *Forgive us our trespasses, as we forgive those who trespass against us . . .* He focused on the words, taking refuge in the repetition, trying to blot out where he was and what was happening.

Kamil turned to face the camera and continued to rant. The men standing in front of the banner were chanting: '*Allahu Akbar.*' God is great.

Johnny began to breathe faster. He concentrated on the Lord's Prayer, using the words to blot out everything else from his mind. *Lead us not into temptation . . .*

The men moved towards Johnny. '*Allahu Akbar, Allahu Akbar, Allahu Akbar.*' They moved like zombies, their eyes wide and unseeing, their hands at their sides.

Johnny tried to get to his feet but his calves cramped and he fell on his side. He coughed as he breathed in dust from the floor. The sandals of the men walking towards him made a swishing sound as they shuffled nearer. It was all over, he knew. Tears sprang to his eyes at the unfairness of it all. He had never harmed them – he had never hurt anyone. He was just a journalist, in Iraq to report on what was happening there. Almost without exception the articles he wrote were against the American-led occupation of the country. *Our Father, who art in heaven* . . . Killing him wouldn't end the war one day sooner. Nothing would change, it made no sense at all. *Hallowed be thy name* . . .

His eyes misted. He tried to lift himself off the ground but the strength had gone from his limbs. He rolled on to his back, gasping for breath. Five pairs of uncaring eyes stared down at him. '*Allahu Akbar, Allahu Akbar, Allahu Akbar.*'

A sixth ski mask appeared. It was Kamil. There was no recognition in his eyes: he wore the blank stare of the other five men. He was muttering, too: '*Allahu Akbar.*' God is great. There was something in Kamil's hand. Something that glittered under the fluorescent lights. A knife.

Johnny tried to roll over but hands grabbed him. One of the men sat on his legs. Another pinned his left arm to the ground. A hand grabbed his hair and yanked his head back. All he could hear was the chanting of the men who were going to kill him. He tried to blank out their voices. He didn't want to die hearing their voices. Hearing them praising their God. The Lord's Prayer whirled faster and faster through his mind. *Thy kingdom come, thy will be done* . . .

The knife sliced through Johnny's throat. There was surprisingly little pain, just a burning sensation. Then he felt blood gush down his neck and heard a roar of triumph from Kamil. He couldn't feel his body, he realised. Everything had gone numb. The knife flashed in front of his eyes and he felt it hack through his windpipe and then everything went black.

The Jaguar pulled up in front of the warehouse. There were two men in the car. The driver was Ian Corben, in his mid-thirties and wearing a sheepskin jacket. He switched off the engine, took a deep breath, then exhaled slowly. 'Into the lion's den,' he muttered.

His companion was a few years older and several kilos heavier. Conor O'Sullivan had left Ireland as a teenager and had lost most of his Galway accent, but he had the black hair, blue eyes and easy charm of a young Pierce Brosnan. His movie-star features were marred only by a jagged scar under his chin. 'Relax,' he said.

'We don't know them. They might—'

'They came through for Mickey Burgess,' said O'Sullivan. 'It'll be fine. Pop the boot.' He climbed out of the Jaguar and adjusted the cuffs of his cashmere overcoat. The boot clicked open and he took out a Manchester United holdall. The two men stood looking at the metal-clad warehouse, with identical buildings, 'To Let' signs above the entrances, at either side.

'If it's a trap, we're fucked,' said Corben.

O'Sullivan smiled easily. 'It's a business transaction,' he said. 'Pure and simple.'

'Yeah, but we're walking in with a bagful of cash and no back-up.'

'They insisted. Two of us and two of them.'

'Yeah, well, we should be the ones setting the rules.'

O'Sullivan thrust the bag at Corben. 'Here, carry this. You're supposed to be the muscle.'

'Second-in-command is how I remember the job description.'

'I don't recall advertising the position,' said O'Sullivan. He glanced at his watch. 'Come on, we're late.'

They walked towards the metal doors of the warehouse's loading bay. O'Sullivan whistled softly. He didn't want to startle anyone inside. He eased himself through the gap between the doors. Corben followed.

Two men were waiting for them, in bomber jackets and jeans. The older one, a heavy-set man in his fifties, was wearing bright yellow Timberland boots; the younger, slightly taller man had on scruffy training shoes and was holding a paddle-shaped black object in his left hand. O'Sullivan knew their names – Graham May and Paul Lomas – but he didn't know which was which. He scanned his surroundings. There were no obvious hiding-places. The warehouse was empty, except for three metal tables against one wall. He relaxed a little.

Corben stood behind him, swinging the holdall. O'Sullivan flashed his companion a quick smile.

'Which one of you is O'Sullivan?' asked the man in the Timberlands. He had an abrasive Scottish accent.

O'Sullivan raised a hand. 'That would be me. Conor to my friends.'

'I'm Paul,' said the man. He nodded at his younger companion. 'He's Graham.'

'How are you doing?' said May, although from his tone it was clear that he didn't care. He gestured at the bag. 'Is that the cash?'

'No it's a Sherman tank,' sneered Corben.

'Ian, be nice,' warned O'Sullivan.

Corben held up the bag. 'It's the cash,' he said. 'Where are the guns?'

'Over there,' said May, gesturing at the tables, on which five metal suitcases were lined up.

O'Sullivan headed towards them.

'Whoa, hoss,' said Lomas. 'First things first.' He nodded at Corben. 'Drop the bag, yeah?'

'What?' said Corben, frowning.

'You heard him,' said May. 'We need to make a few checks first.' He gestured at the paddle he was holding. 'We want to make sure you're not carrying.'

O'Sullivan realised that the paddle was a metal detector, the sort used to screen passengers at airports. Lomas stood with arms folded, staring stonily at Corben.

May stepped forward and ran the metal detector down O'Sullivan's coat. It beeped. May raised an eyebrow and O'Sullivan put a hand into his pocket.

'Slowly,' warned May.

O'Sullivan's hand reappeared with a set of car keys. 'What are you looking for?' he asked.

'What do you think?' snarled Lomas.

O'Sullivan grinned and slipped his keys back into his coat. 'I think you're looking for a gun,' he said. 'But seeing I'm here to buy guns, that wouldn't make any sense, would it?'

'It wouldn't be the first time someone's tried to rip me off,' said May. He ran the detector over the back of O'Sullivan's overcoat.

'Yeah, but rip you off for what?' asked O'Sullivan. 'I've got the cash. You've got the guns. But if I already had a gun, why would I steal one from you? You see what I'm saying?'

'I see what you're saying,' said May.

'If anyone's in danger of being ripped off it's me.'

'I got it the first time. But this is the way it's going to be done, so just shut the fuck up.'

'Plus, this gizmo picks up wires,' said Lomas.

O'Sullivan pointed a finger at Lomas. 'You start calling me a grass and I'm out of here,' he said. 'I came to do business, not to be slagged off.'

'Will you two stop bickering?' said May. He stepped back. 'You're clean.'

'I know I'm clean,' said O'Sullivan. 'I didn't need you to tell me.'

May went to Corben, whose eyes hardened. 'This is a liberty,' he said.

'Let them play their little games, Ian,' said O'Sullivan.

'It's a fucking liberty,' said Corben. 'We came here to do business, didn't we? It's like you said, they've got the fucking guns and we've got the money. We're the ones taking the risk here.'

May lowered the metal detector. 'I'm starting to get a bad feeling about this,' he said.

'Yeah,' said Corben, narrowing his eyes. 'You and me both.' He looked across at O'Sullivan. 'Let's knock this on the head.'

'Ian . . .'

'I mean it. This is all shit.'

'Got something to hide, have you?' said Lomas.

'Why don't we run that thing over you two first?' said Corben. 'See what you've got to hide.'

'You're the visitors,' said Lomas.

'Fuck you,' spat Corben.

'Yeah? Well, fuck you, too.'

Corben stepped towards Lomas, his right hand bunching into a fist. Lomas shuffled backwards, fumbling inside his jacket. He pulled out an automatic and pointed it at Corben's face.

'Easy, easy!' shouted O'Sullivan.

Corben glared at Lomas, his fist pulled back. 'I knew this was a set-up.'

'You started it,' said Lomas.

'Will you both just fucking relax?' said May. 'We're not in the bloody playground here.'

'It's too late for that,' said Lomas, still staring at Corben. 'He's not right.'

'I'm not right?' spat Corben. 'You're the one who pulled a gun.'

O'Sullivan had his hands up, showing his palms. 'Can we all calm down here?' he said.

'I'm calm,' said Lomas. 'I just want to know what he's got to hide.'

'Put the gun down, Paul,' said May.

'Not until I'm sure he's kosher,' said Lomas. 'Check him. And the bag.'

'This is bullshit,' said Corben.

'Just go with the flow, Ian,' said O'Sullivan.

Corben glared at Lomas, took out his mobile phone and car keys, and slowly raised his arms. May ran the metal detector up and down his back and legs, then checked the front of his body. It made no sound.

'Satisfied?' asked Corben.

'No hard feelings?' said May.

Corben lowered his hands. 'I'll decide when there are no hard feelings,' he said.

'The bag,' said Lomas, gesturing with the gun. 'Check the bag.'

May did as he was told, and again the metal detector made no sound. Lomas put away the gun.

'I'm sorry if we got off on the wrong foot,' said May. He patted O'Sullivan on the back. 'Situation like this, it's normal for jitters.'

'The deal was that we all came unarmed,' said O'Sullivan, staring pointedly at Lomas.

'Guns in the cases, guns in a holster, they're all part of the inventory,' said May.

'He pulled a gun on us,' said O'Sullivan.

'Like I said, jitters. Come on, let me show you what we've got.'

May walked over to the tables with O'Sullivan. Lomas and Corben followed, eyeing each other warily. May opened one of the metal cases. Inside six revolvers nestled in yellow foam rubber. May picked up a short-barrelled weapon and held it out to O'Sullivan, butt first. 'Spanish-made Astra .357 Magnum. The foresight has been smoothed down to minimise snagging so it's a perfect concealed weapon.'

'No safety,' said O'Sullivan.

'It's got a long double-action pull,' said May. 'You'd have to be a right twat to fire it accidentally.'

'I prefer Smith & Wesson,' said O'Sullivan.

'Your call,' said May, taking back the Astra. He put it back in its slot in the foam rubber, and handed O'Sullivan a second revolver. 'A J Frame .38 special,' he said. 'Five rounds in the cylinder. The Astra takes six.'

'This is fine,' said O'Sullivan, flicking out the cylinder and peering down the barrel. He put the gun on the table and pointed at another. 'That's an L Frame, right? A .357 Magnum?'

'Sure is,' said May, removing the gun and giving it to him. 'Same action as the J Frame but the cylinder takes six. It's a nice gun, but I have to say I prefer the Astra.'

'How much for the two?' O'Sullivan sniffed the barrel of the Smith & Wesson L Frame.

'Nine hundred.'

'This one's been fired,' said O'Sullivan.

'Test firing, that's all. It's never been fired in anger.'

'Nine is steep.' O'Sullivan gave both of the Smith & Wessons to Corben, who broke them down quickly and efficiently.

'They're quality guns,' said May.

'Nine is still steep.'

'Take it or leave it,' said May.

O'Sullivan sighed. 'Okay. Nine it is. Rounds?'

Corben reassembled the two weapons as fast as he'd stripped them down.

'I'll throw in a box of each,' said May. 'If you need more they'll be fifty apiece.'

'Two boxes of each.'

May smiled. 'Deal,' he said. He opened a second metal case to reveal four Glock pistols. 'Automatics?'

Corben shook his head. 'They spit casings all over the place. And they jam.'

'Guns don't jam,' said May. 'Crap ammunition jams. Used properly, a Glock's as reliable as any revolver.'

'Thanks, but no thanks,' said O'Sullivan. 'We're happy with the revolvers.'

May closed the lid of the case. He opened a third. There was only one weapon inside, a compact shotgun with a pistol grip at the trigger and a second pistol grip under the front of the barrel. 'You wanted a sawn-off, but I thought you might appreciate this.'

O'Sullivan picked up the shotgun. 'Nice.'

'It's a Franchi PA3,' said May. 'The forward pistol grip helps with the pump-action. Special forces use it to blow the hinges off doors for rapid entry. It's a twelve gauge, overall length 470mm so it's easy to conceal. It's only got a three-round capacity but in my experience you only have to fire it once.'

O'Sullivan sighted down the barrel, then gave the weapon to Corben. 'Ammunition?'

'As much as you want.'

'A couple of dozen will see me right,' said O'Sullivan. 'Price?'

'Twelve for the gun. I'll throw in the shells.'

'Twelve hundred quid?' said Corben. 'Do me a favour.'

'Who am I talking to here?' May asked O'Sullivan. 'The organ-grinder or the monkey?'

O'Sullivan's smile hardened. 'He's my partner,' he said, 'and he knows about guns.'

'It's brand new,' said May. 'Return it unfired and I'll pay you nine. So twelve is cheap.'

Corben shook his head. 'It's a shotgun, fancy pistol grips or not. A grand. Give us eight if we don't make it go bang.'

May nodded. 'Okay,' he said. 'But unfired means unfired. Shots in the air count.'

O'Sullivan flashed May a tight smile. 'We got it the first time,' he said. 'What about the heavy artillery?'

May pulled up the lids of the final two cases. Each contained two submachine-pistols.

Corben whistled softly. 'Lovely jubbly,' he said.

May pulled one out and gave it to O'Sullivan. 'The gang-banger's favourite,' he said. 'The MAC-10. Thirty rounds in the magazine and you can let the lot go faster than you can say "drive-by".'

'Sweet,' said O'Sullivan. He passed it to Corben. 'Have you got a silencer?'

'What do you need one for?'

'To keep the sodding noise down – what do you think I need it for?'

'I can get you one.'

'Two,' said O'Sullivan, picking up the second Ingram.

'Fifteen hundred apiece,' said May. He tapped the sub-machine-guns in the second case. 'The Stars are a bit cheaper. Same calibre, same size magazine, a little bit heavier, rate of fire is slower but you can still let rip faster than you can blink.'

'You keep pushing the Spanish gear, don't you?' said Corben. 'You pick up a job lot?'

'Spanish armed forces have been using them since 1985,' said

May. 'Gang-bangers and Hollywood movie producers are the only ones who use the Ingram.'

'We'll take the Ingrams,' said O'Sullivan. 'And two silencers.'

'You planning on going to war?' asked May.

O'Sullivan ignored the question. He ran his eyes over the guns he'd selected. 'Four thousand nine hundred, right?'

'Let's call it a round five grand,' said May. 'I'll give you fifty per cent on the Ingrams if you bring them back unfired.'

O'Sullivan grinned. 'They'll be fired,' he said.

'I don't get you, Conor,' said May. 'You fret about the Glocks because they eject their rounds, but the Ingrams spit them all over the place.'

'Horses for courses,' said O'Sullivan. 'The shorts are for our next job, the Ingrams are for payback that's been brewing for some time. Anyway, what do you care?'

'Just curious,' said May.

'Yeah, well, you know what curiosity did to the cat,' said O'Sullivan. 'And it's four thousand nine hundred.'

'If you want the cases, it's five grand,' said May.

O'Sullivan shook his head sadly. 'You're a cheap bastard.'

'It's a business. I've got overheads and expenses. Do you want the cases or not?'

'Yeah, I want the cases.'

'Good choice,' said May. He packed the weapons O'Sullivan had chosen and clicked the cases shut. 'Now, if we could get the cash sorted . . .'

O'Sullivan nodded at Corben. Corben retrieved the Manchester United holdall, hefted it on to one of the tables and unzipped it. He took out five bundles of fifty-pound notes. Lomas picked up one and flicked through the notes slowly. He nodded at May.

May grinned and held out his hand. 'Nice doing business with you, Conor,' he said.

'Mutual,' said O'Sullivan. The two men shook hands.

Lomas and Corben looked at each other with undisguised dislike.

'Guess they're not going to kiss and make up,' said May.

'Guess not,' said O'Sullivan. He picked up the case containing the shotgun with his right hand and the holdall with the left, then motioned for Corben to carry the rest. The two men walked towards the door.

'If you need anything else, you've got my number,' May called after them.

'Yeah, we've got your number,' muttered Corben.

'Be nice, Ian,' said O'Sullivan.

They walked out into the open air. Corben put down his cases and used the remote to open the boot. They loaded the cases, then climbed into the car. O'Sullivan grinned. 'That went well,' he said.

The two men watched the Jaguar drive away. 'That went well,' said the Scotsman.

'Until you pulled a gun on them,' said his companion. 'What the hell was that about?'

'He was talking about using the metal detector on us. Shit would well and truly have hit the fan if he had done. Anyway, it worked out all right in the end, didn't it?'

The Jaguar pulled out of the industrial estate and accelerated towards the nearby motorway. The two men walked back into the warehouse. They took off their jackets and tossed them on to the tables.

They heard footsteps at the door and turned to see Charlotte Button walking confidently towards them, brushing a lock of dark chestnut hair behind her ear to reveal a moulded plastic earpiece. 'Well done, guys,' she said. She was wearing a belted fawn raincoat and her high heels clicked on the concrete floor.

An Asian man in his late twenties had followed her. Amar Singh was Button's technical specialist. He was carrying a brief-case.

'Sorry about Razor's improvisation, but there was method in

his madness,' said Dan Shepherd. He unbuttoned his denim shirt to reveal a microphone taped to his shaved chest.

'I heard,' said Button. 'If anything, it added to the scenario. There's nothing like a loose cannon to ratchet up the authenticity.'

Singh helped Shepherd to remove the microphone and the transmitter that was taped to the small of his back.

'You wouldn't have shot him, would you, Razor?' teased Button. 'Please tell me you wouldn't have blown a two-month operation by putting a bullet in Mr Corben's chest.'

'I knew exactly what I was doing.' Sharpe scowled.

'You went off menu,' said Shepherd, rebuttoning his shirt. 'I always hate it when you do that.' He grinned to show there was no ill-feeling. He had worked with Sharpe on countless occasions and had total faith in him. It had to be that way when you were under cover.

Four men in black overalls appeared at the doorway, members of the Metropolitan Police's firearms unit, and began to pack up the weapons. Singh put the transmitting equipment into his briefcase and went to Sharpe, who was taking off his shirt. Like Shepherd, he had also been wearing a transmitter.

Shepherd indicated the roof. 'Pictures okay?' The three small cameras that Singh had fitted the previous day were hidden in the metal rafters. They had transmitted pictures to the temporary control centre in one of the adjacent warehouses.

'Perfect,' said Button. 'We've everything we need. The transmitters that Amar embedded in the guns are good for seven days so we'll track them for five and see how many of O'Sullivan's gang we can pull in. Hopefully one of them will roll over on the Hatton Garden robbery in which case O'Sullivan and Corben will go down for life.'

Three weeks earlier a security guard had been shot in the stomach at close range with a sawn-off shotgun. Half a million pounds' worth of diamonds and rubies had been stolen, and the man had died in hospital two days later, his wife and three sons at his bedside. O'Sullivan hadn't fired the fatal shot, but he had orchestrated the robbery, one of more than half a dozen he was thought to have carried out in the previous year. Conor O'Sullivan was a professional criminal who, either through luck or good judgement, had never been to prison. The Serious Organised Crime Agency's undercover operation was about to change that.

'Is that it, then?' asked Sharpe.

'Keep the mobiles going for a week or so just in case,' said Button. 'There's always a chance that O'Sullivan will spread the good word.'

The men in black overalls carried out the cases containing the weapons and ammunition. One, a burly sergeant with a shaved head, flashed Button a thumbs-up as he walked by. 'Thanks, Mark,' she said. 'I'll have the paperwork for you by tomorrow morning.'

'What's next for us?' asked Shepherd.

'Don't worry, Dan, there's no rest for the wicked. I'll have something for you.' She consulted her watch. 'I have to be at the Yard this afternoon. I'll call you both later. But job well done, yeah? O'Sullivan's needed putting away for years.' She headed towards the door, then stopped. 'Oh, by the way,' she said, 'you've both got biannuals this month, haven't you?'

Shepherd and Sharpe nodded. Every six months all SOCA operatives had to be assessed by the unit's psychologist.

'We've a new psychologist on board,' said Button. 'Caroline Stockmann. She'll be getting in touch to arrange the sessions.'

'What happened to Kathy Gift?' asked Shepherd.

'She's moved on,' said Button.

'To where?'

'Academia. Bath University.'

'Couldn't stand the heat?' asked Sharpe.

Button's expression registered disapproval. 'She got married, actually.'

'To a man?' asked Sharpe, unabashed. He raised his hands as if to ward off her glare. 'Hey, these days, who knows?'

'Razor, not everyone gets your sense of humour.'

'But you do, right?'

Button smiled. 'You're a bloody dinosaur,' she said.

'But dinosaurs have their uses,' said Sharpe.

'Actually, they don't,' said Button. 'That's why they're extinct.'

'She got married?' said Shepherd.

'It was all quite sudden,' said Button.

'Probably up the spout,' said Sharpe.

'Jimmy . . .' said Button.

'This Stockmann, what's her story?' asked Shepherd.

'She's top notch,' said Button. 'Very highly qualified. I've known her for ten years.'

'She's worked with undercover agents before?' asked Shepherd.

'Not *per se*,' said Button. 'She was in MI5's Predictive Behaviour Group.'

'Which means what?' said Shepherd.

'The group is used to determine the way various people might react in a given situation. Generally heads of state. So, if you wanted to know how the Iranian government will react to EU pressure to drop their nuclear programme, you'd ask the PBG. The group has other uses, too. Mostly classified.'

Shepherd groaned. 'So a spook'll decide whether or not I'm fit for undercover work.'

'She's a highly qualified psychologist who happened to work for the security services,' said Button. 'It's only because she knows me that she's agreed to work for SOCA. We're lucky to have her.'

'It's not about qualifications,' said Shepherd. 'It's about understanding people – understanding what we go through. And if she's only ever been behind a desk, she's not going to know what life's like at the sharp end.'

'So tell her,' said Button. 'That's the purpose of the biannual, to get everything off your chest.'

'That's not strictly true, though, is it?' said Shepherd. 'It's also a test we have to pass to remain on active duty.'

'Spider, you're fine. I know you're fine and you know you're fine. You have a chat with Caroline and she'll confirm what we both know.' She glanced at her watch again. 'I have to go.'

As she headed for the door, Shepherd saw that Sharpe was grinning at him.

'What?' said Shepherd.

'What happened to Kathy Gift?' said Sharpe, in a whiny voice.

'Behave,' said Shepherd.

'You had a thing for her, didn't you?'

'How old are you, Razor?'

'Spider and Kathy, sitting in a tree . . .' sang Sharpe.

'Screw you,' said Shepherd, walking away.

'. . . K-I-S-S-I-N-G.' Sharpe's voice followed Shepherd out of the warehouse. Button's black Vauxhall Vectra was driving away. She was in the back, reading something.

'You okay?' said Singh, behind him.

Shepherd shrugged. 'What do you make of her?' he asked.

'She's a good boss,' said Singh. 'Gives you room to do your own thing but she's there when you need her.'

Shepherd nodded thoughtfully. 'Yeah, she's growing on me.' He jerked a thumb at the warehouse. 'That went well, from start to finish.'

'She had all the bases covered,' agreed Singh. 'I had to laugh at Razor, though. Pulling a gun like that.'

'Yeah, he's a bugger sometimes. But he's a pro.'

'Fancy a drink?'

'Nah,' said Shepherd. 'I've got to get home. Rain check, yeah?'

'No sweat,' said Singh. 'I'll take Wild Bill Hickok for a drink.' He turned back to the warehouse. 'Oy, Razor, d'you fancy a pint?'

'Do bears shit in the Vatican?' yelled Sharpe.

Shepherd chuckled and headed for his car.

★　　★　　★

Shepherd parked the Series Seven BMW in the driveway. He was going to miss Graham May's vehicle of choice. His own Honda CRV was four years old and he needed to replace it. But a Series Seven was well out of his price range.

The estate agent's sign in the front garden had 'UNDER OFFER' across the top. A young couple, looking for somewhere bigger, had offered the asking price, which was double what Shepherd had paid six years earlier. He had made an offer on a house in Hereford, less than a mile from where his in-laws lived.

His son was in the sitting room, eating a sandwich. A glass of orange juice stood in front of him. Liam's mouth was full so he waved at his father. Shepherd went to the kitchen, made himself a mug of instant coffee, then returned to the sitting room and dropped down on the sofa next to his son. 'Did you do your homework?' he asked.

'Sure,' said Liam, and drank some juice. 'I had to do a book report.'

'Which book?'

'*Animal Farm*. George Orwell.'

'Great story,' said Shepherd. ' "Four legs good, two legs bad." '

'You've read it?' said Liam, surprised.

'At school, same as you,' said Shepherd. 'It's a classic.'

'You don't read books.'

Shepherd raised his eyebrows. 'What?'

'You read newspapers.'

Shepherd wanted to argue but his son was right. The last time he'd read a book for pleasure must have been four years ago when he was on holiday in Spain with Sue and Liam. He rarely had time to read these days, and when he did have a few hours to spare more often than not he'd just vegetate in front of the television. In his younger days he'd been an avid reader – Ian Fleming, Len Deighton, Jack Higgins, John le Carré – but his work as an undercover police officer meant he no longer enjoyed crime stories. Real-life police work was never as cut and dried as it appeared in fiction, and the truly guilty rarely got their just deserts.

Before he could reply, Katra came in. She was wearing baggy khaki cargo pants and a loose sweatshirt. With no makeup and her hair tied back in a ponytail she looked younger than her twenty-four years. 'You're back early,' she said. 'Liam was hungry so I made him a sandwich.' She was from Slovenia, but she had lived with them in London now for two years so her accent had almost gone.

'No sweat,' said Shepherd. 'I'll order a pizza later.'

'Is it okay if I go to the supermarket?'

'Sure,' said Shepherd.

Liam picked up the remote control and switched on the television. 'You don't have time for TV,' said Shepherd, as his son flicked through the channels.

'Anything you want?' asked Katra.

'Toothpaste,' said Shepherd. 'The stuff for sensitive teeth.'

'You have toothache?' asked Katra.

'Just a twinge,' said Shepherd.

'Receding gums,' said Liam. 'It happens when you get old.'

'Older,' corrected Shepherd.

'Your hair gets thinner, your skin gets less flexible and your bones weaken.'

'I'm so glad we had this little chat,' said Shepherd. He held out his hand for the remote control. 'Now, give me that and scoot. And I want to see the book report before you go to sleep.'

Liam tossed him the remote control and Shepherd hit the button for BBC1. On the screen a middle-aged man with a mahogany tan and a woman half his age with gleaming teeth were laughing about nothing in particular. On ITV another woman, with equally sparkling teeth, was talking about the weather as if her audience had learning difficulties. It was going to rain in Scotland. Grin. With a chance of hail in Aberdeen. Bigger grin. But London would be sunny. Mega-grin with sly wink. Shepherd flicked to Sky News. More expensive dental work. Two newsreaders, a man and a woman, with tight faces. In a square frame in the top left-hand corner, a man in an orange jumpsuit was kneeling in front of a banner. Shepherd froze. He increased the volume as the frame expanded to fill the screen. The man in the jumpsuit was in his late thirties, his hair close-cropped. He was glaring defiantly at the camera. It had been six months since Shepherd had seen Geordie Mitchell. Then, his hair had been longer, he had been a few pounds heavier and he had been wearing a Chelsea FC shirt, not an orange jumpsuit.

'A British man working as a security guard in Iraq has been taken hostage by a group calling for the withdrawal of coalition forces from the country,' said the female newsreader.

Shepherd wondered how the former SAS trooper would have reacted to being described in that way.

'Last night Colin Mitchell's captors released a video showing him in apparently good health. They are calling for a complete withdrawal of all British troops from Iraq within the next fourteen days.'

Shepherd hadn't known that 'Colin' was Mitchell's real name. He'd known him for more than ten years as Geordie.

Two men in dark green overalls, scarves over their faces and cradling Kalashnikovs, were standing behind him. A third was holding aloft a rocket-propelled grenade launcher. A fourth masked man was next to Mitchell, addressing the camera in Arabic. A translation of his rhetoric passed slowly across the bottom of the screen.

'Mr Mitchell was taken hostage after the vehicle he was travelling in was ambushed and three of his Iraqi colleagues were killed,' continued the newsreader. 'He is believed to have been working in Iraq as part of a security detail guarding an oil pipeline running through the north of the country. Mr Mitchell's abduction comes just weeks after the beheading of American hostage Johnny Lake. All the indications are that the same group is holding Mr Mitchell. Following Mr Lake's abduction, the American government was given fourteen days to withdraw its troops from Iraq. This morning the Foreign Office refused to comment on Mr Mitchell's abduction.'

Shepherd's mobile rang and he put it to his ear as he stared at the screen. 'Are you watching the news?' said a voice. It was Major Allan Gannon, Shepherd's former boss in the SAS.

'Just seen it,' said Shepherd.

'We have to meet.'

'Absolutely.'

Shepherd got to the Strand Palace Hotel shortly before midnight. Liam was fast asleep and Shepherd had told Katra that he would be back in the early hours. She was used to him coming and going at unusual times so she had said goodnight and that she'd see him in the morning. It had never been as easy getting away when he was married: Sue had wanted to know where he was going, what he'd be doing and how dangerous it was. And she would sit up all night, waiting for him to get back. It was even harder when he was away from home for days at a time. Then he hadn't always been able to phone her, and even when he did his calls had been hurried and whispered. The difference, of course, was that Sue had been his wife and had loved him, while Katra was an employee.

The Major had booked a suite on the seventh floor. Shepherd knocked on the door. It was opened by a man a couple of inches shorter than him but with a similar physique. Like Shepherd, Billy Armstrong was a keen runner and they had often trained together when they were in the Regiment. 'Spider, good to see you,' said Armstrong. He was wearing a brown leather knee-length coat and tight-fitting jeans that were fashionably ripped at the knees. They hugged. It had been more than a year since they'd met.

'Where are you these days?' asked Shepherd.

'Sofia, Bulgaria, babysitting an industrialist who's only just this side of legal. You still a cop?'

'Yeah.'

'Come and work with me. Four hundred quid a day plus expenses.'

'And the chance of getting hurt?'

Armstrong grinned. 'It won't be me they'll be shooting at.'

'I thought you had to throw yourself in front of the bullet.'

'That's just public relations,' said Armstrong. 'When did you last hear of a bodyguard taking a bullet for a client? The boss is through there.'

Major Gannon was standing at the head of a long beech table that seated eight. He was a big man, well over six feet tall, with a strong chin and wide shoulders. His nose had been broken at least once. He was wearing a tweed jacket, an open-necked white shirt and chinos. He jutted out his chin when Shepherd walked in. 'Spider. Good man.' He strode round the table and they shook hands.

A third man was sitting at the table. Martin O'Brien was a former Irish Ranger and an old friend of Shepherd's, even though they had never served together. As he stood up he ran a hand over his shaved head, then slapped Shepherd on the back. He was a big man, and seemed to have got even bigger since he'd left the army. He was wearing a black polo-neck pullover with the sleeves rolled up to his elbows and blue jeans.

'No sign of Jimbo?' the Major asked Armstrong.

'The late Jim Shortt?' Armstrong laughed. 'He'd be late for his own funeral.'

Right on cue, there was a quick double-knock on the main door. Shepherd went to open it. Shortt was a heavy-set man with a sweeping Mexican-style moustache. He was holding a black gym bag and grinned when he saw Shepherd. 'The early worm, hey, Spider?'

'Hey, hey, the gang's all here,' said Shepherd. He jerked a thumb at the bag. 'Are you staying?'

'Just got off a plane from Dublin,' said Shortt. 'The boss said I could kip here.' He winked.

There was another knock at the door. Shepherd opened it. This time, a white-jacketed waiter was outside, behind a trolley loaded with pots of coffee and plates of sandwiches. Shepherd

stood aside to let him wheel it in. O'Brien hurried over to check
the order, then signed the bill. He saw Shepherd grinning at him
and glared defiantly. 'They're not all for me,' he said. 'The boss
said to get some grub in.' He grabbed a handful of sandwiches,
sat down next to Armstrong and offered him one. Armstrong
shook his head.

Shepherd and Shortt helped themselves to coffee as the Major
sat down at the head of the table. 'Right, let's get started,' he said.
'I'm sorry about the cloak-and-dagger, but I obviously can't use
the barracks and I didn't want to take over anyone's home so late
at night.' He was based at the Duke of York Barracks, close to
Sloane Square. From his office overlooking the parade ground he
ran the government's best-kept secret: the Increment. The Increment was an ad-hoc group of highly trained special-forces
soldiers used on operations considered too dangerous for Britain's security services, MI5 and MI6. The metal briefcase that
contained the secure satellite phone they called the Almighty
leaned against the wall behind him. The only people who had
access to it were the Prime Minister, the Cabinet Office, and the
chiefs of MI5 and MI6. When Gannon received a call on it, he
could command all the resources of the SAS and the SBS, plus
any other experts he needed. 'I'll have somewhere else fixed up
for us tomorrow, but this will do as a preliminary briefing room.
Has everyone seen the video?'

Shortt shook his head.

'Spider, do the honours, will you, please?' Gannon pointed at a
video-recorder and television on a stand in the corner of the
room. Shepherd switched on the television and clicked the
remote. The video was the Sky News broadcast that Shepherd
had seen just before the Major had phoned. The men watched it
in silence. The grainy video of Mitchell and his captors lasted
barely a minute. It was followed by a terrorism expert, whom
none of them recognised, talking about the dangers facing civilian
contractors in Iraq, and a representative of the Muslim Council
of Great Britain who denounced the kidnapping and called for

Mitchell's immediate release. 'Kill it, Spider,' said the Major. 'There's nothing else of interest.'

Shepherd hit 'Stop', switched off the television and returned to his seat.

'Colin?' said O'Brien. 'Is that his name, right enough?' He went over to the trolley for more sandwiches.

'How long had he been out there?' asked Armstrong, taking out a pack of Marlboro cigarettes and a disposable lighter. He took off his coat and hung it on the back of his chair.

'It was his third tour,' said the Major. He went to the trolley and poured himself a cup of black coffee. O'Brien offered him a sandwich but the Major declined.

'Geordie always followed the money,' said Shortt.

'Twenty thousand dollars a month,' said the Major. 'One month's paid leave for every three served, plus board and lodging over there, so pretty much everything you earn goes into the bank. It's the new Klondike. We've got guys dropping out of the Regiment early so they can sign on in Iraq. Hard to blame them – they get four times the salary plus the chance to use their skills rather than spending all their time training.'

'I've been offered three jobs out there,' said Armstrong. 'It's getting harder to turn them down. They're desperate for good people. Anyone mind if I smoke?'

'I thought you'd given up,' said Shortt.

'I did,' said Armstrong. He rolled up his shirtsleeve to reveal a white square on his shoulder. 'I'm even using the nicotine patches but they make me want to smoke even more.'

'Smoke away,' said O'Brien, 'but not over my food.'

Armstrong offered the pack around but there were no takers. He lit a cigarette and blew smoke at the ceiling.

The Major waved at the television. 'The money has to be good out there because of the risks. There've been ninety-seven kidnappings so far this year, twenty-six of them Westerners. Of the twenty-six, twenty-four have been killed. They've followed a similar pattern. Kidnapped. No news for a few days, then a video released with the abductors' demands – which are usually totally unrealistic – with a deadline. A second, sometimes a third video, as the deadline gets closer, then nothing for as long as a month, after which we get a video of the hostage being killed. Cards on the table, gentlemen. Geordie's chances do not look good. One of the Westerners who was released was a sixty-eight-year-old nun, the other was married to a Muslim woman and had five Muslim children.'

'Which means what?' said Shortt.

'Which means that it's up to us to swing the odds in his favour,' said the Major. 'Okay, more cards on the table. Officially there's nothing I can do. Unofficially every former member of the Regiment currently active in Iraq is being contacted and brought on side. I've spoken to army contacts out there, but the British Army is based mainly in Basra and Geordie was kidnapped in the Sunni Triangle and that's American-controlled. Since Geordie is a civilian contractor, my bosses won't countenance my using Regimental resources to get him out of the shit. That's why I've called you here. I'm not going to sit on my arse while the Foreign Office huffs and puffs, and I need to know that you all feel the same.'

'Bloody right,' said Shortt.

Shepherd and Armstrong muttered agreement. O'Brien had just taken a big bite of a sandwich but he gave the Major a thumbs-up.

'And I also need you to be aware that if we decide to help Geordie, we're not going to be following the Queensberry Rules or the Geneva Convention,' said the Major. 'We'll be crossing the line.'

'What – again?' Shortt punched Shepherd's shoulder. 'Seems to me that we did that when we got Spider out of bother a while back.'

Shepherd smiled ruefully. Shortt was right. They *had* broken the law before. Shepherd owed all the men round the table, big-time. He owed them and he owed Mitchell, and there was nothing he wouldn't do for them. 'I'm in,' he said, 'whatever it takes.'

'He'd do it for us, no question,' said O'Brien.

'I feel like the four bloody musketeers here,' said Armstrong. 'All for one and one for all.'

'There's five of us,' said Shortt. 'And I'm in.'

'Okay,' said the Major. 'The basics are what you saw on the video. Geordie has fourteen days – thirteen and a half, if we're going to split hairs. He's being held in Iraq by a group who will, unless we intervene, hack off his head. If past experience is anything to go by, our government will do next to nothing, and pleas for mercy will be ignored. Other than a name on a banner, we don't know who's holding him or where he is. We're three and a half thousand miles away from his location—'

'Piece of piss, then,' said Shortt.

The Major ignored the interruption. 'The only thing we have to go on at the moment is that news broadcast. I'm going to have the video analysed, see if there's anything on it that might provide a clue as to who his captors are and where they're keeping him. That's a long shot, frankly. There's a banner up behind Geordie that says it's the Holy Martyrs of Islam – not a name I've ever heard of. Any of you know it?'

All four men shook their heads.

'The problem is, whatever name they use is pretty much immaterial,' the Major went on. 'They seem to pluck them out of the air and there are indications of movement between the various groups. Generally low-level criminal gangs seize the hostages, then sell them on to the militant outfits. The criminal gangs are more likely to take cash. Once the political groups are involved it's not about money any more.'

'I know this is probably a stupid question, but I don't suppose his company had kidnap insurance, did they?' asked Shepherd.

'No, although they've offered a reward of half a million dollars for his return. But, as I said, this isn't about money. It isn't even about foreign policy. It's about terror. The guys holding him want to kill him and they want to do it on camera. The fourteen-day deadline is just a way of generating interest. Now, on a more positive note, the guy Geordie works for is on his way here so we'll have a briefing from him tomorrow. Meanwhile, any thoughts?'

'Nuke the lot of them,' said Shortt.

'Thanks, Jimbo,' said the Major. 'Any serious thoughts?'

'Are the Yanks on the case?' asked O'Brien.

'The military?' asked the Major. 'As much as they can be, but one kidnapped British contractor isn't top of their priorities, not with their own death toll heading towards three thousand.'

Shepherd, Armstrong, O'Brien and Shortt sat back and waited for the Major to continue. The fact that he had called them together meant that he had something in mind.

'If anything is going to happen, it's going to be down to us,' he said. 'There's no question of British troops being pulled out, and no question of the government getting involved in any form of negotiations.'

'Because they don't negotiate with terrorists,' said Armstrong, bitterly. 'Unless they're Irish, of course. Then they invite them to Downing Street for tea. Bloody Paddies.'

'Hey,' said O'Brien. 'Behave. I'm a Paddy, remember.'

The Major raised a warning eyebrow and Armstrong and O'Brien fell silent. 'From what I'm told, Geordie's Sass background won't be revealed,' the Major continued. 'The only family he has is a brother and he knows to keep his head down. The company has been briefed to say only that he served with the army. No details of his career with the Paras or Sass. If the group holding him finds out that he's former special forces they'll make it a lot harder for him. Officially Sass can't be seen to be involved, but unofficially they'll move heaven and earth to find him. But with Geordie in the Sunni Triangle, we're going to need American help. Unofficial American help.'

The Major looked pointedly at Shepherd, who knew what he was suggesting and nodded slowly. 'I'm on it,' he said.

'Assuming we do find where they're keeping him,' said O'Brien, 'what then?'

'Let's take it one step at a time,' said the Major.

'Yeah, but is the plan to let the Yanks try to pull him out, or do our guys go in?'

'I'd hope it'd be a Sass operation but, like I said, they're not in the area. Let's not get ahead of ourselves. First we'll find out where he is.'

'It's al-Qaeda, right?' said Shortt. 'Has to be.'

'It's not as simple as that, Jimbo,' said the Major. 'There is no al-Qaeda any more, not really. These days, it's more of a brand than an organisation. All the groups I mentioned have a similar ideology to al-Qaeda, but the days of a criminal mastermind with overall control are long gone. The guys in these groups were probably trained by al-Qaeda in Afghanistan or Pakistan ten years ago, but now they function as autonomous units. In effect, they've become a terror franchise. It's like Burger King. A franchise in Birmingham doesn't have to call head office every time it cooks a burger. These guys are just out there to cause chaos. If we had an al-Qaeda source, he probably wouldn't even know where Geordie was being held.'

'This is a bloody nightmare,' said Armstrong. 'Why don't we just fly over there?'

'And do what?' asked the Major. 'We wouldn't be able to move around. Any Westerner's a target. We've no intel sources on the ground. No one's going to talk to us. We'd spend all our time just staying alive. At least here we can take a broader view, see the wood for the trees.'

'How about Billy and I head to Baghdad?' said Shortt. 'At least we'd be on the spot.' Armstrong nodded in agreement.

'No one's going to Iraq,' said the Major. 'At least, not yet. We're only eight hours away. We've got just under two weeks, so we don't have to rush into anything, okay?'

Shortt didn't look convinced.

'I want you and Billy trailing the video,' said the Major. 'We need to know how it reached the TV stations. The first to get it was al-Jazeera in Qatar. They usually get the kidnap videos first and pass them on to others around the world. If we can follow that video back to the source, we'll know where Geordie is. Plus, there might be more video with more usable intel on it. I'll get the pictures we already have analysed, see if there's anything there to help us. Spider will look into getting American intel on what's going on in Iraq, and as I said, Geordie's boss arrives tomorrow so we'll have a briefing from him.' The Major stood up. 'It'll be okay,' he said. 'We'll bring Geordie home, whatever it takes.'

Geordie Mitchell put down the paperback book he'd been staring at for the past hour. He hadn't got beyond the first page of *The Da Vinci Code*. It was creased and there were greasy fingerprints on the cover, and Mitchell couldn't help wondering who had read it before and if he had lived to finish it.

The room was fifteen paces long and nine wide. There were no windows and only one door. The inside of the door was featureless except for a peephole at head height. There was no lock, and no handle. Other than a threadbare blanket and a blue plastic bucket, there was nothing. When they fed him it was on paper plates and he had to eat with his hands. Water came in paper beakers. He'd been over every inch of the floor and walls and there was nothing he could use as a weapon – except his hands, of course, and his feet, elbows, knees. Mitchell knew a couple of dozen ways to kill with his bare hands, but despatching one of his captors wouldn't get him out of the basement. He had seen at least six men, and had no way of knowing how many more were upstairs. He could grab one and threaten to kill him unless they let him go, but he doubted they'd be intimidated by threats of violence.

Besides, the chance of catching them unawares was virtually nil. Most of the time he was alone in the basement. When they came to feed him, they shouted through the door that he was to stand against the back wall with his hands out to the side. They wouldn't open the door until he had complied. One man would come in, usually the one called Kamil, with food or water or to empty the bucket. Kamil was the only one who had spoken to him, and he had always been polite and friendly. While Kamil was in the room a second man, wearing a ski mask, would stand at the door cradling an AK-47, his finger inside the trigger guard. It was an intimidating weapon, but Mitchell found it reassuring. It wasn't the sort you'd fire in the confines of a basement: there was a high risk of ricochet, the noise would be deafening and it would be hard to manoeuvre, all of which suggested that the men weren't as professional as he'd first thought.

Mitchell paced round the room on autopilot as he considered his options. During his time on the SAS selection course, he'd gone through Resistance to Interrogation training with the Joint Services Interrogation Unit and passed with flying colours. But it had done nothing to prepare him for what he was going through now.

The training was based on building resistance to physical and mental torture. It came after the Escape and Evasion section of the gruelling SAS selection course – three days of being pursued across the Brecon Beacons by British Army units trying to prove they were every bit as hard as the men who wanted to join the élite special-forces unit. Eventually everyone was caught and handed over to the hard men of the JSIU. The interrogation was open-ended. Mitchell had been grilled for two full days and three nights before he was told that he'd passed and was qualified to wear the SAS badge and beret. It had been sixty hours of hell.

He'd been beasted by four burly paratroopers before he got to the JSIU, so he was already battered and bruised. He'd been stripped naked and doused with icy water. They'd played white noise through huge speakers for hours. They'd shouted at him in languages he didn't understand. They'd blindfolded him and made him stand spreadeagled against a wall with most of his weight on his arms. He'd been screamed at, punched and had his face submerged in a barrel of water until he'd come close to passing out. He'd been tied naked to a chair and interrogated for hours. Under the rules of the test, he had been able to give only his name, rank and number. Divulging any other information meant instant rejection. The interrogators had tried everything. Screaming at him. Cajoling him. Telling him jokes. Asking him if he wanted food or to sleep. They'd even produced a bottle of beer and told him there was nothing in the rules about accepting a drink. He'd refused it and they'd put a cloth bag over his head and dragged him across a field telling him they were going to bury him alive. They hadn't, of course. That was one of the flaws in the test. No matter how convincing the JSIU men were, those they interrogated knew it was an act, that they wouldn't do any permanent damage, and that at some point it would all be over. In the real world bones and teeth were broken – and worse. On the selection course you'd get a little bruised. All you had to do was keep your mouth shut until it was over.

Once he'd joined the Regiment, Mitchell had been on more courses with the JSIU. They'd taught him what was likely to happen if he was captured by an enemy who wasn't bound by the rules of the Geneva Convention. And they'd taught him the skills that would ensure the best chance of survival. But nothing the interrogation experts had taught him had prepared him for what he had been through since he had been brought to the basement.

His initial capture had been by the book: an AK-47 aimed at his chest, a hood pulled roughly over his head, something hard slammed against his temple, and waking up in the back of a van with his hands and feet bound. He'd been kept tied and hooded for the first forty-eight hours, he figured, though it had been hard to keep track of time. He'd been given water to drink through a straw but no food, and no one had said anything to him. He'd been moved from the van to a place that smelled of diesel oil where he'd slept on a dusty concrete floor, then put into the boot of a car and taken to another location where he'd slept on a damp carpet. There, a dog had woken him by licking his hands. Then he was put into a rattling van, with what felt like crates piled round him, and driven for hours to a third location: a room with windows that had been covered with sheets of plywood. He'd been tied to a wooden chair and they had taken his watch, wallet, shoes and belt. The hood had been removed and he had been given cold boiled rice with a piece of barbecued fish.

He'd asked who they were and what they wanted, but their only response was to slap him with gloved hands. After he'd eaten they had left the hood off but sealed his mouth with duct tape. His captors wore ski masks and said nothing to him. He stayed tied to the chair for a day and half a night, then the hood was put back on and he was hit from behind. He'd feigned unconsciousness but they'd hit him again and he'd passed out for real.

When he woke up he was in the basement and everything had changed. He hadn't been bound or gagged. He'd been given food, plenty of water and the paperback book. One of the rules of surviving a hostage situation was to befriend your captors so that they related to you as a human being, not just as a captive, but instead one of the men introduced himself to Mitchell. He said his name was Kamil and apologised for what had happened. He spoke reasonably good English and had a smile that Mitchell was sure would win him more than his fair share of female admirers. Nothing would happen to him, Kamil had promised. A number of hostages had been taken at different locations around the country, but they would all be released within a few weeks. He said he would make Mitchell's stay as pleasant as possible under the circumstances. If Mitchell had any requests for reading matter, Kamil would do what he could to provide it. He was sorry about the poor quality of the food, he said, but assured Mitchell that his captors would eat the same provisions. Mitchell had asked for a beer and Kamil had laughed, then patted his shoulder. They were like two old friends chatting, but for the man in the doorway cradling an AK-47.

Mitchell didn't believe Kamil's assurances. Few hostages were released in Iraq. Most ended up dead. Kamil never raised his voice, never threatened Mitchell, never questioned him. Mitchell knew why. They didn't need anything from him: he was a pawn in whatever game they were playing.

Kamil was the only one of his captors to reveal his face. The others wore ski masks when they were in the room. Mitchell reckoned there were six in addition to Kamil, perhaps seven. There had been five and Kamil in the basement when they had made the video. It had been on the morning of his second day there. They had fed him first: a paper plate of rice with some sort of lamb stew and a paper cup filled with chunks of pickled mango. Then Kamil had brought in a Panasonic video-camera on a tripod and placed it close to the wall on the right of the door. He'd pinned a sheet, on which was printed Arabic script, to the wall on the left. Then he had given Mitchell an orange jumpsuit and asked him to put it on. It had been a request and Mitchell had complied. He was sure that they intended to kill him at some point but there was nothing to be gained from confrontation. He would have to choose his moment to make a stand. Of one thing he was sure: when they came to kill him he would fight back.

Kamil had asked Mitchell to kneel, then tied his wrists together. For a brief moment Mitchell thought he'd misjudged the situation and that they were about to kill him, but he held on to the thought that first they would want to show the world they had him. He had knelt on the hard concrete floor and stared into Kamil's eyes, looking for any sign that his new-found friend had murder on his mind. Mitchell knew that with his hands tied behind his back his options were limited, but he could do a lot of damage with his feet.

Kamil had thanked him, then gone to the camera. Before he switched it on, he had pulled on a ski mask. Again he had apologised to Mitchell, explaining that it was important he wasn't recognised. Five of the captors had lined up in front of the banner. Two were holding Kalashnikovs, one had a Russian-made RPG – Mitchell had smiled inwardly at the sight of it. If it had gone off in the confined space they would all have been killed. It was clearly for show, but he wondered who they were trying to impress.

For a full three minutes Kamil had addressed the camera, speaking in Arabic. Mitchell only knew a few words of the language and wasn't able to follow what was being said, but he could tell that Kamil wasn't promising to release him. Several times Kamil pointed at Mitchell, and once at the banner. When he did that, the guy with the RPG shook it menacingly above his head and all five men chanted in unison.

Throughout Kamil's speech, Mitchell stared defiantly at the lens. He was determined not to show any fear. In any case, he was apprehensive, rather than scared. He was in a dire situation, no doubt about that, but he was sure he wouldn't die that day.

He was right. After Kamil had finished his speech he had switched off the camera, removed his mask and helped Mitchell to his feet. He had untied him and thanked him for his co-operation. 'This will soon be over and you will be back with your family,' Kamil had promised. He had looked Mitchell in the eyes as he'd said it, and had patted his shoulder reassuringly, but Mitchell didn't doubt that the other man was lying.

Over the following days Kamil had been pleasant and polite. He always called Mitchell by his first name – he had found the driving licence in Mitchell's wallet. When he brought the food and water he would sit cross-legged on the floor as Mitchell ate and make small-talk. He asked Mitchell what football team he supported and what cities he knew in England. He talked about English weather, English beer and English food. He never mentioned politics or religion, and didn't ask about Mitchell's work in Iraq or his military background. Mitchell had the feeling that his captors didn't know he was a former soldier or that he had served with the SAS. More likely, they didn't care. All they cared about was that he was British and that he was their prisoner.

Shepherd walked through Harrods' food hall, surrounded by wide-eyed tourists and well-heeled housewives. He wandered past a refrigerated display of fish from around the world, glossy-eyed, open-mouthed and ready for the kitchen. He wasn't there to look at the produce, though: he wanted to confirm that he wasn't being tailed – it was second nature. He did a fifteen-minute sweep through the store, then headed outside and took a circuitous route to the red-brick mansion block that housed the Special Forces Club. The plaque that had once identified it had been taken down in the wake of the terrorist attacks in America and the exterior was identical to the rest of the upmarket residences in the street.

The stocky former SAS staff sergeant who manned the reception desk grinned at him as he signed in. 'Nice day for it, sir.'

'Nice day for what, Sandy?' asked Shepherd.

Sandy shrugged. 'Whatever you had mind, sir.' The 'sir' was ironic – there were no ranks in the club.

Shepherd scanned the names of those who had signed in that day. 'Mr Yokely not arrived?'

'Yokely, sir?'

'American.'

Sandy raised one eyebrow. 'Ah,' he said. 'Mr Yokely doesn't sign in.'

'Really?'

'Far too important for that, I'm told,' said Sandy.

'Seriously?'

'Security issue. The committee okayed it so I put up with it. You know what the Yanks are like – scared of their own shadows half the time.'

Shepherd chuckled and headed upstairs.

Yokely was standing at the bar, nursing a vodka and tonic. When he saw Shepherd, he said, with a faint southern drawl, 'I always expect you to abseil in through the window.' He was in his late forties with short grey hair and thin lips that looked cruel even when they curled into what passed for a smile. He wore a chunky college ring on his right hand, a dark blue blazer, a gleaming white shirt and the same blue tie with black stripes that he'd been wearing the last time they'd met almost a year previously. The shoes were the same, too. Black leather with tassels.

'Thanks for coming, Richard.'

'You were lucky I was in town,' said Yokely. 'Jameson's, soda and ice?'

'Thanks,' said Shepherd.

Yokely smiled and Shepherd realised that the American wanted recognition for having remembered his drink. He didn't rise to the bait. His own memory was virtually faultless, but he figured that the American had simply made notes of what had happened at their last meeting. He seemed the type to keep a file on everyone he met.

Yokely glanced at his wristwatch – a Rolex Submariner, the fiftieth-anniversary edition with the green bezel. 'I can't stay long,' he said. 'A chopper's waiting to take me up to Prestwick. I'm supposed to meet a flight from Afghanistan and then I'm off to Cuba.' He snorted. 'Pity the CIA doesn't give frequent-flier miles.'

'Rendition, they call it – right? Taking suspects to countries where torture isn't illegal?'

Yokely grinned wolfishly. 'It isn't called torture, these days. It's coercive interrogation. And don't go all holier-than-thou on me because it was you guys who invented rendition, way back in 1684.'

'I assume there's nothing I can say to stop you telling me the story?' said Shepherd.

Yokely's grin widened. 'Torture was outlawed in England in 1640, but it stayed legal in bonnie Scotland until the Act of Union in 1707. Now, in 1684 you guys had a suspect and a less than co-operative witness to the attempted assassination of Charles II. They were shipped north of the border and, as a direct result of information obtained under torture, the suspect was tried, convicted and executed. Rendition worked for you then and it works for us now.' He ordered the whiskey for Shepherd, then motioned to a sofa in a quiet corner. They walked across to it and sat down. Yokely swirled the ice in his glass. 'I'm guessing this isn't social,' he said.

Shepherd was sure Yokely knew why he'd asked for the meeting, so the American must be relishing the opportunity to make him sing for his supper. 'Geordie Mitchell,' he said. Yokely pulled a face.

The barman brought the whiskey and Shepherd waited until he had gone back to the bar before he went on. 'He's just been taken hostage in Iraq.'

'Ah,' said Yokely. 'He's one of yours, is he? According to the TV, he's a civilian contractor.'

'He left the Sass a few years back.'

'And I guess he's not shouting about his special-forces background, under the circumstances. The government seems to be keeping that information under its hat, too.'

'They're not doing much.'

'Not much they can do,' said the American. 'You see what they did to that journalist? Just a kid. Father had money, would've paid anything to get the boy back, but they weren't interested. It's not about money.'

'What is it about?' asked Shepherd.

'They want us all dead,' said Yokely, flatly. 'They want us all dead or they want us on our hands and knees praying to Allah five times a day. To them that seems a reasonable request. Hell, they figure they're saving our souls.'

'You believe that?'

Yokely took two gulps of his drink. 'I'm not sure what I believe any more, other than that we're right and they're wrong. A world run by Islamic fundamentalists is not a world I'd want any part of. If the roles were reversed and it was the mad mullahs in charge, I'd probably be setting off bombs myself. I'd kill to protect my way of life, no question.' He smiled thinly. 'Hell, I already have done. You too.'

The American was watching Shepherd over the top of his glass. Shepherd didn't react to the barb. Yes, Shepherd had killed, but not to protect an ideology. He'd killed when he was in the SAS, as a soldier on military operations. He'd killed as a policeman, to save others. But that was his job: it was what he was paid to do. It had nothing to do with ideologies. Shepherd had only met Yokely once, but he knew the American regarded the war against terrorism as a holy crusade, which he was prepared to win at any price.

'So, what do you want from me, Spider? The US government isn't going to go in to bat for a Brit. Not that it would do any good if they did. Your best bet would be to find him an Irish grand-mother.'

'He isn't Irish,' said Shepherd. 'If anyone's going to help Geordie, it'll be us.'

'Us?'

'His friends,' said Shepherd, quietly.

Yokely's eyes narrowed. 'A dangerous road to go down.'

'That's for us to worry about,' said Shepherd. 'We need intel, and we can't get it here.'

'But I'm the oracle so you've come to me?'

'We just need information.'

'What sort of information?'

Shepherd drained his glass. 'Another?' he asked.

'You trying to keep me in suspense?' said the American. He lifted his glass. 'Vodka and tonic with all the trimmings. I keep asking for lime but they give me lemon.'

Shepherd went to the bar for fresh drinks. When he returned he sat down and gave Yokely his glass. 'What do you know about the Holy Martyrs of Islam?' he asked.

'As little as you do, I'd guess,' said Yokely. 'The names these people use mean nothing.'

'When the Lake boy was taken, your people must have looked into it.'

'Johnny Lake was a journalist who was in the wrong place at the wrong time. Plus the stories he was filing weren't going down well in the Oval Office.'

'So the government didn't care?'

'They cared, of course they did. The boy's father was a heavy hitter, with friends on Capitol Hill, but there's a limit to the resources they can put into one missing kid. Don't get me wrong. They looked. And they looked hard. But, so far as I know, no one had ever heard of the Holy Martyrs of Islam.'

'We need to know where Geordie is and who's got him. We're analysing the video, and we'll be talking to his employer so we can gather basic intel on what's happening on the ground. But we need higher-level intel. Electronic traffic and satellite imagery.'

'Sounds like you're planning a war,' said the American.

'We're just mapping out our options,' said Shepherd.

'You find him, then what?'

'We'll cross chickens and count bridges when the time comes,' he said. 'Can you help?'

'Sure,' said Yokely. 'I've got a direct line to the NSA. But why do you need me? You can get the electronic traffic through GCHQ. They're part of Echelon so they have access to all telecommunications and the Internet.'

'It'll take too long to go through official channels,' said Shepherd. 'Paperwork in triplicate, and they'd want to know why we're involved.'

'But presumably your government's on the case. They must be looking for your man.'

'You'd think so, but he's not military, remember?'

'What about your old regiment?'

'They can't help officially,' said Shepherd. 'Unofficially they'll do what has to be done. But first we need to know where he is.'

'Any idea what's being done officially?'

'Downing Street will probably appeal to the kidnappers, but reject any demands they make. The US military will be looking for him, but again Geordie's just a contractor, out there for the money.'

'Guarding a pipeline, they said on CNN.'

'Yeah.'

'Wrong place, wrong time.'

'Yeah. There's no suggestion that it was personal. At this stage we're not sure how well planned the kidnapping was but we're hoping there was phone chatter. What about satellite imagery?'

'I'll see what the NSA has. We might get lucky.'

'And we could do with any intel your contacts have on the Holy Martyrs of Islam. All we've got so far is what's been in the media, which is pretty much zero. Plus we need any info on other militant groups known to be operating in the area where Geordie was taken. According to the TV, he was taken in a place called Dora.'

'I know it,' said Yokely. 'It's a Sunni stronghold on the southern tip of Baghdad. Dangerous place.' He sipped his drink. 'You've seen *The Godfather*? The first one? Was Marlon Brando great in that movie or what?'

'Yeah. I saw it. And I get it.'

'Are you sure?'

'I know how the world works, Richard. You do this for me and at some point you'll be asking me for a favour.'

'And when that time comes?'

'I repay my debts. In full.'

A triumphant smile spread across Yokely's face. 'It's always a pleasure dealing with a professional.'

Shepherd raised his glass in salute. He felt as if he'd just done a deal with the devil. He knew that Yokely would call in the marker, sooner rather than later, and that he would have no choice other than to do whatever the American wanted. Shepherd wasn't happy to be in Yokely's debt, but the only thing that mattered was rescuing Geordie and the American was the one man who might be able to help.

'You know, I've got a lot of respect for you, Spider,' said Yokely. 'I admire the way you handled yourself down the Tube, and on the Eurostar. Both times you did what you had to do.'

Shepherd said nothing.

'I know we're not exactly best buddies, but I want to talk to you as a friend.'

'Go ahead,' said Shepherd.

Yokely took a gulp of his drink. 'He's almost certainly going to die. You know that?'

'Not necessarily. There have been almost two hundred and fifty foreign hostages taken over the past three years. Eighty-six have been killed. That suggests odds of three to one, survival wise.'

'Except that your friend is in the hands of militants. The survival rate at that level is virtually non-existent. And you know as well as I do that so far this year only two Westerners have been released. And how many have been butchered? Twenty-five? They're getting more vicious, not less.'

'Are you telling me we're wasting our time?'

'It's a mess out there, Spider. I'll do what I can to help, but Iraq's not my battlefield, and there isn't a day goes by when I don't thank the Lord for it. My war is against the terrorist threat, and that's hard enough. But in Iraq there's no way of knowing who's friend and who's foe. The enemy doesn't wear a uniform, doesn't follow any of the rules of war. When we first moved into Iraq, the CIA reckoned we'd be facing five thousand insurgents. By the summer of 2004 they'd raised that estimate to twenty thousand. By the winter it had grown to a hundred thousand. Now you can pretty much take any number and double it. And we're not facing a unified enemy. There are Sunni insurgents who want Iraq to go back to the way it was before Saddam was kicked out. There are Baathists from the Return Party, the Fedayeen militia units that kept Saddam in power, Shia guerrillas and, on top of that, all the foreign mercenaries who've flooded into the country. Any one of those groups could be behind the Holy Martyrs of Islam. Or it might not be insurgents. It might be a maverick fundamentalist group, Saudis or Algerians, out to cause as much trouble as they can. If they're fundamentalists, then there'll be no negotiating with them. They'll want to kill your friend to cause a backlash that'll unite Muslims against the West.'

'We're going to do what we can,' said Shepherd. 'Whatever it takes.'

'I empathise, Spider, I really do. If it was one of my friends out there in an orange jumpsuit, I'd be doing the same. But you have to be realistic. I'll get you whatever intel I can, but be aware that you're probably flogging a dead horse.'

Shepherd drained his glass and stood up. 'Give me a call as soon as you have anything,' he said.

'Now I've offended you,' said Yokely.

'No more than usual,' said Shepherd. 'I'll get over it.'

The Major had booked a suite of offices in a building close to the BBC's Broadcasting House in Portland Place. Shepherd took the Tube to Regent's Park, left the station and walked through the park for fifteen minutes. Once he was satisfied that no one was following him, he walked south down Portland Place, heading for the office block. Several yards ahead of him, sitting cross-legged on the pavement, a middle-aged Chinese woman was holding her hands out, palms up, chanting. Across the road a bored armed policeman stood, feet planted shoulder-width apart, in front of the Chinese Embassy. There was always at least one protester demonstrating against the Chinese government's torture of dissidents. Shepherd wondered if the woman thought she could change government policy or if she was there to prove that someone cared. The lone policeman was a token presence, rather than a serious security measure, and there was something very British about the stand-off. Shepherd doubted that the Chinese would have been so tolerant if the woman had been in her own country.

He reached the office block and did a final check that he hadn't been followed. There was an intercom at the main door and Shepherd pressed the buzzer for the second floor. Armstrong answered and let him in.

When Shepherd arrived Major Gannon was sitting at the head of a large boardroom table drinking a mug of coffee. His satellite phone was on a smaller table by the window that looked out over the road. Whiteboards had been attached to three walls, displaying newspaper cuttings, photographs and satellite images of Baghdad. On the fourth wall there was a large-scale map of Iraq. Armstrong was pouring coffee and O'Brien was rummaging through a selection of Marks & Spencer sandwiches. As usual, Shortt was the last to arrive and hurried in, apologising profusely.

'Let's get started,' said Gannon. 'This will be our HQ.' He pointed to a door on his left. 'There's a couple of camp beds in there, and a bathroom. I'll be either here or at the Duke of York Barracks, but my mobile will always be switched on.' He gestured at two laptop computers on a side-table in the far corner of the room. 'They've got broadband and I've rigged up access to the Regiment's databases.' The Major bent down, swung a briefcase on to the table and clicked open the locks to reveal bundles of twenty-pound notes. 'There's cash here, more if we need it.' He closed the briefcase. 'Where do we stand with the video?'

'You were right, boss,' said Armstrong, lighting a cigarette. 'Al-Jazeera got it first, but we're not sure how and they're not prepared to give us any help on that front.'

'What can you tell us about al-Jazeera?' asked the Major.

'It's the largest Arabic news channel in the Middle East,' said Armstrong. 'It means the Island, or the Peninsula. Based in Qatar, it's been around for just over ten years. Tends to show sensational pictures of bodies and the like on its news channel, but also runs sport and children's channels. They came on to the radar after nine/eleven when they broadcast video statements by Bin Laden and his chums. They run a website, too. Aljazeera.net. Not to be confused with Aljazeera.com, which runs really inflammatory stuff.'

'Bush hates them,' interjected Shortt. He rubbed his moustache. 'In 2001 the US bombed al-Jazeera's offices in Afghanistan and a couple of years later they shelled a hotel in Iraq where the only guests were al-Jazeera journalists. They've put several of their journalists in prison and the US-backed government in Iraq has banned the network from reporting there. In 2004, Bush is supposed to have talked about bombing their HQ in Qatar.'

'Am I the only one who doesn't know where Qatar is?' asked O'Brien, running a hand over his shaved head.

'It's a tiny state in the Persian Gulf,' said Shepherd. 'Population just over half a million, it borders Saudi Arabia and the United Arab Emirates. The capital is Doha. So, are al-Jazeera good guys or bad guys?'

'They're neutral,' said Armstrong, flicking ash into a crystal ashtray. O'Brien coughed pointedly and waved smoke away from his face. 'They're an Arab news service, doing the same sort of job that CNN and the BBC do. It's just that America doesn't like the Arab point of view being broadcast. They've also upset pretty much every Arab government in the Middle East at some time or another. For instance, they were the first Arab station to broadcast interviews with Israeli officials.'

'So why do they always get the hostage videos?' asked Shepherd.

'Because if they were sent to CNN there's no guarantee they'd be shown, and if they were, a bloody good chance that they'd been sent to the CIA first,' said Armstrong. 'The BBC would probably refuse to broadcast them on grounds of taste. But al-Jazeera airs them and makes them available to other news agencies.'

'How does the video get to the station?' asked the Major.

'That's the problem,' said Armstrong. 'They won't say. I phoned their news desk in Qatar and I've spoken to senior management, but they're not prepared to give any details.'

'We need to know how they got the video,' said the Major. 'It's the only link we have to Geordie.'

Shortt slid a sheet of paper across the table to him. 'They have a correspondent here in London whose brother works on the news desk in Qatar,' he said. 'His name is Basharat al-Sabah.'

'Have you spoken to him yet?'

'If we call him up, he'll give us the standard line,' said Shortt. 'Unless we get . . . creative.'

'Creative?' said Shepherd.

Shortt placed his hands flat on the table. 'We're going to have to decide here and now how far we're prepared to go to get what we need,' he said. 'If I phone this guy, I'll get the bum's rush. If I turn up on his doorstep, he'll close the door in my face. If I pretend to be a cop or a spook he won't be intimidated. He's a journalist so he knows the ropes.'

'Spider could go in. He's a real cop,' said Armstrong.

'Absolutely not,' said the Major. 'If he makes a complaint, Spider's job'll be on the line. I don't suppose we know what he looks like?'

Shortt grinned and slid another sheet of paper across the table. It was a copy of a Qatar passport. 'A mate in Immigration got it for me,' he said.

'There's no suggestion that this guy's a terrorist?' asked Shepherd.

'He's snow white,' said Shortt. 'He's got a degree in political science, and I ran a CRO check on him through a tame cop. He's never been in trouble, not so much as a parking ticket. His immigration status is clean, and he's worked for several newspapers in London. He even did a work-experience stint on the *Guardian*.'

'Family?' asked the Major.

'Not married. Most of his family are in Qatar, but he has a brother who's a doctor in Saudi Arabia.' Shortt sat back in his chair. 'Here's the thing. This al-Sabah is a model citizen, the sort of guy you'd happily let your sister go out with, if you had a sister, but he's got the information we need. And even if he hasn't, he's got a direct line to a man who has, his brother, Tabarak al-Sabah. The question we've got to answer is how far we're prepared to go to get that information.'

'Sounds like you've got a plan, Jimbo,' said the Major.

Shortt grinned. 'I have,' he said. 'But I'm not sure you're going to like it.'

O'Brien slowed the Transit van as he drove past Brixton Prison. He nodded at the high wall to his right. 'If this goes wrong, we could end up in there,' he said.

'First, it won't go wrong,' said the Major, beside him in the front passenger seat, 'and second, do you think any prison could hold the five of us?'

'The boss is right,' said Shortt, from the back. 'We busted into a prison to get Spider out once before, so I don't think we'd have any problems getting ourselves out.'

'Like I said, it won't come to that,' said the Major. 'Take a left ahead, Martin.'

O'Brien indicated and they turned off Brixton Hill. 'Number twenty-four,' said Shortt. He was sitting on the floor of the van, Shepherd to his left and Armstrong to his right.

'Are we sure he's going to be walking home?' asked O'Brien. He brought the van to a halt down the road from number twenty-four. It was mid-way along a terrace of Victorian houses with weathered bricks, slate roofs and front doors that opened on to the street.

'He doesn't have a car, so he'll be on the Victoria Line home,' said Shortt.

'Unless he gets a lift from a colleague,' said O'Brien.

'If he gets a lift, we'll get him in the house,' said Shortt. 'He's in the office today – I checked. And he was in at ten so I figure with a nine-hour day he'll be here some time in the next hour or so.'

'Unless he goes out for a drink after work,' said O'Brien.

'He's a Muslim, so he doesn't drink,' said Shortt. 'What's with all the doom and gloom, anyway, Martin? Is your blood sugar getting low?'

'Let's relax,' said the Major. 'He'll be here some time tonight, no matter how he comes.'

'Anyone else in the house?' asked Shepherd.

'It's rented. I phoned a couple of times during the day and no one answered,' said Shortt.

Armstrong took out a Browning Hi-power semi-automatic and checked the action.

'No one gets hurt,' said the Major.

'The magazine's empty,' said Armstrong.

'We do what we have to do, but I don't want him in hospital,' said the Major. 'If he gets hurt, the police'll be called in.'

'The cops are already here,' laughed Shortt, and jerked a thumb at Shepherd.

Shepherd flashed him a sarcastic smile. He was far from happy at what they were about to do, but he knew they had no choice. He was a policeman, but Geordie Mitchell was a friend and Shepherd would do whatever it took to save his life.

O'Brien switched on the radio and flicked through the channels until he found one playing bland seventies music. The men listened to the Police, Elton John, and the Eagles as they waited.

It was close to nine o'clock when the Major switched it off. 'This could be him,' he said, looking in the wing mirror.

O'Brien twisted round in his seat. A man in his early thirties was walking from the direction of the Tube. He was wearing a green parka with a fur-trimmed hood and carrying a brown leather briefcase. He had slicked-back black hair and a Saddam Hussein-style moustache. O'Brien had the photocopy of Basharat's passport on the dashboard and passed it to the Major. 'Looks like him,' he said.

'Right, here we go,' said the Major. He watched in the mirror as Basharat strode towards his house. 'Start the engine, Martin.'

O'Brien turned on the ignition.

'Fifty feet,' said the Major.

Shepherd, Shortt and Armstrong pulled on ski masks. They were already wearing gloves.

'Forty feet,' said the Major.

Shepherd took a deep breath. There was no going back once the van door opened.

'Thirty feet,' said the Major.

Shortt slid across to the side of the van.

'Go,' said the Major. 'Go, go, go.'

Shortt opened the side door and jumped out on to the pavement, followed by Shepherd and Armstrong. Basharat stopped when he saw them, his mouth open in surprise. Shortt reached him first, grabbed his left arm and jerked him towards the van. Basharat started to yell but Shepherd clamped a hand over his mouth and seized the hood of his parka with the other. Between them, they hauled him towards Armstrong at the van's door.

Shortt scrambled in, pulling Basharat after him. Shepherd's hand slipped from the man's mouth, but before he could shout, Shortt slammed him on to the floor and put a hand round his throat.

Shepherd and Armstrong piled in and Shepherd pulled the door shut as O'Brien drove off.

Shortt took his hand off Basharat's throat.

'Who the hell are you?' the Arab hissed.

'Shut the fuck up,' said Armstrong, shoving the barrel of his gun under the captive's chin.

'Are you Israelis?' he asked. 'If so, there's been some sort of mistake. I'm just a journalist.'

Armstrong put his masked face close to the Arab's. 'If you say one more thing, I'll smash your fucking teeth with the butt of this gun. Understand?'

The man nodded.

Shortt picked up a roll of electrical tape and used it to bind Basharat's wrists together behind his back. Then Shepherd pulled a sack over his head. 'Breathe slowly and you'll be all right,' he said. There was no sound from the Arab. 'Nod if you understand,' he added. The sack moved up and down.

O'Brien drove south out of London, heading to a farm in Surrey that the Major had cased that morning. It had been put up for auction after the death of its owner. The livestock had gone and the house was empty. The nearest neighbour was half a mile away, a cottage occupied by an old lady and her six cats.

Following the Major's directions, O'Brien turned off the main road, drove through two villages then down a rutted track. He switched off the van's lights and slowed while his eyes grew accustomed to the dark. They passed an auctioneer's sign, then a smaller one that gave the farm's name. O'Brien brought the van to a standstill: there was a barred metal gate across the track and the Major got out to open it.

The farmhouse was a two-storey building with a line of out-houses jutting from the right-hand side. There was a large corrugated metal barn and, lined up in front of it, a range of agricultural equipment, including a tractor and several ploughs. O'Brien parked in front of the barn. 'Get him out,' said the Major.

Shortt opened the van's rear doors. Armstrong and Shepherd seized an arm each and dragged Basharat out. It had started to rain and the Arab slipped on the wet grass as they frogmarched him towards the barn. Shortt hurried ahead and pulled open the wooden door for Armstrong and Shepherd to haul Basharat inside. Shepherd wrinkled his nose at the strong smell of pigs. Shortt switched on a flashlight and played the beam around the interior. There were metal pens to the right and storage bins to the left. Fluorescent lights hung from rafters that ran the length of the barn.

'Down on the floor,' hissed Armstrong. When Basharat hesi-tated, Armstrong kicked his legs from under him and the Arab fell. He landed heavily, his shoulder and head slamming against concrete.

The Major helped Shortt to shut the door, then pulled out his own flashlight. He motioned for Shortt to put his ski mask back on, then pointed at Shepherd and signalled for him to remove Basharat's hood.

Shepherd did so and Basharat coughed, then tried to sit up but Armstrong planted a foot on his chest and forced him back to the floor. The Major stood by the door, his arms folded.

Armstrong glared at Basharat. 'We're going to ask you some questions,' he said. 'Tell us what we want to know and you'll be free to go.' He pointed his gun at the Arab's head. 'If you don't tell us what we want to know, you'll die in this place. You'll die and we'll bury you in a field and no one will ever find your body.'

'I'm a journalist,' said Basharat. 'I'm just a journalist.'

'The videos of the hostages in Iraq – where do they come from?'

'What?' Basharat frowned.

Shortt stepped forward and kicked him in the ribs. Basharat screamed. 'Just answer his questions!' shouted Shortt.

'How do the videos get to the station?' asked the Major.

'Which videos?' asked Basharat.

Shortt kicked him again.

Tears streamed down the Arab's face. 'Why are you doing this?'

'The videos of the hostages,' said the Major. 'How do they get to the TV station?' He walked over to stand next to Armstrong.

'It depends,' said Basharat.

'On what?'

'Sometimes we get a disk. A DVD or a CD. Sometimes it comes through the Internet.'

'You know the Brit who was taken last week – the one being held by the Holy Martyrs of Islam?'

'I saw the story, but I didn't work on it.'

'How did that video get to the station?'

'I don't know. How would I know? I'm a correspondent, I don't work on the desk.'

The Major paced up and down at Basharat's feet. 'What about the American journalist, the one who was beheaded? How did the station get that video?'

'That was a DVD.'

'How do you know?'

'My brother told me. He works on the news desk in Qatar. We spoke about it at the time.'

'And how did the DVD get to the station?' asked the Major.

'From our correspondent in Dubai. It was delivered to his office.'

'Hand-delivered?'

'I don't know. It could have been or it could have been mailed.'

'Why do you think it went to the Dubai office?' asked the Major.

'I don't know,' said Basharat. 'To muddy the waters, I suppose. The CIA watch our head office, bug our phones, follow us to see who we meet.' He squinted up at the Major. 'You're not Israelis, are you? Are you CIA? MI5?'

Shortt stepped forward to kick Basharat again, and the Arab tried to roll out of the way – 'Okay, okay, okay.'

'So the DVD went to your office in Dubai. Then what?' said the Major.

'Someone loaded it into a computer then zapped it over to our news desk. They edited it, then put it on air and on to our website.'

The Major stared down at Basharat. 'What happened to the DVD? Did you pass it on to the authorities?'

'What authorities?'

'The police? The Americans?'

'We're journalists. We protect our sources.'

'Even when they're terrorists?' asked Armstrong.

'We're journalists,' repeated Basharat. 'We just report on what's happening.'

'You broadcast videos of people being murdered,' said Armstrong.

'But that's *all* we do,' said Basharat. 'We report on the people killed by the insurgents, and we report on the killings carried out by the coalition forces.'

'We need to know how the latest video got to the station,' said the Major.

'I told you, I don't know. I assume it came the same way as the Lake video.'

'We have to be sure. I need you to phone your brother and ask him how he got the latest video.'

'It's the middle of the night in Qatar.'

Shortt kicked Basharat in the ribs. He yelped.

The Major knelt down, went through Basharat's pockets and

pulled out his mobile phone. 'Tell him you're doing a story on Mitchell's kidnapping. Tell him a source has told you that the British government might be making a statement first thing tomorrow and you want some background.'

Shepherd and Shortt helped the man to sit up. Shortt used a Swiss Army knife to cut the tape binding his wrists.

'When you talk to your brother, do you normally speak English?'

Basharat shook his head.

'Okay,' said the Major. He gestured at Shortt. 'He speaks Arabic. Not fluently, but well enough to follow what you're saying.'

Basharat looked at Shortt, who spoke a few clipped words in Arabic, then grinned. 'I told him what I'll do to his mother if he screws us around.'

'If he even suspects you're tipping your brother off, you'll get a bullet in your head,' said the Major. 'Do you understand?'

Basharat nodded sullenly. The Major handed him the phone. Armstrong aimed the gun squarely at the Arab's face, his finger on the trigger.

Basharat scrolled through the phone's address book, then hit the green button. He put the phone to his ear, then spoke rapidly in Arabic. It was clear from his tone that he was apologising for waking his brother. Then he was talking in a more measured tone, trying to avoid looking at the gun.

Shortt was listening intently. The Major hadn't been bluffing: Shortt did speak some Arabic but Shepherd was aware that his knowledge of the language was basic, to say the least.

Basharat's voice was trembling and he kept taking deep breaths, trying to steady himself. He closed his eyes and rubbed the bridge of his nose as he spoke. Eventually he ended the call.

'Well done,' said the Major, taking the phone from him. 'What did he say?'

'The video came attached to an email,' said Basharat. 'A Yahoo account. It was about four minutes long. My brother says there was nothing special on the bits they didn't broadcast.'

'Who sent it?'

'The group holding him. The Holy Martyrs of Islam.'

The Major held out the phone. 'Call him back. Get him to forward the email to you.'

'He's mad enough at me as it is,' said Basharat.

'Well, you'll have to decide which is the least dangerous option,' said the Major. 'Your brother being angry with you, or me and these guys. I doubt your brother'll put a bullet in your head.'

Armstrong tapped the gun barrel against Basharat's head to emphasise the point.

'He's at home. The email will be on his office computer.'

'Tell him it's important, that you need it now – tell him what the hell you like but we want that email and we want it now. Do you have a personal email account? Yahoo or Hotmail?'

Basharat nodded. 'I've got a g-mail account.'

'Tell him you're working at home so he should send it to your personal account.'

Basharat took the phone and called his brother again. Shepherd could hear the tension in his voice, and sweat was pouring down his face. He spoke earnestly, his brow furrowed, then fell silent for a while. When he spoke again, he was clearly imploring his brother to do as he asked. Eventually he sighed with relief and switched off the phone. 'He'll do it,' he said. 'It'll take him about half an hour.'

'Good,' said the Major. He opened Basharat's mobile phone, stripped out the battery and tossed the phone back to the Arab.

'What happens to me now?' asked Basharat, looking fearfully at the gun in Armstrong's hand.

'We pick up your email and then you're free to go,' said the Major. He gestured at Shortt, who pulled the hood back over the Arab's head.

'We need a computer,' said the Major.

'Let's run by my house,' said Shepherd. 'I've got broadband.'

Shortt rolled Basharat over and bound his wrists with insulation tape. Then he and Armstrong helped the man to his feet.

'Why are you doing this?' asked Basharat, his voice muffled by the hood.

'You don't want to know,' said Shortt. He put his face close to the Arab's ear. 'If we told you, we'd have to kill you,' he whispered.

As Shortt and Armstrong bundled Basharat outside, the Major put his arm around Shepherd's shoulders. 'Are you okay?' he asked.

'I'm not happy about it,' said Shepherd, 'but it had to be done.'

'We didn't hurt him, not really.'

'We scared him shitless and maybe cracked a couple of ribs.' They walked together towards the door. 'How far would we have gone, boss,' asked Shepherd, 'if push had come to shove?'

'Hypothetical question. No point going there.'

'The guy's done nothing wrong,' Shepherd said. 'He's just a journalist doing his job.'

'And Geordie was doing his,' said the Major. 'We did what we had to do, Spider. Now, let's get that email and Basharat can go home.'

Geordie Mitchell paced up and down, swinging his arms. He always thought better when he was on the move, preferably on a run. The bigger the problem, the longer the run. Most of his former colleagues in the SAS were the same. Running was always the first step on the road to fitness. It built stamina and anyone preparing for the SAS selection course spent six months or more running three or four times a week. At first it was a chore, then it became a habit and eventually it was as natural as breathing.

As he paced around the room, he gazed at the floor. It was bare concrete. It didn't matter how thick it was because he had nothing to dig with. They'd taken his belt and emptied his pockets, and there was nothing in the basement he could use.

Mitchell dropped to the floor and started to do press-ups, keeping his breathing steady and even. He did a slow twenty, then a brisk ten, then another slow twenty, enjoying the burn in his arms. When he'd finished the second set of twenty, he rolled over, linked his fingers behind his head and did fifty sit-ups, lay on the floor for a minute to recover, then did a second set. It was the middle of the night but the light was still on. It hadn't been switched off all the time he'd been in the basement. He'd told Kamil that it was hard to sleep with the light on and Kamil had apologised but said that they had to be able to see him at all times. Every half-hour or so Mitchell would hear a soft footfall outside the door, then a brief silence as one of his captors looked through the peephole. The footfall was a good sign. It meant that there was no covert CCTV coverage of the basement.

Mitchell sat up, breathing heavily. He frowned as he stared at the wall in front of him. There was a small three-pin power socket about six inches above the ground. Mitchell got to his feet and walked over to it. He sat down and stared at it. Two small screws fixed the socket into the wall. The fact that the lights were on meant that there was power to the basement, which meant that the socket was probably live. A live power line could be used as a weapon. And there'd be wires running to the socket behind the wall. Wires could also be used as a weapon. He prodded the screws with his finger. They were in tight. He needed something to loosen them. A coin, or a flat piece of metal. He stood up and walked slowly round the room, even though he knew he was wasting his time: he had already searched every square inch.

The Transit van pulled up outside Shepherd's house. 'You've sold it already, have you?' asked the Major, gesturing at the estate agent's sign in the front garden.

'Under offer,' said Shepherd. 'Should be exchanging contracts later this week.' He opened the van's side door and stood on the pavement looking at the house. The lights were off. It was just before eleven o'clock so Katra had almost certainly gone to bed.

The Major climbed out and walked with him to the house.
Shepherd let them in and they went through to the sitting room.
'Drink?' he asked, as he sat down at his computer. There was a
stack of paper in the printer's tray: Liam had been downloading
information on the space-shuttle programme.

'I'm okay,' said the Major. He pulled up a chair and sat down.
He had written down Basharat's email address and password on a
piece of paper and he handed it to Shepherd, who launched his
Internet browser, tapped in the address of the g-mail home page,
then logged on to Basharat's account.

There were half a dozen unread emails, all but one in English,
the most recent from Basharat's brother in Qatar. The four-
minute video was tagged on to the email as an attachment and
Shepherd clicked on it.

'When are you moving to Hereford?' asked the Major, as they
waited for the file to download.

'Should be about a month,' said Shepherd. 'We've already got
a place fixed up. It's just a question of handling the legal stuff.'

'And the job's okay with you being based out of London?'

'The unit works all over the country so it doesn't matter
where my house is,' said Shepherd. 'The important thing is that
Liam will get to spend more time with his grandparents. It's
important for him and it's important for them. He's all they
have left of Sue.'

Shepherd's wife had died two and a half years earlier in a road
accident, driving Liam to school. She'd jumped a red light and
her VW Golf had slammed into a truck. Since then Shepherd had
juggled being an undercover cop with his responsibilities as a
single parent. Even with Katra's help it hadn't been easy.

'How are you getting on with Liam?'

'Fine,' said Shepherd. 'He's a great boy.'

'He's got over what happened?'

'I don't think either of us will ever get over it entirely, but he
seems okay.'

'What about you? Not seeing anyone?'

Shepherd chuckled. 'Since when have you been all touchy-feely, boss?'

'Three years is long enough, Spider. No one expects you to stay in mourning for ever.'

'It's two and a half. And I'm not in mourning.' Shepherd grimaced – he had sounded defensive.

'How long has it been since you went on a date?'

Shepherd laughed. 'Do people still go on dates?'

'I was trying to ask you subtly how long it'd been since you got laid.'

'I don't have much opportunity,' said Shepherd. 'Most of the women I've met recently have been either planning to have their husbands killed or blowing themselves to kingdom come. And I'm so busy that speed-dating is probably the only dating I'd have time for.'

The video finished its download and Shepherd opened the Windows Media Player so that they could watch it. The video had evidently been edited before it had been sent to the television station as it started in mid-sentence as a masked man with a Kalashnikov paced up and down in front of the camera.

The first thirty seconds hadn't been shown on television, and there was no station logo as there had been on the transmitted version. 'It's clearer than the version we taped off Sky News,' said the Major. 'If there's anything in it that'll help us find Geordie we'll stand a better chance of seeing it on this.'

They heard footsteps padding down the stairs and looked around to see Katra walk into the room, wrapped in a pink towelling robe. 'Oh, it's you,' she said.

'What were you expecting, burglars?' asked Shepherd.

Katra looked confused. 'No, I locked the doors,' she said. Since she had arrived from Slovenia her English had improved by leaps and bounds, but she still hadn't grasped Shepherd's sense of humour.

Shepherd introduced Major Gannon.

'Are you hungry?' she asked. 'I could make sandwiches.'

'We're fine,' said Shepherd. 'We're doing a bit of work, so you can go back to bed. Sorry we woke you.'

'I was waiting for you to come back,' said Katra. 'Would you like some coffee?'

'Really, we're fine,' said Shepherd. 'Now scoot.' Katra giggled and went back upstairs. When Shepherd turned back to the Major, the boss was grinning at him. 'What?' he asked.

'Nothing,' said the Major.

'She's a kid,' said Shepherd.

'She's, what – mid-twenties?'

'Twenty-four. And I'm thirty-six.'

'So when you're ninety, she'll be seventy-eight.'

'And she's an employee.'

'I didn't say anything, Spider.'

Shepherd burned the video on to a CD, then copied the original email on to the same disk.

'Anything interesting in his in-box?' asked the Major.

Shepherd clicked through Basharat's emails. There was nothing out of the ordinary, mainly gossip to friends in Qatar and his brother in Riyadh. 'Just chit-chat,' he said. He ejected the CD and gave it to the Major. 'What's the plan now?'

'We'll give the video a full working over, and I'll run a check on the email,' said Gannon. 'We should be able to track it back to its source. Let's just hope it's in Iraq.'

Shepherd walked the Major out to the van. Overhead the moon was full, so clear that they could see the craters on its surface. 'Geordie's boss is in town tomorrow,' said the Major. 'Can you come to Portland Place in the afternoon?'

'Sure,' said Shepherd. 'We're on a loose rein at the moment.'

The Major climbed back into the Transit van and drove off. As Shepherd walked to the front door he switched on his mobile. He had one voicemail message and he listened to it as he locked the front door. It was Caroline Stockmann, the unit's new psychologist.

★   ★   ★

Shepherd walked into the King's Head and looked around. Brown coat, brown hair and glasses, was how she'd described herself. Arranging to meet in the pub down the road from his house was a smart move, he thought, as he walked through the bar. If he didn't turn up she didn't have far to walk to his house. That had been one of Kathy Gift's tricks, turning up on his doorstep unannounced.

Caroline Stockmann was sitting in a quiet corner with a pint of beer in front of her. Chestnut hair rather than brown, a bit shorter than shoulder-length, glasses with rectangular frames. She was reading a copy of the *Economist* and looked up from it as he walked over. 'Dan?' He frowned at the pint glass and she smiled. 'You expected me to be sipping orange juice?' she asked.

Shepherd was lost for words. That was exactly what he'd thought. It was late afternoon but, even so, their meeting was business rather than social. And a pint of beer was the last thing he'd have expected a female psychologist to be drinking. 'Sorry. Yes. Dan – Dan Shepherd.'

'You can have orange juice if you want, but I'm off home after this and I've had a rough day,' she said.

'No, I could do with a drink, too,' said Shepherd. Stockmann extended her hand and he shook it. She had a firm grip. He noticed the engagement and wedding rings on her left hand. 'Do I call you Dr Stockmann, Mrs Stockmann or Caroline?'

'Caroline is fine.'

Shepherd went over to the bar and returned with a Jameson's, soda and ice. He sat down opposite her. 'Do you do a lot of interviews in pubs?'

'I pretty much go where I have to,' said Stockmann. 'You guys don't work office hours, and it's not as if you can pop into the local police station, is it? Where did Kathy see you?'

Shepherd grinned. 'She used to turn up at my house, but that was because I kept missing appointments.'

'Deliberately?'

'As you said, we work odd hours. It's hard to plan ahead.'

'Which is why pubs are a good idea,' she said. 'And they pull a good pint here.'

'I'm not really a beer drinker,' said Shepherd.

'Watching your weight?'

'It's an undercover thing. If I drink beer, everyone knows how much I've had. If I'm on whiskey and soda, I can add more soda and ice and no one's any the wiser. I can stay sober while everyone else drinks themselves stupid.'

'Vodka and tonic would make more sense. There's no colour to show how weak it is.'

'Okay, but I like the taste of Jameson's,' admitted Shepherd. 'You'll find most of the undercover guys stick to spirits and mixers.'

'You like undercover work?'

'You couldn't do it if you didn't,' said Shepherd.

'What do you like? The challenge?'

'Sure. You're putting yourself up against some very heavy guys. One false move and it's all over.'

'That must be scary at times.'

'Challenging.'

Stockmann smiled but said nothing.

'You don't take notes,' said Shepherd.

'I've got a good memory,' she said. 'Something we have in common.'

'Photographic?'

'I wish,' she said. 'But I can remember conversations almost verbatim. And I'm good with facts. And vocabulary. I speak five languages almost fluently.'

'I envy you that. I'm bad at languages. My memory's infallible with facts, faces and events, but I can't process information the way you have to if you want to speak a foreign language.'

'We've something else in common. I have a son called Liam, too.'

Shepherd raised his glass to her. 'Great name,' he said.

'My husband thought so,' said Stockmann. 'And we've a daughter. Rebecca.'

'Kids are what it's all about,' said Shepherd.

'Your boy must make your life complicated.'

'That's one way of putting it.' Shepherd laughed. 'He's ten so most of the time he still does as he's told, but I'm dreading his teens.'

'Being a one-parent family can't be easy at the best of times, but the pressures of your job must make it even more difficult.'

Shepherd shrugged. 'I have an au pair, and we're moving closer to my in-laws, Liam's grandparents.'

'You're leaving Ealing?'

'The house is under offer,' said Shepherd, 'and there's a place in Hereford we're interested in.'

'Bereavement, divorce and moving house are the three most stressful events in anyone's life. That's what they say.'

'Yeah, well, only someone who's never been shot would say that,' said Shepherd.

'You've been shot?'

'Isn't it in my file?' asked Shepherd.

'I didn't see it,' said Stockmann. 'What happened?'

'It was when I was in the SAS,' said Shepherd. 'Afghanistan. A sniper got me in the shoulder.'

'Ouch,' said Stockmann.

'It was a bit more than ouch,' said Shepherd. 'If I hadn't been helicoptered out, I might not have made it.'

'That's not why you left the SAS, though, is it?'

'Nah. I was back on duty two months later. I left the Regiment when my wife fell pregnant. She thought I should spend more time at home.' He snorted. 'That's not how it worked out, though. I was probably away more as a cop than I was when I was with the Regiment.'

'Out of the frying-pan into the fire?'

'Exactly how she put it,' said Shepherd. 'Though Sue was a bit more expressive.'

'More adjectives?'

'A lot more.'

She raised her glass and winked. 'I do like a good pint.' She took a sip and put the glass down in front of her. 'Kathy Gift was doing your biannuals for how long? Three years?'

'Pretty much,' said Shepherd. 'Do you know her?'

'We met a couple of times to go over her cases.'

'Is that what I am? A case?'

Stockmann smiled, and Shepherd forced himself to relax. Or at least to appear relaxed – he could never really let go when he was talking to the unit's psychologists. There was too much at stake. They chatted and nodded sympathetically but at the end of the day they decided whether or not he was fit to do his job.

'It makes the transition easier, allows me to hit the ground running, as it were,' she said. 'But I suppose it does give me the advantage. I know a lot about you but I doubt that you were able to find out much about me.'

Shepherd smiled thinly. She would have expected him to check her out – he was a policeman, after all – but while his MI5 contacts had heard of her, none had met her and none had been able to add anything to what Charlotte Button had told him. She was right: she did have the advantage. 'So, let's get on to an even playing-field,' she said, smiling brightly. 'What would you like to know?'

'I'm not sure there *is* anything,' said Shepherd. 'It's not like we're best buddies, is it? Kathy went off and got married and we knew nothing about it.'

'You expected a wedding invitation?'

Shepherd swirled his whiskey around his glass. 'No, of course not. But it's a strange situation. You get to know our innermost thoughts, you get closer to us than our families and friends do, yet there's no emotional context. You care, but you don't care.'

'Kathy liked you, I've no doubt about that . . . Sounds like we're at primary school, doesn't it? Who likes who, who's best friends with who.'

'It's not a question of liking, it's a question of trust.'

'My security rating is about the highest there is, but I don't suppose that's what you mean,' said Stockmann. 'You mean emotional trust.' She leaned forward. 'Dan, I believe in what I do, and I'm absolutely committed to doing the best possible job I can for the unit.'

'A friend of mine once explained the difference between commitment and involvement,' said Shepherd.

'The breakfast analogy? The chicken is involved and the pig is committed?'

'Well, that spoils that story,' said Shepherd.

'I do understand that when you go into a situation under cover your life is on the line. And the worst thing that can happen to me is that I break a nail typing up a report. But that doesn't mean I don't understand or that I don't empathise with what you do. Anyway, come what may, we're stuck with each other. I have to do the biannual thing for Charlie, so let's have a chat and a few drinks and then we can go our separate ways.'

'Are you full-time with SOCA now?'

'I'm a sort of consultant,' she said. 'I'll still be doing some work with Five.'

'You've been with them for a while?' asked Shepherd.

'Almost a decade,' she said.

'Charlie said you were with something called the Predictive Behaviour Group.'

'The mind-readers,' she said. 'Getting inside other people's heads.'

'Which is what you're doing with the undercover unit now.'

She smiled. 'Bit different,' she said. 'In the unit's case, I'm there to help. The PBG was more about stitching people up – finding their weaknesses and advising others on how to exploit them. It was fun at times.'

'In what way?'

'How much did Charlie tell you?'

'Not much.'

She took another sip of her pint. 'I don't suppose there's any harm in telling you – you've signed the Official Secrets Act.'

'And I'm one of the good guys,' said Shepherd.

'Indeed you are. Anyway, when the group was first set up its main task was to advise ministers on how foreign politicians would react to certain situations. Then our brief widened and we started giving briefings on major criminals to the security services. How would Gangster A react if approached by an attractive female undercover agent? What would Gangster B do if asked to give evidence against a competitor? That sort of thing.'

'Interesting,' said Shepherd.

'It got a lot more so when we started to get more proactive,' said Stockmann. 'MI5 set up a unit whose brief was basically to unsettle some of the biggest villains in the UK, the really heavy guys, the ones who are virtually untouchable by conventional policing. The idea was to put them under pressure by screwing with their lives.'

'In what way?'

Stockmann giggled. 'We had *carte blanche*,' she said. 'That didn't mean they did everything we suggested, but we were free to let our imaginations roam. From simple things like scratching their cars or arranging for roadworks outside their house, to mortgage loans being called in or flights cancelled.'

'How does that help anyone?' asked Shepherd.

'It's about putting them off-balance,' she said, 'annoying them until their life is in total disarray. The idea is that they spend so much time worrying about all the fertiliser that's being thrown at them that they row with everyone close to them. They start making mistakes, being more hands-on, which means you guys stand a better chance of catching them in the act.'

'You're telling me you were paid to annoy people?'

'That's about it,' she said, 'but we got results. We'd been looking at a heroin dealer in Wolverhampton and we suggested that his wife's dog was kidnapped. It was obvious that she loved it more than him, but then it was around more than he was. Cocker spaniel with lovely eyes. Anyway, the dog duly went missing and she nagged him so much that he belted her and a neighbour called the police. They went in to sort out the domestic and found two kilos of heroin in his kitchen. He was fairly low down the food chain but the Drugs Squad turned him and we put half a dozen very heavy guys behind bars.'

'Who does the dirty work?'

'You mean who kidnapped the dog? The spooks, bless them. They love playing games. Now, one thing's not in your file and that's your nickname – Spider.'

'I ate one once,' he said.

'Lovely,' said Stockmann.

'It was in my SAS days. Jungle training. We had a competition to see who could eat the most repulsive thing. I ate a tarantula.'

'And you won?'

Shepherd shook his head. 'Came second.'

'What did the winner eat?'

'You don't want to know.'

'I've got a pretty strong stomach.'

'Really, you don't want to know. It all got a bit silly.'

'Boys will be boys,' said Stockmann. She raised her glass to him. 'How did the tarantula taste?' she asked. 'Like chicken, I suppose.'

'Like a spider,' said Shepherd. 'Bit chewier than a caterpillar.'

Stockmann chuckled. 'Must come in handy, your SAS background,' she said, 'insect-eating notwithstanding.'

'I don't behave like a cop who's spent ten years pounding the beat,' said Shepherd, 'and I'm fitter than most.'

'And there's the weapons training.'

'I wondered when you'd get around to that.'

'We've got to talk about it, Dan. It happened.'

'It happened,' agreed Shepherd.

'Any thoughts on it?'

Shepherd sat back in his chair. 'I talked it through with Kathy. They made me have several sessions with her.'

'You understand why. You shot three people, two men and a woman.'

'I took out three suicide-bombers who, if they'd had their way, would have killed hundreds of innocent people.'

'But being right doesn't make killing any easier.'

'Actually, it does,' said Shepherd.

'There's as much stress-induced illness on the winning side as there is on the losing side,' said the psychologist.

'You're talking about war,' said Shepherd. 'War's a different sort of stress, the stress of never knowing if you're next to be killed. Law enforcement is different. You make a decision and go with it. Providing you make the right decision, everything falls into place. If I'd shot three innocent people I'd be feeling guilty, no question, but the three terrorists I shot were just about to blow themselves and others to kingdom come. If your question is whether or not I regret what I did, then the answer is no. Definitely not.'

'Because you were in the right?'

'Because I did what had to be done,' he said.

'Do you believe in the death penalty?'

'In general, no. For paedophiles and serial-killers, probably. But we're never going to have the death penalty in this country again. The way things are going, our penal system does all it can to put murderers back on the streets.' He frowned. 'You're not suggesting that I executed them, are you?'

'No, that's not what I meant.'

'Because I didn't shoot them as a punishment. I shot them to stop them killing others.'

'Do you want to hear my theory on murder victims?' asked Stockmann.

'Sure.'

'It's the victims-generally-ask-for-it theory. Not very politically correct, I'm afraid, in this day and age.' She took another sip of her beer. 'I'm not talking about terrorism or random killings, but they really are a tiny minority of murders.'

'Most victims know their killers,' said Shepherd.

'Absolutely,' said Stockmann. 'Family members or neighbours account for ninety per cent of murders.'

'And the victims ask for it – is that what you're saying?'

'Don't get me wrong, that's just my way of describing how I think it works. No one deserves to be murdered. But in the vast majority of cases, the behaviour of the victim leads to their death. It's the wife nagging at her husband when he gets back from the pub. Should he be coming home drunk? No, of course not. Does she have the right to nag him? Of course she does. But it's the fact that she nags him when he's drunk that leads him to pick up a kitchen knife and stick it into her heart.'

'Cause and effect?'

'Exactly. Two guys in a pub, both the worse for wear. They start to argue. Punches are thrown, a bottle gets smashed and is shoved into a guy's throat. If the victim had walked away before the bottle was smashed, he'd still be alive.'

'But if you take that argument further, you could say that anyone who walks down a dark alley deserves to be mugged. Or a woman who goes out alone at night is asking to be raped.'

'Would you walk alone down a dark alley if you didn't have to?'

'No, but we live in a country where anyone should be able to walk anywhere without fear of being attacked.'

'Dan, I'm not on the side of the murderers, muggers and rapists. And of course I'm not saying that anyone deserves to be robbed or raped. But murder is different. It's a lot easier to mug or rape than it is to kill. Murder is a big step – the biggest. And I believe that, more often than not, the victim is controlling the situation.' She smiled. 'Like I said, it's not a politically correct view. But I'd say that the terrorists you killed brought about their own deaths by virtue of their actions. So I can see why there wouldn't be much guilt attached to what you did.'

'Is that really your theory?' asked Shepherd.

'What do you mean?'

'I mean, is it really your theory or is it a way of assessing how I feel about killing?'

Stockmann smiled. 'Do you think I'm that devious, Dan?'

'You work for MI5 and they don't come more devious than that.'

'And now I work for SOCA. And we're just chatting. Do I believe that the behaviour of a murder victim results in their death? Yes, I do. Cross my heart and hope to die.'

'OK. So, how does it look? Am I fit for duty?'

'No question about that,' said Stockmann. She handed him a business card. 'That's got my mobile number, Dan. If ever you want a chat, give me a call. I'm not just there for the biannuals or when Charlie wants reassurance. I'm a resource you can use whenever you want.'

'Thanks,' said Shepherd, slipping the card into his wallet. 'Have you met Razor yet? Jimmy Sharpe?'

'He's next on my list. Why?'

Shepherd grinned. 'No reason.'

'He's a character, I gather,' she said.

'Oh, yes,' said Shepherd. 'For sure.'

Rob Manwaring cradled the twelve-gauge automatic shotgun and wished for the thousandth time that he could fire the weapon in anger. He was one of a dozen marines in Baghdad who had been selected to try out the Auto Assault 12 but although he had been on two patrols a day for the best part of a month he'd yet to fire at anything other than a range target.

The AA12 was a street sweeper. It could empty its twenty-round drum magazine in two seconds, and came with a full range of ammunition including non-lethal rounds, shot and solid bullets, and high-explosive armour-piercing projectiles that could pierce quarter-inch-thick steel plate. Manwaring was carrying all the different types of ammunition, and was itching to fire them. Along with the AA12, he had been given all the latest combat equipment. He had an Advanced Combat Helmet, which was three and a half pounds lighter than the old Kevlar helmet, a pair of Wiley X goggles, Infantry Combat Boots Type II, which were more comfortable and durable than the old army boots, with the added benefit that they never needed polishing – at least that was the theory, but they got just as dusty and muddy as the old ones ever had. He also had on the army's latest Interceptor Body Armour, guaranteed to stop a 9mm bullet, with the Armour Protection Enhancement System, for further protection to the groin, arms and neck. He'd been offered the Deltoid Extension pack, for the shoulders and the sides of the ribcage, but it added an extra five pounds in weight and limited the movement of his arms so he'd turned it down. It was all very well looking like Robocop, Manwaring figured, but it was no good if he couldn't use his weapon effectively. Several of the guys in his unit had discarded the heavy body armour to save even more weight but Manwaring had heard too many stories about snipers for that.

He and three members of his unit were on foot patrol, and their armoured Humvee rolled about fifty feet ahead of them. The top brass had decided that more troops should be out and about, mixing with the locals, winning hearts and minds. Manwaring considered it a waste of time: there was no way he could laugh with the locals when he was dressed in full combat gear and carrying a weapon that could kill a couple of dozen with one burst. All the chewing-gum in the world wasn't going to change the view of ordinary Iraqis that the Americans were an occupying power. They just wanted their country back.

A group of children in threadbare shirts and shorts ran over, their bare feet kicking up dust. 'Hey, dudes!' shouted one. He couldn't have been more than seven. 'High five!' He held up his hand.

Manwaring grinned. He held the AA12 against his chest and raised his right hand. The boy had to jump to reach it. 'What's your name?' asked Manwaring, and took a swig from his water bottle.

'Chiko!' shouted the little boy.

'Chiko? That's a Mexican name, isn't it? Are you Mexican?'

'Chiko!' yelled the little boy. 'Chiko! High five!'

Manwaring gave the boy a second high five, then called to the other guys in his unit, 'Anyone got some gum?'

'You getting soft in your old age, Rob?' said the guy to Manwaring's right. Ben Casey was a ten-year veteran: he had served in Afghanistan three times and was on his second tour in Iraq. Casey pulled an open pack from one of his vest pockets and tossed it to Manwaring, who fumbled with his gun.

'Butterfingers!' shouted Casey, as the gum bounced off Manwaring's helmet. The sticks tumbled out of the pack and landed on the ground. The children yelled and scrambled for them.

One of the older boys pushed Chiko aside and the little boy fell, scraping his knees. He rolled on to his back, sobbing.

'Hey!' shouted Manwaring. 'Be careful!' He bent down and reached for the child's arm.

As the body armour rode up to his waist, the Sniper's bullet smacked into the base of his spine and ripped through his gut. Manwaring fell forward, on top of the now screaming boy, blood pooling around them. The AA12 fell from his grasp and clattered on to the road.

The Sniper smiled as he watched the Americans run for cover. '*Allahu Akbar*,' he whispered. God is great. The man's name was Salam, but he no longer answered to that name. He was Qannaas, the Sniper. He had killed two hundred and thirty-seven Americans in less than three years, every one with a single bullet.

The man next to him also smiled. '*Allahu Akbar*,' he echoed. He was the Spotter. He had been with the Sniper for two years. Before that there had been another, but he had been shot by the Americans when the car he was in hadn't slowed for a roadblock on the outskirts of Baghdad. In a perfect world the Sniper would have chosen to work alone. But the world wasn't perfect and a sniper always needed a spotter. A sniper could be so focused on his target that he would no longer be aware of what was going on around him. And while the Sniper was concentrating, the Spotter could keep an eye on the wind. A palm frond swaying, a flag fluttering, a column of smoke dissipating gave clues to the direction and strength of the wind. The Spotter would whisper his estimation of its characteristics and the Sniper would adjust his aim accordingly. A good spotter meant the difference between a good shot and a perfect shot, and so far all two hundred and thirty-seven of his shots had been perfect. Two hundred and thirty-seven shots, two hundred and thirty-seven kills.

The Spotter waited by the Sniper's side to see what he would do next. Sometimes the Sniper would shoot once, then move on. Sometimes he would wait and select a second target. They were on top of a building overlooking the street and it was clear that the soldiers, frantically seeking cover, had no idea where the shot had come from.

The Humvee had stopped but the men inside stayed where they were. The children were running down the street, screaming in terror, but the Iraqi civilians just stood and stared at the dead soldier. The Iraqis knew they had nothing to fear. The Sniper only shot Americans in uniform.

He slotted another round into the breech. He had decided to wait for the second shot. At some point the soldiers would go to retrieve their fallen comrade and that was when he would make his second shot of the day. His second shot and his second kill. He pressed his eye to the rubber cup of the telescopic sight and waited.

Driving into Central London was a pain at the best of times but early evening meant tackling the rush-hour and Shepherd was in no mood to be sitting in traffic. He caught a Central Line train at Ealing Broadway and read the *Daily Mail* as he headed east. A former general turned military commentator had been given two pages to detail the problems facing the coalition forces in Iraq. His line was that while it had been a mistake to invade Iraq in the first place, it would be an even bigger mistake to pull out before democracy had been established. That would lead to only one thing: all-out civil war in which hundreds of thousands would die. Shepherd wasn't an expert on military affairs, but he agreed with the former general's conclusions. He had always felt that invading

Iraq had been a huge mistake. Saddam Hussein had been a tyrant, who had maimed and murdered his people, but Shepherd figured that other countries should be left to work out their own problems. If America felt justified in invading Iraq because it disagreed with the way the country was being run, what was to stop China deciding that they could do a better job of running America than the President?

The decision of President Bush Senior to go to war against Iraq to liberate Kuwait had made perfect sense, politically, morally and legally. His son's motives in invading made less sense to Shepherd, and he was even more bewildered by the British Prime Minister's decision to commit British troops to the fight. If Shepherd had still been in the SAS when the war had started he would happily have gone to Iraq. He was a soldier and a good soldier obeyed orders, even when they knew that those orders were wrong.

Shepherd left the train at Notting Hill Gate and flagged down a black cab. He had it drop him a couple of hundred yards from the shopping street where Button wanted to meet. He spent fifteen minutes checking he wasn't being tailed, then headed to the high-class butcher's whose window was full of organic beef and free-range chickens. On the way he spotted Sharpe, sitting in a coffee shop and pretending to read the *Evening Standard*. Shepherd slipped in through the door and moved cautiously behind him. He was just about to put a hand on Sharpe's shoulder when Sharpe spoke without looking around: 'Don't play silly buggers,' he snarled.

'Just checking you were on the ball. How long have you been here?'

'An hour,' said Sharpe. 'Her Majesty went in fifteen minutes ago.'

'And you're waiting for what, exactly?'

Sharpe put down his paper. 'Always arrive early, you know that.' He looked at his watch. 'Okay, let's go.'

'I'll take her a tea,' said Shepherd.

'You didn't bring teacher an apple?'

'I want a coffee so I'll take her a tea. It's not brown-nosing. If we were meeting Hargrove in a pub we'd buy him a drink.' Sam Hargrove had been their boss in the days before their undercover unit had become part of the Serious Organised Crime Agency. He had always preferred to hold his meetings in pubs or at sporting events. Unlike Charlotte Button, who had moved to the unit from MI5, Hargrove had been a career cop with almost thirty years in the job.

Shepherd went to the counter and ordered. 'I'll have a *latte*,' said Sharpe, at his shoulder.

Shepherd paid, the girl behind the counter slotted the cups into a cardboard tray and Sharpe took it from her. 'Least I can do is carry them,' he said.

He followed Shepherd across the road. The door that led to the offices above the shops was between the butcher's and a florist. There were three brass nameplates at the side of the door and an entryphone with three buttons. Shepherd pressed the middle one and smiled up at the CCTV camera that monitored the entrance. The door buzzed. He went in and climbed up with Sharpe to the second floor.

Charlotte Button had the door open for them. She was wearing a white jacket over a floral dress and looked as if she had just come from a christening. 'Everything all right?' she asked.

'I brought you a tea,' said Sharpe.

'Razor, that's so sweet,' she said, and took the paper cup from him.

Sharpe looked at Shepherd and winked. Shepherd mouthed an obscenity at him.

The office was lined with filing cabinets and volumes on tax law. There were four desks, one in each corner, and a door leading to another office.

'Through there,' she said. The two men stood aside to let her go in first.

A single large oak desk dominated the interior office, with a high-backed executive chair behind it. A large whiteboard stood beside it, with a couple of dozen photographs stuck to it, head-and-shoulder shots and surveillance pictures taken through a long lens. They were all of Asian men in their early twenties to mid-thirties. From the street backgrounds Shepherd decided that they had been taken in the UK, but he couldn't identify the locations. Sharpe handed him his coffee.

'This is going to be a joint operation with SO13, the Anti-Terrorist Branch,' said Button, coming up behind them. 'They've been running a long-term penetration of an Islamic terrorist cell in the Midlands and need a weapons connection. They made an approach to SOCA and, as luck would have it, you two are already up and running. You can continue your covers as May and Lomas.'

She went over to the whiteboard. Five of the photographs were grouped together, head-and-shoulder shots in colour, all the faces staring, unsmiling, at the camera. They appeared to be blown-up passport or driving-licence photographs. 'These are the five guys you'll be meeting. One is the Branch's man, but they're not prepared to say which.'

'What?' said Shepherd.

'They're insisting, and I've agreed,' said Button. 'It's not that unusual a request. We did similar deals in Northern Ireland all the time. Sass, Army Intelligence, RUC, MI5, everyone wanted to protect their resources.'

'Yeah, but this isn't Northern Ireland,' said Shepherd. 'We're not going to blow anyone's cover, are we?'

Sharpe studied the photographs. Under each was a printed label with the man's name and details of height and weight: Asim, Salman, Ali, Hassan and Fazal. Asim and Salman shared the same family name.

'I know this is a bit obvious, but can't you just run checks on these five guys?' said Sharpe. 'The new SOCA database would give you an idea of who's been naughty and who's been nice. It's so packed with information that I hear Santa Claus has started using it.'

'It's a matter of trust, Razor,' said Button. 'You're right, of course. If we wanted we could run the names, but I'd assume that the anti-terrorism boys will have already covered for their man. But leaving aside the matter of trust, I see their point of view. If anything goes wrong, the fact that you don't know who the agent is means he can't show out.'

'Which means we can't protect him,' said Sharpe.

'He doesn't need our protection,' said Button. 'All you're doing is handling the weapons side. They're Islamic fundamentalists so they won't be getting into bed with you. We have to respect their wishes. And remember, the day might come when you want to keep your anonymity. This sets a precedent.'

'When and where?' asked Shepherd.

'They'll make contact tomorrow,' said Button. 'They'll be given the Graham May phone number. Play hard to get – you don't like dealing with people you don't know, where did you get the number. You know the drill. You make contact and you go in unwired. Just a meet-and-greet. If they're not spooked, we use the warehouse again, wired for sound and vision. That's if they go for it. If they want to choose the turf, run with it. You'll be the outsiders, so let them make the running.'

'Do we go armed?' asked Shepherd.

Button looked pained. 'I'd rather you didn't.'

'It fits in with our cover. We're arms dealers.'

'These guys aren't professionals, so far as I'm told, just hot-heads who want to go out and commit mayhem.'

'Sounds like they've already got enough to charge them with conspiracy,' said Shepherd.

'The Branch wants more,' said Button, 'and the chance to distance their man. A Muslim undercover agent is like gold these days. They want him away clean before they bust them.'

'Makes sense,' said Sharpe.

'Why, Razor, I'm so glad you approve,' said Button. 'Any questions?'

Shepherd tapped the whiteboard. 'These names, are they real?'

'They're the names the Branch gave me with the photographs,' said Button.

'If we don't know them, what's our connection? Who's going to make the call?' said Shepherd.

'The agent is going to be putting your name forward tomorrow, but on the basis that a friend of his says you might be in a position to supply weapons. One of the gang members will make the call.'

'So the man who calls won't necessarily be the agent?' said Sharpe. Button gave him a withering look and he held up his hands. 'Just thinking aloud,' he said.

'What sort of weapons?' asked Shepherd.

'Submachine pistols,' said Button. 'The intel suggests they're planning an attack on a shopping mall.'

'What the hell are they thinking?' asked Sharpe.

'It's terrorism,' said Button. 'They're probably not thinking about anything other than causing the maximum amount of terror. And shooting families out shopping is as good a way of doing it as any.'

'And we're going to supply the weapons, are we?' asked Shepherd.

'You make contact and set up a buy. Once the buy is set up we'll decide how to play it.'

'We'll decide, or the Branch?' asked Shepherd.

'It's their operation,' said Button.

'That's my worry,' said Shepherd. 'If it's a SOCA operation, we have control. Suppose they decide we sell the guns, then something goes wrong and people die? Which fan is the shit going to hit? I don't want it heading in my direction.'

'Let's take it one step at a time, Spider. I'll be watching your back.'

Shepherd hadn't been working with Charlotte Button long enough to trust her as a matter of course, but she was his boss and he had no choice other than to give her the benefit of the doubt.

'Okay, then,' said Button. 'Give me a call as soon as you have a meet set up. Everything else okay?'

'No problems here,' said Sharpe.

'Everything okay in your life, Spider?' she asked.

'Sure,' said Shepherd.

'Nothing on your mind?'

Shepherd wondered if she was getting at something, then decided she was simply checking on his welfare. 'The sale of my house is taking for ever, but other than that everything's just fine.'

'You know what they say, moving house is just about the most stressful thing you can go through. That and bereavement.' A look of horror passed over her face as she realised what she'd said. She reached out to touch his arm. 'I'm sorry, I said that without thinking. I'm an idiot.'

'No,' he said. 'Caroline Stockmann said the same thing. People can't tread on eggshells around me for ever. And you're right, moving house is stressful. But it's going okay.' Selling his house had been hard, but it hadn't come within a million miles of the pain Shepherd had felt when Sue died. He wouldn't tell Button that, of course. He wouldn't tell her about the nights he'd cried himself to sleep either, or that the worst moments came when he'd wake up after dreaming about her, only for the memory of her death to hit him again. Each time it happened was like the first. But as the years passed the dreams had become less frequent and the pain had numbed. He would never forget Sue, he had loved her too much for that, but he had meant what he'd said to Button. He didn't expect people to pussyfoot around him. His wife had died. He had dealt with it and his son had dealt with the loss of his mother. End of story. They were moving on now, and selling the house was part of the process.

'I won't be putting any more cases your way until the Branch operation is over,' she said, 'so work your move round that.'

'Thanks,' said Shepherd. He felt a twinge of guilt at not mentioning Geordie's kidnapping, but at least he hadn't lied.

'Oh, and Caroline was impressed with you,' said Button. 'Very impressed.'

There were two pots of coffee on the hotplate. One regular and one decaffeinated. Shepherd poured himself a cup of regular. He had never seen the point of removing caffeine from coffee. It made as much sense as taking the alcohol out of whiskey. 'Get me one, Spider,' called O'Brien, who was spreading strawberry jam over a croissant. Armstrong and Shortt were sitting at the long table, flicking through the day's newspapers. Whenever they came across an article about Mitchell they ripped it out and stuck it on one of the whiteboards. An ashtray filled with cigarette butts sat in front of Armstrong.

Shepherd poured coffee for O'Brien and gave it to him. He picked up one of the torn-out articles. It was from the *Daily Telegraph*, a report on the Foreign Secretary's reaction to the kidnapping. 'This is a very, very difficult and very worrying situation,' said the politician. 'We remain in touch with his family.' He had been speaking at a press conference and had been asked if the government would be prepared to pay a ransom for Mitchell's release. His reply had been emphatic: 'The government of the United Kingdom does not pay ransoms.' According to the article's author, sources close to the Foreign Secretary were convinced that the militant group intended to kill Mitchell, come what may.

The door to the conference room opened and the Major ushered in a tall man with swept-back grey hair and a neatly trimmed moustache. The Major was carrying his sat-phone and his companion had a brown leather document case tucked under one arm. The Major closed the door and put the phone on the floor. 'This is John Muller,' he said. 'He heads up the company Geordie works for.'

Muller shook hands with them all, then took off his jacket and sat down next to the Major at the head of the table. O'Brien poured a mug of coffee for him as he rolled up his shirtsleeves.

'John's here to give us a quick briefing on what's happened over in Iraq,' said the Major.

Muller stirred his coffee. 'Geordie was in charge of security for a fifty-kilometre length of pipeline,' he said. 'Most of it was underground. There were a couple of pumping stations, and he also ran security for our personnel. He had about a hundred Iraqis under him, along with a dozen expats, mainly South African. He was driving back to our compound with three Iraqis. They were killed and he was bundled into a vehicle and driven away.'

'Was Geordie the target, then?' asked O'Brien.

'Almost certainly not. They'd just taken one of our executives to the airport and it wasn't his responsibility. A South African was supposed to do it but he was sick. Geordie was in the wrong place at the wrong time.'

'He was armed, right?' said the Major.

'Of course,' said Muller. 'But the abductors blew up my men's Jeep with an improvised explosive device.'

'Were they planning to kill them, or was it about taking a hostage?' asked Shepherd.

'Personally, I think they were out to kill them. Then they saw Geordie and decided to take him and sell him on to a fundamentalist group. It was opportunistic. If they'd been planning a kidnap from the start, I don't think they'd have used the IED.'

'I'm missing something here,' said Shepherd. 'Are the guys who took Geordie criminals or fundamentalists?'

'Almost certainly criminals,' said Muller. 'Or at least guys who are motivated by money. They would have sold Geordie on to the fundamentalists.'

'So why are criminals setting off IEDs?' asked Shepherd.

'Because there are bounties on offer,' said Muller. 'There's a whole load of wealthy fundamentalists out there funding the trouble. They're the same guys who pay off the families of suicide-bombers. The going rate is three thousand dinars if they toss a hand grenade at an infidel. That's about three dollars. They get two hundred thousand dinars if they fire an RPG and up to a million if they take out a vehicle with an IED. The guys who took Geordie were after the million, but when they saw they had a live foreigner they knew they'd be able to get even more.'

'But there was no ransom demand after they took him?' said the Major.

'The first I heard was the video on al-Jazeera,' said Muller. 'It was never a question of money. We've offered a reward for his safe return but we've had no response. It's purely political.'

'There's no way that your company can negotiate for his release?' asked Armstrong. He flicked open his pack of Marlboro, tossed a cigarette into the air, caught it between his lips, then lit it.

Muller shook his head. 'There's no one to negotiate with,' he said. 'It's a fucking minefield over there, literally and figuratively. There's no central organisation we can deal with, and we've no idea who has any sort of influence on the various groups. The militants are in a state of constant flux, too. I liken it to a virus, constantly evolving. We have a hard time keeping track of who's who. The Holy Martyrs of Islam only came to light when they kidnapped the Lake boy. The main group out there is called Al-Qaeda In Iraq, and used to be led by a Jordanian, Abu Musab al-Zarqawi. They killed an Egyptian envoy and a couple of Algerian diplomats a while back. Al-Zarqawi was killed some time ago but his group is still active. Thing is, they usually target the hostages they take, but it looks as if Geordie's abduction was opportunistic – they blasted his vehicle and he could easily have died, so we don't think al-Zarqawi's mob's behind it. But there are dozens of other groups out there who are just as dangerous. Al-Jaysh al-Islami fi Iraq, The Islamic Army in Iraq kidnapped an American recently; seized two French journalists and killed an Italian in 2004. They've probably butchered a dozen people in the last three years. The Ansar al-Sunnah Army killed a Japanese security manager and a Turkish contractor. The Islamic Army of Iraq seized two French journalists, and killed a dozen Nepalese workers. The al-Saraya Mujahideen took a group of Japanese and

Italians two years ago. Al-Tawhid wal-Jihad, which translates as Unity and Holy War, has abducted and decapitated seven civilian contractors. The Green Battalion killed an Italian security guard. The Holders of the Black Banners have been taking hostages but so far haven't killed any. Ditto the Islamic Movement for Iraq's Mujahideen. Those are the groups that issue the demands and perform the executions, but they rarely carry out the initial kidnappings.'

'Criminal gangs, right?' said Shepherd.

'Exactly. The insurgents who captured Geordie have probably passed him on to one of the militant groups. Probably got money for him.'

'If we can get to them, could we pay them off?' asked Shepherd.

'Almost certainly not,' said Muller. 'I'm sorry, guys, but these bastards aren't in it for the money. We've put the word out that we'll pay half a mill for his return, but it won't do any good. Between you and me and these four walls, the reward is just public-relations bullshit.'

'Is there any way of telling which side this group is on?' asked Shepherd.

'They're almost certainly Sunnis,' said Muller. 'They pretty much ran Iraq when Saddam was in charge. Most of the Sunni clerics in Iraq regard the *jihad* as a legitimate reaction to what they see as the American invasion of their country whereas the Shias tend to regard the Americans as a temporary presence. So the attacks on the coalition troops tend to be from Sunni insurgents. The Shias make up most of the Iraqi Army and police force, which is why there are so many attacks against them. More than thirty thousand dead so far.'

'What's been done on the ground?' asked Shortt, rubbing his moustache.

'My guys are gathering intel. The Blackwater boys are on the case. We have a number of shared contracts and I've got a pretty good relationship with their top brass. But once they're dug in, the militants aren't going to put their heads above ground until Geordie's dead.' He pulled a face as if he had a sour taste in his mouth. 'I'm sorry, guys, it doesn't look good.'

'What about the military?' said Armstrong.

'They're looking, but you have to know what it's like out there. The American troops ride around in convoys and hardly ever get out of their Humvees. The locals are on the ground, but with the best will in the world they're not going to stumble across Geordie. Our best bet is going to be human intel, either an informer or someone who gets hauled in for something else and wants to cut a deal.'

'Yeah, or maybe we could call in a psychic,' said Shortt, bitterly.

'Easy, Jimbo,' said the Major. 'No need to go shooting the messenger. John's just telling us the way things stand.'

'I'm heading straight back there,' said Muller. 'I wanted to brief you guys, and I'm paying a courtesy call on Geordie's brother. But then I'll be in Baghdad until this is over. One way or the other.'

'Let's suppose we identify the guys who are holding him,' said the Major. 'What are our options?'

'If we know who they are, we can reach out to them through groups they might be sympathetic to. Religious figures, for instance. It's a question of who should make the approach.'

'Has that worked in the past?' asked Shepherd.

'A few times,' said Muller. 'It depends on the agenda of the hostage-takers. Sometimes they'll make more capital out of showing they can be reasonable. Or it could be seen as a way of boosting the status of someone sympathetic to their aims. Like I said, it's a minefield.'

A mobile phone rang. Shepherd winced and fished his two out of his jacket pocket. 'Sorry, I've got to take this,' he said, and hurried out of the room.

'That Graham May?' asked a voice. Youngish, a nasal Birmingham whine.

'Who wants to know?' said Shepherd, shutting the door behind him.

'A friend of a friend said you might be able to supply us with what we need.'

'Do I know you?'

'No, but I've got the cash.'

'Who gave you my number?' asked Shepherd. He was an underworld arms dealer and they were suspicious of anyone they hadn't dealt with before.

'A friend of mine,' said the voice.

'Yeah, well, unless he's a friend of mine, and a bloody good one at that, we're going to end this conversation right now.'

'You are May, right?'

'Like I said, who the hell are you?'

'My name's . . .' the voice hesitated '. . . Tom.'

'Tom?'

'Yeah, Tom.'

'Tom, Tom, the piper's son?'

'What?'

'I don't know anyone called Tom. This conversation is over—'

'Wait! Wait!' said the man, panicking.

Shepherd smiled to himself. 'Tom' was behaving like a rank amateur.

'The man who gave me your name said I wasn't to tell you who he is.'

'That makes no sense at all,' said Shepherd.

'He gave me your number and your name.'

'And what is it you want?'

'To buy some gear from you. I already said.'

'I know that, you moron. I meant what exactly do you want to buy?'

'I want to talk to you, in person.'

'You *are* talking to me in person,' said Shepherd. 'That's how phones work. Now, get to the point or piss off.'

'I mean, I want to meet you. To talk about what we want to buy. We haven't done this before.'

'That's blindingly obvious,' said Shepherd.

'So we want to meet you, face to face, see if we can trust you.'

'I'm the one who should be worried about trust,' said Shepherd. 'Where do you want to meet?'

'We thought maybe Hyde Park. Near the memorial to Princess Diana.'

'We? How many of you are there?'

'Two.'

'Tom and Jerry?'

'What?'

'You're Tom, right? Is your mate Jerry?'

'No, his name's . . . James.'

'Tom and James?'

'Yes. Tom and James.'

'And how will I recognise you?' said Shepherd. 'I'm assuming you don't know what I look like.'

'Better you tell me what you look like.'

'I'm devilishly good-looking with a twinkle in my eye,' said Shepherd. 'Does that help? Of course it doesn't. Look, be at the memorial tomorrow at noon. You and your mate carry a copy of the *Financial Times* and the *Guardian*. One each. And stand together. I'll approach you. If I spot anything I don't like, you won't see me for dust. Understand?'

'Okay. Yeah.'

'Tomorrow, then,' said Shepherd. He ended the call and put away the phone.

Back in the room, the Major was leaning back in his chair, tapping a pen on the table.

'Do we have a plan?' asked Shepherd.

'We're working on it,' said the Major.

There were three loud bangs on the door. 'Please stand against the wall, Colin,' shouted Kamil.

Mitchell stood up, went to the far wall and stood against it, arms outstretched. The door opened. Kamil was holding a paper plate loaded with rice and chunks of lamb, and a bottle of water. Behind him, a man in a ski mask held an AK-47. It was feeding time.

Kamil walked into the centre of the room and sat down cross-legged. He placed the food in front of him and beckoned Mitchell to join him. 'I shall eat with you, Colin,' he said.

Mitchell hadn't told Kamil that nobody had called him Colin since he'd left school. Even his brother called him Geordie. It had been his army nickname, and once his parents had passed away it had been the only name he answered to. But he wanted Kamil to keep calling him Colin. It was a constant reminder that he was the enemy; an enemy that Mitchell would have to kill if he was to escape from his prison.

'Can you play chess?' asked Kamil.

Mitchell nodded.

Kamil reached into a pocket and brought out a travel chess set, a plastic board that folded in half with circular magnetic pieces. He placed it on the floor and set out the pieces as Mitchell chewed a chunk of lamb.

'How long have you been in Baghdad?' asked Kamil.

'Six months, just about,' said Mitchell.

'Can you speak any Arabic?'

'*Allahu Akbar*,' said Mitchell.

'Ah, good,' said Kamil. 'God is great.'

'*Inshallah.*'

'God willing,' said Kamil, nodding. 'If you speak only two phrases in Arabic, they are the two to know. "God is great" and "God willing". He is all powerful and everything that happens is because of Him.'

'You believe that, do you?' asked Mitchell.

'Of course. All Muslims do. And all Christians do, too. Are you not a Christian?'

'I suppose so,' said Mitchell. He used his fingers to shovel rice into his mouth. Sometimes they gave him a plastic spoon and sometimes they didn't.

'Either you are or you aren't,' said Kamil. He finished placing the pieces on the board and waved for Mitchell to go first. Mitchell pushed his king's pawn two spaces forward. 'I was christened a Catholic,' said Mitchell, 'but I'm lapsed.'

'You don't believe in God any more?' said Kamil. He moved his king's pawn.

'Not the sort of God my parents believed in,' said Mitchell.

'What sort of God do you believe in, then?'

'It's hard to say,' said Mitchell.

They played for a while in silence. Within the first half-dozen moves Mitchell realised that Kamil was by far the better player. He was methodical and stared at the board for a full two minutes before each move. Mitchell played impulsively and rarely looked more than a couple of moves ahead. He had never much cared for board games and preferred to play cards, ideally for money. 'Have you always been a Muslim?' he asked.

'Of course,' said Kamil.

'The reason I ask is that a lot of people become Muslims, right?'

'When they realise that Allah is the true God and that only He can be worshipped. And that Muhammad was Allah's messenger.'

'And you pray five times a day?'

'That is what is required of us. But there is more to being a Muslim than praying five times a day. One is a Muslim every second of every minute of every hour until one draws one's last breath.'

They continued to play. Kamil took one of Mitchell's bishops in a fork attack with his knight, then gradually pressured his queen. Even though he clearly had the advantage, he continued to study every move carefully, bent forward over the board, deep creases in his brow. Mitchell knew that he could kill Kamil. He could grab him and break his neck as easily as snapping a twig.

He could smash his windpipe and watch him die on the floor clutching his throat. He could punch his nose so hard that the cartilage would splinter and spear the brain. He could kick him in the stomach with such force that his spleen would rupture. There were a dozen ways that Mitchell could end the life of the man sitting in front of him, but it would serve no purpose. The door was locked and on the other side there were men with guns.

Kamil looked up. 'You are in a bad position,' he said, smiling.

'I know,' said Mitchell, 'and I fear it can only get worse.'

Shepherd sipped his coffee and looked at the Serpentine. 'The two over there, throwing the Frisbee,' he said quietly. A homeless man in a grimy overcoat and wellington boots was throwing bread to a group of Canada geese; he grinned at them, showing a mouthful of blackened teeth.

'They know me,' he said.

'Great,' said Sharpe. He looked casually to where two Pakistani men in their twenties were half-heartedly tossing a blue disc back and forth. 'Yeah,' he said. They were close to the Princess Diana memorial, a concrete water feature in the shape of a battered oval. Several dozen tourists were sitting on the edge, paddling their feet in the water that gushed around as if it was a natural stream.

It was a quarter to twelve and Shepherd and Sharpe had been in the park since eleven. 'They're the brothers,' said Shepherd. 'Asim and Salman. I'm guessing they're there to keep an eye on things because they don't have newspapers.'

It was a warm day so Shepherd was in khaki trousers and a pale blue polo shirt, with a pair of sunglasses perched on top of his head. There was little risk of anything happening in the open but he wanted the men to see that he wasn't carrying a weapon. From the phone conversation he'd had, he was sure that the men weren't professionals. 'Tom' had been clearly out of his depth, and the brothers playing with the Frisbee seemed ill at ease and hadn't once looked in their direction.

Sharpe drank his coffee and grimaced. 'This is horrible,' he said. He was wearing a Glasgow Rangers shirt over baggy blue jeans.

'Good job you didn't pay for it, then,' said Shepherd.

'Didn't say I wasn't grateful.'

'There's Hassan,' said Shepherd, 'blue baseball cap, white shirt, walking over from the road.'

'You and your photographic memory,' said Sharpe. He glanced towards the man. 'Yeah, that's him, all right.'

'I wasn't asking for confirmation, Razor,' said Shepherd, drily. 'I just wanted to make sure you'd seen him.' He sipped his coffee. Sharpe was right: it wasn't good.

Hassan strolled through a gap in the fence round the water feature and wandered over to a clump of trees. He sat down in the shade, his back to a trunk, took out a pack of cigarettes and lit one with a cheap plastic lighter. A camera with a telephoto lens hung from a strap round his neck.

Shepherd and Sharpe walked towards the Serpentine then continued beside it. Two groups of teenagers were racing in rowing-boats, laughing and jeering at each other. Sunbathers were out in force, although it was too early for lunchtime office workers to put in an appearance. An overweight girl with a crash helmet and knee pads whizzed by on roller-blades. 'They don't look like hardened criminals,' said Shepherd.

'The men who blew up the Tube were in their twenties and thirties,' said Sharpe. 'These guys aren't out to rob a bank. They're terrorists.'

'Terrorists, or wannabe terrorists,' said Shepherd.

'The only difference is having the tools,' said Sharpe.

'So why are they coming to us? That's what I don't get. If they're al-Qaeda, why don't they have their own weapons?'

'Because they're not al-Qaeda, they're home-grown terrorists. British born. Invisibles, they call them. You know that.'

'But this seems so . . . amateurish.' He took another sip of his coffee and tossed the paper cup into a rubbish bin. 'Tom and

Jerry are here,' he said. The final members of the group were walking across the grass towards the water feature. According to the names under the photographs on Button's whiteboard, they were Ali and Fazal. Ali was the smaller of the two with a shaved head and a slight stoop. Fazal was a good six inches taller with a long, loping stride. Both men had moustaches and wore sunglasses. Ali was carrying the *Financial Times* and Fazal had a copy of the *Guardian* in the back pocket of his jeans. They headed straight for the water feature.

'Just the five,' said Sharpe.

'Looks that way,' said Shepherd. 'Lying little bugger. He said there'd be two of them.'

'Like you said, amateurs.'

'Thing is, amateurs are unpredictable. You know what a professional will do, but an amateur can go off the rails.'

'I don't see any heavy artillery,' said Sharpe.

'Yeah, I know. Come on, let's go.' They walked across the grass. Ali and Fazal stood with their backs to the memorial. To their left, an old couple were placing a small bunch of flowers on the ground. There were tears in the woman's eyes and she dabbed at them with a little white handkerchief.

Ali saw them first and nudged Fazal in the ribs. Fazal pulled out the *Guardian* and held it in both hands.

'Which one's Tom?' said Shepherd, as he reached them.

Ali waved his *Financial Times*. 'That's me,' he said.

'I'm May, the guy you spoke to,' said Shepherd. He nodded at Sharpe. 'This is Lomas.' Ali held out his hand, as if he wanted to shake, but Shepherd ignored it. 'This isn't a date,' he said. 'Let's walk as we talk.' They started across the grass. 'So,' said Shepherd, 'what's on your shopping list?'

'We want submachine-guns,' said Fazal.

'Really?' said Shepherd. 'What country are you planning to invade?'

'Can you supply us or not?' asked Ali.

'Do you even know what a submachine-gun is?' asked Sharpe.

'It's a gun that can fire bursts of bullets,' said Fazal.

'Right, and they're bloody dangerous,' said Sharpe.

'So what? You sell them with health warnings, do you?' asked Ali. 'We have the money and we want to buy. If you can't supply us, we can go elsewhere.'

'What make?' asked Shepherd.

Fazal shrugged. 'Uzi, maybe.'

'How about MP5s, the guns the SAS use?'

'You can get one?'

'We can get you anything, for a price,' said Shepherd, 'but you'd be better off telling me what you want them for.'

Fazal and Ali looked at each other and Fazal began to speak in Urdu, but Sharpe held up his hand. 'Use English,' he said.

'We've got problems with a gang,' said Fazal. 'A big gang. We want guns that show we mean business.'

Shepherd stopped walking. They were close to the wire fence that separated the memorial from the rest of the park. 'Are you planning to fire them?'

Fazal frowned. 'What do you mean?'

'We generally offer a deal. You buy the guns from us, but if you don't fire them we'll buy them back. It's like renting.'

'Why would anyone rent a gun?' asked Fazal.

Sharpe sighed theatrically. 'Say a guy wants to knock over a bank. He wants a shooter but he doesn't fire it, just uses it to get the money. Once he's got the cash, he doesn't need the gun any more so he sells it back to us. But if he fires it the gun can be traced so it's no use to us. Got it?'

'Yeah,' said Fazal. 'I get it.'

'So, will you be wanting to sell the guns back after you've finished with them?' asked Shepherd.

Ali and Fazal exchanged another look. 'Maybe,' said Fazal. 'But we have to pay the full amount up front, right?'

'Right.'

'How much?'

'Depends on how many you want. And how many rounds.'

'Five guns.'

'Okay. Look, if you want something with a high rate of fire, maybe you should think about the Ingram MAC-10. It's like an Uzi but smaller. The magazine holds thirty rounds and it'll fire them all in less than a second.'

'How much?' said Fazal.

'Two thousand pounds each,' said Shepherd. The going rate on the street was five hundred less but he wanted to see if the men knew how much the weapons were worth.

'So, ten grand for the five?' asked Fazal.

'Studied maths at university, did you?' asked Sharpe.

'Ten grand, that's right,' said Shepherd.

'And what about the bullets?'

'We call them rounds,' said Sharpe.

Fazal glared at Sharpe. 'Have you got a problem with me?' he said.

Sharpe glared back. 'I don't like dealing with amateurs. If they get caught, they tend to sing to the cops.'

'We won't be talking to the police,' said Fazal. 'You can count on that.'

'Let's keep to the matter in hand,' said Shepherd. 'Five Ingrams is ten grand. I can sell you a hundred rounds for five hundred quid.' That was way over the going rate, too, but the men just shrugged.

'We'd need six hundred,' said Fazal.

'Six hundred rounds?' said Shepherd.

'Is that a problem?' asked Fazal.

'It's not a problem,' said Shepherd, 'but it's a lot.'

'You can get them?'

'Of course.'

'We'd expect a discount,' said Ali.

'Six hundred rounds? I could let you have them for two and a half grand.'

'Two,' said Ali. 'Ten for the guns, two for the ammo. Twelve thousand pounds in all.'

Shepherd nodded slowly. The two men clearly had no idea of the true value of the weapons they were buying.

'The magazines,' said Fazal. 'How many magazines would we get?'

'One for each weapon,' said Shepherd, 'plus a spare. That's standard.'

'We need more.'

'How many?'

'Thirty bullets in each, right?'

'Yes. But, as Lomas said, we call them rounds.'

'So we need twenty.'

'Twenty magazines? You want all the rounds loaded into magazines?'

'Yeah, we want twenty magazines. How much?'

'Another five hundred.'

'So twelve and a half grand for the five guns, twenty magazines and six hundred rounds?' said Ali.

'That's it,' said Shepherd. 'Do we have a deal?'

'Yes,' said Fazal.

'When do you need them by?'

'As soon as possible,' said Fazal.

'I'll call you tomorrow to fix a time and place,' said Shepherd. 'I'll tell you where and when. The time and location are non-negotiable.'

'I understand,' said Fazal.

'Make sure your mobile is on. If I call and you don't answer, the deal's off. One more thing.' Shepherd turned and gestured at Hassan. 'Tell your mate over there to come here.'

'What are you talking about?' said Fazal.

'Your mate with the camera. The one that's been snapping away at us for the past five minutes. Tell him to come here now or I'll roll up that copy of the *Guardian* and force it so far up your arse that you'll be spitting out the crossword clues for the next two days.'

Fazal stared at him for a few seconds, then waved Hassan over to him. The man pretended not to understand and looked away, but then Ali called over to him in Urdu.

'English,' said Sharpe.

'Come here!' shouted Ali.

Hassan walked towards them, swinging the camera back and forth, eyes darting nervously between Shepherd and Ali. He went to stand beside Ali. Shepherd held out his hand for the camera. Hassan put it behind his back, like a guilty schoolboy.

'Don't screw around, sonny,' said Shepherd. 'Give me the camera.'

Hassan held it out reluctantly and Shepherd snatched it. It was a digital Nikon. 'What were you thinking?' he asked Ali.

'We don't know you,' said Ali.

'So how does having our picture help?'

'We thought it would give us some security,' said Ali, 'if anything went wrong.'

'If anything goes wrong, I will personally shoot you both,' said Shepherd, 'and those idiots playing with the Frisbee. I'll put you all on crutches, whether or not you've got photographs of me.' He flicked open the slot that contained the memory chip. Hassan protested as he pulled it out: 'Hey! That's a gigabyte!' he said.

'Yeah?' said Shepherd. He tossed the camera into the water. 'And that's an underwater camera.'

Hassan yelped and jumped into the water memorial.

'That camera cost two thousand pounds!' said Ali. 'His father lent him the money.'

Hassan was groping around in the water, moaning.

'Well, he should be more careful about where he points it,' said Shepherd.

He and Sharpe walked away, hands in their pockets. 'Did you make out the agent?' asked Sharpe, as they reached the entrance to the park.

'Not sure,' said Shepherd.

'I figured it can't be the brothers, right? No way would a guy want to put his own brother away. I'd put my money on Fazal. The tall dark silent one.'

'Could be.'

'Five Ingrams is one hell of a lot of firepower,' said Sharpe, 'and they want all the rounds in magazines, which suggests they're going to keep blazing away. Can you imagine what five guys with Ingrams could do in a shopping mall?'

'Yeah,' said Shepherd, frowning.

'What's wrong?'

'Nothing.'

'Something on your mind?'

'Just my bloody house. Estate agents, solicitors, removal men. It's a bloody nightmare. I'll be glad when it's over.'

'Fancy a pint?'

'I'll take a rain check, Razor. I want to get home.'

Kamil picked up his queen, smiled apologetically at Mitchell and put it down next to Mitchell's king. 'Checkmate,' he said quietly.

'You play well,' said Mitchell.

'My father taught me, when I was a boy,' said Kamil.

'He taught you well.' Mitchell put the last piece of lamb into his mouth, then Kamil took the paper plate and stood up. 'Can I borrow the chess set?' asked Mitchell. 'I want to practise some openings.' He smiled. 'Maybe I'll be able to give you a better game next time.'

Kamil looked as if he was going to refuse, but then handed it to Mitchell. 'We shall play again tomorrow,' he said.

'I'll look forward to it,' said Mitchell, then went to stand against the wall. Kamil knocked on the door. It opened and he slipped out.

Mitchell waited until the door had been bolted and the sound of footsteps had faded, then knelt in front of the plug. The chess pieces were circular, each about the size of a penny, metal discs covered with plastic, black or white and embossed with a symbol denoting the piece they represented. He took a black pawn and pushed the side into the top screw in the socket. He wiggled the

disc until he felt it bite, then pressed hard and twisted anti-
clockwise. The screw moved a quarter of a turn and Mitchell
grinned. It was going to work. He pulled out the disc and
examined it. The plastic was indented, where it had been forced
into the screw head, but not ripped. He smoothed it between his
finger and thumb, then put it back on the board and picked up
another. He used that to turn the screw another quarter turn.
This time it moved easily.

Yokely walked into the interrogation room carrying a mug of
coffee. The Saudi was wearing an orange jumpsuit and his hands
and legs were shackled. He was a lot thinner than he had been the
last time Yokely had seen him. He had grown a beard, too, but his
hair was cut short. There were dark patches under his eyes and a
rash of acne across the right side of his neck, which was raw where
he'd been scratching it. 'So how are you, Abdal-Jabbaar bin
Othman al-Ahmed?' asked Yokely, stretching out the syllables.
    The Saudi sneered at him, then pointedly looked away.
    'Taking care of you, are we? Plenty of clean underwear, and
there's an arrow on the ceiling of your cell pointing towards
Mecca. Food prepared in accordance with your religious beliefs.'
Yokely sat down and adjusted his shirt cuffs. 'How long have you
been here now? Six months? I've lost track of time.'
    The Saudi said nothing.
    'You think you're smart, don't you?' asked Yokely, leaning
back in his chair and putting his feet on to the table. He saw
distaste in the Saudi's eyes. 'Public-school education, first-class
degree from the London School of Economics. Well travelled.
And me? What am I? The ugly American. Big, stupid, insensi-
tive.' He raised his coffee mug. 'Guilty as charged. In the words of
the great philosopher Popeye, I am what I am.' He sipped his
coffee. 'I'd offer you some but I know that any form of stimulant
is against your Islamic principles,' he said. 'So I won't be putting
temptation your way.' He took another sip and sighed. 'The thing
is, if you're so smart, why are you the one in chains wearing an

orange jumpsuit, and why am I sitting here drinking coffee with an inch-thick T-bone steak waiting for me outside? One of life's little mysteries, I guess.'

He swung his feet off the table and sat with his hands round the mug. 'When do you think the modern Islamic movement started, Mr Ahmed?'

The Saudi stared sullenly at the floor. The door behind Yokely opened and a man in starched fatigues walked in. He put a tray on the table, then left without a word. A plate piled high with fried chicken, two steaming freshly baked hunks of cornbread and a bowl of coleslaw lay before them.

'I think it goes back to 1928. The Muslim Brotherhood was formed by Sayyid Qutb. There are those who say he just stole the ideas of Muhammad Ibn Abd al-Wahhab, but I think he was very much his own man. Sayyid felt that the only way to stop the decline of Islam was if a small devoted team of what he saw as true Muslims applied themselves to forming as many Islamic governments as possible. I'm paraphrasing, of course.'

The Saudi was trying not to look at the fried chicken.

'There were those who thought the Muslim Brotherhood was too soft, so one of Sayyid's *protégés*, Sheikh Taqiuddin al-Nabhani set up the more radical Hizb ut-Tahrir, the Party of Liberation. Nabhani thought that Islam and Western civilisation were mutually exclusive, that the two could not co-exist and that the only way to liberate Muslims would be to overthrow the existing nation states and replace them with a borderless world ruled by a new caliph. Since nine/eleven Hizb ut-Tahrir has been arguing that all Muslims are in a state of war.' Yokely grinned. 'Which would make me the enemy, of course.' He waved at the fried chicken. 'I've got a steak waiting for me outside, so please help yourself.'

The Saudi wiped his mouth on the back of his hand and looked away.

'Go on, Mr Ahmed. I know the processed rubbish they feed you here must be getting you down. You used to eat in some of the best restaurants in the world, didn't you? How did you rate The Ivy in London? It's just about my favourite restaurant anywhere. Their fish and chips – out of this world. A simple dish, traditional British food, but perfectly cooked.'

The Saudi said nothing.

'The funny thing is, fish and chips isn't the British national dish any more. Did you know that?'

The Saudi didn't speak.

'These days, the British eat more chicken tikka masala than they do fish and chips. Amazing, when you think about it. Indian food – the Brits eat more of it than anything else. More than roast beef, more than steak and kidney pie, more than fish and chips. More than KFC, McDonald's, all the fast food that we Americans try to get them to eat. And you know what all those Indian restaurants refuse to serve? Pork. And why's that? Because most chefs in Indian restaurants are Muslims. You know, if I was an al-Qaeda strategist, I'd be suggesting that their operatives infiltrate the country's Indian restaurants and organise a mass poisoning. I reckon that over one weekend they could probably kill twenty per cent of the population.' Yokely grinned. 'I know, I know, I'm wandering, so let me get to the point. The Muslim suicide-bombers that you sent against the London Tube were members of a splinter group of Hizb ut-Tahrir. Yet they attacked London, one of the most multi-racial cities in the world. Have you wandered around Riyadh lately? How many white faces did you see? How many Orientals? I doubt that you ever went on the Tube, Mr Ahmed, but I did and I can assure you that you'd be hard pushed to find a more mixed sample of humankind than in a London Tube carriage. You'd be lucky to see more than a handful of white faces. So my question, I suppose, is what you thought you'd achieve by blowing up Africans, Asians, Orientals, Muslims and Buddhists? You're a smart man, can you explain it to me?'

Yokely smiled at the Saudi, his eyebrows raised.

The Saudi said nothing.

'I guess not,' said Yokely. 'It'll have to remain one of life's little mysteries. But it makes no sense to me. New York is just about the world's most multi-racial city yet that was al-Qaeda's prime target. The thing is, you and your friends are bound to fail. Long term, everything you do is a waste of time. Do you know why?'

The Saudi folded his arms and stared at the floor.

'Let me tell you,' said Yokely. 'It's Turkey.' He smiled and waved at the plate of chicken. 'And I'm not talking about the sort you roast and serve up with cranberry sauce. You see, Mr Ahmed, the wealthier and more prosperous a country, the less religious it becomes. It's sad but true. Religious attendance is falling throughout the West. Just about the only exception is Israel and, of course, that's because you can't be an Israeli unless you're Jewish. Your foot-soldiers are poor Muslims with no prospects – homeless Palestinians, Iraqis with no jobs, Armenians with no health care. They're angry because they're poor, and you and your friends feed on that anger. But what's going to happen when Turkey joins the European Union? And it will.' He chuckled. 'We'll make sure of it. They'll become part of Europe, and then what? Their living standards will shoot up – they'll be buying cars and second homes like there's no tomorrow, and pretty darn soon they'll be thinking that perhaps there's no real need to be down on a prayer mat five times a day, and that the odd bottle of wine with dinner is no bad thing. Then Muslims around the world might start to think that perhaps there's a better way to live, and that if the seventy-odd million Muslims in Turkey can make better lives for themselves then maybe there isn't much point in strapping explosives round your waist to blow up innocent civilians. And we'll be there, the good old US of A, ready to sell them as much Coke and Starbucks, as many CDs and DVDs as they want. You see, you think I'm stupid, Mr Ahmed, but I know my history and I can use that to predict the future. We'll win this crusade, and you'll lose. In fact, you've lost already, it's just that you don't know it.'

The Saudi snorted softly but said nothing.

'You don't say much, do you? My colleagues tell me you haven't said a word since you arrived here.' He pushed the tray closer to the Saudi. 'I suppose you know that we're finding it harder to operate in Guantánamo Bay. The world is watching, and all that nonsense. Anyway, we'll be moving you out. Sooner rather than later.'

The Saudi's eyes darted to Yokely's face. The American smiled at his reaction. 'We'll get your Combatant Status Review Tribunal out of the way first, just to make sure the paperwork's in order, but then we'll move you to the Ukraine,' he said. 'They're very keen to help us, the Ukrainians, and they have some skilled technicians over there. Former KGB. Very heavy guys, Mr Ahmed. They make me look like a Boy Scout.'

'This is a violation of my human rights,' said the Saudi. It was the first thing he'd said since Yokely had walked into the room.

'Of course it is,' said Yokely, 'but what about the rights of the innocents who died in London? In Sydney? In Madrid? In Bali?'

'You are going to torture me again.'

'We're going to get you to tell us what you know by whatever means we deem necessary,' said Yokely. 'It's your call, Mr Ahmed. The ball is firmly in your court. If I was you, I'd take a piece of that mouth-wateringly delicious chicken and start talking.'

'*Hill 'annii*,' spat the Saudi.

Yokely smiled amiably. 'I wish I spoke Arabic, but sadly I don't. Just one of the many gaps in my education.'

'I will kill you,' said the Saudi. 'One day I will kill you.'

'That's what we call an idle threat. How are you ever going to hurt me?'

The Saudi stared at the American with flint-hard eyes. 'Not everyone held here is held here for ever. Word will get out, Mr Yokely. Word will get to those who can do you harm. And they will get to you one day. Maybe not here. Maybe not in Baghdad. But maybe in your home town. Maybe you'll get into your car one day, turn the ignition and bang!' The Saudi shouted the final word and Yokely jumped. The Saudi laughed scornfully. 'You have tortured me already – you tortured me before you brought me here. You killed my cousin, Husayn. You burned my brother, Abdal-Rahmaan, alive. You brutalised my sister. What more do you think your former KGB thugs can do to me?'

'Did I say thugs?' said Yokely, regaining his composure. 'I'm sorry, I gave you the wrong impression. They're doctors. Or at least they've been medically trained. They've got a host of chemical cocktails they're keen to try on you. None has been FDA approved, of course, and the chances are that you'll end up a vegetable, but you'll tell them everything you know. Every single thing.' Yokely pushed back his chair and stood up. 'This will be the last time we meet, Mr Ahmed. I'll be getting full reports from the Ukrainians, so I'll have everything I need. You might as well enjoy the chicken. I gather the food over there is every bit as bad as it is here.'

Yokely picked up his mug and walked out of the room, down a corridor past two armed marines, and through a door. There were two plasma flat-screen TVs on the wall, relaying images from the two CCTV cameras in the interrogation room. A tall man with receding grey hair was sipping a can of Sprite as he watched the Saudi stare at the plate of fried chicken. 'Ten bucks says he takes a piece,' he said. Carl Bulmer was the type to bet on which of two raindrops would be first to reach the bottom of a windowpane.

'You're throwing your money away,' said Yokely. 'He knows we're watching him.'

Bulmer was with the CIA, a twenty-year veteran of South America, Afghanistan and Iraq. Not that his CIA credentials were ever referred to in the Guantánamo Bay camp. The CIA operatives were described as OGA personnel, working for Other Government Agencies. It was, as Yokely knew, a rose by any other name. Bulmer wore the standard OGA attire of long-sleeved black shirt, black trousers and impenetrable sunglasses. It was as much a uniform as the orange jumpsuits they forced the inmates to wear.

'If you don't want to bet, fine,' said Bulmer. He stretched out his legs and balanced his can of Sprite on his lap as he watched the Saudi.

Yokely raised his eyebrows. 'Want to bet a hundred?'

Bulmer hesitated, then nodded acceptance. 'A hundred it is.' He kept his eyes on the screen. 'I heard you were in The Hague a while back,' he said.

'My itinerary is classified these days,' said Yokely. 'You know how it is.'

'Day you flew out, Slobodan Miloševic had a heart-attack.'

'An unhappy coincidence.' Yokely laughed. 'No great loss to the world.'

'Word is that the two events were not unconnected.'

Yokely chuckled. 'A butterfly flaps its wings in China and there's a hurricane in Florida?'

'I think the word is that the connection is a bit closer than that.'

Yokely continued to chuckle but said nothing.

Bulmer levelled a finger at the monitor. 'You know, he said more to you in there in five minutes than he's said to us in six months,' said Bulmer.

'I'm not sure that death threats count as conversation,' said Yokely, helping himself to a bottle of water from a small fridge beside one of the desks.

'You got him angry. That's a start.'

'I killed his brother and cousin,' said Yokely, 'but if he hates me enough, he might open up to you.'

'Anything specific?'

'The Holy Martyrs of Islam,' said Yokely. 'They're new boys on the block but they've started killing hostages in Iraq.'

'Yeah, the Lake boy. Just goes to show, all the money in the world won't help if these bastards get you. What's your interest?'

'Nothing special,' said Yokely. 'Just want to do a favour for a friend.' He nodded at the screen. 'Are we putting a time limit on this, by the way?'

Bulmer glanced at a digital clock up on the wall. 'Half an hour?'

'Up to you,' said Yokely. 'He's never going to eat it. He seems to think he can get information out – what do you think?'

'He's in solitary most of the time.' Bulmer drank the last of his Sprite, crumpled the can with one hand and tossed it into a wastepaper basket on the far side of the room. He pumped his fist in the air. 'I think he was bluffing.'

'Yeah, me too. He's got an ego and we can use that. He's not seen anyone from the embassy, has he?'

'Which? He's got dual, right? Saudi and British?'

'I don't think the British Embassy staff would pass on messages to al-Qaeda, do you?'

'Two-faced lot, the Brits,' said Bulmer.

'That's the French, Carl. Anyone from the Saudi lot been to see him?'

Bulmer leaned forward and tapped on his computer keyboard. A spreadsheet filled the screen and he stared at it, brow furrowed. 'No visitors,' he said. 'No requests for visits, either.'

'Okay, so just check that he doesn't come into contact with any other inmates.'

'Richard, please, don't teach me how to suck eggs,' said Bulmer. 'I know what solitary means.'

'There's solitary and there's solitary,' said Yokely. 'I don't want anyone even to hear him fart.' He headed for the door.

'Aren't you going to wait and see if he eats the chicken?' asked Bulmer.

'I trust you,' said Yokely. 'Send me a cheque.'

Shepherd opened one of the three metal cases and looked at the handguns inside. Two Ingrams. Four magazines. He ran a hand over them and remembered the old cliché: guns don't kill people, people kill people. Like most clichés, it was true. But when it came to killing people, guns made the job a whole lot easier. Knives were too personal: it was hard to look a man in the eye and shove one into his chest. Guns could kill at a distance: you just pointed and pulled the trigger. Technology did the rest. And the

Ingram was one of the best, just pray and spray. It wasn't even necessary to aim it because its rapid rate of fire meant that anything within range would be ripped apart. Killing with a gun was a relatively simple matter. But coping with the emotional burden afterwards . . . That was different. He closed the case with a dull thud. The other two contained spare magazines and a hundred rounds. Button had decided they shouldn't come up with all the weapons and ammunition up front but make the guys work for it. It would give the Branch detectives a chance to follow the weapons back to Birmingham. If they knew that more weapons and ammunition were on the way, Ali and Fazal would probably wait to launch their attack.

'The world is going to hell in a handbasket,' said Sharpe, pacing up and down by the entrance to the warehouse.

'What does that mean?' asked Shepherd.

'It means the world's going crazy,' said Sharpe scornfully.

'I know what it means, but what's the story with the handbasket? What the hell's a handbasket?'

'A basket that you hold in your hand,' said Sharpe, patiently.

'Right. So how does the world fit into it? And who's taking it to hell?'

'It's an expression,' said Sharpe.

'I know it's an expression, Razor. I'm just saying, it's an expression that doesn't make the least bit of sense.'

'You're missing the point.'

'No, Razor, you're not getting to the point. What's got you all riled up this time?'

'Did you see the racial-identity memo that came round?'

'I don't read memos,' said Shepherd. 'I figured if it was important someone would talk to me about it.'

'You write reports, don't you?'

'Sure.'

'So you need to know how to describe the bad guys. And the PC brigade have gone and moved the goalposts again. We used to know where we were, right? You and I are IC One males. Anyone from the Mediterranean is IC Two, blacks are IC Three, Asians are IC Four, Chinks are IC Five and Ragheads are IC Six.'

'You did go on the course, didn't you?' asked Shepherd.

'What course?'

'The course about not offending ethnic minorities,' said Shepherd.

'I'm not saying it to their faces,' said Sharpe.

'But you would, wouldn't you?'

'The point I'm trying to make is that the six classifications were all you needed. You're on the trail of two Yardies and you hit the radio to say that they're IC Three males. Do you know what the Yardies are now?'

'B Ones,' said Shepherd. 'M One if they're mixed race.'

Sharpe's eyes narrowed. 'I thought you hadn't read the memo?'

'The classifications were changed a while back.'

'And you know how many there are now?'

'Sixteen,' said Shepherd. 'Plus one.'

'The one is if the bad guy doesn't want to say where he's from. How stupid is that?'

'If they don't say, we get to guess. That's all the plus one means.'

'Spider, you can see what a crock of shit this is, can't you? It's political correctness gone mad. In the old days, a white guy was an IC One, end of story. Now a white guy can be W One, white British, W Two, white Irish, or W Nine, White Other. Now, I'm on the trail of a white guy. Is he British, Irish or a bloody Kiwi? How do I know? I don't, right? He's just a white guy. So how do I call it in? W One, W Two or W Nine? And what happened to W Three, W Four, W Five and all the rest of the Ws?'

'Fair point,' said Shepherd, who was already bored with the conversation.

'Am I supposed to ask him?'

'I don't know,' said Shepherd.

'And they've subdivided the Asians into A One Indian, A Two

Pakistani, A Three Bangladeshi, and A Nine Asian Other. Now, I ask you, can you tell the difference between a Paki and a Bangladeshi?'

'Razor, "Paki" is offensive,' said Shepherd.

'Screw that,' snarled Sharpe. 'Brit is short for British, Scot is short for Scottish, and Paki is short for Pakistani. The point is, how the hell are we meant to tell them apart? And what about the Ragheads? They've done away with the IC Six Arab classification but under the new codes there are no Arabs. They fall under O Nine, Any Other Ethnic Group. How stupid is that? The Ragheads are the biggest threat to the free world, and we don't even have a classification for them. What are we going to say over the radio next time we're on the trail of a Raghead suicide-bomber? That we're following someone from Any Other Ethnic Group wearing an explosive vest?'

Shepherd had no answer for that because what Sharpe had said was absolutely correct. In their bid to be politically correct, the powers-that-be had done away with the Arab classification. Oriental had gone too, with the new definitions having room only for Chinese. Thais, Vietnamese and Koreans were lumped together under A Nine, Any Other Asian. It made no sense. The original classifications could be criticised as not specific enough, but at least the guys on surveillance knew who they were looking for. But the new classifications veered from being too specific to too vague. They were worse than useless.

'Like I said, the world's gone mad,' said Sharpe, his voice loaded with bitterness.

'You don't have to use the new classifications on surveillance, you know that,' said Shepherd. 'They're an admin thing, that's all.'

'It's nonsense,' said Sharpe. 'What does it matter if a villain is Irish or Welsh? If he's a Bangladeshi or an Indian?'

'It helps the collation of statistics,' said Shepherd.

'Yeah, well, where's the classification for Turks? They're behind most of the drugs being brought into London. Where's the classification for Jamaicans? They're responsible for most of the gun crime. What about the Bosnians and their ATM frauds?'

'You should write a memo,' said Shepherd.

'I'm a dinosaur,' said Sharpe. 'They're not going to pay me any attention.'

'You're a cop with almost thirty years' experience,' said Shepherd.

'Which counts for nothing,' said Sharpe. 'They don't care what we think. We're just pawns in a bigger game.'

'It's not a game, Razor. None of this is.' Shepherd's mobile phone vibrated and he took it out. Charlotte Button. He pressed the green button. 'Yeah?' he said. He wasn't being rude: it was standard procedure not to identify himself over the phone unless he was in character.

'Would you be so kind as to tell your prehistoric colleague that we're recording everything that's being said.'

'Ah, right,' said Shepherd, and gave Sharpe a warning look. 'I'll do that.'

'And tell him that we have more than enough already to put an end to his career. We'll reset the recording as of now, but it's my last warning.'

'I'll tell him,' said Shepherd.

Button ended the call.

'Tell me what?' said Sharpe.

'Enough of the racist stuff,' said Shepherd, putting away his phone.

'Me? Racist?' said Sharpe, genuinely offended. 'I had a Chinese last night and an Indian on Monday.'

'I hope you're talking food,' said Shepherd. 'Just remember we're on tape.'

'Message received and understood,' said Sharpe, saluting Shepherd. He waved up at one of the hidden cameras in the roof. 'Testing, testing, one, two, three.'

Sometimes Razor's sense of humour could be infuriating, Shepherd thought. He heard a car engine outside. 'Here they are,' he said, and went to the metal door that led out to the car park. Ali was at the wheel of a five-year-old Ford Mondeo. Fazal had just climbed out of the front passenger seat. Hassan sat in the back, glaring. Shepherd stood in the doorway, arms folded, the hard man.

Ali climbed out of the car and waved at him. Shepherd looked pointedly at his watch. 'Are you going to stand there all day, or are we going to get on with this?' he said.

Ali hurried over with Fazal. Hassan stayed in the back of the car. Shepherd gestured at him. 'Still mad about his camera, is he?'

'It's ruined,' said Ali. 'They said it would cost at least two hundred pounds to repair.'

'Yeah, well, maybe next time he'll be more careful where he points it. Is he staying in the car?'

'If that's okay.'

'He can turn cartwheels round the car park so long as he doesn't try to take my picture again.' Shepherd held the door open for them, and they walked into the building. They stopped short when they saw that Sharpe was holding a metal detector.

'What's that?' said Fazal.

'It's a thermostat,' said Sharpe. 'It stops things overheating. We know you're not going to do anything silly but just hold up your arms and let me check you out.'

'You don't trust us,' said Ali.

'We don't trust anybody,' said Sharpe.

'What about you?' said Fazal. 'How do we know you don't have guns?'

Shepherd grinned. 'Of course we've got guns,' he said. 'You're here to buy guns, remember? Now, hold out your arms or piss off.'

Ali and Fazal glanced at each other nervously. Ali was sweating and wiped his brow with his sleeve.

'Is there a problem, ladies?' asked Sharpe.

Fazal reached into his jacket and took out a machete, the blade wrapped in newspaper. Sharpe took a step back, transferred the metal detector to his left hand, then pulled out an automatic with the right.

'It's okay – it's okay!' shouted Ali.

'Put the knife down!' shouted Sharpe, pointing the gun at Fazal's chest.

Fazal bent down slowly and placed the machete on the floor. He reached into his trouser pocket, pulled out a flick knife and put it next to the machete, then straightened up.

'Knives?' said Sharpe. He sneered at Fazal. 'You bring knives to a gun deal? What was going through your tiny little mind? You were going to pull a knife and we hand over the guns 'cos we're pissing ourselves?'

'They're for protection,' said Ali. He reached into his jacket and pulled out a hunting knife in a nylon sheath. He dropped it on to the floor, then pulled a carving knife with a wooden handle from the back of his trousers, the blade in a cardboard sleeve. It clattered on to the concrete.

'Against what? You think a knife is gonna stop me putting a bullet in your leg?'

'Not against you,' said Ali.

'Against who, then?' asked Shepherd.

'You don't know what it's like for Muslims after seven/seven,' said Ali. 'It was rough before but we're all marked men now. You can't walk down the street without getting abuse and worse.'

'And a knife stops the name-calling, does it?' said Shepherd.

Ali pulled up his sweatshirt to reveal a half-inch-thick scar that ran from his left side to his navel. 'Maybe not, but it'll stop this happening again.'

Shepherd stared at the scar. It was a full ten inches long and, from the way it had healed, it had been a deep wound. 'You were lucky,' he said.

'Lucky?'

'Lucky you didn't die.'

'Yeah, well, it wasn't for want of them trying. That was two weeks after the London bombings. I was in Birmingham, for fuck's sake, on the way to collect my winnings from the bookie.'

'I thought Muslims didn't gamble,' said Shepherd.

Ali frowned. 'What's being a Muslim got to do with anything? I'm British, mate, as British as you. If I want to bet on the horses, I will.'

Sharpe put away his gun and transferred the metal detector to his right hand. Ali held out his arms to the side and Sharpe ran the detector over him. Then he did the same with Fazal. It beeped when it went over the man's trouser pocket but it was only his keys and loose change.

'They kicked the shit out of me and slashed me because to them I was the wrong colour,' said Ali. 'And do you know what the police did? Nothing. They couldn't care less. Sent a white cop who was younger than me. He took a few notes and I never saw him again. Hospital was great but you want to know why? Because hardly anyone working there was white, that's why.'

'Sounds like a racial thing, rather than a religious one,' said Shepherd.

'It's the same,' said Ali. 'You think the guys who did this to me knew I was Muslim? Or cared? They didn't ask – they didn't need to. The guys who blew up the Tube were Asian so all Asians are the enemy.'

'And what do you want the guns for? To even the score?'

'What do you care why I want the guns? You sell, we buy.'

'Can't say fairer than that,' said Shepherd. 'Come and see what I've got.'

He took the two men to the metal cases and opened the one containing the Ingrams. 'The good news is that these are brand new, unfired,' said Shepherd. 'The bad news is that it'll take me a few days to get the other three.'

'We said five,' said Fazal.

'Yeah, I know, but they're difficult to get. When you called you didn't say you wanted five. I can get five, but it'll take a couple of days.' He opened the case containing the magazines. 'I got all the magazines but only a hundred rounds. The other five hundred are on the way.'

'You can get them?' pressed Ali.

'I said I could, didn't I? I had a hundred in stock but my guy in Croatia is going to have to ship the rest and that'll take a few days.'

'A couple? Or a few? Which is it?' asked Fazal.

'Why? Are you up against a deadline?'

Ali picked up one of the Ingrams and sighted along the top. 'When can we get the rest?' he asked.

'Three days max,' said Shepherd.

Ali reached for a magazine. 'Can I try it?'

Sharpe laughed. 'No, you can't bloody try it!' he said. 'One, you'll hear the noise half a mile away and, two, there's no way we're going to trust you with a loaded submachine-pistol, not after your stunt with the knives.'

'How can we be sure they'll work?' asked Fazal, picking up the second gun.

'They're not second-hand cars,' said Shepherd. 'They're fire-arms. You strip them, you check the working parts. It's the ammunition you should be worried about.'

'What do you mean?' said Ali, frowning.

'A gun's a gun,' said Shepherd, 'just a mechanical tool. If the individual parts function correctly, it'll work. But with the ammu-nition, you're dependent on a chemical reaction. A crap round can ruin your whole day. Basically guns don't jam, bad ammunition does.' He opened the case containing the boxed rounds. 'But this is the best of the best. You'll have no problems with it.'

'I'd be happier firing them first,' said Fazal.

'Fine,' said Shepherd. 'Buy them and you can fire them all you want. Speaking of which, where's the money? I'll take five grand for what you have here, and you can give me the rest on delivery of the other three Ingrams and the rounds.'

'I'll get Hassan to call for the cash,' said Fazal.

'What?' said Sharpe.

'We don't have the money with us,' said Ali.

Sharpe took a step forward. 'What do you mean you don't have the money?'

'We wanted to see that you were for real.'

'Are you winding me up?'

'We just wanted to see what you had. Now we know you can come up with the goods, we'll do business with you.'

'Screw you, Paki,' said Sharpe, prodding Ali in the chest. 'We're not fucking Argos – you don't place an order and queue up at the desk.'

Fazal moved towards Sharpe, who pre-empted him by pulling out his gun and pointing it at the man's face.

Ali held up his hand. 'It's okay,' he said to Fazal.

'No, it's not okay,' said Shepherd. 'I don't know who you think you're dealing with but this isn't how business is done.' He took the two Ingrams from the men and put them in the case.

'We couldn't be sure you'd have the guns,' said Ali.

'You're time-wasters,' said Shepherd, slamming the case shut. 'I think you'd better go before my partner decides to use you as target practice.'

'I want the guns,' said Ali, 'and I've got the money. Just not here.'

'Okay, but here's the thing. We don't know you, so we don't trust you. For all we know you could be working for the cops. Or you could be trying to roll us over. Either way, you can see how you not having the cash would set alarm bells ringing.'

'Look, don't get the wrong idea,' said Ali. 'We've got the money, we just didn't bring it with us. I'll tell Hassan to make a call and it'll be here in fifteen minutes.'

'Yeah, or maybe he makes a phone call and the cops come. Or your mates turn up with more knives.'

'I swear to you, all that will happen is that the money will be brought to you,' said Ali.

Shepherd looked across at Sharpe. 'What do you think?'

'I think we should just pop them both, then go out and put a bullet in the one outside,' said Sharpe. 'Something's not right.'

Ali held up his hands. 'Please, you have my word. We have the money. We want to buy as much as you want to sell. Let me get my colleague to make a phone call.'

'I'll tell you what we'll do,' said Shepherd. 'We'll stand at the door with you. You shout at him to come to us. We listen while he makes the call. And if anything other than a bag of money arrives, you'll have a bullet in your head. Okay?'

'Okay.'

Shepherd pushed him towards the door, then motioned for Fazal to follow him. Sharpe kept his gun levelled on Ali as he walked behind him. 'Stop at the door,' said Shepherd. The two men did as they were told. Ali beckoned to Hassan.

'Over here, slowly,' said Shepherd. 'And keep your hands out of your pockets.' He didn't believe the men intended to rip them off, but an underworld arms dealer like Graham May would be suspicious of everybody and everything.

Sharpe waved his gun at Hassan. 'Make the call,' said Sharpe. 'Get the money and make sure every word is in English. If I hear one word of Paki I'll shoot all of you.'

'Urdu,' said Fazal. 'We speak Urdu.'

'I don't care what the hell you speak. I just want to hear English coming out of his mouth.'

Hassan reached inside his jacket.

'And if that hand appears with anything other than a mobile phone in it, I'm going to start shooting.'

Hassan's hand reappeared with a Motorola phone. He flipped it open, scrolled through the address book and called a number. 'Yeah, everything's okay,' he said. 'Bring the cash.' He flipped the phone shut and glared at Shepherd.

'You can stop giving me hard looks,' Shepherd said to Hassan. 'They don't worry me, and it was your own fault for thinking you could take my photograph without me minding. Now, get inside and sit down on the floor.' He gestured at Ali and Fazal. 'That goes for you too.'

The three men went to sit by the metal tables.

'What do you think?' whispered Sharpe.

'I think they thought they were being clever, that's all,' said Shepherd. 'It's not a problem.'

They stood by the door, but kept a close eye on the three men. Just under twenty minutes later, a Volvo estate car drove up.

'They don't go in for posh motors, do they?' said Sharpe.

It parked next to the Mondeo. Asim was driving and Salman was in the passenger seat.

'Tom, get over here,' said Shepherd. Ali got to his feet. The circulation had gone in his legs and he walked unsteadily over to the door. 'Go and get the money,' said Shepherd. 'Five grand. Don't make any sudden movements, don't do anything that will make Lomas here get the least bit jittery because that gun he's holding so casually has a hair trigger.'

'Okay, okay,' said Ali, and hurried over to the Volvo. Asim wound down the window. They were too far away for Shepherd and Sharpe to hear what was said, but Salman had a briefcase on his knee. He opened it, took out half a dozen bundles of notes, then closed the case and handed it through the window to Ali. Ali hurried back with the briefcase in both hands.

Shepherd followed him to the metal tables while Sharpe stood at the door, holding his gun in plain view.

Ali opened the briefcase. Inside there were bundles of used banknotes, a mixture of tens and twenties. Shepherd flicked through one, then tossed it back into the case.

'Aren't you going to count it?' asked Ali.

'If you're short, I'll shoot you in the legs,' said Shepherd. 'Now, do you want to count it or are you happy?'

'It's all there,' said Ali.

'Well, then, there's no need to count it, is there?' said Shepherd, cheerfully. He nodded at Hassan and Fazal. 'You guys can get up now.' They got to their feet. 'I'll call you once we have the rest of the guns and ammunition,' said Shepherd. 'Now that we know each other, we can bring them to you. Where are you guys from?'

'Birmingham,' said Fazal.

'Two hours up the motorway,' said Sharpe. 'We can do that.'

'Okay,' said Ali, picking up the case of guns. He carried it towards the door. Fazal picked up the cases with the magazines and ammunition and followed him. Hassan took one from him.

'Drive carefully,' said Shepherd. Hassan gave him a final glare and Shepherd grinned back.

Ali and Fazal put their suitcases into the Mondeo's boot, then climbed into the car. Hassan put his in with theirs, slammed the boot and joined them. They drove away, the Mondeo leading, as Shepherd and Sharpe watched them.

'Those guys really are amateurs,' said Shepherd. 'Did you see the way they handled the Ingrams? I don't think either of them had ever held a gun before. And they didn't ask any of the questions they should have asked.'

'Amateurs can do a lot of damage with guns like that,' said Sharpe.

'They won't do anything until they've got the rest,' said Shepherd.

'Nice twist offering to take the guns to them,' said Sharpe. 'Weren't you going off menu, though?'

'Yeah, I didn't think they'd go for it but they took the bait. We'll see what Charlie says, but I think SO13 will want a chance to get a video of them with weapons on their own turf.'

Sharpe opened the briefcase of money. 'Doesn't look much, does it?' he said.

'It isn't much,' said Shepherd. 'It's less than my estate agent's charging me and not much more than I'll pay my solicitor.'

They heard footsteps behind them and turned to see Button and Singh at the door. 'Well done, gentlemen,' said Button. She was wearing a dark blue blazer over a white shirt with pale blue Levis, and carrying a small transceiver in her right hand.

'You got it all?' asked Shepherd.

'Sound and vision,' said Singh.

Shepherd and Sharpe took off their jackets and shirts so that Singh could remove the transmitters and microphones. 'What do you think?' Shepherd asked Button.

'Not the most professional bunch in the world,' she said, 'but you don't have to be al-Qaeda trained to start blasting away in a shopping mall.'

Shepherd nodded at the knives and machete on the floor. 'You'll be able to get prints off those and I'm pretty sure they're using their own vehicles.'

'SO13 have them identified already,' said Button.

'I meant so we could get full IDs on them,' said Shepherd.

'It's an SO13 case,' said Button. 'We don't need to duplicate their work. And I'm not sure we need you hotfooting it up to Birmingham.'

'I thought it might help,' said Shepherd.

'Seems a bit over-keen,' said Button. 'Better we let them come down here.'

'Yeah, let Muhammad come to the mountain,' said Sharpe.

Button gave him a withering look. 'Razor, you're going to have to be careful with the racial epithets.'

'It was a joke,' said Sharpe.

'I meant in general,' she said. 'Your language isn't acceptable.'

'I was in character,' said Sharpe.

'You can't go hurling words like "Paki" around any more.'

'With respect, ma'am,' said Sharpe, 'I'm using the slang appropriate to the legend I've been given. I can't start talking like an Oxbridge graduate just because the Commission for Racial Equality might get on my back.'

'I appreciate that, but the tape was running and if one day it gets to court the defence will have a field day. We don't want another OJ, do we?' Sharpe opened his mouth to reply but Button silenced him with a wave of her hand. 'So, next time you feel like mouthing off, call him a prick or a moron, but don't pick on racial characteristics.'

'Heard and understood, ma'am,' said Sharpe.

'You're grinning, Razor.'

'It's my sunny personality, ma'am.'

'And stop calling me "ma'am". I know you only do it to wind me up. Okay, today went well, all things considered. We've got them on tape with weapons, but I want to take it a step further.'

'How?' asked Shepherd.

'According to SO13, the group is considering a suicide mission. I want you to offer them explosives and detonators.'

Shepherd stared at her, stunned. 'You what?'

'We need to ratchet it up a notch. When you call them about delivering the rest of the guns, let them know you can get explosives.'

'They didn't ask us for explosives, though, did they?' said Shepherd.

'Because you were put forward as an arms dealer,' said Button. 'They've accepted you, now it's time to raise the stakes.'

Shepherd's eyes narrowed. 'Is this SO13's idea, or yours?' he asked.

'Does it matter?'

'It smacks to me of entrapment,' said Shepherd.

'They contacted you,' said Button.

'For guns. Now we're suggesting that they set themselves up as suicide-bombers.'

'We give them the option,' said Button. 'It's up to them whether or not they take it. Spider, what's the problem?'

'No problem, I guess,' said Shepherd.

She looked at Sharpe. 'Razor?'

Sharpe grinned. 'No problems here,' he said.

Three loud bangs on the door jolted Mitchell out of a dreamless sleep. He groaned and rolled over. 'Colin, stand by the wall, please.' It was Kamil. Mitchell put a hand against it to steady himself as he got up. He had slept in some uncomfortable places but nothing compared with lying on a concrete floor with just a threadbare blanket.

He stood with his back to the wall, arms outstretched. A key rattled in the lock and the door opened. Mitchell caught a glimpse of a man holding a Kalashnikov, then Kamil was there with a paper plate and a plastic bottle of water. Kamil smiled. 'I have food,' he said, 'and water.'

'Thank you,' said Mitchell.

Kamil gave him the plate. It was covered with a round slice of pitta bread on which lay a chicken leg, a chunk of feta cheese and a handful of green grapes. 'Looks like you've got all four food groups covered,' said Mitchell, 'but a beer would be nice.'

'To be honest, I'd happily give you one, but my colleagues out there are stricter than I am and they would not be happy if there was alcohol in the house.'

'That's okay. I was joking,' said Mitchell. He sat down with his back to the wall and started to gnaw at the chicken leg. Kamil unscrewed the bottle top and handed the water to him. During the day it was stiflingly hot in the basement and Mitchell needed at least three litres of water to replace the fluid he lost through sweat. But at night it was so cold that even wearing his clothes and wrapped in the blanket he still shivered.

'Have you been using the chess set?' asked Kamil, sitting cross-legged on the floor.

For a moment Mitchell thought that the other man knew what he had been doing with the pieces, then realised he was only asking if he'd been practising. He nodded and popped three grapes into his mouth.

'Do you want to play?'

'Sure,' said Mitchell. 'How about we play for money?'

Kamil chuckled. 'Muslims do not gamble, Colin. We can't bet money in any form.'

'Sorry. I didn't know.'

'That's okay,' said Kamil. 'Where is the chess set?'

Mitchell pointed to *The Da Vinci Code*. 'Under the book.'

Kamil crawled over to the paperback and moved it to the side. He picked up the magnetic chess set and opened it.

Mitchell chewed and tried to appear unconcerned. He had kept changing the pieces as he had worked on the screws in the socket so that they would all show the same wear and tear, but there was a chance that Kamil would notice the damage if he looked carefully.

'Can I ask you a few questions about Islam?' asked Mitchell.

Kamil seemed surprised. 'What do you mean?'

'I don't know much about your religion,' said Mitchell. 'I've worked in Iraq for six months and I've seen the mosques and the men praying but I've never understood what the religion was about. What you were saying about there being just one God, it sounded like what I was told at church years ago.'

'There are many similarities between our religions,' said Kamil. He put the chess set on top of the book, 'but we don't believe that Jesus Christ was the son of God.'

Mitchell smiled. 'I've always had trouble with that myself,' he said. 'I don't see how a God could have a flesh-and-blood son.'

'We believe that Jesus was a good man, but he wasn't the son of God,' said Kamil. 'We believe that Muhammad was the only true messenger of God.'

'So you don't believe in the Bible?'

'We don't believe that the Bible is the word of God,' said Kamil. 'We have the Koran, which was written on golden tablets in Paradise. It has to be read as if God Himself was speaking.'

'Would you be able to get me a copy?' asked Mitchell.

'But you cannot read Arabic,' said Kamil.

'There are translations, aren't there?'

'The Koran must be read in Arabic,' said Kamil. 'If it is not in the original Arabic, it is not the true word of God.'

'So how does a non-Muslim learn about Islam?'

'If you are serious, I could read from my copy, then explain to you what it means.'

'Would you do that?'

Kamil smiled. 'I would be more than happy to, Colin. We could start now.'

'I'd like that,' said Mitchell. 'I'd like that a lot.' He popped another grape into his mouth.

Shepherd parked the BMW in the driveway and let himself into the house. It was just before three o'clock so Katra had probably gone to pick up Liam. He stripped off his clothes, showered and had just slipped on his bathrobe when the phone rang. He picked up the extension in the bedroom. It was Linda Howe, the solicitor who was handling the sale of his house: 'It's bad news, I'm afraid,' she said. 'Has your estate agent been in touch?'

'No,' said Shepherd. 'What's up?'

'The buyer's having trouble meeting his commitments and has asked if you'd be prepared to drop your asking price.'

Shepherd cursed under his breath and sat down on the bed. 'So I've been gazumped?' he said.

'Well, strictly speaking, it's gazumping when the vendor increases his price at the last minute,' said the solicitor.

'So I've been reverse gazumped,' said Shepherd. 'Either way he's taking a liberty, Linda. We agreed a price.'

'Absolutely we did,' she said, 'but until the contracts are exchanged and they've paid their ten pcr cent deposit, either party is free to renegotiate or even to pull out altogether.'

Shepherd had thought the couple who had offered for the house pleasant enough. He was a financial adviser in his late twenties, working in the City, and she was a couple of years younger, a personal assistant at a public-relations company near Oxford Circus. They had said they were planning to start a family and wanted a house they could grow into. They owned a small flat in Bayswater and had already accepted an offer on it; the husband had arranged a mortgage through his company. They had seemed the perfect buyers. 'What exactly did they say?' asked Shepherd.

'That their buyer has dropped his offer by fifteen thousand pounds. They can't proceed unless you agree to the same.'

'So I have to suffer because their buyer's playing hardball?' asked Shepherd.

'We can tell them we're not prepared to accept a lower offer. The ball's in your court, Dan.'

'And if I agree to take the hit, everything goes through?'

'We amend the contract accordingly and as all the searches have been done we'll probably be able to exchange the day after tomorrow, with another two weeks to completion. I could probably do it quicker if the other side co-operates.'

'Their timing's impeccable, isn't it?' mused Shepherd.

'What do you mean?' asked the solicitor.

'From their point of view, it's perfect timing. They presumably know that I've made the offer on the place in Hereford, and I told them about Liam, that he was moving schools. I even told them about Liam's grandparents. They know I want to move as quickly as possible. And then, right at the last minute, they throw a spanner into the works. No doubt they think I'll knock off the fifteen grand for the sake of a quiet life.'

'It wouldn't be the first time someone tried that,' admitted the solicitor. 'But what do you want to do about it?'

'I'm on a tight budget with this,' said Shepherd. 'If he leaves me fifteen grand short, that's fifteen grand I don't have. I'm not sure that the bank will increase my mortgage.'

'It's a difficult situation, I know,' said the solicitor.

Shepherd tried to clear his thoughts. If he'd been Graham May he'd have gone round with a gun and threatened to put a bullet into the man's leg, maybe threaten to rape his wife as well. But he wasn't Graham May, he was Dan Shepherd, SAS trooper turned undercover cop, and as angry as he was at what the couple had done, they had still acted completely within the law.

'What do you want to do?' asked the solicitor.

'I don't know,' said Shepherd. 'If we pull out now, will I still have to pay your fee?'

'The bulk of the work has already been done,' said the solicitor. 'I could probably knock ten per cent off our agreed fee, but that would be as far as I could go.'

'So either way I lose out,' said Shepherd. 'I stump up the fifteen grand or I start from scratch – *and* lose the house I'm buying.'

'That's the problem with a chain,' said the solicitor. 'If one link breaks, the whole thing collapses. There is another option. We could tell the seller of the Hereford house that we want to drop our offer by fifteen thousand.'

'Do you think she'd agree?'

'We could try.'

The woman selling the house in Hereford was a widow in her seventies. Her husband had died two years earlier and she was planning to move closer to her married daughter in Essex. She was buying a small bungalow so she would have money to spare, but Shepherd had felt that he was getting a good deal on the house and didn't like the idea of trying to snatch back fifteen thousand pounds at this late stage. 'No, I don't want to do that. It's not . . .' He hesitated. The word he wanted to use was 'fair' but he'd sound so naïve. As a serving police officer, he knew that life wasn't fair – in fact, it was a long way from it. More often than not the bad guys got away with villainy and the good ones got hurt. The richer and more successful the villain, the more likely he was to stay free. The poorer the victim, the less likely he or she was to see justice done. So, life wasn't fair and only the naïve or stupid thought it was. 'Necessary,' finished Shepherd. 'Let me think about my options.'

'The buyer says he'll give us three days,' said the solicitor. 'Seventy-two hours.'

'Now he's setting deadlines?' said Shepherd, exasperated. 'This is extortion. He's deliberately putting me under pressure hoping I'll crack.'

'I dare say that the buyer of his property has set the same deadline,' said the solicitor.

'I know, I know,' said Shepherd. He ran his hand through his hair. 'Let me think about it. I'll get back to you.'

He ended the call and tapped in his mother-in-law's number. She answered in her usually crisp manner, but when she realised it was him she was immediately chatting away: 'Daniel, I'm so glad you called. The headmistress wants to confirm Liam's start date, and I said he'd be with them next Monday. I've already bought his uniform but he'll need white plimsolls and I wasn't sure what size to get.'

'Moira, there's been a hitch . . .' He explained what had happened.

'Oh, Daniel,' she said. She was the only person who used Shepherd's full name and had never called him anything else, even though he'd asked her to call him Dan. To his friends and colleagues, Shepherd was either Spider or Dan. His wife had called him Dan. Or 'lover'. Even Moira's husband, Tom, called him Dan. But to Moira he had always been Daniel and always would be, just as trainers would always be plimsolls. 'Look, if it's a problem with the financing, Tom and I can tide you over. Tom would talk to his bank. I'm sure they'd agree a bridging loan.'

'Really, it's okay,' said Shepherd.

'Whatever happened to honesty and decency?' asked his mother-in-law. 'A man's word used to be his bond.'

'It's every man for himself, these days,' said Shepherd.

'Well, it shouldn't be. They agreed to buy your house for a price and now they're going back on it. You should be able to sue them.'

'Sadly, the law's on their side,' said Shepherd.

'Then the law's wrong,' said Moira.

'No argument there,' said Shepherd. 'Look, it's not the end of the world.'

'You're still moving, aren't you?' said his mother-in-law. Shepherd could hear the apprehension in her voice. He knew how much she wanted Liam close by. Since Sue had died, Moira and Tom had seen their grandson mainly during school holidays and for the occasional weekend. Shepherd knew that they deserved more. Sue had been their only child and Liam was their only grandchild. He was all they had left of her, and Shepherd was determined that Liam would be a bigger part of their life in future.

'Of course we are,' said Shepherd. 'I'll talk to my bank about a bridging loan, but if they won't play ball I might have to pull out of the house I'm buying in Hereford.'

'Oh, Daniel . . .'

'It's okay, really. Worst possible scenario, Liam can come and stay with you again.'

'I hope you don't mean that's the worst possible scenario,' said Moira.

'I'm sorry, that's not what I meant,' said Shepherd. 'I meant if I can't sort it out, it would be great if he could stay with you for a while.'

'Of course,' said Moira. 'His room is here whenever he needs it.'

'Thanks,' said Shepherd.

'What about Katra?'

'If the house sale falls through, she can stay in Ealing. I'll stay there too. It might work out, Moira, but if it doesn't I want Liam settled in his new school as soon as possible. I know the headmistress moved heaven and earth to get him in mid-term.'

'Is everything else okay, Daniel?' she asked.

'Everything's fine,' he said.

'You sound a bit stressed, that's all.'

'It's been a stressful week.'

Richard Yokely was watching the flat-screen computer monitor with Marion Cooke, one of the CIA's top video analysts, whom he had known for almost a decade. This video was a little less than two minutes long and only one man spoke; he wore a ski mask and brandished a Kalashnikov. It was the seventh time they had viewed it. Now Cooke sat back and exhaled through pursed lips. 'Not much of a plot,' she said. 'I'll give it both thumbs down.'

'Anything on the ringleader?'

She looked pained. 'My Arabic's good but I'm not a linguistics expert so I can't even tell you his nationality. But I'll run it past our guys and we'll get it nailed down. I can cross-check it with voices on file and I'll let you know if we get a match.'

'The banner?'

' "The Holy Martyrs of Islam. Death to the Infidels." The sort of rhetoric we usually see in this sort of thing.'

'Can you cross-check it with previous videos? Use of language, handwriting – I need to know if they have links to other fundamentalist groups.'

'Yeah. I'd never heard of the Holy Martyrs of Islam before now.'

'No one has,' said Yokely, 'but this is their second kidnapping and they haven't made any mistakes so I'm assuming they've got experience.'

Cooke tapped the keyboard and zoomed in on the face of the man in the orange jumpsuit. 'He's a Brit, right?'

'Yeah. Civilian contractor.'

Cooke pressed another button and the video began to play again, but this time the man's face filled the screen. 'You know what's interesting?' she mused.

'Tell me,' said Yokely.

'He's not afraid,' said Cooke. 'I've seen a few hostage videos and you can see the fear on their faces. Wide eyes, hyperventilating, shaking. This guy's like a rock. And look at his eyes – he's watching everything. He's not at all scared.'

'Ah,' said Yokely. 'Perhaps I understated his background. He was in special forces for a while.'

'The SAS?' She grinned. 'Then, from what I've heard, his captors are the ones who should be worried.'

'They don't know what he was before,' said Yokely. 'So far as they're concerned, he's just a hired hand.'

'Probably best,' said Cooke.

'What about the other men in the video?'

'Can I see through the masks, you mean? Sadly, the technology isn't there yet, Richard.'

'You know what I mean, Marion.'

Cooke grinned. She started the video again and waited until the masked men standing in front of the banner were in view, then froze the picture. She pointed at the man on the left cradling one of the weapons. 'Kalashnikov AK-47,' she said. 'Barrel length sixteen point three inches, overall length thirty-four point two five inches.' Then she pointed at the second Kalashnikov. 'This is the newer variant, the AK-74,' she said. 'See the bigger muzzle? Cuts down on the recoil. It's a bit longer at thirty-seven inches overall but the barrel is around half an inch shorter. Using those numbers as a reference, I can get the height and body measurements of all the men in the video, plus a pretty close approximation of their weight.'

Yokely patted her shoulder. 'Excellent,' he said. 'What else?'

'You don't ask much, do you?' she said. She tapped on the keyboard again. The screen showed the full view of the video's first frame: the five masked figures standing in front of the banner. 'Do you know much about RPGs?' she asked.

'Just that they go bang and do a lot of damage,' said Yokely.

Cooke froze the picture and zoomed in now on the man holding the RPG. 'Funny things, RPGs,' she said. 'Most people think that it stands for rocket-propelled grenade but it actually stands for *ruchnoy protivotankovy granatomyot*. That translates as hand-held anti-tank grenade-launcher. But our military and most of our allies don't use the word "grenade" to describe an anti-tank weapon. So RPG, strictly speaking, is only used to describe the Russian variant.'

'So what *do* we call them?'

Cooke smiled. 'Shoulder-launched missile weapon systems,' she said. 'Or shoulder-launched rockets. You see, under our definition, grenades can't be self-propelled.'

'Marion, you never cease to amaze me,' said Yokely.

'Sweet-talker,' said Marion. She nodded at the screen. 'This one is the guerrilla's favourite,' she said. 'The RPG-7. It was RPG-7s that brought down the Blackhawk helicopters in Somalia. The Mujahideen used them in Afghanistan and Unita rebels had them in Angola. Now they're all over Iraq.'

'Any way of identifying it?' asked Yokely.

Cooke went in close on the RPG. 'I don't see a serial number,' she said. She frowned thoughtfully. 'I've seen an RPG in another Iraqi video,' she said. She rubbed the back of her neck. 'When the hell was it? Not recently, that's for sure.' Her voice had dropped to a whisper and she closed her eyes. 'Come on, Marion. Come on, come on.'

'In my experience, you relax and you remember,' said Yokely.
'Please, Richard, don't even think of offering me a massage.'
Yokely laughed. 'I was thinking of getting you a coffee.'
'Sure – caffeine. That'll relax me.'

Mitchell dropped to the ground and did twenty rapid press-ups,
then ten slow ones. He rolled on to his back and started doing
brisk sit-ups. Fitness was crucial if he stood any chance of
surviving the next few days. He would only get one opportunity
and when it presented itself he would have to be ready to seize it
with both hands.

He had loosened the screws and removed the socket from the
wall. Two wires led to it, a red live one and a blue neutral. There
was quite a bit of slack in them and he had been able to pull out
almost two feet. The question was where he went from there. He
lay on his back, staring up at the ceiling and taking deep breaths,
feeling the burn in his abdomen.

He had no way of knowing if the socket was live. Even if it was
it would almost certainly be on a different circuit from the lights.
If he touched the two wires together there was a good chance he'd
blow a fuse or throw a circuit breaker but that probably wouldn't
knock out the lights and even if it did he'd still be locked in the
basement.

He started doing sit-ups again, this time slowly with his right
leg crossed over the left. The wire was a weapon. He had at least
two feet to play with, maybe more if he pulled it hard. He could
use it as a garrotte, which would be a killing weapon. He could
grab Kamil, wrap the wire round his neck and threaten to kill him
unless he was released. Kamil was the leader but Mitchell didn't
know how committed the other men were to him. Threatening to
kill Kamil might be his ticket out, but it might also be his death
warrant.

He crossed his left leg over the right and started a new set of sit-
ups.

If the socket was live he might be able to use the electricity in some way. If he had more wire he could run it over to the door and use the power to disable the men when they came into the room. But he didn't have extra wire and even if he had he wasn't sure there'd be enough current to electrocute his captors. There were so many uncertainties that it was laughable, but Mitchell was sure of one thing: he wouldn't go down without a fight.

Yokely's mobile phone rang and he took the call.

'Tell me I'm a genius, Richard,' said Marion Cooke.

'You're a genius,' said Yokely.

'The most wonderful analyst you've ever met.'

'The most wonderful analyst I've ever met,' he repeated.

'And smarter than the average bear.'

'Way smarter,' said Yokely. 'Is there something you want to tell me, Marion, or do you just need your ego stroked?'

'I have a match on the RPG in the Mitchell video.'

'No way,' said Yokely.

'Total way,' said Cooke. 'The same RPG was in a video that went online six months ago, but from a totally different group. They called themselves Islamic Followers of Truth. They kidnapped three Egyptian electricians and later released them. Word is that a ransom was paid but the Egyptian authorities denied it. The three men are back with their families and the Islamic Followers of Truth were never heard from again.'

'So it's good news, bad news?' asked Yokely.

'O ye of little faith,' laughed Cooke. 'It's great news. The organisation, or whatever it was, vanished, but we have one of its members in custody. One Umar al-Tikriti.'

'An illustrious name, indeed,' said Yokely. Tikriti was Saddam Hussein's family name, taken from Tikrit, the name of his home town.

'No relation,' said Cooke. 'At least not a close one. Umar was pulled in after a mortar attack on the Green Zone three months ago. He was in the vicinity and chemical tests showed traces of explosives residue on his clothes. He is presently a guest at your old stamping ground, the Baghdad Central Detention Centre. Intel we have says he was a member of the Islamic Followers of Truth, though that came from an informant and Umar has denied it.'

'Well, he would, wouldn't he?' said Yokely.

'Exactly,' said Cooke. 'Seems to me, if you want to know who's holding that RPG in the video, Umar is the man to talk to.'

'Marion, you're an angel,' said Yokely.

'I know.'

Three mobile phones in charging units were lined up on the bedside table. The middle one was ringing and Shepherd grabbed for it as he sat up. It was Richard Yokely. 'You awake?' asked the American.

Shepherd squinted at the digital clock behind the phones. 'Richard, it's three o'clock.'

'So that's a yes,' said Yokely, cheerfully. 'How do you fancy having a chat with someone who might know one of the guys in your friend's video?'

'Is this some sort of riddle?' asked Shepherd.

'There's a car on its way,' said Yokely. 'Should be with you in half an hour.'

'Where am I going?'

'Oxfordshire,' said the American. 'But bring your passport to be on the safe side.'

Shepherd showered, then put on a denim shirt and black jeans. He took a brown leather jacket from the cupboard under the stairs and made himself a coffee.

Katra came into the kitchen, rubbing her eyes. She was wearing her bathrobe and had her hair tied up. 'What's happening?' she asked.

'Sorry,' he said. 'I have to go out. I'm not sure when I'll be back.'

'Is everything okay?'

'Everything's fine,' said Shepherd. 'You go back to bed.' She headed for the stairs. 'Oh, Katra, we've had a problem with the house sale. It might be that Liam has to stay with his grandparents until I get it sorted.'

'Okay,' she said.

'He's going to the school in Hereford from Monday – can you make sure he knows?'

'What about you?'

'I'll stay here, you too. I'm really busy at the moment so I'll need you to show people round.'

'I thought the house had been sold,' she said.

'Yeah,' said Shepherd, ruefully. 'So did I.' The doorbell rang. 'That'll be my ride.' He pulled on his jacket and opened the front door. A thick-set man with a square jaw and a crew-cut, wearing a charcoal grey suit and a Paisley patterned tie, looked at him with unsmiling eyes. 'Dan Shepherd?' he asked.

'That's me,' said Shepherd. He closed the door behind him. The man was already walking towards a black Lexus parked in the road. He opened the rear door for Shepherd, who would have preferred to sit in the front but he sensed that the man expected him to get into the back so he climbed in and fastened his seat-belt.

The man was a good driver, clearly a professional. He was also uncommunicative: he virtually ignored Shepherd's attempts to make small-talk so Shepherd settled back in the leather seat and wondered what in Oxfordshire warranted a visit in the early hours. Just over an hour later he got his answer when he saw a sign for RAF Brize Norton. 'Oh, terrific.' He sighed.

The Lexus purred up to the main entrance of the airbase. The driver wound down the window and handed a sheet of paper to a uniformed airman who peered at Shepherd. 'ID,' he said. Shepherd handed him his passport. The airman scrutinised it and gave it back with a curt nod. The window rolled up and the Lexus drove on to the airfield.

Yokely was waiting beside a white Gulfstream jet with an American registration number. He was dressed casually in a black leather bomber jacket, khaki trousers and brown loafers with tassels. He grinned as Shepherd got out of the car.

'What's going on, Richard?' asked Shepherd.

'There's someone I think you should talk to,' said the American. The Lexus drove off.

'Please tell me he's on the plane.'

'Ah, if only life were so simple.' Yokely gripped the handrail of the stairs that led up to the aircraft door. 'Come on. The captain's already filed his flight plan.'

'To where?'

'Strictly speaking, that's classified,' said Yokely.

'Richard . . .'

'Baghdad,' said Yokely. 'Now come on, time's a-wasting.'

Yokely and Shepherd went up the stairs and sat in two leather armchairs facing across a table that was strewn with early editions of the morning newspapers. The captain came out of the cockpit, square-jawed and sporting a crew-cut like the Lexus driver, dressed in a short-sleeved white shirt with yellow and black epaulettes.

'Five minutes, gentlemen,' he said, and shut the door. 'We crash, we die,' said the pilot. 'That gets the safety briefing out of the way. Fasten your seat-belts and try not to use the head as there's blood in there and we haven't had time to clean it up.'

'Blood?' said Shepherd, as the pilot disappeared into the cockpit.

Yokely held up his hands. 'Nothing to do with me.'

'This is a rendition flight, is it?'

'Strictly speaking, it's only rendition if we're transporting a prisoner,' said Yokely. 'So the answer's no. But on the way back, now that would be a different kettle of fish.'

'You're going to pick someone up?'

'Again, nothing to do with me,' said Yokely. 'We're just hitching a ride.'

The engines whined and they fastened their seat-belts. The jet taxied to the runway and two minutes later they were climbing through cloud, heading east. Yokely glanced at his watch. 'Why don't you get some shut-eye?' he said. 'As comfortable as these jets are, the powers-that-be refuse to let us have in-flight entertainment or stewardesses. I can make us a coffee before we land but in the meantime I suggest we get some sleep.'

Shepherd pressed the button to recline the seat and was asleep within minutes.

Shepherd opened his eyes to find Yokely smiling at him. 'You snore,' said the American, 'like a train.'

'It's an inherited defence mechanism,' said Shepherd, stretching his arms. He undid his seat-belt and stood up, rubbing the back of his neck. 'It goes back to caveman times,' he said. 'When a hungry lion wandered by and heard my ancestors snoring he gave them a wide berth, figuring they were as dangerous as he was. The guys who slept silently were eaten. Darwinian selection. That's why I snore. That's how I used to explain it to my wife, anyway.'

'Did she buy it?'

'Not really.'

Yokely pointed to a mug of coffee on the table. 'Didn't know if you took sugar.'

'I don't. Thanks. When do we get there?'

'We'll be starting our descent in five minutes,' said Yokely. 'Best you finish your coffee before we do.'

'Why's that?'

Yokely grinned. 'You haven't been to Baghdad before, have you?'

'First time,' said Shepherd.

'You'll need your seat-belt and a strong stomach.'

'Why?'

'Now that'd spoil the surprise, wouldn't it?'

Shepherd swallowed the last of his coffee as the pilot's voice came over the intercom. 'Make sure you're strapped in, gentlemen. We're heading on down.'

The engine noise quietened as the pilot throttled back, then the left wing dipped and the jet went into a steep left turn. Shepherd's stomach churned as the nose pointed down and they began a dive, still turning to the left.

'Yee-ha!' bellowed Yokely.

Shepherd tasted bile at the back of his throat and he swallowed. The last thing he wanted was to throw up in front of the American. The jet levelled, still in a dive, but as soon as it had levelled out the left wing dipped again and the plane banked so sharply that Shepherd was thrown to the side. Their downward spiral continued, the plane descending so quickly that Shepherd was continually working his jaw to equalise the pressure in his eardrums. 'What the hell's going on?' he asked.

'It's the safest way to get down,' said Yokely. 'The insurgents have a habit of shooting at planes coming in to land.'

The plane levelled, then banked once more. It broke through the clouds but all that Shepherd could see through the window was the desert spinning round. His stomach heaved and he took a deep breath.

'The sick bags are under the table,' said Yokely.

'I'm fine,' said Shepherd.

Their rate of descent increased as they got closer to the ground and they were diving so steeply that Shepherd couldn't see how they'd be able to pull up in time but at the last minute the wings levelled, the nose came up and the plane's wheels slammed on to the ground. The jet taxied off the runway and made a series of turns that took it away from the main terminal building, then came to a halt.

'Welcome to Baghdad,' said Yokely.

Shepherd opened his mouth to reply but felt nauseous again and instead took a deep breath.

The captain came out and opened the main door. Outside were two dirt-encrusted Humvees, engines running. 'Our chariots await,' said Yokely. He was carrying a laptop computer case. Shepherd followed him out. Within seconds his face was bathed in sweat.

At the bottom of the stairs an American soldier, a huge man made even bigger by his helmet, goggles and body armour, cradled an M16 in his arms. 'Good to see you back, Mr Yokely,' he said, in a broad Southern drawl.

'They can't keep me away, Matt,' replied Yokely, patting him on the shoulder.

'Gear's in the rear,' said the soldier.

Shepherd followed Yokely to the second Humvee and climbed into the back. Two sets of body armour and two helmets lay on the floor. Yokely handed a set to Shepherd and the two men struggled to put it all on in the confines of the vehicle.

The soldier grinned at them from the doorway. 'The armour's a pain but it's necessary,' he said. 'Three men were killed yesterday when an IED went off just two miles from here.'

'No problem,' said Shepherd, tightening the straps that adjusted the collar. He sat down on a narrow seat of torn, dirty canvas over foam rubber. The soldier climbed in and sat next to him. He pulled the door closed and sat with the M16 between his legs. Behind the driver a blue cooler was filled with water bottles. Everything in the vehicle was covered with reddish dust.

'Much happening?' asked Yokely, as the Humvee drove away from the plane.

'Same old, same old,' said the soldier. 'How long are you here for this time?'

'Flying visit,' said Yokely, fastening the strap of his helmet.

They reached the airport perimeter. The barrier went up as they approached and the two Humvees roared through and out on to the road.

'That's it?' asked Shepherd. 'No Passport Control, no Customs?'

'I don't exist,' said Yokely, adjusting the straps of his body armour. 'And as long as you're with me, neither do you.'

The Humvee picked up speed. Through the window Shepherd saw a convoy of trucks heading towards the airport, topped and tailed by nineteen-ton eight-wheeler Stryker light-armoured vehicles, their 105mm cannons sweeping the roadsides. Metal mesh screens were wrapped round them, offering some protection against rocket-propelled grenades. In the middle of the convoy there were three soft-skinned Nissan pick-up trucks in which uniformed Iraqi troops were strap-hanging. None was wearing body armour although they had Kevlar helmets. Shepherd glimpsed one of the drivers as they raced by, an Arab wearing a baseball cap the wrong away around and headphones. His head was bobbing back and forth in time with whatever music he was listening to.

A strip of land more than a hundred feet wide separated the carriageways, sandy reddish soil dotted with dried grass. Emaciated cattle grazed on what little vegetation there was, seemingly oblivious to the speeding traffic.

'Can you tell me where we're going? Or is that classified?' asked Shepherd.

'Now we're on the ground I can tell you,' said the American. 'The Baghdad Central Detention Centre.'

'That would be Abu Ghraib prison, right?'

'The name changed a while back,' said Yokely, 'but yes. That's where our man is being held.'

'That's where you abuse your prisoners, isn't it?'

Yokely chuckled at Shepherd's attempt to rile him. 'In 1984 alone, Saddam Hussein had more than four thousand men executed there, so let's not make out that a bit of teasing is on a par with what the great dictator got up to. He held his enemies for up to twenty years, often packed fifty into a tiny cell with standing room only, and he used a lot as guinea pigs in his chemical and biological weapons programmes. And while we're on the subject, it's worth mentioning that you Brits built the place for him.'

'I didn't know that,' admitted Shepherd.

'Back in the swinging sixties, when the West was more than happy to do business with Iraq,' said Yokely. 'Funny old world, isn't it?' He tightened the Velcro straps on his body armour.

'Most of our troops take out the reinforcing plates,' he said. 'They complain about the weight.'

'They're heavy all right,' said Shepherd, 'but given the choice between carrying a few extra pounds or taking a bullet in the chest . . .' He banged his fist against the Kevlar chest plate.

'It's not snipers you've got to worry about,' said Yokely, as the Humvees accelerated past a pick-up truck with half a dozen live goats in the back. 'They call this road Sniper's Alley but most of the casualties are from IEDs. The insurgents rarely use snipers.' He grinned. 'And you know who's to blame for the boom in IEDs?' he said. 'No pun intended.'

'I'm sure you're going to tell me,' said Shepherd.

'One of yours,' said the American. 'Lawrence of Arabia. The fag who drove the motorcycle. Way back in the Arab Revolt of 1916 to 1918. He pioneered the use of explosives as a terrorist tool. He blew up seventeen of the Turks' locomotives over a four-month period and after that they were scared shitless of travelling by train. Fear's the greatest tool of a terrorist, and IEDs are a great way of spreading fear. The insurgents here have taken what Lawrence did and raised it to the tenth power. Do you have any idea how much the Department of Defense spent last year on counter-IED measures?'

'Again, I'm sure you're going to tell me.'

'Three and a half billion bucks. That's billion, not million.'

Shepherd raised his eyebrows. 'That's one hell of a lot of money, all right.'

Yokely smacked his palm against the side of the Humvee. 'They've just poured almost four hundred million dollars into reinforcing these babies. Imagine what you and I could do with that amount of money.'

'Retire?'

Yokely chuckled. 'You'll never retire,' he said. 'You're the same as me. You love the thrill of the chase, the eternal struggle between good and evil.'

'I don't see life as simply as that,' said Shepherd.

'You won't admit it, but you're addicted to the adrenaline rush,' said Yokely. 'We all are.' They drove past the burned-out shell of a saloon car. 'The IED is the terrorist's weapon of the future,' he said. 'They're perfecting the technique here, but before long they'll be using them all over the States and Europe.'

'We've had that before, with the IRA,' said Shepherd.

'Different animal,' said Yokely. 'The IRA were interested in spectaculars. Big showy explosions and, more often than not, they gave warnings. The fundamentalists are concentrating on small explosions designed to kill and maim. No warnings. Imagine the havoc devices like that would wreak on our freeways. Or in New York City. Or London. They already account for two-thirds of all American combat deaths in Iraq. And how many of the bastards placing the devices do we catch? Hardly any. The bad guys love odds like that. Maximum terror, minimum risk. It's a hell of a lot easier to recruit a guy to plant IEDs than it is to recruit a suicide-bomber. I tell you, they can fight like this for ever. It doesn't matter how many troops we send, how much equipment we give them, we can't win. Because the enemy is untargetable. Overwhelming fire-power is all well and good, but in Iraq we've got nothing to shoot at.'

The Humvee slowed to walking pace. Ahead a flock of bleating sheep were wandering across the road, guided by two Iraqis wearing dusty *dishdashas*, their heads swathed in black and white checked scarves. 'You have to be careful of livestock out here,' said the driver, over his shoulder.

'Ambushes?' said Shepherd.

The driver grinned. 'Ambushes we can handle,' he said. 'It's the compensation claims that bust our balls. If you kill a sheep, you don't just pay to replace the animal. You have to pay for the generations of sheep that would have been produced by the animal you killed. So you run over one and you pay out twenty thousand dollars.'

The drive from the airport to the prison took just over half an hour. They were waved through several roadblocks manned by American and Iraqi soldiers, and barrelled across road junctions without slowing. The first time they came to a complete stop was when they pulled up in front of a sandbagged barrier outside the main entrance to the prison.

Two soldiers with M16s spoke to the driver of the first Humvee, then a red and white striped pole was raised to allow both vehicles to approach the main gate. It rattled back and the Humvees drove through. Ahead, a second metal gate barred their way until the one behind was shut. Two more soldiers with M16s looked down on them. Both men wore impenetrable sunglasses.

'Who are we here to see?' said Shepherd.

'An Iraqi by the name of Umar al-Tikriti,' said Yokely. 'I've reason to believe that he knows the guy holding the RPG in the video of your friend.'

'And he'll tell us who he is?'

Yokely grinned. 'Hopefully, if we play it right,' he said.

The inner gate rattled open and the two Humvees drove into a central courtyard. The soldier opened the rear door and Shepherd and Yokely climbed out. Shepherd shaded his eyes against the unrelenting sun. His shirt was soaked under the body armour and he was holding his leather jacket.

'You can strip the Kevlar off now, gentlemen,' said the soldier. 'You're among friends here.'

Shepherd and Yokely took off their helmets and armour and tossed them into the back of the Humvee. Yokely picked up his laptop computer case.

A tall man with close-cropped red hair, freckles and desert camouflage fatigues strode across the courtyard holding a clipboard and a transceiver. 'Can't keep you away, can we?' he said.

Yokely grinned. 'Dan, this is Bob Winmill,' he said. 'He's with the sixteenth Military Police Brigade and is the power behind the throne here.'

Winmill shook hands with Shepherd. 'Like "windmill" but without the *d* in the middle,' he said. His little finger was missing and there were burn scars round his wrist, but his grip was strong. 'Welcome to our facility, Dan,' said Winmill.

'I assume our man's in the hardsite?' said Yokely.

'He is now,' said Winmill. 'We had him in Camp Redemption but we moved him last night.' He saw Shepherd's confusion. 'Sorry, Dan,' he said. 'The hardsite is the old part of the prison, the cell box complexes. It's where Saddam kept his prisoners. We've had them refitted to US specifications, but because we can't pack them in the way he did, they now hold only a fraction of our inmates. The rest we keep in tents in compounds. We've just under three thousand in Camp Redemption. We only put the most dangerous prisoners and those with intelligence value in the hardsite.' He waved at the building to their left. 'He's in there now.'

'So he's not dangerous?' said Shepherd, putting on his jacket.

'We found traces of explosives on his clothes. To be honest, that means nothing out here, but it's enough to hold him for as long as we want. He hasn't told us much, but we don't really know what to ask him.'

'He was in a group called the Islamic Followers of Truth, right?' said Yokely.

'That came from another inmate,' said Winmill. 'The intel is probably good but the group was more criminal than insurgent so we didn't pack him off to Guantánamo.'

'What can you tell us about him?' asked Shepherd.

'He's twenty-six, a Sunni, and this is his second time inside the prison. Eight years ago he was a guest of Saddam Hussein, serving time for robbery. He was released in 2002 after Saddam announced an amnesty for most of the country's prisoners.'

'What incentives can I offer him?' asked Yokely.

'A room with a view,' said Winmill. 'A change of clothes, maybe.'

'Early release?'

'It's that important?'

Yokely looked at Shepherd. 'Yes,' he said. 'It is.'

'It's not as if we caught him with a detonator in his hand, and the Egyptian electricians the group was holding were released unharmed. If it helps, I don't see why we couldn't send him on his way.'

'We'll see how it goes,' said Yokely. 'Thanks, Bob. I owe you one.'

'You owe me several,' said Winmill, 'but who's counting? Come on, I'll walk you in.'

He took them to a metal door, unlocked it with a key on a chain attached to his belt, pulled it open and waved the two men through.

A corridor ran the length of the ground floor. At regular intervals, barred doors opened on to individual cells. Each was about four metres wide and eight deep. Winmill locked the door behind them and took them down the corridor. Shepherd looked into a cell as they walked by. Four Iraqis were sitting on the floor, looking out through the bars. All four were wearing traditional long white *dishdashas*. 'I've got him in an interview room on the second floor,' said Winmill. 'We've had him there since this morning and we haven't told him why.'

'Does he speak English?' asked Yokely.

'Some,' said Winmill.

'I'd like to try it without an interpreter first,' said Yokely.

'Fine by me,' said Winmill. Two uniformed military policemen walked by, their shirts perfectly ironed and their boots gleaming. They nodded at Winmill, who nodded back.

At the end of the corridor they came to another locked door. Winmill unlocked it with the key he'd used previously. The three went through and he relocked it.

'Do you video your interviews?' asked Shepherd.

'No,' said Winmill. 'The only record is what is written down by the interrogating officers.'

'And we won't be writing anything down,' said Yokely. 'I've already explained that we're not really here.'

'Just a mirage,' laughed Winmill. 'See the cell there?' He indicated a cell to their left. 'Andy McNab was held there for a while. The *Bravo Two Zero* guy. Great book. You want to know how the Iraqis treated their prisoners, read it. What happened here, what they called abuse, was a tiny fraction of what Saddam's people did.'

They headed up a flight of stairs and Winmill unlocked yet another door. They went through and found a uniformed military policeman standing outside a metal door, an M16 rifle at his side. Unlike the doors on the ground floor, which were composed of bars, the one being guarded was solid with a square observation hatch at eye level. 'Any idea how long you'll be?' asked Winmill.

'How long's a piece of string?' asked Yokely.

'Okay, let the guard know when you're done and he'll call me to come and get you. Try not to break anything this time, Richard.'

'That guy fell off his chair. How many times do I have to tell you?' He turned to Shepherd. 'A prisoner gets one small fracture and they make out you're the Spanish Inquisition.'

'Things are different here now. We're more accountable. Even you OGA guys.'

Yokely threw him a mock salute. 'Yes, sir,' he said. Winmill shook his head and walked back to the stairs, twirling his key chain. 'I thought we'd do this as good cop, bad cop,' said Yokely. 'We'll tell him you're Mitchell's brother, and at some point you should get heavy with him. I'll threaten to leave him alone with you. Then we'll play it by ear.'

'Any limits?'

'Don't worry,' said Yokely. 'No one's going to be photographing you. You can go as far as you want . . . You're not listening to any of this, are you, son?' he asked the guard.

'Deaf as a post, sir,' said the man, staring straight ahead.

'Okay, let's do it.'

The guard opened the door for them. Umar was sitting at a plastic-topped table, his hands clasped as if in prayer. He had a thick, straggly beard and his head had been shaved although the hair was now starting to grow back. He was wearing a grubby *dishdasha* and plastic flip-flops.

The guard closed the door behind them and Yokely put his case on the table and unzipped it. He took out a sleek grey laptop with no manufacturer's logo, opened it and switched it on. Umar watched him, but said nothing. Yokely sat down, folded his arms and waited for the computer to boot up. Shepherd stood by the door and continued to stare at the Arab, who steadfastly refused to look at him. Once the computer was running, Yokely turned the screen so that it was facing Umar. He pressed a button and a video began to play. It was jerky and grainy, and showed five men, in green fatigues with scarves covering their faces, standing over three terrified men who were kneeling. Four of the men in fatigues were holding Kalashnikovs, the fifth an RPG above his head. There was no sound but the men in fatigues were clearly chanting. Yokely froze the picture. 'The Islamic Followers of Truth,' said Yokely. He smiled at Umar. 'But, of course, you know that.' He tapped his finger on the figure furthest to the right. 'This, we think, is you.'

Umar stared at the video but said nothing.

'The three Egyptians were released six weeks after this video was taken. How much ransom did you get?'

Umar remained silent.

'Quite right,' said Yokely. 'None of my business. Besides, the money doesn't concern me.' He tapped the man who was holding the RPG. 'What does concern me is this man. We want to know who he is.'

Umar continued to gaze at the screen, his chest barely moving as he breathed. Yokely tapped a button on the keyboard and the video started to play. 'After the hostages were released, the Islamic Followers of Truth were never heard from again. A cynic might think that the group was only formed to carry out the kidnapping and that once the money had been paid they disbanded.' The screen went blank. Yokely tapped another button and a second video started. 'I doubt you've seen this seeing as how you've been behind bars for the last few months.' He let the Mitchell video play in full before he spoke again. 'Have you heard of the Holy Martyrs of Islam?'

Still Umar said nothing.

'You do speak English, don't you?' asked Yokely, frowning. 'Please say you do because I really don't want to have to get an interpreter involved.'

Umar stared at Yokely, then slowly closed his eyes.

'I do hope that doesn't mean you're being uncooperative,' said the American. He pointed at Shepherd, even though Umar's eyes were still closed. 'This man is the brother of the man being held hostage,' said Yokely. 'The man who will be beheaded in the not-too-distant future. If you continue to be uncooperative, he's going to be a very angry man.' Yokely stood up and stretched. 'I think I'll just visit the men's room,' he said. He banged on the cell door and the guard unlocked it.

Shepherd moved aside to let Yokely leave. Yokely gave him a broad wink as he slipped out of the door.

Shepherd took off his leather jacket and put it on the back of the chair. Umar opened his eyes a fraction, then closed them again. Shepherd shut the laptop and slid it across the table. He walked in front of the Iraqi and stood looking down at him. Umar squinted up at him, then yelped as Shepherd grabbed him by the neck of his *dishdasha* and yanked him to his feet, then pushed him backwards. The Iraqi tumbled over the chair and hit the floor. Shepherd kicked the chair away, bent down and hauled him to his feet. 'No,' was all the Iraqi managed to say before Shepherd slammed him against the wall. His legs buckled and he slumped to the floor, leaving a smear of blood on the plaster. Shepherd grabbed him and pulled him up again. He knew that Umar hadn't hit the wall hard enough to be knocked unconscious. He pushed him back against the table and slapped him across the face. 'I'll kill you,' said Shepherd. 'I'll kill you here and now.' Umar tried to get up but Shepherd slapped him again. 'They're going to kill my brother,' he said, 'so you tell me what you know or I'll kill you, so help me I will.'

Umar put up his hands to ward off the blows, but Shepherd was too strong for him. He screamed and Shepherd clamped his hand over the man's mouth, then twisted him round and slammed him against the wall once more. He pushed his mouth close to the man's ear. 'He's not coming back until you've told me what I want to know, or you're dead,' hissed Shepherd. 'And I don't think he cares either way.'

Umar tried to push himself away from the wall. Shepherd used the man's momentum to swing him round, then grabbed his wrist and twisted his arm savagely. Umar bent low to take the pressure off his arm but Shepherd reversed the lock and forced him back. Umar screamed in pain and Shepherd stamped on his instep. Umar yelled louder and his right leg buckled. Shepherd let him fall, then kicked him hard in the back, twice. Umar curled up into a ball.

Shepherd dropped down on top of him, trapping the Arab's arms with his thighs. Umar thrashed from side to side but Shepherd was too heavy for him. He put his hands round the man's throat and squeezed, felt the cartilage click and relaxed a little, not wanting to do permanent damage, but he kept enough pressure on to stop him breathing.

Umar's mouth opened and closed and his eyes bulged. Shepherd counted in his head to twenty and removed his hands. Umar gasped for breath.

'Talk,' said Shepherd. 'Or I'll kill you.' Flecks of his saliva peppered the man's face.

Umar shook his head, so Shepherd started to strangle him again, staring into his eyes, watching for the moment when he would begin to lose consciousness. Just as his victim was about to pass out, Shepherd took his hands away, pulled him to his feet, grabbed him by the *dishdasha* and threw him up against the wall.

Umar was panting and there was blood on his lips. 'Please, no more,' he gasped.

'Talk,' said Shepherd. He took away his right hand and bunched it into a fist. 'Or don't talk. I'm happy enough to beat you to a pulp.'

'Enough,' said Umar. The strength had gone from his legs and only Shepherd's grip kept him upright.

'The man holding the RPG?' said Shepherd. 'You know him?'

'Yes, I know him,' said Umar, rubbing away tears.

'He was in your group? The Islamic Followers of Truth?'

Umar was still gasping for breath. Shepherd raised his hand to slap him and Umar covered his face. 'Yes,' he said. 'He wanted to kill the Egyptians. He said it was more important that we kill them than take the money.'

'But you wanted the ransom?'

Umar nodded, and started to sob, tears running down his cheeks. Shepherd helped him to the table, picked up the chair, and sat him down. 'What happened to the group?' he asked.

'There was no group. We wanted money for the Egyptians. That is all. Once we had the money, it was over.'

'The man with the RPG, who is he?'

'His name is Wafeeq bin Said al-Hadi.'

'And he wanted to kill the Egyptians?'

'He said he didn't care about the money. He is very religious. We just wanted the money.'

'What do you know about the Holy Martyrs of Islam?'

'Nothing,' said Umar. He lowered his hands. 'I swear I know nothing. I have never heard of them.'

The door opened. Yokely was holding a plastic bottle of water. 'How's it going?' he asked.

'He's given me the name,' said Shepherd.

'Anything else?'

'I don't think he knows any more.'

Yokely put the water on the table and picked up the laptop. 'Let's be on our way,' he said. He gestured at Umar. 'Did you promise him anything?'

'We never got round to it,' said Shepherd.

Yokely put the laptop away. 'Bob'll be pleased to hear that,' he said.

The flight out of Baghdad was as hair-raising as the landing had been. The Gulfstream went up at an almost impossibly high rate of climb in a tight corkscrew that nearly had Shepherd throwing up again. When they were at cruising altitude Yokely unfastened his seat-belt and made coffee.

There were two other passengers on the flight. One was an Arab who had clearly been drugged. Handcuffed and manacled, in khaki fatigues, he was carried on to the plane by two soldiers. A black nylon blindfold covered his eyes but he was unconscious and stayed that way, his head slumped against the side of his seat, a trickle of saliva dripping down his clothing.

He was accompanied by an American in black, with impenetrable sunglasses. He had nodded at Yokely and Shepherd as he'd boarded the plane but hadn't said a word to them. He sat next to the Arab and read a copy of *Newsweek*. Yokely offered him coffee, but he shook his head and continued to read.

Yokely hadn't asked Shepherd what had happened in the room. He hadn't had to. Shepherd wasn't proud of what he'd done, but he wasn't ashamed either. The man he'd assaulted was a terrorist, there was no doubt about that, and he'd had the name Shepherd wanted, which justified what he'd done. Shepherd hadn't enjoyed acting like a thug – he didn't take pleasure in inflicting pain. His performance in the prison had been just that – a performance, an act. He had been playing a role, as he did whenever he went under cover. He'd done it well, too, because it had been clear from the fear on Umar's face that he believed Shepherd would kill him.

Yokely handed him a cup of coffee.

'You do a lot of this sort of thing?' asked Shepherd.

'Define your terms,' said Yokely.

'Transporting prisoners around the world.'

'It's not unusual,' said Yokely, 'but I'm more often involved with information retrieval than I am with transportation.'

'Interrogation,' said Shepherd.

'Retrieval covers a multitude of sins,' said Yokely.

'Can I ask you something?' said Shepherd.

'Fire away.'

'Does it worry you, what you do?'

'I could ask the same of you, couldn't I?'

'We're bound by different rules, though,' said Shepherd. 'I'm an undercover cop. I've got to follow PACE.'

'Pace?'

'The Police and Criminal Evidence Act of 1984, which defines what we can and can't do. You don't seem to follow any rules. You operate outside the normal structure of things.'

'What are you saying? That because you follow the rules you don't need a conscience?'

'I have a conscience, but most of the time I'm following rules rather than my conscience. It seems to me that you make your own rules.'

'I'm not a maverick. I've got a boss – a very big boss – but I'm not micromanaged the way you cops are. Don't all the rules and regulations get to you? All the paperwork?'

'It's a nuisance but it's got to be done. There have to be checks and balances.'

'The bad guys don't see it that way. If they don't follow rules, why should we?'

'But how do you know who the bad guys are if they don't go to trial?'

Yokely grinned. 'That's where information retrieval comes in,' he said. 'You're not going all liberal on me, are you? This is a war. We're not playing games. The winners win and the losers die. And I for one am glad that I'm not bound by the same rules you are.'

'Yeah, maybe you're right, it's the rules and regulations that give me a sense of fairness. Providing I follow the rules, everything I do is morally justifiable.'

'Sure. Let's not forget that you've killed in the line of duty. Anyone else who kills gets put in jail. You got an award.'

Shepherd sipped his coffee.

'My offer's still open,' said the American, quietly. 'I can use a man like you.'

'I need rules,' said Shepherd. 'I really do. I'm not sure how I'd be able to cope in an arena where there are no checks and balances.'

'You need a strong moral centre,' said Yokely. 'You need to believe one hundred per cent that you're right.'

'Isn't that what most dictators would say?' said Shepherd.

Yokely pointed a warning finger at Shepherd, but he was smiling. 'Now you're trying to upset me,' he said. 'You're very good at that.'

When the plane started to descend, Shepherd looked at his wristwatch. They had been in the air for less than three hours. Fifteen minutes later they landed at an airfield that appeared to be in the middle of nowhere. 'Where are we?' asked Shepherd.

'Classified,' said Yokely.

'Yeah, right,' said Shepherd. 'You could tell me, but you'd have to kill me.'

'No, I just won't tell you,' said Yokely. 'I'm serious, Spider. It's classified.'

The pilot emerged from the cockpit to open the door. Two soldiers in green uniforms and peaked caps entered the cabin and walked to the back of the plane, their gleaming boots squeaking with each step. Shepherd didn't recognise the uniforms or insignia but they were definitely from one of the former Soviet Union countries.

They picked up the unconscious Arab and dragged him to the front of the plane. The man in black followed them, carrying his magazine. Yokely flashed him a mock salute as he went by and the man saluted back. Shepherd looked out of the window. The soldiers dragged the Arab across the Tarmac towards a waiting vehicle. Shepherd couldn't identify the uniforms but he knew the vehicle: it was an open-topped Waz, the Russian equivalent of a Jeep. The soldiers threw him across the back seat and climbed into the front. The man in black was talking to a uniformed officer. Both were smoking.

The pilot closed the door and went back into the cockpit. They taxied to the runway and were soon in the air again. Shepherd fell asleep and didn't wake until the wheels touched the runway. 'Where are we?' he asked, rubbing his eyes. 'Or is it still classified?'

'Gatwick,' said Yokely. 'I'm just dropping you here.'

'Where are you going?'

Yokely grinned. 'Sadly, that's classified,' he said. 'While you were asleep I had my guys in Langley run some basic checks on Wafeeq and the driver who'll take you back into London has an envelope for you. There's a picture, I gather. The rest is up to you.'

As he left the plane Shepherd shook the American's hand. 'Thanks,' he said. 'I owe you one.'

'Yes, you do,' said Yokely. 'And don't think I won't remember.'

The pilot closed the door as Shepherd walked away from the plane. A Lexus was waiting for him, this time a white one, and the driver was black, in a grey suit. He handed Shepherd an envelope and held open the rear door. Shepherd climbed in.

He called the Major on his mobile. Gannon was at the office in Portland Place, with Armstrong, Shortt and O'Brien. Shepherd said he was on his way and ended the call.

The Lexus drove to the airport perimeter where a uniformed security guard, accompanied by two police officers cradling MP5s, waved them through without asking for identification. Shepherd stared out of the window, trying to gather his thoughts. It was hard to believe that in less than eighteen hours he'd flown to Baghdad on a plane that probably didn't officially exist, then assaulted and beaten up a man for information with absolutely no comeback, and delivered another prisoner to a country where he was sure to be tortured. And it had all been arranged by a man who seemed able to travel the world without Customs and immigration checks. Shepherd wondered how much power Yokely had. He seemed to be beyond all limits.

Shepherd opened the envelope. Inside he found a computer printout with a few paragraphs of type and a blurry surveillance photograph of two Arabs drinking coffee at an open-air café. One had been circled with a black pen.

The driver dropped him in Portland Place. Shepherd pressed the intercom buzzer and was let in.

The Major was sitting at the head of the table, talking into a mobile phone. He waved at Shepherd to take a seat. O'Brien was pouring coffee and asked Shepherd if he wanted some.

'Cheers, Martin,' said Shepherd. There was a stack of Marks & Spencer sandwiches and rolls next to the coffee maker and Shepherd helped himself to a salmon and cucumber sandwich before sitting at the table.

The Major ended his call. 'How did it go?' he asked Shepherd.

'I've identified one of the men in Geordie's video – the one with the RPG,' said Shepherd. 'His name is Wafeeq bin Said al-Hadi. He's almost certainly in Iraq, but no one knows where exactly.' He opened the manila envelope. 'This is all I have, picture-wise.'

'Where did you get it?' asked O'Brien.

'Friends in high places,' said Shepherd, and exchanged a look with the Major. Gannon knew where the information had come from but Richard Yokely was protective of his privacy.

'So we know who, but we don't know where,' said Armstrong. He took out a Marlboro, tossed it into the air and just managed to catch it between his lips.

Shepherd tapped the computer printout. 'According to this, he's got a brother in Dubai, a legitimate businessman. He's not hiding so we can get to him.'

'John Muller's got an office in Dubai,' said the Major. 'He's visiting Geordie's brother but he'll be in London tonight. I'll get him on the case. What's the guy's name?'

Shepherd slid the printout across the table to the Major. 'It's all there,' he said.

'Diane, isn't that your boyfriend over there?' said the sergeant, nodding at the group of civilian contractors who were piling out of an SUV. Three were Americans but the fourth was a good-looking Iraqi. His name was Kevnar and he described himself as a Kurd, rather than as an Iraqi. He was in his late twenties and Diane Beavis thought he was just about the most attractive man she'd ever seen. He looked like the young Omar Sharif in the movie *Doctor Zhivago*. It was one of her all-time favourites. And, like Omar Sharif in the movie, Kevnar was a doctor. At least, he'd trained as a doctor. Now he worked as a translator for an American logistics company. Doctors were much needed in Baghdad but they were paid about two hundred dollars a month by the government. Translating earned him three times as much. She'd laughed at his name the first time he'd introduced himself because it sounded so like Kevlar, the bullet-proof material that had saved so many American lives.

'He's not my boyfriend, Sarge,' she said, flushing. She'd met Kevnar a few times and he always had a smile for her; they'd chatted twice. She doubted he'd be interested in her. She was thirty-seven next birthday and had been career army for eleven years. She'd had the occasional sexual partner over the past decade but no one who could have been described as a boyfriend. She was pretty much resigned to spinsterhood and had persuaded herself that she'd never wanted children anyway.

'Go on, we can spare you for five,' said the sergeant. They were waiting to rendezvous with an Iraqi repair crew who were going out to fix a mobile phone mast on the outskirts of the city. The last time a crew had gone out their truck had been blown apart by an RPG and the phone company had requested armed support.

'Thanks, Sarge,' she said. John Petrocelli was career army, too, but had only joined up five years ago. He was on the fast-track to greater things, but Beavis had more or less given up on promotion, as she had marriage and motherhood. She'd joined as a grunt and she'd leave as one.

It was her second tour of duty in Iraq, and she was enjoying it as much as the first. Iraq was one of the few theatres where women were put in combat roles, usually on searches and raids. The reason was simple: many Iraqi women were covered from head to foot in the traditional burkha and would resist to the death any attempt by a man to search them. But they had to be searched because the burkha was perfect for concealing weapons and explosives. This meant that on every mission involving potential contact with locals there had to be at least one woman in the unit.

Beavis had come under fire several times and had already been awarded the Combat Action Badge. Many of her male colleagues complained about being in Iraq. They hated the heat, the food, the lack of entertainment and, most of all, being pitted against enemies who refused to fight like men. Combat in Iraq consisted of ambushes, sniper attacks and IEDs. The insurgents specialised in sneak attacks and killing from a distance, taking lives without risking their own. It wasn't a form of combat for which the infantry had trained, and it meant that every time they left the Green Zone they were in a constant state of tension, not knowing if or when they would be under attack. Beavis had never complained about being posted to Iraq. It was stressful, and at times uncomfortable, but she had never felt more alive than when she was out on patrol with an M16 in her hands.

She held the weapon barrel down and strolled over to the group, trying not to appear over-keen. The contractors were big men from West Virginia, whose bellies hung over their belts. They wore sidearms and carried shotguns.

Kevnar grinned when he saw her. He had a great smile, thought Beavis. It was the first thing she'd noticed about him. He was always smiling, always happy. She smiled back and wished she'd been able to put on a smear of lipstick. His smile revealed perfect teeth, not a filling to be seen. Beavis's parents hadn't bothered with fluoride when she was growing up so she had half a dozen crowns at the back of her mouth. She realised that she was staring at his and forced herself to look away.

'You are busy today, Diane?' asked Kevnar.

She loved his accent. The only word she could come up with to describe it was 'treacly'. It was soft and sweet, and made her shiver. 'We're guarding some phone technicians,' she said.

'Be careful,' he said.

She was touched by his concern. The last time they'd spoken she'd asked about his family, and what he'd told her had reduced her to tears. He'd had a wife and two small children, a boy aged three and a girl just about to turn one. He'd been working as the doctor in the small Kurdish village where he'd been born. Late one evening a farmer had turned up on his doorstep. The man's daughter was about to give birth to her first child and was in a lot of pain. The farmer had brought his tractor with him and had driven Kevnar to the farm. It had been a difficult birth but finally the woman produced a healthy girl. When Kevnar got back to his village the next morning, the first sign he saw that something was wrong were the dead dogs lying in the street. Then he'd seen an old woman face down in the gutter, mouth open, blood running from her nose. Further along the street there were more dead dogs, and the village baker was lying on the ground outside his shop, dried blood all over his face.

Kevnar had leaped off the tractor and raced home. His wife and children were dead in their bloodstained beds. Saddam Hussein had decreed that the Kurdish village should be used to test a new batch of nerve gas that his scientists had been developing. Two hundred and nineteen people had died that night. It hadn't been war, it hadn't been punishment; it had been nothing more than a scientific test. Beavis couldn't imagine how Kevnar must have felt, but he had smiled and shrugged, and said it was in the past and he had to live for the future.

'We're going for a meal tonight, myself and two of the Americans,' he said. 'There is a restaurant I have suggested they try, just outside the Green Zone. You would like it, I'm sure.'

Her breath caught in her throat. Was he asking her on a date? Her heart began to race. 'That sounds fun,' she said.

'Are you allowed to eat out of the Green Zone?' he asked.

'Sure,' she said. 'We're not prisoners.' She undid the strap of her helmet and removed it, shaking her dyed blonde hair and wishing she had a comb. 'I'd love to come, Kevnar,' she said.

'Perhaps afterwards I could show you where I live,' he said.

'That would be great,' said Beavis. 'Where shall I meet you?'

The bullet smacked into the side of her head, just above her right temple. It exited on the opposite side, blowing out a chunk of brain matter and blood that splattered across the road. Kevnar was running for cover before her body hit the ground.

Shepherd held the phone to his ear, listening to the ringing tone. A wire led from the bottom of his Nokia to a laptop computer in front of Amar Singh. Charlotte Button was sitting behind the desk, sipping a cup of tea. Ali answered.

'Tom, it's Graham May,' said Shepherd. 'Everything okay?'

'Fine.'

'You haven't fired those guns yet, have you? Remember, I'll only take them back if you haven't, and that goes for practice shots.'

'When can we have the rest?' asked Ali.

'Two days max,' said Shepherd. 'I've been thinking maybe it's not a good idea for me to drive up to you. You can collect them from here, same as last time.'

'Same place?'

'Probably,' said Shepherd. 'I'll let you know the day before. Listen, Tom, I might have something else you'd be interested in.'

'Yeah?'

'You heard of C4?'

'It's an explosive, right?'

'Damn right. Top of the range. The American military use it.'

'And you've got some?'

'It's on the way. Should be here at the same time as the Ingrams.'

'I don't think this is the sort of thing we should be talking about on the phone,' said Ali.

'It's not a problem,' said Shepherd. 'We've both got throwaway mobiles. I'll be dumping this one as soon as our deal's done. Now, are you interested or not?'

'How much can you get?'

'As much as you need.'

'What's it cost?'

'Five hundred pounds a kilo.'

'What would a kilo blow up?'

'Half a kilo would blow up a car, no problem,' said Shepherd.

'And what about detonators? Explosives are no good without detonators.'

'As many as you want,' said Shepherd. 'Fifty quid a go.'

'I'll have to talk to my friends,' said Ali.

'Don't leave it too long,' said Shepherd. 'I've got other buyers.'

'For explosives?'

'Sure,' said Shepherd. 'I can shift all I've got coming. I'll need to know soon.'

'But we get the guns, right?'

'Don't worry, like I said, they're on their way.'

'I'll call you when I've talked to my friends,' said Ali.

'Do that,' said Shepherd. He ended the call, put the phone on the table and sat back. 'Okay?' he said to Button.

She stood up. 'It was fine,' she said.

Singh disconnected the phone from the computer.

'Do we wait for them to call, or do I call again in a day or two?' asked Shepherd.

'Let's leave the ball in their court,' she said. 'SO13 has them under surveillance. Nothing's going to happen without them knowing.'

'Okay,' said Shepherd. 'Look, I need a favour – some personal time over the next few days. Are you okay with that?'

'Spider, we're in the middle of an operation.'

'All I have to do is take a phone call.'

'And hand over the guns, plus the explosives.'

'I've plenty of days owing.'

'What's the problem?'

'I'm in the process of moving house.'

'To Hereford, right?'

'I want my boy to be closer to his grandparents. Look, I'll be around.' He held up his mobile. 'I'm always at the end of the phone.'

'Okay,' said Button, reluctantly. 'I won't put you down for any more cases, but if the Birmingham business starts moving, I'll need you back.'

'About that,' said Shepherd, 'there's something else I need to ask you.'

'Fire away.'

'You won't like it.'

'I consider myself warned,' said Button. 'Get it off your chest.'

'It's an Anti-Terrorist Branch case, right?'

'That's what I said.'

'How much of the operation is theirs?'

'Most. We're just providing the arms dealers. It'll be an SO13 case when it gets to court.'

'And, hand on heart, you don't know who their undercover guy is?'

Button's eyes narrowed. 'I'm not in the habit of lying, Spider, to you or anyone else. Now, what's your problem?'

Singh headed for the door with his laptop. 'I'm off,' he said.

'Thanks, Amar,' said Button.

Shepherd waited until Singh had closed the door behind him. 'The problem is, I think Ali's their undercover guy.'

Button shrugged. 'You might be right.'

'But you don't know for sure?'

'That's twice you've suggested that I've been less than honest with you. SO13 wouldn't tell me and, frankly, I didn't feel that I had to know.'

'You heard that story about him being knifed after seven/seven? Well, it didn't ring true. I've told enough cover stories in my time and his lacked conviction. Anyway, the scar wasn't right. It wasn't a machete or a knife that did it. Looked to me like an industrial injury.'

'So, as I said, you might be right. What of it?'

'Ali's running the show, you've seen that. He's the top dog. Without him they'd just be a group of disaffected kids.'

'Except that they're in their twenties and three of them have been to Pakistan for six months, which would have given them plenty of time to slip away to an al-Qaeda training camp.'

'Which three?'

'The brothers, Asim and Salman, and Fazal.'

'That's your intel or SO13's?'

'It came out during the briefing,' said Button. 'These guys want to buy guns and explosives, Spider. They're not planning a stag weekend.'

'It felt to me as if Ali was the one in charge. Which means he's been acting as an *agent provocateur*.'

'No one forced them to go along with him,' said Button.

'Agreed. But you have to wonder what would have happened if he hadn't been around to gee them up.'

'In all probability someone else would have spotted their potential. But if it had been someone else, maybe we'd be dealing with four more suicide-bombers down the Tube.'

'But we were the ones who mentioned explosives,' said Shepherd.

'You suggested they were available.'

'And Ali said he'd talk to the others. He was the first to mention detonators. I reckon I've just been pitching to an SO13 agent. I'm getting a bad feeling about this, that's all I'm saying. I think we set them up. I think Ali was setting them up from the start and we helped him.'

'No one forced them to buy those guns,' said Button. 'The Ingram isn't the weapon of choice for the country set. It's for mass killing. It's a gun you fire on a crowded bus knowing you're going to kill and maim dozens of people. And the fact that we're the ones offering him the explosives and detonators is a good thing, Spider. What if they'd ended up dealing with the Russians or the Serbs? Then they'd be on the loose with the real thing and we'd be none the wiser.'

'Would they, though? Or would they just be sitting in their mosque up north mouthing off?'

'There's a parallel here,' said Button, patiently, 'in a case you worked on a while back under Hargrove. A woman who wanted her husband killed. You posed as a hitman and she asked you to kill her husband. The premise is the same. You were giving her the opportunity to hire a killer and once you made contact you suggested various ways in which her husband could be killed.'

'She was already looking for someone to kill him,' said Shepherd. 'It wasn't as if we put the idea in her head.'

'Spider, we're going round in circles. Anti-Terrorist wouldn't have called us in if they didn't think these men were a real threat. They don't have the resources to go on wild-goose chases. But your feelings are on record, okay?'

Shepherd had pushed it as far as he could. 'And you're okay with me having a few days off?'

'Providing you're available for this Birmingham case, yes. Are you okay? You look tired.'

'I didn't sleep much last night,' he said.

'Maybe a couple of days off is what you need,' she said. 'I've been working you pretty hard over the last couple of months.'

Shepherd felt a twinge of guilt at her concern for his welfare, but he could hardly admit to her that the reason he was tired was because he'd spent the previous night flying to and from Baghdad.

Shepherd was in his bedroom packing clothes into a holdall when his personal mobile rang. It was Jimmy Sharpe. 'Razor, what's up?'

'I'm in deep shit,' said Sharpe. 'Can you talk?'

'I'm on my way out but, yeah, what's the problem?'

'That new shrink's pulling the plug on me.'

'She's *what*?'

'Racist tendencies make me unsuitable for undercover work, she said.'

'She told you that?'

'Button called me. And that pisses me off – she didn't have the balls to tell me face to face. Had to do it on the phone.'

'Bloody hell, Razor, what did you say to her?'

'Told her to stuff her bloody job.'

'I meant to Stockmann. What did you tell the shrink?'

'It was just a chat, same as it always used to be with Gift. To and fro, a bit of banter, showing her I hadn't lost my marbles and that I can still walk in a straight line without falling over my feet.'

'So how did the racism issue come up?'

'We talked about the recent cases. About the Pakis and that.'

'And you called them Pakis, of course?'

'Don't you bloody start,' snapped Sharpe. 'Paki is short for Pakistani. I'm a Scot, you're a Brit, a Paki's a Paki. What am I supposed to say? A citizen of Pakistan?'

'Anything else?'

'It was just chit-chat, Spider – and, okay, I might have let my guard down – but now Button says I should be looking for a transfer.'

'Did she say you were off the unit?'

'Not in so many words. She didn't flat out sack me, but the writing's on the wall.'

'What do you want me to do, Razor?'

'Put in a good word. Tell Button how it is. She listens to you.'

'She's our boss, Razor. It's her unit.'

'If you don't do something, I'm out. And I'm not going back into uniform at this time of my life.'

'It won't come to that, and you know it. There are other options.'

'I don't want other options. I want to stay in SOCA.'

Shepherd looked at his watch. He had four hours before his flight left Heathrow. 'Let me see what I can do,' he said.

He ended the call, fished Caroline Stockmann's business card out of his wallet, then called her mobile. She was surprised to hear from him, and even more surprised when he asked to meet her. She lived in North London but he figured he had just about enough time to swing by her house on the way out to the airport.

Shepherd's minicab was waiting outside, and half an hour later he was sitting in Stockmann's kitchen with a mug of coffee. When he'd told her he wanted to talk about Jimmy Sharpe she'd at first refused to let him into her house, but Shepherd had begged for ten minutes of her time.

'My report's done and dusted,' she said, stirring her coffee. 'There's nothing more I can do.'

'Jimmy Sharpe's a good cop,' said Shepherd, 'one of the best I've ever worked with.'

'I'm not disputing that,' she said.

'But you've said he's racist.'

Stockmann frowned. 'Who said I did?'

'He did. Charlie's told him to leave the unit.'

Stockmann stirred her coffee thoughtfully. 'I hardly think she's done that on the basis of my evaluation,' she said.

'That's the way Razor tells it,' said Shepherd. 'Did you say he was racist?'

'I said he uses racist language and that could be an indication of underlying racism.'

'It's just the way he talks,' said Shepherd. 'I know that most of your work has been with MI5, but there's a world of a difference between the security services and what the cops have to face on the streets.'

'I'm aware of that,' said Stockmann.

'I'm sorry, I don't mean to be patronising, but let me run a few things by you. I've gone undercover against big-time cannabis and crack dealers. Now, over the years I've been a cop, I've never even seen a cannabis dealer with a gun. Cannabis dealing and guns don't go together. On the other hand, I've never seen a crack dealer without a gun and more often than not they come with a complete arsenal. And your average crack dealer only has to think he's been looked at wrong for him to start shooting. You get the difference?'

'Yes – though you're bordering on patronising now. Look, I see where you're heading. Cannabis dealers are generally white, crack dealers are black. So when you treat them differently it's because of their profession, not their colour. I understand that. And I understand that street muggers are generally black and serial killers are generally white. But that doesn't excuse your colleague's attitude.'

'He uses antiquated phraseology, I admit.'

Stockmann chuckled. 'He calls Arabs "ragheads" and Pakistanis "Pakis". That's not antiquated, that's offensive.'

'He's not racist,' said Shepherd. 'I can unequivocally promise you that Razor is not racist.'

'Then perhaps you might explain to me what your definition of racist is?'

'Is this about me, now, or him?' asked Shepherd, cautiously.

'We're talking about him,' said Stockmann. 'I've already given you a clean bill of health.'

'Okay. My definition of racism would be treating people differently on the basis of race. Razor doesn't treat people differently because of their colour. He treats good people with respect and bad people with distrust. Doesn't matter what colour they are. Now, in these politically correct days, that's actually not the way to do things. As cops we're supposed to bend over backwards to be sympathetic towards minorities. In my experience they get cut more slack than the majority. Razor doesn't see life that way. If you treat him with respect, he'll treat you the same way. Doesn't matter who or what you are.'

'And his language doesn't bother you?'

'I find it annoying more than anything. And sometimes he plays on it. But I don't think his use of language is a good enough reason to take him off the unit.'

'I'm not the one doing that. It's Charlotte Button's decision.'

'Based on your recommendation.'

'I make observations rather than recommendations,' said Stockmann.

'And your observation is that he's racist?'

'That he expresses racist tendencies,' corrected Stockmann.

'Razor is a cop,' said Shepherd, 'an old-school policeman who spent years pounding the beat. His language is anachronistic at times, but he is the most honest and trustworthy cop I've ever met. If he saw anyone in trouble, no matter what race or creed they were, he'd help.'

'Is his use of racist language common among officers?'

'No, of course not.'

'And is it something you approve of?'

'You said this wasn't about me,' said Shepherd.

'It isn't. I'm trying to ascertain how you guys think.'

'Look, it's all very well saying that everyone deserves to be treated the same, but the real world isn't like that. People conform to stereotypes. I could stand with you in Oxford Street and pick out the muggers for you, not based on their race but on their attitude and the way they dress. Muggers are predators, and I can spot that. The fact that most muggers are black is incidental. I can also spot the pickpockets, the pimps and the drug dealers. And I can pick out the guys who have been inside. Yes, of course it's environment, not race, that determines criminality but if I'm kicking down the door of a crack house I'm going to be more nervous than if I'm knocking on the door of a mansion in Mayfair. Does that mean I'm off the unit, too?'

Stockmann smiled. 'Of course not.'

'You know, I'm not allowed to use the expression "nitty-gritty" in any report I write. Do you know why that is?'

Stockmann shook her head.

'Because "nitty-gritty" was the detritus at the bottom of slave ships – the shit, old food, skin cells and all the rest of the stuff that accumulated during the voyages. I'm not allowed to use the phrase in case it causes offence – to whom? To a crack dealer who's causing misery and death on the streets, who's put three bullets in a rival dealer and who's terrorised his neighbourhood? I work undercover against those guys, and you should hear the racial slurs they use about cops. That's what we mean by racial attacks, these days. It's not about getting physical, or even about applying mental pressure, it's about use of English. It's ridiculous, Caroline. It's nonsense. And if you start acting like the thought police there isn't going to be a cop worth his salt left on the force.'

Stockmann wrapped her hands round her mug. 'Why did you come to me?' she said. 'Why didn't you go to Charlotte?'

'Because if I went to her, I'd be going above your head, and I didn't want to do that. It would put her in a bad position. If she agreed with me she'd have to overrule you. This way you can say you've reassessed your assessment.'

'Reassessed my assessment?' she said, smiling.

'You know what I mean,' said Shepherd. He glanced at his wristwatch. He was running late. 'Look, I know my coming here is unethical but I wanted to plead Razor's case in person.'

'Man to man?'

Shepherd laughed, despite the seriousness of the situation. 'Person to person,' he said. 'Please, just think about what I've said. I can guarantee one thing. If Razor stays on the unit I will personally give him an attitude adjustment.' He stood up. 'Thanks for the coffee, and for breaking the rules for me.'

'Your boyish charm got you over the threshold,' she said. 'Seriously, we're all on the same team here. My function is purely to help you guys, and girls, do the job to the best of your ability. Let me sleep on it.'

She showed him out and Shepherd hurried back to his waiting minicab.

Wafeeq stripped the Kalashnikov down into its component parts and began to clean and oil them. Kamil sat opposite, watching him work. 'Where did you learn to do that?' asked Kamil.

'Afghanistan,' said Wafeeq. 'You can strip a gun, can't you?' Kamil shook his head.

'A gun is a tool,' said Wafeeq. 'It has to be looked after if it's to function properly.'

They were sitting in the kitchen. Rahman and his younger brother Azeem were downstairs, outside the door that led to the room where the infidel was held. Abdul-Nasir was up in the front bedroom that overlooked the road and Sulaymaan was in the main room, sleeping. Wafeeq had known all the men for at least a decade. He never worked with anyone he didn't know and trust. He had been taught well and he had been taught by the best.

'You met him, didn't you? When you were in Afghanistan?'

Wafeeq's eyes narrowed. 'Who told you that?'

Kamil shrugged. 'People talk.'

'And people who talk die,' said Wafeeq.

'It was nothing,' said Kamil. 'Rahman said that you had met, that's all.'

'It was a long time ago,' said Wafeeq. 'Before nine/eleven. Before everything.'

'What was he like?'

'He is a great man,' said Wafeeq. 'A great man and a great Muslim. He has given up a lot to be where he is.'

'I would give anything to meet him,' said Kamil.

'It will not happen,' said Wafeeq. 'He can meet no one now. He can talk to no one. The infidels are watching and waiting.' He glanced at the ceiling. 'They have satellites searching for him, they monitor all telephone calls, listening for his voice. They have a bounty on his head.'

Kamil stood up and stretched. 'I shall take Colin some food,' he said.

'You should not use his name,' said Wafeeq.

'It means nothing.'

'It means you think of him as human,' said Wafeeq. 'He is not human. He is an infidel. He is here to trade on the suffering of Muslims and he deserves to die.'

'There's nothing wrong with making his last days comfortable,' said Kamil.

'You are soft, Kamil.'

Kamil sat down again and watched as Wafeeq reassembled the

AK-47. 'You know that's not true,' he said. 'I have killed many people. You know that.'

'It is not how many you kill, my friend,' said Wafeeq. 'It is the way you do it.' He grinned. 'But you are learning.'

The Major was waiting for Shepherd at the entrance to the departure terminal. 'Hell's bells, Spider, you're cutting it close,' he said.

'Sorry, boss,' said Shepherd.

'The rest of the guys have already gone through. Get your skates on.'

The Major headed for the departure gates as Shepherd hurried to the check-in. He had only hand luggage and a business-class ticket so he was soon boarding the plane. They were all sitting separately on the Emirates Boeing 777. Muller flew frequently and was upgraded to first class. The Major and Shepherd sat on opposite sides of the forward section in business class, Armstrong, O'Brien and Shortt behind them. When they arrived in Dubai, after an eight-hour flight, a dark-skinned man with a thick moustache and a tan safari suit was waiting for them, holding up a card with Muller's name on it. Muller introduced him to Gannon and Shepherd. 'This is Halim,' said Muller. 'He'll get us through Immigration. Give him your passports.'

The Major and Shepherd did as he had said. Ahead they could see long queues in front of bored immigration officials, many of whom were women in black headscarves.

'Don't worry, we'll be fast-tracked,' said Muller. He waved for Armstrong, O'Brien and Shortt to join them, then they followed Halim to a much shorter line. Five minutes later they were waiting for their bags.

Halim took them through Customs, then outside the terminal building. He asked them to wait and hurried off to the car park. A group of Arab men walked by wearing gleaming white *dishdasha*s with white *ghutra* headdresses held in place with black ropes. They were pushing trolleys loaded with Louis Vuitton suitcases and Harrods carrier-bags. Shepherd had seen them go to the first-class cabin of the plane. They had boarded in jeans and designer jackets but as the jet had begun its descent into Dubai they had hurried to the lavatories to change.

'They're locals, right?' Shepherd asked Muller.

'Could be,' said Muller. 'Or they might be from Jordan. The Saudis generally have red and white *ghutra*s. And Saudi men insist that their women wear the full burkhas so that they're covered from head to foot in black.'

'Seems a bit cruel, that,' said O'Brien. 'White would reflect the sun, wouldn't it? Black absorbs it.'

Muller chuckled. 'The men get to wear white,' he said. 'It's a man's world out here.'

'But the women can work, right?' said Shepherd. 'There were women in Immigration.'

'Sure. They can work, drive cars, wear pretty much what they want – even bikinis on the beaches. At times you can forget you're in an Islamic country.'

Two white Toyota Land Cruisers pulled up. Halim was at the wheel of the first, and a man who looked like his younger brother was driving the second. Halim parked, then got out to open the rear door. 'Spider and I'll take the first one with John, you guys take the other,' said the Major.

O'Brien, Armstrong and Shortt carried their luggage to the second vehicle while Halim helped Shepherd load his own and the Major's bags. There were already two metal suitcases there, slightly bigger than the one the Major usually carried.

'Can we run by the house first?' the Major asked Muller.

'Sure,' said Muller. 'It's not on the way but at this time of night there's hardly any traffic.'

The Major told Armstrong, O'Brien and Shortt to go straight to the hotel, then he and Shepherd got into the back of the SUV while Muller climbed into the front. As Halim drove away from the airport, the Major flashed O'Brien a thumbs-up.

Shepherd sighed and ran his hands over his face. The business-class seat had been comfortable enough but several small children close by had spent most of the flight bickering and squabbling so he had barely slept.

'You okay?' asked the Major.

'I'm fine,' said Shepherd. 'What's the plan?'

'We'll do a quick recce now, then John can brief us at the hotel.' The Major checked his watch. 'It's two a.m. so we can sleep after the briefing, then hit the house tonight. When's nightfall, John?'

'Between seven and eight,' said Muller.

The SUV powered down a modern road towards a cluster of futuristic tower blocks in the distance, glass and steel towers that glinted in the moonlight. Closer by, huge construction sites sprouted from the fawn-coloured earth. Everywhere that Shepherd looked buildings were going up and roads being widened. 'It's like one massive building site,' he said.

'Yeah, it's a boom town at the moment,' said Muller. 'They reckon that a third of the world's cranes are here. A couple of years ago the ruling sheikh allowed foreigners to buy places and the money has poured in. They plan to double the population over the next decade, and want to make themselves the financial and technological hub of Asia.' He grinned. 'The shopping's good, too. Plus there's booze and hookers. We send our guys here on R and R mainly because they flatly refuse to go anywhere else in the region.'

'But Dubai is Muslim, right?' said Shepherd.

'Sure, but they're pretty tolerant of other religions, and of Western ways generally. You can drink here though alcohol licences are always tied to hotels. This is as liberal as it gets in the Middle East. Westerners are queuing up to buy property, but there's a lot of Arab investment money coming in, too.'

'It's got to be a risk, though, hasn't it?' asked Shepherd. 'Infidels living in a Muslim country? I thought that was what the *jihad* was about.'

'I wouldn't buy here,' agreed Muller. 'Allowing foreigners to buy land was a whim, and they could just as easily change their minds.'

'I was thinking terrorism,' said Shepherd. He indicated a line of crane-festooned tower blocks to their left. 'I can't see the likes of Iran and Syria wanting hordes of Europeans and Americans setting up here. The shopping malls and hotels would be perfect for suicide-bombers.'

Muller twisted around in his seat. 'Exactly my thoughts,' he said. 'Although there are rumours that serious money is being paid to keep the place terrorist-free.'

'They'd do that?'

'Why not? Dubai's all about business. Besides, the Brits had an unspoken arrangement with the fundamentalists for years, you know that. They were allowed to pass through London, even to live there, so long as they didn't shit on their own doorstep. It used to drive our State Department up the wall. It was only after the bombings on the Tube that your lot clamped down. What they're doing here is no different. No one wants to rock the boat because they're too busy making money.'

They drove down the al-Shindagha tunnel, which cut under a creek that divided the north of the city from the south, then emerged into the night. To their right was the blackness of the Persian Gulf, dotted with the navigation lights of passing ships. They drove past Port Rashid, then the Dubai dry docks, following the beach road south. Although the city had first-world roads and cars, driving standards were definitely third world, with little attention paid to keeping in lane, and most drivers pounded on their horns to proclaim their right of way.

'We're coming up to Jumeirah,' said Muller. 'It's not quite Millionaire's Row but it's where the wealthy expats live.' He unfolded a map and held it up against the dashboard.

Ahead, they could see a huge steel and glass structure shaped like the sail of a ship, on an island three hundred metres or so offshore. A gently curving causeway linked it to the mainland. It was the tallest building for miles, and easily the most impressive. As Shepherd watched, the lights illuminating it gradually changed from green to blue. 'Wow,' he said.

'Yeah, it's one hell of a thing, isn't it?' said Muller. 'It's the Burj Al Arab, designed to look like the sail of a dhow. It's a thousand feet high, the tallest hotel in the world, pretty much the most expensive, and allegedly has seven stars, although that's really just PR bullshit. But cheap it isn't. Pretty much everything is gold-plated, they ferry guests from the airport in white Rolls-Royces, and you get your own personal butler.'

'We're not staying there, are we?' asked Shepherd. 'My credit cards are almost maxed out.'

Muller laughed. 'I figured we were on a budget,' he said. 'We're in the Hyatt, back near the airport.'

Halim turned away from the beach, past the wall of the city zoo, and headed east along a road lined with huge villas. 'We're coming up to it,' said Muller, running his finger along the map. Halim indicated left, and turned into a side-road. He slowed the Land Cruiser to walking pace. Muller pointed to their right. 'The white villa with the blue roof,' he said.

The house was two storeys high, with large balconies on the upper floor. It was surrounded by a white wall, about ten feet high, and through an ornate barred gate they saw a black Mercedes and a green Jaguar XJS parked in front of a fountain.

'Nice,' said Shepherd.

'Two or three million dollars' worth,' said Muller. He motioned for Halim to drive faster. 'Fariq's in business with a couple of local wheeler-dealers. One of them's a minor member of the royal family, which opens a lot of doors out here. Locals have to be in partnership with every foreign business that opens up, but having a royal on board makes things a lot easier.'

'I didn't see any CCTV,' said Shepherd.

'There isn't any,' said Muller, settling back in his seat as Halim accelerated down the road. 'Security's minimal. There's almost no crime in Dubai. It's pretty much a police state. They keep tabs on the entire population, local and expatriate. The locals don't need to steal and the expats are here to work. There aren't many muggers or robbers, and those there are get caught pretty quickly.

So, no armed guards, no CCTV, just a basic alarm system, and I doubt he even switches it on most of the time.'

Halim drove back towards the airport, and fifteen minutes later they pulled up in front of the Hyatt Regency Hotel. Bellboys in long grey jackets rushed over to carry in their bags. Muller insisted on taking the two metal cases himself.

Halim handled registration, then went outside to wait with the SUV while the three men headed for the lifts. The Major and Muller were on the ninth floor, and Shepherd was on the twelfth. 'I've got a suite so let's do the briefing there,' said Muller. 'Say, fifteen minutes?'

'Fifteen it is,' said the Major. 'I'll ring round and tell the guys.'

Muller and the Major got out of the lift and Shepherd went on up. His room was a decent size with a view over the sea. A coaster-sized metal disc with an arrow pointing to Mecca was stuck to the window sill. It was the only indication that the room was in an Islamic country.

Shepherd had a quick shower and shave, then headed down to Muller's suite.

Armstrong, O'Brien and Shortt were already there, sitting at a dining-table and watching Muller stick a large satellite photograph on to the wall. A red arrow pointed at a walled villa. 'This is Fariq's house,' said Muller. 'Eight bedrooms, swimming-pool, servants' quarters, garaging for four cars.' He rattled off the details like an estate agent.

'The servants live in?' said Shepherd.

'A man in his sixties drives Fariq around during the day and acts as a watchman when he's out of town,' said Muller. 'The man's wife does the housework and cooks if needed. According to my guys, the old man has a hearing aid that he takes out when he's in bed, and the wife's an early riser so she's usually asleep by ten.' Muller ran his finger along a wing that jutted out of the left-hand side of the house. 'They have three rooms here, above the garage. Their bedroom overlooks the main road so they can't see the rear garden.'

'But their wing has access to the main house?' said Shepherd.

'A small staircase leads down from their sitting room into a hallway. From there, there's a door into the garage, then another that leads into the kitchen of the main house.'

Muller took half a dozen photographs from a manila file and stuck them on to the wall in a vertical line beside the first. The top one showed Fariq bin Said al-Hadi. Below that they saw a woman in her mid-thirties, taken with a telephoto lens. Muller tapped it. 'This is the wife, Fatima. She's almost always at home.' The three other photographs were of two teenage boys and a younger girl. 'These are his children. The two boys are at boarding-school in the UK. The girl is at home. She's seven.'

'No guns?' asked Shepherd.

'No permits have been requested, so any guns in there would be illegal. But Fariq is just a businessman, no reason to have a gun.'

'Lucky for us, right enough,' said O'Brien.

'What about our weaponry?' said the Major.

'I know you Brit special forces prefer the Browning Hi-power but they're few and far between in Asia,' said Muller, as he walked to one of the metal cases. He swung it on to the table and clicked open the combination locks to reveal four Glock automatics and a dozen magazines. 'Are you okay with these?'

'Glocks are fine,' said the Major. He pulled one out and checked the mechanism, then looked down the sights. 'Besides, the idea isn't to shoot anybody.'

O'Brien took out another and handed it to Shortt, then gave one to Shepherd.

'So I don't get one?' asked Armstrong.

Muller grinned and opened the second case. Inside was a Taser. 'I figured something non-lethal might be of more use,' he said. He handed it to Armstrong. 'Effective up to twenty feet but ideally you make contact at ten. I'm sure you know the drill. Two prongs shoot out and the perp gets enough current to drop like a stone.'

Armstrong weighed the Taser in his hand. 'I've used one before,' he said. 'In fact, I've been hit with one.'

'Get away,' said Shepherd.

'Did a non-lethal weaponry course a year or so back,' said Armstrong. 'Part of the deal was that we all had to experience the products on offer.'

'Did it hurt?' asked Shortt.

'What do you think?' replied Armstrong. 'It hurt like hell. You just go into spasm and feel like you're dying, but you're not, and half an hour later you're fine. But John's right – you drop like a stone and you don't even think about getting up until it's switched off.' He grinned and pointed the weapon at Shortt. 'Wanna give it a go, Jimbo?'

'I'll take your word for it,' said Shortt.

'Yeah, but until you've tried it for yourself . . .'

'When you two ladies have finished, I'd like John to get on with his briefing,' said the Major.

Armstrong put the Taser back into its case, and O'Brien, as usual, picked up a sandwich.

Muller pointed at a photograph of the rear of the house. 'The wall here is only overlooked by one other house. Halim took a look yesterday evening and he tells me it's empty. We go over the wall here,' he tapped the picture, 'and we're straight into a clump of date palms that runs almost up to a conservatory next to the pool. We should be able to get access through the conservatory and the chances are that the door into the house will be open.'

'That's a gamble, isn't it?' said Shortt.

'Like I said, Dubai is almost crime-free. Most people leave their doors unlocked. But we can cut the phone lines first and I've got a mobile-phone jammer, so we can always break in if need be.' He opened an architect's drawing of the villa.

The Major grinned. 'How did you get that?' he asked.

'Fariq's villa is a standard design – there's a hundred of them in the city.' He stuck it on to the wall. It showed the ground and upper floors of the house, and a front, rear and side view. He pointed to the rear of the left-hand side of the house. 'This is the master bedroom,' he said. 'Fariq will almost certainly be there.'

'With his wife?'

'I assume so,' said Muller. 'Arab married couples generally sleep together, but if she's in a different room it'll probably be this one at the back.'

'Both overlook the rear garden and the conservatory,' said Shepherd.

'But the palms will provide cover,' said Muller, 'and there are heavy curtains at the windows.'

The Major studied the drawing. 'So, Spider and I will go in through the conservatory. Martin, you and Jimbo skirt round the house to the front door in case anything goes wrong. Billy, you open the front door while Spider and I check the ground floor and move to the stairs. Once we've secured the ground floor, Spider and I will go up first, Jimbo and Martin following. Billy, you move to the kitchen just in case Mr and Mrs Driver sleepwalk.'

'And where exactly will I be while this is going on?' asked Muller.

'With respect, John, you'd get in the way. We've all worked together before.'

'Well, fuck you very much,' said Muller, folding his arms and glaring.

'Like I said, with respect,' said the Major. 'You'll be more use with the vehicles. We don't want too many of us in the house. I need you outside, to check that everything is as it should be. If there's a siren, you'll know if it's a cop car or a fire engine. If you see a patrol go by, you'll know if it's routine or not. Anyway you've got a business here. If anything goes wrong, you've got far more to lose than we have.'

'Geordie's my man,' said Muller.

'He's our man, too,' said the Major.

The Sniper's weapon was a 7.62mm Dragunov SVD Sniper Rifle. It had a distinctive wooden stock with two cut-out sections and a chunky ten-round magazine jutting from the bottom. It had originally been used by a Russian sniper in Afghanistan, but he had been killed by the Taliban and the weapon was used to shoot dead more than a dozen Russian soldiers before it made its way to Iraq and ended' up in the hands of Qannaas, the Sniper.

The Dragunov had been built for one purpose: to kill at a distance. It came equipped with a bayonet but from the day in 1965 when the rifle was first produced, by Evgeniy Fedorovich Dragunov, no one had ever been injured, let alone killed, with it. It was a sniper's weapon, pure and simple. The Sniper had a copy of the manual for it, which he had paid a teacher to translate from Russian into Arabic. The manual claimed that the rifle was accurate up to one thousand metres but the Sniper knew that was Russian hyperbole. It was only accurate to about six hundred metres and the Sniper preferred to engage his targets at less than half that distance.

He laid the rifle on the table and stroked the polished wooden stock. It was shorter than that of most American sniping rifles because it had been designed for use by Soviet soldiers who often fought in cold climates and wore bulky clothing. The gun had been well designed but, like most things made during the Communist era, the workmanship and materials were less than perfect and the weapon required constant maintenance and cleaning.

The Sniper shook the bottle of cleaning solution to make sure that the contents were thoroughly mixed: drinking water, ammonium carbonate and potassium bichromate. The solution was used for cleaning the inside of the barrel. He placed the bottle on the table next to the rifle, with a small can of rifle oil for cleaning and lubricating the weapon's moving parts, a scouring rod for cleaning the bore, and some cloths, which were spotless. He had a chest full of new ones, and threw them away after one use. It was one of his many eccentricities.

When the Sniper had been in the Republican Guard, he had been taught to clean his weapon immediately after he had fired it. But now that he was on his own crusade, he had his own way of doing things. He still cleaned and oiled the weapon each evening, but he did it again in the morning. It was as much a part of his routine as his personal ablutions. The Sniper was a good Muslim and he prayed five times each day, and before he prayed, he bathed. And he had always bathed before he went out on a mission. He had washed his body from head to foot, then washed his hair three times, then washed his body again. When he had started his crusade against the occupying Americans, he had decided to accord his weapon the same treatment he gave his body.

His schedule was the same each day. He rose, bathed and prayed. Then he ate a simple breakfast of bread and fruit. He stripped and cleaned the weapon, taking at least an hour to do the job. Then he bathed again, prayed and went out to kill. It was what he did. It was his life.

He had no regrets about what he was doing. The infidels had no right to be in his country – they were not even Muslims – and he would continue to kill them, one by one, until they left. That they would leave one day was beyond doubt. Iraq was not their country and the longer they stayed the more they were hated and the more they died. He picked up the rifle and began to disassemble it, humming to himself.

John Muller opened the small stepladder and steadied it against the wall. He nodded at the Major, who was wearing a pair of dark slacks, black training shoes and a dark shirt with long sleeves. He had a Glock in a nylon holster tucked into the small of his back and next to it a transceiver from which a black wire ran up to an earpiece. He pulled on a pair of black leather gloves and a ski mask, patted Muller on the back, then climbed the ladder and pulled himself on to the wall. He grunted, slid over and a second later there was a dull thud as he hit the ground.

Shepherd pulled on his own ski mask. Like the Major he was wearing dark clothing, with a holstered Glock and a transceiver with an earpiece. He moved smoothly up the stepladder, hauled himself on to the wall and dropped down on the other side, his knees bending to absorb the shock. He was in a clump of half a dozen date palms, their trunks as thick as a man's waist. The Major signed for him to move to his right. In quick succession Shortt, Armstrong and O'Brien dropped down to join them. Shortt and O'Brien had Glocks, but Armstrong had the Taser in a black nylon holster clipped to his belt.

The Major pointed at Shortt and O'Brien, and signalled for them to move along the side of the house. The two men slipped away in a low crouch, keeping close to the wall. The Major nodded at Shepherd and Armstrong, then headed through the date palms towards the rear of the house. They moved from palm to palm, keeping low, their feet making no sound on the close-cropped grass.

Shepherd looked up. The windows were blank, the curtains drawn. An airliner flew high overhead, navigation lights flashing. The garden wasn't overlooked, so no one could see them moving to the conservatory at the rear of the house. There was no CCTV camera, and no sign of an alarm box. The top of the wall they'd climbed over had been smooth: in London broken glass would have been set into the concrete, or metal spikes. Muller had known what he was talking about when he'd said that the average Dubai resident didn't expect intruders.

The Major reached the conservatory door and waited for Armstrong and Shepherd to join him before he gripped the handle and twisted. He swore softly when he found that it was locked.

Armstrong took a piece of sticky-backed plastic from his pocket, tore off the protective film and pressed it gently against the glass close to the handle. He waited until another airliner was flying overhead, then took a deep breath and jabbed his elbow at the centre of the patch. The glass made a dull crumpling sound as it broke. Carefully, Armstrong peeled back the plastic while Shepherd held his gloved hands underneath it to catch any loose shards. The Major reached inside, found the key in the lock, and turned it. He pushed open the door and crept inside.

Shepherd followed him. As they moved through the conservatory, Shepherd pulled out a little black box with two stubby antennae – the mobile-phone jammer. He pressed a switch on the side and a green light blinked. The jammer would kill all mobile-phone signals within a radius of thirty metres in case anything went wrong and Fariq tried to call the police. Muller had already cut the landlines to the house – he had a transceiver that matched those carried by the Major and Shepherd and it wouldn't be affected by the jammer. He would use it to warn them of any police activity in the area.

The french windows linking the conservatory to the spacious sitting room weren't locked, as Muller had predicted. The Major eased them open and the three men moved silently into the house, switching on small Magnalite torches. The Major pointed at the hallway, and Armstrong moved on tiptoe towards the front door.

Shepherd noticed a huge oil painting above a shoulder-height marble fireplace. It was a family group, Fariq standing behind his wife, his hand on her shoulder, and in front of them their three children. Evidently it had been commissioned a few years earlier and the artist had done a good job. Despite the stiff pose, the faces were real and natural, and the love and pride the man felt for his family poured out of the canvas. In the painting, Fariq had an honest face. There was perhaps a touch of arrogance, but it wasn't the face of a schemer or a liar. He looked like a good man, and Shepherd had just broken into his house and was about to go up the stairs with a loaded gun. He felt as if Fariq's dark brown eyes were burning into his own and forced himself to move on. The Major was looking at him, his Glock in his hand, and Shepherd went past him, towards the hallway. Gannon always knew what was on Shepherd's mind and the last thing Shepherd wanted just then was a heart-to-heart about the morality of what they were about to do. He reached behind him and pulled out his Glock.

Armstrong was already on his way back, accompanied by O'Brien and Shortt. The Major indicated that Armstrong should head for the kitchen, then waited for O'Brien and Shortt to unholster their weapons and started to go up the stairs.

The Major was on the left of the sweeping staircase, with Shepherd on the right. It was made of thick marble slabs and their trainers made no sound on it. There were large framed photographs on the walls: Fariq with his sons, Fariq with his daughter, a younger Fariq on his wedding day, his wife with beautiful olive skin, doe-like eyes with lashes that seemed to go on for ever, and hair that glistened as the light from the Major's torch passed over it.

Shepherd and the Major reached the top of the staircase and moved towards the master bedroom, O'Brien following. Shortt waited at the head of the stairs.

The Major eased his fingers round the door handle, nodded at Shepherd and pushed the door open a few inches. From inside the room they could hear gentle snoring. The Major pushed the door wide. The room was in near darkness and the two men waited a minute to allow their eyes to get accustomed to it, then crept across the threshold. The bed was on the far side of the room, with an ornate carved headboard and a matching wooden chest at the foot. To the left a sliding panelled door led to the dressing area and bathroom. The windows were covered with thick curtains. Fariq lay on his back on the left of the bed. His wife was facing away from him, her hair forming a black curtain over the pillow.

Shepherd moved to her side of the bed. The Major crept to Fariq, and aimed his gun at the man's face, his finger on the trigger. Shepherd slid his Glock back into its holster and took a roll of insulation tape from his pocket. He had already doubled over the end of the tape so that he could grip it easily with his gloved fingers. He put it on the bedside table, close to a glass of water on a white marble coaster, then took a deep breath to steady himself.

He exhaled slowly, then reached across the sleeping woman, cupped his right hand over her mouth and clamped the left at the back of her neck. Her eyes opened and she kicked out. Shepherd pulled her out of the bed, tightening his grip on her mouth. She flailed with her arms, her hands curled into talons. Shepherd kept her off balance, moving her from side to side so that she couldn't grab him, then swept her feet from under her and lowered her to the ground. Her foot caught the bedside table, which scraped across the floor. A second later, the water glass smashed.

Fariq woke with a start. The Major grabbed his hair and pushed the barrel of his Glock under the man's chin. 'Say nothing,' he hissed.

Shepherd put his knee in the small of the wife's back. He kept his right hand over her mouth and groped behind him with the other for the roll of insulation tape. She struggled, thrashing from side to side, and Shepherd leaned down so that his mouth was just inches from her right ear. 'Stop moving,' he said. 'Stop moving or I'll shoot you.'

'Fuck you,' she said, through clenched teeth, and continued to struggle. Shepherd was surprised to hear an American accent.

'I just want to tie you up,' he whispered. 'We're not here to hurt you.'

Her foot lashed out at the bedside table again and the lamp wobbled.

'Please, don't hurt my wife,' said Fariq, his voice shaky.

'Shut up!' hissed the Major.

Shepherd managed to get the woman's hands together behind her back but she continued to wriggle about so much that he couldn't reach for the insulation tape. He shuffled forward, used his thighs to pin her arms to her sides, then grabbed the roll of tape.

'Get off me!' she shouted, and Shepherd clamped his hand over her mouth. She tried to bite him, but he cupped his hand so that she couldn't.

He could smell her perfume and saw sweat glistening on her neck. 'Think of your daughter,' he murmured. The woman stiffened. 'Think of what we could do to her if you continue to mess us around like this.'

She twisted her head to the side. 'You're not a man,' she said slowly, then fell silent and lay still. She offered no resistance as Shepherd bound her wrists. He felt his cheeks redden under his ski mask and his stomach was churning. She was right. He wasn't behaving like a man. He'd threatened a child. He'd spoken instinctively, going for the one thing he knew would stop a mother in her tracks, but he was ashamed. He was behaving as badly as any of the criminals he'd ever put behind bars. There was nothing lower than a man who threatened someone's family, and that was what he'd done. Part of him wanted to apologise, to tell her that he'd spoken in anger and frustration and that he'd never, ever, consider hurting a child, but it was too late. He'd said it and nothing he could do would take it back.

He gripped her shoulders and lifted her to her feet. She glared at him and Shepherd knew that if she'd had a knife in her hand she'd have thrust it into his chest and smiled as she'd twisted the blade. She hated him and he knew that he deserved it. He pushed her back so that she sat down on the bed, still glaring at him.

'Finally,' said O'Brien, who was standing by the door.

'What did you want me to do? Knock her out?' said Shepherd.

'Who are you?' asked Fariq. 'What do you want?'

He tried to sit up but the Major pushed him down and tapped the barrel of his Glock against Fariq's head. 'Keep quiet while we get everyone settled. Any more noise from you and we'll gag you and your wife.' He looked at O'Brien. 'Get the girl.'

'Wait,' said Shepherd. 'Maybe it'd be better if we let the mother do it.'

'I can handle a seven-year-old,' said O'Brien.

'I was thinking from the child's point of view,' said Shepherd. 'If you go thundering in there with your mask on you'll scare her half to death. You don't look much like Santa Claus.'

'What's your plan?' asked the Major.

'I'll take the mother in. The mother can put her at ease.'

'I wouldn't recommend untying her, not after all the effort it took to tie her up,' said the Major.

'Why do you want my daughter?' asked Fariq's wife.

'We don't want her,' said Shepherd. 'We just need to keep you together.'

'Why? What are you going to do?' Her voice was low and deep, almost a whisper, and there was no trace of fear in it.

'We need you in one place. We're going to take you to the servants' quarters where you'll be safe.'

'Safe from what?'

'Look, all I want to do is move you and your daughter to the servants' quarters. I'll happily send *him* in to grab your daughter but I'd imagine that would be pretty traumatic for her.'

'It's pretty traumatic for all of us,' said the woman. 'Why don't you get the hell out of our house and we'll all be a lot happier?'

Shepherd fought the urge to smile. He motioned for her to stand up and she did as she was told. Fariq tried to sit up again but this time Shepherd pushed him back. 'Not you,' he said.

'Where are you taking my wife?' he asked.

'I told you not to talk,' said the Major.

Shepherd held the woman's upper arm and walked her to the door. 'You're hurting me,' she said.

'Live with it,' said Shepherd. He took her into the hallway. Shortt was outside the daughter's bedroom. 'I'm letting the mother talk to her first,' said Shepherd. Shortt moved to the side. Shepherd kept his grip on the woman as he reached for the door handle. 'Just tell her there's nothing to worry about, and that she's to do as we say.'

'And is that true? Do we have nothing to worry about?'

Shortt tapped her on the shoulder with his Glock. 'Worry about me,' he said. 'Now, get in there and do as you're told.'

'Don't you touch me!' she hissed. 'You touch me again and I'll kill you.'

'Feisty, huh?' said Shortt.

'She's okay,' said Shepherd. 'Leave her alone. Please, Fatima, we don't want to upset your daughter, do we?'

'And you can stop patronising me,' she said.

'I'm not patronising you, I'm just telling you the way things are,' said Shepherd. 'If you want, we can storm in there and grab her but this way will be a lot less stressful.'

'Then untie me,' she said.

'Like fuck we will,' said Shortt scornfully.

Fatima ignored him and continued to look at Shepherd. 'Seeing me tied up like this will upset her,' she said. 'It's going to be bad enough with you wearing those masks and carrying guns. Please, untie me so that I can comfort her.'

'After all the trouble I took to get the tape around your wrists?'

'That was then,' she said. 'Now I'm asking you. Please. Untie me so that I can hold my daughter.'

'You'll scratch my eyes out,' said Shepherd, only half joking.

She smiled sadly. 'I want to comfort my daughter,' she said quietly. 'You have my word that if you untie me I will do nothing to provoke you.'

'You can't believe a word she says,' said Shortt.

'We've got guns, and she knows her husband is back there,' said Shepherd. He took a small Swiss Army knife from his pocket, pulled out a blade and gently cut the tape.

'Thank you,' she said, massaging her wrists.

'Just explain to her that she has to come with us, and not to make a noise,' said Shepherd. He opened the door and let her go in first.

The little girl was asleep on her back, her mouth open, her left arm round a toy leopard. Fatima walked to the bed and sat down next to her daughter. She put a hand on her arm and whispered in her ear. The little girl's eyes fluttered and she turned away. '*Anaa na' saan*,' she muttered sleepily.

'I know you are, little one,' said Fatima. 'But you must wake up.'

The child opened her eyes. Fatima put her face close to her daughter's, then kissed her nose. 'Now, listen to me, little one. There are some men here. They are visiting us for a while.'

'*Maa l-mushkila?*' asked the girl.

'No, there's nothing wrong,' said Fatima, 'but while they're here, let's be polite to them and speak in English so that they can understand. Okay?'

'Okay,' said the child. 'Where are they?'

'They're outside,' said Fatima. 'They're wearing masks, but you mustn't be frightened. It's no different from when I wear the burkha when I go out sometimes. They just want to cover their faces. Now, sit up.'

The little girl brushed her hair from her face. 'I'm sleepy,' she said.

'I know you are,' she said. 'We're going to see Mr and Mrs Yazid.'

The child slid her legs out of bed and saw Shepherd standing at the door. He had put his gun back into its nylon holster and he waved both hands at her. 'Hi,' he said.

'This is ridiculous,' said Shortt. 'We're not bloody child-minders.'

'Why don't you go downstairs while I get this sorted?' said Shepherd.

'We don't have to treat them with kid gloves.'

'They haven't done anything wrong,' said Shepherd. 'They're not the enemy.'

'No, but they're related to the enemy,' said Shortt.

Fatima put her arm around her little girl. '*Laa tkhaaf*,' she said. 'Don't be scared.'

Shortt headed downstairs. Shepherd took a step inside the room. 'Everything's going to be all right,' he said.

The little girl buried her face in her mother's hair. 'That mask isn't helping,' said Fatima.

'I'm sorry,' said Shepherd, 'but there's nothing I can do about that.'

'You should be ashamed of yourself, frightening a child.'

'I'm not proud of this, believe me. You're just in the wrong place at the wrong time.'

'I'm in my home,' she said. 'You're the one in the wrong place.'

Shepherd pointed at the hallway. 'Come on,' he said.

'Where are we going?' said the little girl.

'To see Mr Yazid.' Fatima scooped up her daughter.

'My leopard!' cried the little girl.

Shepherd picked it up and gave it to her. Fatima walked slowly to the door, stroking the child's hair. Shepherd followed them down the stairs, along the hallway and into the kitchen. O'Brien was standing by the sink, holding his Glock. Fatima flashed Shortt a baleful look as she walked across the marble floor. She whispered something in her daughter's ear as she carried her into the servants' quarters, which consisted of a sitting room with a small dining-table and two sofas, and a bedroom with two single beds and two wardrobes. Armstrong had taken the old couple into the bedroom and bound and gagged them. They lay on their backs on the beds, gazing up at him fearfully. He was standing by the door, Taser in hand. 'How did it go?' he asked.

'No problems,' said Shepherd. He nodded at Fariq's wife. 'The kid's a bit upset.'

'Of course she's upset,' snapped Fatima. 'We're all upset.'

'Do you want something from the kitchen?' asked Shepherd.

'I want you all out of my house,' she said.

'Shall I gag her?' asked Armstrong.

Fatima glared at him over the top of her daughter's head. 'You so much as touch me and I'll kill you!' she said. Her daughter began to sob. 'Now see what you've done,' she hissed at Armstrong.

'If anyone's upsetting your daughter, it's you,' said Shepherd. 'Can we calm down? Nobody's going to hurt you. Now, please, sit on the sofa.'

Fatima looked as if she might refuse but her daughter was still sobbing so she sat.

'We're going to have to tie your hands again now,' said Shepherd.

'No,' she said.

'I'm sorry, but we have no choice,' said Shepherd.

'You are scared of a woman?' she said.

'Not scared, just careful,' said Shepherd. 'If your hands are tied you're less likely to try something. And my colleague over there is a lot less understanding than I am.' He pulled the roll of insulation tape from his pocket.

'You're not tying my daughter up, are you?'

'We have to.'

Fatima laid her on the sofa, and the little girl curled up with her leopard. Fatima stroked her hair. 'Don't worry,' she said. 'I won't let them hurt you.' She held out her hands and Shepherd bound her wrists together.

'If I was you, I'd do them behind her back,' said Armstrong. He took out a cigarette and lit it.

'Put that out!' snapped Fatima.

'Go screw yourself,' said Armstrong. He took a long pull on his cigarette and blew smoke at her.

'You do not smoke in my house,' she said.

'I'll do what the hell I want,' said Armstrong.

'Put it out,' said Shepherd, quietly.

'What?' said Armstrong.

'Let's not annoy them more than we have to.'

'You're getting soft in your old age,' said Armstrong, but he stubbed the cigarette out on the sole of his trainer.

'And take the butt with you,' said Shepherd. 'DNA.' He checked that the tape wasn't too tight around the woman's wrists, then put the roll back into his pocket. 'Now, do you want me to bring you anything from the kitchen?' he asked.

'A knife,' she said drily. 'A big knife.'

Shepherd grinned. He left Shortt in the sitting room with Armstrong. He reflected wryly that one man on his own probably wouldn't be able to keep Fatima under control.

The Major was waiting for him in the master bedroom. 'Okay?' he said.

'All under control,' said Shepherd, 'but she's a handful.'

The Major waved his Glock at Fariq and told him to sit on a

chair beside a large gilt mirror. He was wearing yellow silk pyjamas, and his belly wobbled as he sat down. 'Right, Fariq, we can end this quickly and painlessly,' he said. 'If you tell us what we want to know, we'll be out of here.'

'Who are you?' asked Fariq.

'I suggest you listen carefully to what I'm saying,' continued the Major. 'This isn't about you, it's about your brother. We need to contact him, and once we have, we'll leave you and your family alone.'

'What have you done with my wife?'

'She's fine, and so is your daughter. We're not here to cause anyone any harm. We just want to talk to your brother.'

'I have four brothers,' said Fariq.

'Wafeeq.'

'I haven't seen Wafeeq for three years,' said Fariq.

'Where is he?'

'I just said, I don't know.'

'No, you said you hadn't seen him. That doesn't mean you don't know where he is.'

'You are playing with words,' said Fariq. 'I'm telling you the truth. I do not know where he is. If I knew, I'd tell you. I swear.'

The Major prodded Fariq in the chest with the Glock. 'We're not playing anything,' he said menacingly. 'Now, where is Wafeeq?'

'Iraq, I assume.'

'Where in Iraq?'

'I don't know.'

'Does he have a house there?'

'I don't think so.'

'You don't think so?'

'We are not close. I see him at family functions, that's all. Three years ago there was a funeral for an uncle. That was when I saw him last.'

'Do you have a phone number for him?'

Fariq shook his head.

'What about other family members? Do you have the number of anyone who would know how to contact him?'

'We are not a close family.'

'Where's your mobile?' asked the Major.

'My what?'

'Your mobile phone – your cellphone.' The Major mimed putting a phone to his ear.

'It's there.' Fariq nodded at the bedside table.

The Major gestured to Shepherd, who went to the table where a new-model Motorola lay next to a diamond-encrusted gold Rolex watch. Shepherd picked up the sleek black phone and flipped it open, examined the screen, then shook his head.

'What's wrong?' asked the Major.

'It's Arabic,' said Shepherd. 'Everything's Arabic, even the menu.'

'Can't you change the language?'

'Sure, but that won't convert the data in the phone book. That'll stay Arabic.'

'You're wasting your time,' said Fariq. 'I don't have Wafeeq's number.'

'I'd prefer that we check that for ourselves,' said the Major. 'Where's your Filofax? Your business diary – whatever you use to keep track of your movements?'

'You're wasting your time,' repeated Fariq.

The Major stuck the barrel of his Glock under Fariq's chin. 'It's our time to waste,' he hissed. 'Now, tell me where your Filofax is.'

'The study. Downstairs. On my desk.'

Shepherd hurried out and down the stairs. The study was to the left of the main hallway, a book-lined room with leather chairs and a large oak desk with an IBM laptop computer. The leather-bound Filofax was next to the laptop. Shepherd picked it up and flicked through the pages. All the writing was Arabic. He sat down at the desk and switched on the laptop. Once it had booted

up he scanned the icons. All were in English. He clicked on the
Outlook Express icon and smiled when he saw that everything
was in English. He went through the address book, but there was
nothing for Wafeeq, then the inbox and the messages-sent folder.
There was nothing to or from Fariq's brother.

He closed Outlook Express and found a folder containing
letters that Fariq had written. Half were in Arabic, the others in
English. The latter were business-related and none were to
anyone called Wafeeq. Shepherd left the computer and went
back upstairs.

'What took you so long?' said the Major, when Shepherd
walked into the master bedroom.

'I was checking his computer,' said Shepherd. 'His emails are
in English. There was nothing from his brother that I can see.' He
showed the Filofax to the Major. 'This is all Arabic, too.'

'Take it outside with the phone. See if he can make sense of it.'

Shepherd knew that 'he' meant Halim. He was the only one in
the group who could read Arabic. Shortt spoke a bit and understood some, but he couldn't read or write it. Shepherd took off his
ski mask, headed downstairs and walked along the main drive to
the gate. There was a large gate for vehicles and a smaller one set
into the wall. It was bolted but not locked. Shepherd drew back
the bolt and stepped on to the pavement. A top-of-the-range
Mercedes with heavily tinted windows drove by and Shepherd
turned his face away. He walked briskly along the pavement, then
down the side-road where Muller had parked the Land Cruiser.
Muller was sitting in the front passenger seat, Halim next to him,
both hands on the steering-wheel.

'Everything okay?' asked Muller, as Shepherd climbed in.

'The house is secure, but we're not getting anywhere yet,' said
Shepherd. He gave the Filofax and mobile phone to Halim and
asked him to check if there was any entry for Wafeeq.

'How's Fariq taking it?'

'Not happy, but co-operating. His wife's a hard nut.'

'Just one kid?'

'The daughter,' said Shepherd. 'Fariq says he's had no contact with his brother.'

Halim handed back the phone. 'All the Iraq numbers are business-related except three, which are women's names,' he said.

'He could be using a coded name,' said Muller.

'That's possible,' agreed Shepherd. 'Or he could have memorised the number. Either way, we'll have to get pretty heavy to get the truth out of him.'

Halim flicked through the pages of the Filofax.

'If he's lying, he'll probably come up with the number when we record the video,' said Shepherd. 'We've made it clear that all we want is a contact number for his brother. Once we make the video we move it up a notch.'

Halim gave Shepherd the Filofax. 'There is nothing in there for Wafeeq,' he said.

'I think he's probably telling the truth,' said Shepherd. 'I don't think he's a hard-line Muslim. The house is Western and the daughter speaks good English, so I'm guessing she goes to an international school. Anyway, if he was hard-line he wouldn't live in Dubai, which is relatively Western, and for Western read "decadent".'

'You think Wafeeq would resent his brother's lifestyle?' asked Muller.

'That's what I'm thinking,' said Shepherd. 'What do you think, Halim?'

'It would be hard for a fundamentalist to remain close to someone with more liberal views,' said Halim. 'Even a brother.'

'Which means we go to Plan B,' said Muller.

'I'm afraid so,' said Shepherd. 'And life is going to get complicated.'

'I'll come in with you,' said Muller. 'Halim can hold the fort here.' He handed his transceiver to Halim and followed Shepherd into the house. Shepherd told Muller to wait in the kitchen and went upstairs to the master bedroom. Fariq was still sitting in the chair, his hands tied. The Major was by the bed and Shortt was at the window, peering through the curtains.

'A word,' said Shepherd to the Major, who followed him out of the bedroom, down the stairs and into the kitchen. Shepherd pulled up his ski mask and the Major did the same. Both men were bathed in sweat and had flecks of wool sticking to their cheeks. 'There's nothing for Wafeeq in the Filofax or the phone. I reckon he's telling the truth.'

'Okay,' said the Major. 'That means we do as we planned – take him away and make the video.'

'We can't leave the wife here,' said Shepherd. 'She's as hard as nails. She'll go straight to the cops.'

'Not if she believes her husband will die.'

'She knows we're Brits and that we won't chop his head off.'

'She thinks we're Brits, but she doesn't know for sure. But who we are doesn't matter. She'll believe it's a kidnap for ransom. It's up to us to convince her that if she comes up with a ransom she'll get him back. That'll give us time to work on getting the brother.'

'So we're gambling on how much she loves him? For all we know she'd like nothing better than to have him out of the way. She's a Muslim so she can't divorce him, remember?'

'So we take her too.'

'And leave their daughter behind? You think she's going to behave rationally? She's a seven-year-old – and you'll be leaving her with the old couple. Will they care about anything other than where next month's salary's coming from? If we take Fariq and his wife, who's to say the old couple won't just run off with the family silver? Or go running straight to the police? You see where I'm going with this, don't you? The only way to make sure that the cops aren't called in is to keep all five under wraps. And there's no way we can get them all out of here.'

'So we stay put, is that what you're suggesting?'

'We keep the husband in the bedroom, the wife and everyone else stay in the servants' quarters under guard. That way they're all together so no one panics. John stays outside and can tip us off if we have visitors. If anyone does call we let the old man answer the door and all he's got to do is say that the family's away and won't be back for a few days. We make the video and keep them under wraps here. I know it's not what we planned, but I don't think we can risk splitting them up.'

The Major nodded thoughtfully as he considered what Shepherd had suggested. 'Okay,' he said eventually. 'You're right.' He nodded at John. 'Can you bring in the gear?'

Muller went back out to the car while Shepherd and the Major went back upstairs. Shortt had his gun levelled at Fariq's chest.

As they walked into the bedroom, Fariq said, 'Can I see my wife and daughter?'

'Soon,' said Shepherd, pulling his gun out of its holster.

'You are Americans? British? Israelis?'

'Don't worry about who we are,' said Shepherd. 'Just do as you're told.'

'I don't know where my brother is, you must believe me, but I am sure of one thing. He is not in Dubai.'

Shepherd gestured with the gun. 'Shut up,' he said.

Fariq opened his mouth to say something, but Shepherd pointed the gun at his chest. The man sagged in the chair, head bowed.

A few minutes later, there was a knock at the door. The Major opened it and took a black nylon backpack from Muller. He unzipped it and pulled out an orange jumpsuit, which he tossed to Shepherd. Shepherd put the barrel of his gun under Fariq's chin. 'Listen to me carefully,' he said. 'We need you to put this on. Understand?'

'What do you want?' asked Fariq. 'If you want money, I have money.'

Shepherd pushed the gun harder under the man's chin. 'We just want you to put this on. Do you understand?'

'Yes.'

'We have your wife, and we have your daughter, so please

don't do anything stupid.' He untied Fariq's hands and thrust the jumpsuit at him. 'Now put it on.'

Fariq stood up, took off his pyjama jacket, then turned around as he slid off his trousers. The rolls of fat at his waist jiggled as he put on the jumpsuit. He turned back to zip it up. 'Why are you doing this?' he asked.

Shepherd reached over to touch the man's hair. Fariq flinched. 'Stay where you are,' said Shepherd. 'I'm not going to hurt you.' He messed Fariq's hair, then looked at the Major, who took a digital video-camera out of the backpack and went to Fariq.

'Listen to me, and listen to me very carefully. I want you to identify yourself, and I want you to say what day it is. You are to speak in Arabic.' The Major nodded at Shortt. 'My colleague here speaks reasonable Arabic, but we will be showing the video to a native speaker before we send it on so if you say anything that I haven't told you to say your family will suffer. Do you understand?'

Fariq nodded.

'I'd like to hear you say that you understand,' said the Major.

'I understand,' said Fariq.

'So, you identify yourself, and you say what the date is. Use yesterday's date. Yesterday's date,' he repeated. 'Do you understand?'

'Yes.'

'Then I want you to say that you are in Iraq, that you have been kidnapped and that you will be killed within forty-eight hours if the Holy Martyrs of Islam do not release the civilian contractor called Colin Mitchell.'

Fariq began to tremble. 'Please, you can't do this to me,' he said.

'Do you understand what I said?'

Fariq nodded fearfully.

The Major gestured with the Glock.

'Yes, I understand,' said Fariq.

'Repeat it to me, in English,' said the Major.

'I have been kidnapped in Iraq and I will be killed within forty-eight hours if the Holy Martyrs of Islam do not release the civilian contractor called Colin Martin.'

'Colin Mitchell,' said the Major. 'His name is Colin Mitchell.'

'Colin Mitchell.'

'You are to say that in Arabic. And if you add anything – anything at all – your family will suffer.'

'Who are you?' said Fariq. 'Why are you doing this? I know nothing about the Holy Martyrs of Islam. And I have never heard of this Colin Mitchell.'

'Just do as you're told,' said the Major.

'You can't treat me like this. I'm not a terrorist – I'm nothing to do with what's going on in Iraq. That's why my family are here. We have made a new life in Dubai.'

'Your brother is threatening to kill an innocent man. We are doing the same.'

'But it's nothing to do with me,' wailed Fariq, tears welling in his eyes, 'and it's nothing to do with my family. My brother is like a stranger to me. Do you think he'll care if you threaten me? If he's a terrorist, like you say, he won't stop what he's doing because of me.'

'You're his blood,' said the Major.

'It won't make any difference. Look, why don't you offer to pay a ransom for the return of your friend? I have money. I'll pay. A million dollars. Two million dollars. I will give you the money and you can give it to them. Just let my family go, please.' Fariq fell off the chair on to his knees and clasped his hands together. 'Please, I beg of you, you're a good man, I understand that you're only trying to help your friend, so let me help you. Don't hurt my family – please!' Tears ran down his cheeks and he threw himself forward, placing his forehead on the Major's feet. 'Please, I beg of you.'

The Major took a step back but Fariq grabbed his ankles. The Major almost fell but steadied himself against the wall.

Shepherd loosened the man's grip and helped him to his feet.

Fariq sobbed and held on to Shepherd's shoulders. 'I don't want to die!' he cried.

Shepherd lifted Fariq's head so that he was looking into his eyes. 'Be a man,' he said quietly.

Tears were streaming down the Arab's face now. 'Please, don't kill me.'

'Then do as we say.'

'I will – I will! But let my family go. They have done nothing.'

'You know we can't do that, Fariq,' Shepherd said. 'We all have to stay together. And crying isn't going to achieve anything. Just do as you're told and everything will work out fine.' He turned to the Major. 'Where shall we do it?'

The Major pointed at one of the walls on which a picture hung: a desert scene, a lone Bedouin leading a camel away from an oasis. 'Move that and we've got a blank wall.'

Shortt took it down and tossed it on to the bed. He pulled out the picture hook, and moved a winged chair to the side. Fariq had stopped sobbing but the tears still flowed. Shepherd led him to the wall and stood him with his back to it.

The Major held up the video-camera. 'You remember what you have to say?' he asked.

Fariq nodded.

'Colin Mitchell, remember?'

Fariq nodded again. 'Colin Mitchell,' he repeated.

Shortt moved to stand next to the Major. He frowned at Fariq and aimed his Glock at the man's groin.

The Major pressed 'record' and Fariq started talking, but after a few seconds he was stammering and blubbering, then collapsed against the wall, his hands over his face.

Shepherd stepped forward and pulled him to his feet. The Major stopped recording.

'We could use the wife,' said Shortt.

'No!' said Fariq. 'I can do it.' He wiped his face with his hands and took a couple of deep breaths. 'I can do it,' he repeated to himself.

The Major pressed 'record' again. Fariq spoke more confidently this time as he stared fearfully into the camera lens. His
voice was wavering and there was no doubting his turmoil, but he
continued to speak, and after twenty seconds or so Shepherd
heard him say Mitchell's name. He talked for almost a minute,
then dried up. 'Was that okay?' he asked Shepherd.

Shepherd looked at Shortt. 'Sounded okay,' said Shortt.

Shepherd smiled. 'Well done,' he said.

'Now can we go?' asked Fariq.

'You know that's not possible,' said Shepherd, patiently. 'You
can't go until this is over.'

'You can let my family go. They won't do anything as long as
you have me.'

'You're all staying here,' said Shepherd. 'That's the way it has
to be.'

'My brother doesn't know me any more,' said Fariq.

'Yeah, you said,' said Shepherd. 'Now shut up or I'll gag you.
You can get changed.'

'Do I have to wear my pyjamas?'

'Whatever you like.'

The Major was checking the recording.

'Okay?' asked Shepherd.

'Looks fine,' said the Major. He handed the camera to Shortt.
'Get our guy to look it over. Anything suspicious, anything not a
hundred per cent kosher, I want to know.'

Shortt took the camera and headed for the stairs.

Shepherd waited until Fariq had pulled on a pair of trousers
and a white shirt then bound his hands behind his back and took
his arm. 'We're going to the servants' quarters,' he said. 'You can
stay with your family.'

'Thank you,' said Fariq.

'Don't thank me,' said Shepherd. 'It's easier for us to keep you
in one place.'

'You're a good man,' whispered Fariq. 'I know you are.'

'I'm not a good man,' said Shepherd, 'and don't bother trying to play me. Now, move.' He pushed Fariq out of the door, along the hallway and down the stairs.

O'Brien was in the kitchen, inspecting the contents of a huge stainless-steel refrigerator. 'Do you want anything?' he asked Shepherd.

'I'm okay.' Shepherd's stomach was churning.

'It's mostly Arab food,' said O'Brien.

'It would be,' said Shepherd.

'Hey, Fariq, where do you keep the bread?' asked O'Brien.

'It's in the cupboard there, by the coffee-maker. If you want, my cook can prepare something for you.'

'She's staying where she is,' said Shepherd, and pushed Fariq across the kitchen towards the stairs to the servants' quarters. 'Coming up,' he called.

Armstrong was waiting at the entrance to the sitting room with the Taser.

He stepped aside to allow Fariq and Shepherd into the room.

Fariq sighed with relief when he saw his wife and daughter sitting on the sofa. '*Anaa aasif,*' he said. '*Saamihnii.*'

'English!' snapped Armstrong. 'Speak only English.'

'He was saying he's sorry,' said Fariq's wife. 'He was apologising for you, you moron.'

Armstrong pointed the gun at her. 'I warned you, shut up!' he said.

'What's wrong?' she said, her chin up. 'You don't like it when we speak Arabic and you don't like it when we speak English.'

'Don't, darling. They'll leave soon.' Fariq smiled at his daughter. 'Are you all right?' he asked. The little girl's wrists had been bound together with tape.

'*Al-umuur aadiyya,*' she said, close to tears.

'English, little one, these men want us to speak English so that they can understand what we're saying.'

'Did they hurt you?' she said.

'No.'

'But you've been crying.'

'I was worried about you, that's all.'

'Are they going now?'

'They'll stay just a little longer,' said Fariq. He turned to Shepherd. 'Can I hold her for a bit?'

Shepherd cut the tape binding Fariq's wrists. The Arab sat down on the sofa next to his daughter and put his arms around her. 'Can you untie her?' he asked.

Shepherd shook his head.

'Scared of a child?' said Fariq's wife.

'I warned you,' said Armstrong.

'*Ughrub annii*!' hissed the woman, and spat at him.

'Right, that's it,' said Armstrong, and moved towards her.

Fariq slid across the sofa to his wife. 'Please – she's stressed, that's all,' he said. He tried to put his arms around her but she shrugged him away.

'*Laysa ladayka ash-shajaa'a al-kaafiya*!' she said.

'What can I do?' he said. 'They've got guns.'

'You can stand up for yourself,' she said.

Armstrong pushed Fariq to the side, then started to wind tape around the wife's mouth. She struggled but Armstrong was too strong for her. The child was crying in Fariq's arms. 'Please, do not let him hurt my wife,' he begged Shepherd.

'The bitch hasn't shut up since we brought her here,' said Armstrong. Fatima tried to headbutt him but he shoved her back on the sofa.

Shepherd pointed at her. 'You, sit still. If you behave, we'll take the gag off. If you carry on being a pain in the arse, we'll put you in a wardrobe. It's your choice.' He went to Fariq. 'I'm going to have to tie you up again now.'

'Please, I just want to hold my daughter.'

'I understand that,' said Shepherd, 'but there's less risk of anything happening to you if you're restrained.'

'Daddy, I want them to go,' whispered the girl.

Fariq kissed the top of her head. 'I know you do, honey,' he said. 'Don't worry, they will soon.'

Shepherd taped Fariq's wrists behind his back, then taped his feet together.

He stood up. 'I'll leave you to it,' he said, to Armstrong.

'I wouldn't mind a coffee.'

Shepherd went downstairs. O'Brien was slicing a loaf of bread. 'Billy wants a coffee,' said Shepherd, 'and you might take up some water for the family.'

'How did the video go?'

'He looked scared to death.'

'Should do the trick,' said O'Brien. He held up a slice of bread. 'You want toast?'

'Maybe later,' said Shepherd. The front door opened. He grabbed for his Glock and brought it to bear on the figure that stepped across the threshold but relaxed when he saw it was Shortt.

Shortt closed the door carefully. 'Halim says the video's fine. Fariq stuck pretty much to the script, just added a bit about please do what we say because he's sure we mean to kill him.'

'How do we get the video to al-Jazeera?' asked O'Brien. 'Email?'

'Too risky,' said Shepherd. 'They could track it back to its source. Maybe not to the exact computer but certainly to the server and definitely to the country. We need them to think that Fariq's in Baghdad. If the police suspect he's in Dubai they'll tear the country apart. We'll copy the DVD and have it hand-delivered to al-Jazeera's office here, the same way they got Geordie's video.'

The Major came down the stairs. Shortt gave him the camera. 'It's fine,' he said. The Major pulled a small cable and a blank DVD from his pocket. 'Give me a hand,' he said to Shepherd.

Shepherd followed him to the study. The computer was still on, the fan in the main unit whirring quietly. Shepherd sat down in front of it, slotted in the DVD and connected the camera to one of the computer's two USB sockets. It took several minutes to download the video, then Shepherd edited out the first few seconds and ended the video at the point where Fariq was about to ask if what he'd said was okay. He and the Major watched it through from start to finish, checking that nothing on screen would identify the location.

'Looks good to me,' said the Major.

Shepherd burned the video on to the DVD, ejected it and handed it to him. 'Do you think it'll work?' he asked.

'I hope so,' said the Major.

'What Fariq said, about not being close to his brother, he might have been telling the truth.'

'Blood's got to be thicker than water,' said the Major. 'Close or not, I can't see a man standing by and seeing his brother killed.'

'Unless he's a dyed-in-the-wool fundamentalist who reckons his brother's in the pay of the infidels. I figure the hard-liners have got to see Dubai as a threat to what they're trying to achieve in Iraq and Iran. Fariq's taken his family from Baghdad and set up home here. Maybe Wafeeq would be happy to see him dead.'

'You're a cynical bugger, Spider.'

'I'm a realist.'

'Any other suggestions?'

'I wish I had,' said Shepherd. 'I just worry that this is all we've got.'

'It's our best shot. Let's see how it works out.' He waved the DVD. 'I'll take this to John. He can get Halim to have it delivered first thing. With any luck it'll be on air by lunchtime.'

'Do you think they'll believe he was kidnapped in Iraq?'

'I don't see why not. Fariq travels back and forth. Worst possible scenario, the local cops will come around to see if the wife's here. We get the old guy to answer the door and say the family's away for a few days. I don't see there'll be any reason for them to be suspicious.'

'I can't believe we're doing this,' said Shepherd.

'Believe it, Spider, because it's the only chance we've got of freeing Geordie.'

★　　★　　★

Richard Yokely's mobile rang. There were two men in the office with him, both wearing Bluetooth headsets. They were in their early thirties and were wearing dark sweatshirts with the sleeves pulled up to the elbows, jeans and heavy workboots. They could have been brothers they looked so alike, but one had a broken nose and the other a thick scar above his lip. 'Excuse me, guys, I have to take this,' he said. He went out into the corridor. A marine in dress uniform with an M16 in his hands stood to attention. 'Marion, sweetheart, how are you?' said Yokely.

'Where are you, or is that classified?' she asked.

'London,' said Yokely. 'The embassy.'

'Information retrieval?' she said.

He laughed. 'Embassies are a lovely grey area,' he said. 'American soil, yet not American soil, and safe from prying eyes.'

'Anyone I know?' she asked.

'One of the Invisibles,' said Yokely. 'British-born Pakistani. He's been under the radar here but NSA picked up some interesting phone traffic that suggests he might be a link to some heavy-hitters in Afghanistan. We've just brought him in for a talk, see if there's any way we can persuade him to change sides. You know how it is.'

'Sadly, I know exactly how it is,' she said. 'Have you been watching al-Jazeera?'

'It's on my must-watch list,' said Yokely. 'Right after Larry King on CNN.'

'I heard he died three years ago and that it's all computer-generated, these days,' said Cooke.

Yokely chuckled. 'I heard that, too,' he said. 'How can I help you, Marion?'

'I just wanted a chat,' she said. 'There's a new kidnap video, just been released. An Iraqi businessman by the name of Fariq bin Said al-Hadi.'

'Ah,' said Yokely.

'Coincidence, or not?'

'I'm in London, Marion,' said Yokely. 'Cross my heart and hope to die.'

'I know you wouldn't lie to me, Richard. We go back way too far for that. But is this something I should be worried about?'

'It's absolutely one hundred per cent nothing to do with me,' said Yokely. 'Mitchell is a Brit and Brits are out there causing mischief.'

'This Fariq is not a player, Richard. He's a businessman. He's been looked at in the past and there's not a black mark against him. And you know who his wife is?'

'I did a bit of digging, yes, but what's happening is nothing to do with me. Or you.'

'Well, that's reassuring,' said Cooke. 'I have to say, it's a nice spin, isn't it? Kidnap a close relative of someone who's holding one of your friends. Tit for tat. You let yours go and we'll let ours go.'

'That seems to be their thinking.'

'Do you think it'll work?'

'Actually, Marion, I don't,' said Yokely.

O'Brien was frying eggs, splashing fat over the yolks with a spatula and humming. Muller had visited a local supermarket and delivered two carrier-bags filled with Western groceries including eggs, bread, Heinz ketchup, Nescafé, breakfast cereal and milk. 'Easy over, Spider?' asked O'Brien.

'As they come,' said Shepherd. Since they'd broken into Fariq's house, he'd lost his appetite, not from fear but because he had a growing sense that, despite their intentions, what they were doing was fundamentally wrong.

The Major and Armstrong were in the servants' quarters keeping watch on their captives, and Shortt was in the front bedroom, watching through the window. Halim had delivered the DVD to the television station's office just before noon, and by three o'clock they had seen it on the al-Jazeera website. Fariq was described as an Iraqi businessman and the story with the video reported that he had been kidnapped in Baghdad.

O'Brien slapped an egg so hard on to a slice of bread that the yolk burst. 'Help yourself to sauce,' he said.

One of Shepherd's two mobile phones rang inside his leather jacket, which was hanging on the back of a chair. He fished it out and cursed under his breath. It was the Graham May phone and Ali was calling. 'Martin, keep quiet, yeah? This is business.' He pressed the green button to take the call. 'Yeah?'

'Graham?'

'Yeah, what's up?'

'It's Tom,' said Ali. 'Where are you?'

'Why do you care?' snapped Shepherd. 'You're not my mother.'

'When I called the ringing tone was different, like you were out of the country.'

'I'm checking on the gear,' said Shepherd.

'That other stuff we talked about – you know what I mean?'

'Yeah.'

'We want some. Can you get ten kilos? And twenty of the things you said were fifty quid.'

'Sure,' said Shepherd. 'But it'll be another eleven grand.'

'We've got the money,' said Ali. 'When can you get the stuff here?'

'Birmingham or London?'

'London's fine,' said Ali. 'We want it as soon as possible. The other gear, too.'

'Are you on a deadline?'

'We don't want to hang about,' said Ali. 'When will it be ready?'

Shepherd rubbed the back of his neck. He had no idea how long he was going to be in Dubai. He could tell the Major he had to go back to London and he would understand, but Shepherd knew where his loyalties lay. 'A few more days,' he said. 'There's been a hiccup but we're getting it sorted.'

'A problem?'

'Not any more. But this is difficult stuff to move around – we're not shipping bananas. As soon as I've got it in the UK, I'll call you.'

'How long?'

'Not long,' said Shepherd.

'You're not fucking around with me, are you?' asked Ali.

'Tom, I want to sell you this gear as much as you want to buy it. Keep your mobile on, I'll call you as soon as we're sorted.'

Shepherd cut the connection and cursed again.

'Problems?' asked O'Brien, laying more eggs on to slices of bread.

'Work,' said Shepherd.

'How much do they pay you to be a cop?' asked O'Brien.

'Not enough,' said Shepherd.

The transceiver on the kitchen table crackled, then they heard Muller's voice. 'We've got visitors,' said Muller. 'Cops. They've pulled up outside.'

'Shit,' said O'Brien. 'Just when I'm ready to eat.'

The Major's voice came on. 'What's the story, John?'

'They're locals, just one car. Two guys are getting out now, not drawing their weapons. Looks routine. Make that three guys. Two men and an officer.'

'Let me know if more arrive,' said the Major.

Shepherd rushed up the stairs to the servants' quarters. The Major was already at the door. 'They're off the mark quickly,' he said. 'Get the old man. Explain to him what he has to say, then take him downstairs.' He nodded at Armstrong. 'Gag them all. Quickly.'

'I'm on it,' said Armstrong.

Shepherd went through to the bedroom and used his Swiss Army knife to cut the tape from Yazid's feet and wrists. He helped him to sit up. 'The police are here,' he said. 'You are to tell them that your boss is in Baghdad, with his wife and daughter. You think they'll be back in a week. You don't know where they went or where they're staying. Do you understand?'

The old man nodded.

'My friends will be up here with their guns. If the police make trouble, people here might get hurt – your wife might get hurt. It will be best for everyone if you make sure that the police go away.'

Yazid nodded again.

'My friend will be listening to you and he speaks Arabic. If you say anything to the police, he will know. There is one thing you must understand, my friend. If the police force their way in here, they will only care about your boss and his family. They won't care what happens to you. You and your wife could easily be killed.'

'I understand,' said Yazid, rubbing his wrists. He was still wearing his pyjamas.

'Get changed quickly,' said Shepherd. He waited while the old man pulled on a pair of brown trousers and a wool shirt.

'I haven't shaved,' he said.

'It doesn't matter.' Shepherd took the man's arm and led him out of the bedroom. Fariq, his wife and daughter were sitting together on the sofa, bound and gagged. Fatima glared at Shepherd as he walked by. The Major was standing at the top of the stairs with Shortt, both holding their Glocks.

'Okay?' said the Major.

'He understands,' said Shepherd.

'I will do as you ask,' said the old man. 'I will make them go away.'

The Major put the transceiver to his mouth. 'Sitrep, John.'

'They're walking up to the gate. No weapons drawn, it looks like a friendly visit.'

There was a buzzing sound in the hallway. 'The intercom,' said the old man.

'Answer it, and open the gate,' said the Major. Yazid went down the stairs with Shepherd beside him and Shortt following. O'Brien was in the kitchen, Glock drawn, eating an egg sandwich.

'Keep the back covered,' said Shepherd. 'It looks like there's only the three coming to the front door, but just in case, yeah?'

'I'm on it,' said O'Brien, through a mouthful of food.

Shepherd and Shortt took the old man into the hallway and he showed them where the intercom was. He pressed a button and kept his eyes on Shepherd as he listened to the officer on the intercom. Then he pressed a chrome button. 'They are coming in,' he said.

'They didn't say what they wanted,' said Shortt. 'They just asked to come in.'

Shepherd put a hand on Yazid's arm. 'You are not to let them into the house,' he said. 'On no account are they to come inside. Do you understand?'

'Yes.'

Behind them the transceiver crackled. 'They're inside the gate,' said Muller.

Shepherd hurried into the kitchen and picked up the transceiver. 'Radio silence until they've gone,' he said, and switched off the device. He got back into the hallway as the front doorbell rang.

Shepherd ducked into the study with his Glock at the ready. Shortt nodded at Yazid and pointed at the door. Then he stood in the corner behind the door, the gun aimed at the old man's stomach.

Yazid opened the door. Only one of the policemen spoke and Shepherd assumed it was the officer. The old man replied in Arabic. He sounded deferential but firm, and there was a lot of head-shaking. He kept a tight grip on the door. The conversation went on in Arabic for several minutes, then the old man smiled and started to close the door, head bobbing. Shepherd half expected to hear the officer protest and force his way in, but eventually the door clicked shut and Yazid sighed. 'They have gone,' he said.

Shepherd looked at Shortt.

'I didn't follow it all but they asked for the wife first,' said Shortt. 'Then they wanted to know when he'd last heard from the husband. He stuck to the script, as far as I can tell.'

Shepherd patted Yazid on his shoulder. 'You did well,' he said. 'Thank you.'

'I did it because you said my wife might die if I didn't,' he said flatly.

'I'm sorry about this,' said Shepherd. 'I really don't want to hurt anyone.'

'Then why are you carrying guns and wearing masks?' asked Yazid.

Shortt pushed him in the back. 'Come on, upstairs,' he said.

'Hey, easy with him, he's an old man,' said Shepherd.

'If he keeps his mouth shut, I'll go easy on him,' said Shortt. 'And you don't have to justify yourself to him. We're doing what we're doing and that's the end of it.'

Shepherd wanted to argue, but he knew there was no point. And there was no way to justify what they were doing. Nothing he could say to make their actions morally or legally right. He went back into the kitchen and picked up the transceiver as Shortt and Yazid went to the servants' quarters. He switched it on and pressed 'transmit'. 'All clear,' he said. 'They've gone.'

Mitchell heard shouting behind the locked door, and the sound of a round being chambered. Then he heard more shouting and a key rattling in the lock. He was sitting with his back to the wall, the paperback book in his lap. His stomach turned over as he realised that his time might have come. There was no shouted command for him to stand against the wall but the door was flung open and one of the men was there, holding a Kalashnikov. He didn't have his face covered and Mitchell saw rotting teeth and a scar that zigzagged across the right cheek. The man screamed something at him in Arabic. Mitchell had no idea what he was talking about, but his intention was clear.

He struggled to his feet but his left leg cramped and he stumbled against the wall. As he pushed himself up the man slammed the butt of the Kalashnikov into his stomach and he pitched forward, the taste of bile in his mouth. As he fell forward the man hit him again, this time on the back of the neck. Mitchell hit the ground hard and fought to stay conscious. He tried to roll on to his back, but the man kicked him in the ribs. Mitchell grunted and tried to grab his assailant's leg. The man stepped back and pushed the barrel into Mitchell's throat. Mitchell lashed out with his foot and caught him in the groin. He fell back and the Kalashnikov went off. The bullet smacked into the concrete just inches from Mitchell's head. The noise was deafening and his ears were ringing as he rolled on to his front and pushed himself up.

'You bastard!' screamed the Arab, in heavily accented English. He brought the gun to bear on his stomach and Mitchell kicked out, knocking the barrel to the side. He took a step forward but the kick in the ribs had slowed him down and the Arab slammed the butt of the Kalashnikov into his sternum.

Mitchell slumped to the ground. By design or luck the blow had disabled him: he opened his mouth but couldn't breathe. The Arab pointed the Kalashnikov at his face and screamed again. Mitchell was unable to move or speak, and waited for the bullet to end his life. The Arab screamed again and his finger tightened on the trigger. The only thought that went through Mitchell's head was that at least it would be quick, and that dying from a bullet to the brain was a thousand times quicker than being beheaded. He closed his eyes.

He heard more shouts from outside the room, then rapid footsteps. He opened his eyes and saw Kamil blocking the man's way. 'Wafeeq, *tawaqqaf*!' he shouted.

The man glared at Mitchell over Kamil's shoulder. '*Sa' aqtuluk!*' he screamed. 'I'm going to kill you!'

'*Isghi limaa aquuluh*,' said Kamil, softly.

'*Ihtamm binwaa huwa min sha'nik*,' said the man, gesturing with the Kalashnikov and trying to get past him.

Kamil pulled at Wafeeq's arm, then wrapped his arms around him and whispered in his ear. Gradually Wafeeq calmed, but he still had his finger on the trigger. Mitchell lay where he was, not wanting to attract attention to himself. Kamil might have calmed the man down, but he still had a loaded assault rifle in his hands.

Kamil kept talking to Wafeeq as he led him to the door and ushered him out. Mitchell crawled to the wall and sat against it. His ribs hurt and, gingerly, he pressed his side where Wafeeq had kicked him. Nothing seemed broken. He turned his head slowly from side to side checking for damage to his neck. Again, there was pain but nothing serious.

A figure appeared in the doorway and Mitchell flinched, then realised it was Kamil. He was carrying a cloth and a bottle of water. He closed the door, hurried over to him and knelt down beside him. 'I am sorry for what happened,' he said. He opened the bottle of water, poured some over the cloth and dabbed it on Mitchell's face. 'Are you okay?'

'Thanks to you,' said Mitchell. 'He was going to kill me.'

'I only just got back,' said Kamil. 'The others, they are too afraid of him to try to stop him.'

'What set him off?' asked Mitchell.

'His brother has been kidnapped,' said Kamil.

'Well, now, isn't that ironic?' said Mitchell, bitterly. He took the bottle of water from Kamil and drank slowly, then wiped his mouth with the back of his hand. 'But I don't see why his brother being kidnapped gets him ticked off at me.'

'The people who have taken his brother say that he will be killed unless you are released.'

'What?' said Mitchell. It was the last thing he'd expected to hear.

'There is a video of his brother saying that unless you are set free, he will be killed. Do you know who would have done such a thing?'

Mitchell was genuinely confused. 'Kamil, I have no idea what you're talking about.'

'Who are you, Colin?' said Kamil.

'You know who I am. I'm just a guy out here trying to make a living.'

'A security guard?'

'Yes.'

'Yet you have friends who are willing to kill to set you free?'

Mitchell stared at him. Suddenly he knew what had happened and fought the urge to smile. That was it. He had friends who would kill to set him free. 'Kamil, I swear to you, on my mother's life, I have no idea what's going on,' he said. He had no problem with lying to the Arab and, if he got the chance, he would have no hesitation in killing him.

Muller walked around the sitting room. 'The waiting's driving me crazy,' he said. He stopped by the grand piano and peered at a collection of photographs in ornate silver frames. It had been a full thirty-six hours since the video had gone online and there had been no news from Mitchell's captors.

'Yeah, well, at least you're not in a basement wearing an orange jumpsuit,' said Armstrong, who was stretched out on one of the sofas smoking a cigarette and reading a magazine. Shepherd was sitting at the desk, stripping his Glock and watching CNN with the sound muted on a plasma TV. If there was anything about Geordie, he expected to see it on the American news channel first, although he had been checking the al-Jazeera website every hour on the computer in Fariq's study.

'What do you mean?' asked Muller.

'Nothing,' said Armstrong. He blew a smoke ring up at the ceiling.

'No, what do you mean?'

'I mean we're all sick of waiting, but we're not the ones whose lives are on the line.'

'Leave it, Billy,' said Shepherd.

'Geordie's the one at risk here, so let's not complain about waiting.'

'I wasn't complaining,' said Muller. 'I just wish things were moving, that's all.'

'You and me both,' said Armstrong, putting down his magazine. 'You don't hear me bitching and moaning. And I'm not the one who got Geordie kidnapped.'

'What's that supposed to mean?' said Muller.

Armstrong swung his feet off the sofa. He dropped his cigarette onto the floor and stamped on it. 'It was your company he was working for. Geordie's a pro so he'd have known what he was doing, which means one of your guys let their guard down.'

'Leave it out, Billy,' said Shepherd.

'I don't need you to fight my battles,' said Muller. He went over to Armstrong and pointed a finger at his face. 'It was an IED that took out their vehicle. Don't blame me for that.'

'Get your finger out of my face or I'll break it,' said Armstrong.

'Billy, come on,' said Shepherd.

Armstrong stood up, his hands loose at his side, fingers curled. It wasn't an overly aggressive stance, but Shepherd knew he was a heartbeat away from laying into the American.

'We're all tense,' said Shepherd. 'Let's not start taking it out on each other.'

'It wasn't my fault,' said Muller, slowly and deliberately.

'Billy, why don't you go up and relieve Martin?' said Shepherd. 'He probably wants to eat by now.'

They heard footsteps from the kitchen and the Major walked in with a mug of coffee. 'What's going on?' he asked.

'Nothing,' said Armstrong, lighting another cigarette.

'Just a discussion about strategy,' said Muller. 'No big deal.' He turned and went back to the piano.

'Everything okay?' the Major asked Shepherd.

'Sure. Billy was just going up to relieve Martin.'

'Good idea,' said the Major. 'He gets cranky if he doesn't get a snack at this time of the day.' Armstrong headed for the servants' quarters. 'There's coffee in the kitchen if you want it,' the Major said to Shepherd.

'I'm okay,' said Shepherd.

'Nothing on the website?'

Shepherd shook his head. 'They've got to be monitoring all the usual channels to see what reaction their kidnapping is having, so they must know by now that we've got him.'

Muller walked over to a large gilt sideboard on which more than a dozen framed photographs were lined up like soldiers on parade, larger than the ones on the piano.

'What if we don't hear from them?' asked Shepherd.

'We're screwed,' said the Major. 'But let's not assume the worst. There's still time.'

'There's time today and tomorrow. But what if two days pass and we hear nothing? Do we have a Plan B?'

O'Brien came in from the kitchen. 'What's that about a Plan B?' he said.

'We don't have one,' said Shepherd. 'That's the point.'

'Nothing from the bad guys?' said O'Brien.

'It could be that Wafeeq would be happy to see his brother dead,' said Shepherd. 'Or it might make him so angry that he kills Geordie on the spot.'

'Let's stick with Plan A for a bit longer,' said the Major.

'Yeah, but we don't have a Plan B, do we?'

'Maybe we do,' said Muller. He picked up one of the framed photographs and took it to the Major. It was a wedding photograph: Fariq and his wife, with an elderly couple standing to Fariq's left and another couple, slightly younger, to his wife's right. 'I'm guessing that's the parents. His and hers.'

The Major took the photograph from him. 'You recognise someone?'

'The guy standing by Fariq's wife is a top Sunni politician, one of the survivors of Saddam's regime. The Americans helped groom him for government because they need someone speaking for the Sunni minority.'

'So she'd be his daughter, presumably?' said Shepherd.

'Let me Google it,' said Muller.

'Try the computer in his study,' said Shepherd.

Muller took back the photograph and headed for the study.

'If he's right, we might have that Plan B,' said the Major.

'The wife?' said Shepherd.

'A guy like him would probably have a direct line to the Sunni insurrectionists. Put pressure on him and he can put pressure on them.'

'By pressure you mean put her in the orange jumpsuit?'

'Have you got a problem with that?'

Shepherd slotted the magazine into the butt of the Glock. 'I guess not,' he said.

'It's no different from what we've done so far,' said the Major. 'We just make another video.'

Shepherd's mobile rang. Jimmy Sharpe. 'Razor, what's up?' he asked.

'You're the man, Spider. You're the bloody man.'

'I'm busy with something, Razor. Can we keep this short?'

'I don't know what you said to the shrink but the pressure's off.'

'Stockmann?'

'Yeah. She's had a change of heart and that's got to be down to you.'

'I'm glad it worked out. But we've got to have a chat when I get back.'

'Where are you?' asked Sharpe.

'Working on something,' said Shepherd. 'Personal. I'll be back in a day or two. And we have to talk, Razor, your language has got to change.'

'Yeah, yeah, yeah.'

'I'm serious. That was the deal I reached with Stockmann. She revises her report, but you have to watch what you say.'

'No more Pakis?'

'Razor . . .'

'I was joking. Yeah, we'll have a chat when you get back. You can teach me how to be more politically correct.'

'I'm looking forward to it,' said Shepherd. He cut the connection.

'Problem?' asked the Major.

'Just house-training a dinosaur,' said Shepherd.

Dean Hepburn opened the bottom drawer of his desk and took out a bottle of Jack Daniel's. He waved it at Richard Yokely. 'A quick one?' he said.

'Why not?'

Hepburn pulled two glasses from the drawer and poured two hefty slugs into them. He handed one to Yokely and they clinked. 'To the bad old days,' he said.

'Ah, yes,' said Yokely. 'I remember them well.' He sipped his Jack Daniel's. 'The new technology's all well and good, but it takes a lot of the fun out of it.'

Hepburn swung his feet on to his desk and balanced the glass on his expanding waistline. 'I hate it here,' he said. 'They don't let me drink in the office.'

'Bastards,' said Yokely.

'If it wasn't for the pension, I'd go freelance. But I've got three kids in college and a wife who wants a holiday home in Florida.'

'The NSA's not so bad, Dean,' said Yokely. 'At least you don't spend half your life at thirty thousand feet.'

'And what brings you to Crypto City?'

Crypto City was what the forty thousand or so employees of the National Security Agency called their huge headquarters in Forte Meade, Maryland, half-way between Baltimore and Washington. More than fifty buildings, hidden from prying eyes with acres of carefully planted trees. Some of the best brains from the country's top universities worked in the NSA's offices and laboratories. However, Hepburn was not a graduate of one of America's leading educational establishments: like Yokely, his training ground had been Nicaragua, Colombia, Panama and Afghanistan.

'A little off-the-record help,' said Yokely. 'I'm looking for any traffic regarding an Iraqi by the name of Wafeeq bin Said al-Hadi, and his brother Fariq.'

Hepburn scribbled down the two names.

'Location?'

'Wafeeq is in Iraq. Fariq is in Dubai. You'll see traffic saying he's been kidnapped in Baghdad but my intel is that he's in Dubai.'

'And what are you expecting?'

'If I'm really lucky you'll hear Wafeeq, but he's a pro so I won't be holding my breath.'

'Is this connected with the Colin Mitchell kidnapping you asked me to keep an eye on?'

Yokely chuckled softly. 'That's the million-dollar question,' he said.

'I'll take that as yes,' said Hepburn. Behind him a poster for *Breakfast at Tiffany's*, with a coyly smiling Audrey Hepburn, was stuck to the wall. He claimed that the actress was a distant cousin but Yokely had run a few checks and could find no blood link. Not that it mattered – there was no point in spoiling a good story.

'I doubt there'll be much international phone traffic,' said Yokely, 'but if they use the Internet something might go through the satellites.'

Most of the telecommunications traffic into the United States came via one of thirty Intelsat satellites that circled the Earth some twenty-two thousand miles above the equator. Calls from the Middle East, Europe and Africa were beamed down to AT&T's ground station in West Virginia whence they were routed round the country. The NSA had its own listening station fifty miles from the phone company's station. Like its Fort Meade headquarters, the station, and its massive gleaming white parabolic dishes, was shielded from prying eyes by thick woodland. Its signals, and those from another in Brewster, Washington, which monitored traffic from Asia, were sent to Fort Meade for analysis. The agency's supercomputers sifted through the millions of daily calls and transmissions for key words or voices, and anything red-flagged was passed on to human experts for analysis.

'I'll put a watch on it for you. Any idea who he might contact?'

'The usual suspects,' said Yokely. 'Frankly, I think what's more likely is that there'll be local traffic. Can you get the Baghdad CSG on the case?'

The Cryptologic Support Group was a miniature version of the NSA that could be sent into trouble spots for as long as they were needed. They monitored all phone and radio communications in their area and sent the data to Forte Meade for processing. A large CSG contingent was based in the Green Zone in Baghdad.

'I'll get them right on to it,' said Hepburn. 'What's your interest?'

'Wafeeq is in the hostage business. His brother Fariq has been kidnapped.'

'I suppose the irony isn't lost on him,' said Hepburn.

'Wafeeq is going to want to know what's happened to his brother so there's a chance he'll let his guard down.'

Hepburn tapped on his computer keyboard. He sipped his Jack Daniel's as he studied the screen. 'Wafeeq is known, and there's a list of numbers that he's used before. He's a heavy hitter, all right.' He looked at Yokely. 'If we get a trace on him, do I go public?'

'I'd prefer a quiet word,' said Yokely. 'Lets me consider my options.'

'So it's unofficial?'

'Totally.'

'Cool.' Hepburn tapped away at the keyboard again. 'Nothing on the brother.'

'Fariq's clean,' said Yokely, 'and he won't be using a phone in the near future. If you put his name into the search engine I'll need the wheat separating from the chaff.'

Hepburn nodded. 'There'll be a lot of chaff.'

'Well, that's what billion-dollar supercomputers are for, isn't it?'

Hepburn raised his glass in salute. 'To the great American taxpayer.'

'I'll drink to that,' said Yokely.

★   ★   ★

Muller came into the kitchen with a grin on his face. 'Jackpot,' he said. 'Fariq's wife is the youngest daughter of Abu Bakr al-Pachachi, and that's him in the photograph. I was so busy looking at Fariq that I didn't realise who he'd married.' He handed the framed photograph to the Major, who was sitting at the kitchen table with Shepherd. 'He's number two in the Foreign Ministry, he's met personally with Bush and Blair and is one of the few Sunnis that the Shias respect.'

'Am I the only one here who doesn't know the difference between a Sunni and a Shia?' asked O'Brien, buttering a slice of toast.

'Mostly you can't,' said Muller. 'They speak the same language, generally look and dress the same.'

'Like Protestants and Catholics in Northern Ireland then,' said O'Brien.

'There are funny little differences,' said Muller. 'When Sunnis pray they hold their hands towards their chests while Shias have theirs at their sides. The ultra-religious Sunnis are more likely to have long beards and their women will cover themselves like the Saudi women, just revealing their eyes. The Shias are more likely to adopt Western dress. But, really, you'd be hard pushed to tell them apart.'

'So why don't they get on?' asked O'Brien. 'They're all Iraqis, right?'

Muller chuckled. 'Why don't the Protestants and Catholics get on? They're all Irish, right? On the surface the issue in Iraq is religious, but at the end of the day it's about power. The Sunnis had it under Saddam and now that we're running the show the majority Shias are calling the shots. But the fact that al-Pachachi is a Sunni means he'll have leverage with the insurrectionists. Hopefully.'

'That explains why the cops came around as quickly as they did,' said Shepherd. 'Al-Pachachi must have contacted them as soon as he heard Fariq had been kidnapped.'

'Sure, but it's his daughter he's concerned about. Remember, it was her the police asked for first. And if he was bothered about Fariq, he'd have done something already.'

'Maybe he tried.'

'Or maybe he's pissed off with Fariq for bringing his daughter and grandkids to Dubai,' said the Major.

'All we've got is maybes,' said Muller, 'but now we know about his daughter we can put more pressure on him.'

The Major handed the picture frame to Shepherd. 'Let's get her into the study.' He pulled on his ski mask and went up the stairs to the servants' quarters, O'Brien following.

Shepherd looked at the photograph. Assuming their first child had been born a year or so after the marriage, the wedding must have taken place sixteen or seventeen years earlier. The years hadn't been good to Fariq – his waistline had thickened, his jowls had dropped and his hair had thinned. But Fatima had barely changed. If anything, the woman he had wrestled with in the bedroom was even more beautiful than the shy-looking girl in the picture. She was glacing sideways at her father, as if looking for his approval, while al-Pachachi was staring at the camera, his lips pressed together, one hand resting lightly on his daughter's shoulder. He was a Saddam Hussein lookalike, jet black hair and thick moustache, square face, the skin pockmarked with old acne scars. His eyes were as hard as flint. He must have been tough to survive in Saddam's inner circle, but only an astute politician could have managed the switch to the new regime. He went through to the sitting room and put the picture back on the sideboard among the rest of the framed photographs. He picked up another of Fatima and the children standing in front of the Eiffel Tower. The boys were handsome, as tall as their mother even though they were only in their early teens, and with the same soft brown eyes. Fatima was holding her daughter's hand. They were both wearing long red scarves and gloves.

Shepherd envied Fariq his family. Three lovely children and a spirited, beautiful wife. Shepherd had lost his wife and he doubted he'd have more children. He had Liam, and he loved him more than life, but there was a world of a difference between single parenthood and being a husband and father. There were several photo albums at his house in Ealing, tucked away in a chest of drawers in the spare bedroom. They were filled with family snaps, usually taken on holidays, at school concerts or sports days. They stopped when Liam was seven. The last ones in the album had been taken on a trip to Wimbledon Common, a picnic sitting under a tree, then kicking a football. Just a family outing, nothing special, except that it had been their last. The day after the picnic Shepherd had gone under cover as an armed robber, and two weeks later he'd been sent to a Category A prison. While Shepherd had been inside, Sue had died in a senseless traffic accident. Shepherd still couldn't look through the albums without crying so he kept them hidden away.

He stared at the photograph of Fatima and her children and wondered what Sue would have said if she'd known what he was doing. She'd never liked his undercover work but at least she had accepted that he was doing a worthwhile job under difficult conditions. He was one of the good guys. He had been a good guy in the SAS and he was a good guy working for SOCA. But in Fariq and Fatima's sitting room, with a holstered Glock and a ski mask, he wasn't one of the good guys any more. He went back to the kitchen and up the stairs. He heard Fariq's wife arguing with the Major before he got to the door that led to the servants' quarters. 'I'm staying here with my daughter,' she was saying.

'I need you in the study,' said the Major.

'I don't give a shit where you need me.'

O'Brien was standing at the doorway. He grinned as Shepherd walked up. 'Balls of steel, that one,' he said, gesturing with his Glock.

Fariq was in the armchair by the window, wrists and ankles taped together; more tape held him to the chair. Fatima's legs were free, but her wrists were taped. She was sitting on the sofa next to the little girl. Through the door that led to the bedroom,

Shepherd could see the old couple, bound but not gagged, watching what was happening in the sitting room.

Armstrong was standing with the Taser in his hand, but the Major had holstered his Glock. 'I'm just asking you to go with us to the study. That's all,' he said.

'And I'm telling you I want to stay here,' she said.

'I'm not arguing with you,' said the Major.

'What are you going to do? Use that stun gun on me?' she said, nodding at Armstrong's Taser. 'Or are you going to shoot me?'

'Darling, please do as they say,' said her husband.

Fatima ignored him. 'This is between you and Fariq,' she said. 'It has *nothing* to do with me.'

Despite himself, Shepherd smiled. She was outmanned and outgunned but she had no qualms about standing up for herself against five men in ski masks.

'It has just become about you,' he said. 'Now, stand up and walk downstairs with me or, God help me, I'll put you over my shoulder and carry you.'

'Are you proud of yourself,' she asked, 'terrorising women and children?'

'You don't seem terrorised,' said the Major.

'Do you call yourself men?' she said. 'You're not men. You're scum.'

'We're not going to hurt you,' said the Major. 'We need to do something in the study.'

'What? What is it you want me to do?' She glared up at him defiantly.

'I need a word, in private,' said Shepherd.

The Major looked around. 'Now?'

'Yeah, now.'

The Major nodded. 'The kitchen,' he said. 'Gag her,' he told Armstrong. 'And be careful. She bites.'

The two men went downstairs and took off their ski masks. The Major opened the refrigerator, took out a carton of orange juice and held it up. Shepherd shook his head. The Major poured himself a glass. 'What's the problem?' he asked.

Shepherd jerked his thumb at the servants' quarters. 'What's going on up there is the problem. It's so bloody wrong.'

The Major took a long pull at his juice. 'We knew that before we started. We knew we'd be crossing the line.'

'Agreed,' said Shepherd. 'But we're moving further and further away from it. I could just about convince myself that threatening Wafeeq's brother was acceptable, the ends justifying the means and all that, but we've got his wife and kid at gunpoint now and we're threatening to hurt her.'

'We're not going to harm them, Spider.'

'That's like an armed robber saying he's carrying a sawn-off shotgun to scare people. It's not really the point, is it?'

'So what is the point?'

'She's right,' said Shepherd. 'She said we're not behaving like men and she's right. We're behaving like the terrorists that we despise. What we've done is every bit as bad as what those bastards are doing to Geordie. I'm not saying that as a policeman, or talking about the legality of what we're doing. This has nothing to do with breaking the law, and everything to do with the way we're behaving. There's no honour in what we're doing, and I think it's time to stop.'

The Major drank some more of his juice.

'I accepted what we were doing in London,' continued Shepherd. 'We needed that information and we needed it quickly. I could convince myself that it was acceptable to kidnap Fariq to put pressure on his brother. But we've moved beyond that and I can't justify what we're doing any more.'

The Major put down his glass. 'You're right,' he said.

'But?'

'There's no "but", Spider. You're right.'

'So, what now?'

The Major folded his arms and leaned against the sink. 'We either carry on upping the ante, threaten to kill the wife in the hope that her family can influence the kidnappers, or we call it a day.' He took a deep breath and let it out slowly. 'Like I said, you're right. My heart isn't in threatening women and children – but the way things are, with what little time we have left, I don't see any other way of getting Geordie out alive.'

'I might have an idea,' Shepherd said.

'A good one?'

'Better than threatening women and kids,' said Shepherd.

Shepherd sat down next to Fatima. 'Are you okay?' he asked. She glared at him with undisguised hatred. 'Are you okay to talk?' he asked. 'If I take that gag off you, will you promise not to start shouting and screaming?' She nodded, but continued to glare at him. Shepherd reached up slowly, undid the gag and pulled it away from her mouth. 'Fatima, I want to talk to you without you screaming at me or trying to bite me.'

'Just say what you have to,' she said. 'You bore me.' They were alone in the sitting room. The Major and Armstrong had taken Fariq and his daughter to join the old couple in the other room. Shortt and Muller were in the hall.

'Okay. I'm sorry for what's happened here, and for threatening you and your family. I'm not proud of what we've done.'

'You shouldn't be! You're scum, worse than—'

Shepherd put his hand over her mouth and she stopped talking immediately. 'Please, just let me speak,' he said, then took away his hand slowly. Her chest rose and fell as she breathed, and her cheeks were flushed. She had been held hostage for two days, had not a trace of makeup on her face, hadn't combed her hair or showered, but she was still one of the most beautiful women Shepherd had ever seen. He felt sorry for Fariq. He had a stunning wife, but he must spend every waking hour worrying that one day he would lose her.

'What we did was wrong, and I don't expect you to understand why we did it, but we truly believed that what we were doing was for the best.' She opened her mouth to speak but Shepherd held up his hand to pre-empt her. 'What we have to decide now is where we go from here,' he said.

'I want you out of my house,' she said quietly, 'and away from my family.'

'I understand that,' said Shepherd.

'You are a father. You know how a parent feels when their child is threatened.'

Shepherd's mouth fell open. 'How do you know I'm a father?' he asked.

She snorted contemptuously. 'Men change when they become fathers,' she said. 'I see that change in you. Just go.'

'We can't just go,' said Shepherd. 'That's the problem.'

'Because you think I will go to the police?'

'Yes.'

She sneered at him. 'Of course I will go to the police. What do you think I will do? Forgive and forget?'

'I don't expect forgiveness, and I'm sure you won't forget what we did to you.'

'We haven't seen your faces. You've worn masks and gloves all the time you have been here. I'm sure you have been careful to leave no DNA. What can I tell the police? That five Westerners kidnapped us? Do you have any idea how many Westerners there are in Dubai? Hundreds of thousands. I can tell them nothing that will help identify you.'

'Agreed,' said Shepherd. 'But we'd feel better if no one was looking for us.'

'You want me to promise not to call the police?'

Shepherd nodded.

'And why would I agree to that?'

'Because if you don't, you'll stay tied up here and someone will watch over you with a gun.'

'For how long?'

'For as long as it takes. We won't be threatening you. We'll just have to keep you out of circulation until we know it's safe.'

'But if I tell you we won't go to the police, you'll leave?'

'Yes.'

She narrowed her eyes. 'Why would you believe me? Why wouldn't I tell you what you want to hear, then call the police as soon as you've gone?'

'Because you've got something we haven't,' said Shepherd. 'Honour.'

She looked into his eyes with a slight frown. 'And if I give my word, you will go?'

'Yes.'

She continued to stare at him, then nodded. 'Then I give my word,' she said.

The Major sat at the head of the table, tapping a pen on the gleaming wood. Muller sat to his right, Armstrong to his left. O'Brien and Shortt stood with their backs to the window. In the distance, a plaintive wail called the faithful to prayer. They had just got back to the Hyatt and they were dog-tired.

Shepherd sat at the far end of the table, opposite the Major. He was hunched forward, head down over his interlinked fingers. 'I don't know what to say,' he said.

'You don't have to say anything,' said the Major. 'We understand how you feel.'

'Fariq's not the enemy,' said Shepherd. 'He just happens to be from the same gene pool. If we—'

The Major interrupted him. 'Spider, it's done. We're all in this together. That's the way it has to be. We all have to agree with what we're doing, or we're wasting our time.'

'With due respect to everyone's sensibilities, what the hell are we going to do about Geordie?' asked Muller. 'Do I have to remind you that the clock is ticking and we've blown the only chance we had of getting him out alive?'

'John, please . . .' said the Major.

Muller got up and paced in front of the photographs on the wall. 'The only plan we had has been blown out of the water – everything we've done over the past week has been a total waste of time. If we don't do something – and fast – they'll hack his fucking head off. The deadline runs out in four days.'

'I've got an idea,' said Shepherd.

'We all go home and forget this happened?' snapped Muller.

Shepherd lifted his head. 'No,' he said quietly. 'I've got an idea that might work, but I'll have to go back to London first.'

Drugs had got Samuel Brown into Iraq, and drugs meant that his time in the hellhole of Baghdad was at least profitable, if not exactly enjoyable. Brown had been nineteen when he'd been caught by an undercover drugs cop in Philadelphia. He had been working his way up the food chain but he was still just a small-time foot-soldier for one of the city's minor gangs and when he'd been busted he'd been down to his last few grams of crack cocaine, which meant that they hadn't been able to charge him with dealing. He'd already had a fistful of juvenile convictions, however, mainly for vandalism and theft, so the possession charge would probably have earned him rather more than a stern word from the judge. It had been his older brother, Luke, who suggested he enlist. He persuaded Samuel that if hc signed up the judge would probably let the matter drop. What the brothers hadn't expected, though, was for the judge to stipulate that if Samuel failed to serve a full five years in the army, he might still face the drugs charge.

Brown had hated basic training, hated the rules and regulations, hated the mindless boredom that was life in the infantry, even hated his M4 carbine. On the streets of Philadelphia, he had carried a handgun and used it whenever he had to. He'd liked the feel of a gun in his hand and the way it earned him respect. He'd shot three men, all rival drug dealers, and he'd enjoyed seeing them slump to the ground in agony. None had died, although one had been in intensive care for a week. Not that Brown had cared.

Once in the army, he'd assumed that shooting would be the one thing he'd enjoy. He was wrong. The army took all the fun out of it. It had to be done by numbers, the army way. And all he ever got to shoot was range targets. At least in Philadelphia he'd been free to shoot rats and cats. In the army every round had to be accounted for and he spent far more time cleaning and oiling the carbine than he did firing it.

When Brown had been told he'd be shipping out to Iraq, he'd assumed that at last he'd be able to fire his weapon at living, breathing targets, but once again he'd been wrong. He'd been in the country for five months, assigned to guard duty within the Green Zone for his entire tour of duty, and had yet to fire his gun in anger.

Brown found Baghdad just as boring as life in the army Stateside. It was too hot during the day, too cold at night, and most of the time he stood outside the headquarters of the Iraqi Governing Council, a massive marble building that had once been the home of the Military Industry Ministry. Back in Philadelphia, Brown had been a user and a dealer. He preferred crack cocaine, but it was hard to find in downtown Baghdad. Heroin, however, was plentiful, and he soon found that chasing the dragon helped him get through the long shifts of guard duty.

Brown's supplier was an Iraqi called Jabba. The heroin came from Afghanistan and it was better than anything available on the streets of Philadelphia. It was cheaper, too, almost a third of the price it fetched in the States. Brown had met Jabba in the Green Zone when he'd stopped to use the men's room attached to his unit's canteen. Jabba had been cleaning the toilets, on his knees in yellow gloves, a bottle of bleach in one hand, a brush in the other.

He'd looked up and Brown had known straight away that Jabba was more than just a cleaner. He'd nodded, Jabba had wished him a good day in perfect English and Brown had stood at the urinal, pissing. He had asked casually if Jabba knew of any way that a guy might be able to get high and Jabba had said that, funnily enough, he did. He had been working on Saddam Hussein's chemical warfare programme, and he'd lost his job with thousands of others when the coalition forces took over the country. He'd managed to get work as a cleaner in the Green Zone but it didn't pay enough for him to take care of his wife and five children so he was selling drugs on the side.

At first Brown had bought just enough for himself, then one of the guys in his platoon had complained that he'd been unable to get high and Brown had sold him a few grams. Word spread, and soon he was supplying half a dozen of the guys he was bunking with. Within two months he had almost fifty regular customers. He'd become a major supplier and without even trying, unlike in Philadelphia, he hadn't had to shoot anyone to win his market share.

Jabba seemed to have no problems getting as much heroin as Brown wanted. He said that the heroin came from Afghanistan, and since the Americans had thrown out the Taliban, production had soared. Brown didn't know how he got it into the Green Zone, and didn't ask.

He lay on his bunk and wondered if he had time to smoke a little before his shift started. He was lying on his back, flicking through an old copy of *Mad* magazine, a can of Coke in his hand.

Brown and Jabba had talked about what would happen when Brown returned to the States. Jabba had a brother who worked for an import-export company in Singapore and he reckoned he could easily ship large quantities of heroin to the east coast. If Brown could connect with major distributors, they'd make a fortune.

A lieutenant threw open the door to Brown's dormitory, shattering his reverie. 'Brown, grab your gear. We're short a man in the Bradley. Outside, two minutes.'

The lieutenant hurried away, and a few seconds later Brown heard him shouting at another soldier. He threw on his body armour and helmet, picked up his carbine and rushed outside. Three dust-covered Humvees were in the courtyard, revving their engines as the gunners standing in their turrets checked their .50 calibre machine-guns. In front of them stood the massive tank-like Bradley Fighting Vehicle. There was room for six men and three spaces were filled. Brown fastened his helmet strap, climbed in and sat down with the carbine between his legs. The camouflaged legs of the turret gunner were between the two lines of seats. Seconds later the lieutenant and another soldier ran to the vehicle, climbed in and the door slammed.

The Bradley was the safest way of moving around in Iraq. Its hi-tech armour would stop virtually anything the insurgents could throw at it, and the driver was safe as he looked through the three forward periscopes and the one mounted to the left. The Bradley's main weapon was a 25mm Bushmaster chain gun, which had been converted to fire at five hundred rounds a minute, while a 7.62mm machine-gun was mounted to its right. To the left of the turret there was a twin-tube Raytheon anti-tank missile system.

Once the door was closed, the soldiers couldn't see where they were. It was claustrophobic, unbearably hot, and the noise of the massive Cummins engine was deafening. 'Where are we going, sir?' shouted Brown.

'Nahda, to the east of the zone,' shouted the lieutenant. 'Insurgents blew up a car and a patrol has them pinned down.'

The engine roared and the Bradley shook, like an amusement-park ride. Brown said a silent prayer of thanks that he hadn't chased the dragon. The adrenaline was coursing through his system and he had to stop himself yelling. His hands were shaking – from excitement, not fear. With any luck he'd get a chance to fire his weapon at a living, breathing target.

He looked at the other men in the Bradley. They were tense but he could see they were excited, too, at the prospect of combat. Most of the time the infantry were waiting for the next IED or a sniper's bullet, but now they were cavalry riding to the rescue, armed to the teeth with all the firepower they needed.

They drove hard for a good fifteen minutes, then the Bradley screeched to a halt. 'Okay, rock and roll!' shouted the lieutenant, as the doors opened.

The men fanned out behind the vehicle. About fifty feet in front of the Bradley a burnt-out car lay on its side. The body of the driver was half out of the window, the flesh blackened and still steaming. Brown heard a burst of gunfire to his left and ducked instinctively. There was more gunfire to his right and bullets screeched off the Bradley's armour.

The three Humvees had pulled up behind and the gunners were aiming their roof-mounted machine-guns to the right. Brown peered around the Bradley. To his left four marines were crouching behind a Humvee, firing at a pick-up truck that had slammed into a telegraph pole. Brown's eyes stung from the cordite in the air.

There were three men behind the pick-up truck, and another lying down in its flatbed, all holding Kalashnikovs, their faces hidden behind red and white chequered scarves. The one in the back of the truck fired and more bullets ricocheted off the Bradley's armoured steel. Brown shouldered his M4 and fired a quick burst at the man at the front of the truck. The top of his head blew off in a shower of red and Brown grinned, his heart pounding. 'Did you see that?' he shouted. 'Did you fucking see that?' He turned to the soldier next to him. 'Blew his fucking head off!'

The last thing Samuel Brown ever saw was the contempt on his colleague's face. The bullet ripped through his throat at eight hundred metres a second and virtually severed his spinal cord. He was dead before he hit the ground, the M4 still in his hands.

'*Allahu Akbar*,' whispered the Sniper, as he chambered a second round.

'*Allahu Akbar*,' echoed the Spotter. The dead soldier in the street below was his two-hundred-and-fortieth kill. The attack on the vehicle had been fortuitous. The Sniper had been waiting for an American foot patrol, and he had watched from his vantage-point on top of the building as the insurgents had placed the IED at the side of the road and hidden it under a pile of garbage. Their target was a civilian, probably a government official, and the Sniper had watched dispassionately as the car, a Mercedes, had been blown on to its side and the occupants burned to death. He had watched without emotion as the Humvee had turned up and the marines had shot out the tyres of the pick-up truck that the insurgents were using, and he had waited as the gun battle raged below. More soldiers would arrive, he knew. The insurgents were pinned down and had nowhere to go. The Americans would call for reinforcements, and the insurgents would fight to the death.

One of the soldiers knelt beside the dead man, checking for a pulse. He was wasting his time, the Sniper knew. It had been the perfect killing shot. The Americans were constantly improving their body armour and their new helmets would stop a rifle round, but there were always gaps. The face was the perfect target. And the back of the head. There was a gap at the bottom of the body armour, and at the sides. The more difficult the Americans made it, the more the Sniper enjoyed the challenge.

The officer hurried to the dead man. The Americans had no way of knowing where the shot had come from. They would assume it had been the insurgents. It was the best sort of killing zone, one where confusion reigned, and the gunfire down below had covered the sound of his shots. He sighted on the officer's neck and tightened his finger on the trigger. '*Allahu Akbar*,' he said.

The Emirates flight landed at Heathrow Terminal Three just after midday. The queue through Immigration snaked back almost a quarter of a mile. Shepherd could have short-circuited it by identifying himself as a police officer but he didn't want to draw attention to himself. He joined the line and forced himself to be patient. It was a full ten minutes before he got to the immigration hall. Shepherd smiled to himself as he realised that Sharpe would have had a field day if he had been there. Terminal Three dealt with flights from Asia and Africa, and few of the passengers ahead of him in the EU line could be classed as IC1s. Clearly a plane had recently arrived from India: he could see a group of two dozen overweight women in saris and headscarves, all clutching British passports. Four Arab businessmen, who had been in the first-class section on his plane, were ahead of him and appeared to have French passports. Several Nigerians with bulging hand luggage and ill-fitting suits had British ones and a Pakistani in a long coat was juggling three. Eventually he chose an Irish one and put the other two back into his pocket.

Shepherd looked to the front of the queue. Three men and a woman were processing the EU queue, barely glancing at the passports handed to them. It had never made sense to Shepherd the ease with which the British allowed people to move in and out of the country. As an island, its borders could easily have been policed. But the checks were cursory and the immigration officials were more interested in the passports than they were in those carrying them. More often than not an official didn't speak to the person, just checked the passport and handed it back. It was only after the bombs on the London Tube system that the authorities had begun to check who was leaving the country. The government had long since admitted that it had lost control of its borders and that it had no idea how many immigrants, legal or illegal, were in the country. And, as far as Shepherd could see, it was in no hurry to remedy the situation. At the very least, he thought, the British should be following the example of the Americans, photographing and fingerprinting every foreigner who entered the country, but there was no sign of that happening.

The queue moved quickly, almost at walking pace, and soon Shepherd was in a black cab heading to Ealing.

When he went into his house Liam was engrossed in his Sony PlayStation. The game seemed to involve mowing down pedestrians with a high-powered sports car. 'Hi, Dad, where've you been?' he asked, eyes fixed on the screen.

'Working,' said Shepherd. 'I need a shower. Where's Katra?'

'Getting some herbs from the garden. Hey, she said I had to go and stay with Gran and Grandad.'

'We might not be able to get the new house in Hereford so Gran said you can stay with them until I get everything sorted,' said Shepherd. 'That way you can still go to the school.'

'You'll be there, too?'

Shepherd pulled a face. 'I'll have to stay here until we've sold it,' he said.

'With Katra?' Liam grinned mischievously.

'What are you grinning at?' asked Shepherd.

'Nothing,' said Liam.

'Tell me.'

'Nothing,' repeated Liam.

'She has to stay here to take care of the house,' said Shepherd. 'Once we have the new house in Hereford she can move there.'

'You like her, don't you?'

'Of course I do. But not in the way you mean.'

'What way is that?' said Katra, behind him.

Shepherd jumped. Katra was standing behind him in a baggy pullover and pale blue jeans that had worn through at the knees. She was holding a basket of the herbs she'd picked. 'Liam was teasing me,' said Shepherd, 'for which he'll pay next time he comes to me for pocket money.'

'Are you in for dinner?' she asked. 'I'm making *cevapcici*.'

'What's that?' asked Shepherd.

Liam sighed theatrically. 'Slovenian meatballs, shaped like sausages,' he said. 'Don't you know anything?'

'I know that your pocket money's just been halved,' said Shepherd, ruffling Liam's hair. He smiled at Katra. 'I'll have to pass on the *cevapcici*,' he said. 'I'm just dropping in to pick up some clothes and then I'm heading off, probably for a few days this time.'

'Anywhere interesting?' she asked.

'Just work,' he said. 'I'll shower and change and then I'm off.'

'Your solicitor called. She wants you to phone.'

'Thanks,' said Shepherd. As he went upstairs, he called Linda Howe on his mobile.

'Thanks for calling back,' she said. 'I wanted you to know that the buyer of your house has agreed to pay the original price.'

'That's great news,' said Shepherd. 'What brought about his change of heart?'

'I thought you might be able to tell me,' said the solicitor.

'What do you mean?' said Shepherd. He went into the bed-room and tossed his holdall on to the bed.

'The buyer said he'd spoken to a friend of yours. A detective.'

'Ah,' said Shepherd.

'Apparently the detective explained that you were working on a stressful case and that the last thing you needed was to be worried about the sale of your house.'

Shepherd put his hand on his forehead. Only one person would have done that. Jimmy bloody Sharpe.

'And suggestions were made about a possible Financial Services Authority investigation into the buyer's company, I gather.'

'Nothing to do with me,' said Shepherd. 'I was out of the country. I've only just got back.'

'Well, whoever it was and whatever he said, it did the trick. The buyer came in this morning and signed the contract. He's not happy, but the sale has gone through and all we need to do now is hand over the keys.'

'That's great news,' said Shepherd. 'I'll get my au pair to arrange the move. The purchase of the Hereford house is still okay, right?'

'Absolutely,' said Howe. 'We should have everything sorted within the next day or two.'

'I'll probably be out of the country again, but my mobile will still work,' said Shepherd. He ended the call, unzipped his holdall and emptied the contents on to the quilt. He tossed his dirty clothes into the wicker basket in the bathroom, took clean under-wear and socks from his chest of drawers, then put them with three polo shirts into his holdall.

He heard footsteps on the stairs and turned to see Liam in the doorway. 'You were joking about my pocket money, weren't you?' he said.

Shepherd took out his wallet and gave his son a ten-pound note. 'That's for two weeks,' he said.

'Thanks, Dad,' said Liam. He picked up the hardback book

Shepherd had been reading on the flight from Dubai. 'Hey, you're reading a book,' he said, sitting down on the bed.

Shepherd pretended to clip his son's head. 'I can read, you know,' he said. He'd picked up the copy of the Koran at Dubai airport. He knew next to nothing about the religion of the men who were holding Geordie hostage and he had decided it was about time to fill in the gaps.

Liam flicked through it. 'The Koran?' he said. 'That's like the Bible, right? Why are you reading it?'

'I wanted to learn about Islam,' said Shepherd, sitting down on the bed next to his son. 'Muslims read the Koran, so I thought I would too.'

'They want to kill Christians, don't they?'

'Where did you get that idea?'

'That's what they do. The men who exploded the bombs on the Tube were Muslims. And the men fighting the troops in Iraq are Muslims.'

'Sure, but that doesn't mean all Muslims want to kill Christians. It's a really peaceful religion.' He nodded at the book. 'You should read it. If everyone behaved the way the Koran tells people to behave, the world would be a much better place.'

'What does it say?'

'It says that a good Muslim follows five rules. They're called the five pillars of Islam, a bit like the Ten Commandments. You know the Ten Commandments, right?'

'I think so.'

'You think so?'

'We did them at school. "Thou shalt not kill." That's one.'

'Sure,' said Shepherd. 'And honouring your father and mother is another you could try to remember. The five pillars are pretty simple. The first is that Muslims have to have faith that Allah is God and that only He can be worshipped, and that Muhammad was Allah's messenger. It's a bit like when the Bible says there's only one God.'

'So God is Allah?'

'Yes. But Muslims don't believe that Jesus was the son of God. The second pillar says that Muslims have to pray five times a day. Between dawn and sunrise, after midday, between midday and sunset, right after sunset and one hour after sunset. That's why you hear that wailing noise from mosques. It's telling Muslims it's time to pray. The third pillar is called *zakah*, which means giving to charity. Every year Muslims are supposed to give a percentage of their wealth to the needy.'

'We do that,' said Liam. 'We give to charity at school.'

'Sure,' said Shepherd, 'but Islam makes giving to charity part of the religion. The fourth pillar is fasting. Once a year Muslims have to fast for a month during daylight. No food or drink from dawn to dusk. The idea is that it teaches patience and self-control.'

'Like giving stuff up for Lent,' said Liam.

'Absolutely,' said Shepherd. 'There are lots of similarities between Christianity and Islam. The fifth pillar's a bit different, though. Once in their lifetime, Muslims have to make a pilgrimage to Mecca in Saudi Arabia, if they can – it's their big holy place. According to the Koran, those are the main rules that Muslims have to follow.'

'So why do they kill so many people?' asked Liam.

'It's not because they're Muslims,' said Shepherd. 'The people who set off the bombs are terrorists. It's like with the IRA. The IRA were Catholics, but the men who set off the IRA bombs were terrorists first and Catholics second. The Bible says it's wrong to kill, so the IRA men who set off the bombs couldn't be called real Christians. It's the same with the Koran. The Koran doesn't say that killing is right. It talks about defending the religion, but not about violence. So Muslims who kill aren't good Muslims. And the vast majority of Muslims are good people. We mustn't let what's happening in Iraq, or what happened in London, change how we view a whole religion. That's what the terrorists want.'

Liam nodded thoughtfully. 'It'd be a better world without any religion, though, wouldn't it?'

Shepherd exhaled through pursed lips. 'Tough question,' he said. 'Religion causes conflict, there's no getting away from that, but following a religion tends to make people behave better. Terrorists notwithstanding.'

'Because they're scared of God?'

'Not necessarily scared,' said Shepherd, 'but if you believe that a God, any God, is watching over you, you'd tend to be nicer to those around you.'

'What about you, Dad? Do you believe in God?'

Shepherd grimaced. 'You're full of tough questions today, aren't you?' He lay back on the bed and stared up at the ceiling – as he had thousands of times before, most of them with Sue lying next to him. Now she was dead and Shepherd didn't believe she was sitting on a cloud, strumming a harp. Dead was dead and death was for ever. No heaven, no hell. Did that mean he didn't believe in God? Shepherd had seen so much evil that it was hard to believe an omnipotent being was somehow in control. But he remembered, too, that when he'd been shot in Afghanistan, he had asked God, through gritted teeth as he lay bleeding on the sand, to keep him alive. It hadn't been God, of course, who'd stemmed the blood and packed the wound, it had been Geordie. And it hadn't been God who'd called in the helicopter and carried him to it. That had been Geordie, too.

'Dad . . .' said Liam.

'I'm thinking,' said Shepherd.

'About what?'

'About how to answer your question,' he said. He sat up. 'I'm not sure,' he said. 'I'm honestly not sure. God has never spoken to me, that much I know. And I see a lot of bad in the world. But there are people who truly believe that God has spoken to them, and they often do a lot of good. It's something that everyone has to decide for themselves. You either believe, or you don't.'

'Gran and Grandad do, don't they? They go to church every Sunday.'

That was true, Shepherd knew. But the God Moira and Tom

believed in would abhor gay marriage, abortion and women clergy. They had insisted that he and Sue were married in church, and he had been happy to go along with it. Whenever he had been at their home on a Sunday he'd accompanied them to church. He'd enjoyed the hymns and laughed at the vicar's occasional jokes, but he'd always seen it as a way to keep Tom and Moira sweet rather than as a way of communing with God. Shepherd's photographic memory had always come in handy when he was leaving: he'd shake the vicar's hand, smile warmly and quote an obscure passage from the Bible, word perfect. Sue had always been noncommittal on religion, and they hadn't talked about it much. There was a Bible in the house, a gift from Tom and Moira, but he and Sue had never opened it. 'Going to church is a good thing,' said Shepherd.

'But you don't go, do you?'

'I do if we're with Gran and Grandad.'

'But you don't believe in God, do you?'

'It doesn't matter what I believe,' said Shepherd. 'What matters is what you believe.'

'I don't think there's a God. If there was, why would He let Mum die?'

'It's a tough question.'

'You always say that when you don't want to answer me,' said Liam.

'I'm being honest,' said Shepherd.

'Mum didn't do anything wrong, but she died. That's not fair. If there was a God, wouldn't He make sure that bad things only happened to bad people?'

Shepherd shrugged.

'I know, it's a tough question,' said Liam.

'But it is,' said Shepherd. 'It's almost impossible to answer. Every day when I'm working I see good, honest people get hurt. And often I see bad people do terrible things and get away with it. But that doesn't mean I don't try to do my job. Just because the world isn't fair doesn't mean we shouldn't try to make it fair.'

Liam frowned and Shepherd saw that another tough question was on its way. 'I've got to go out for a while.'

'Where are you going?'

'It's work,' said Shepherd. 'I'll be away for a few days.'

'You're *always* away. It sucks.'

'It what?'

'It sucks.' Liam rolled off the bed and headed for his bedroom. Shepherd hurried after him. 'What's wrong?' he asked.

'Nothing,' said Liam.

'Look, when this is over, I'll spend more time with you, I promise.'

'Okay.'

'I mean it.'

'I know you do.'

Shepherd peered at his watch. 'I've got to go, Liam. We'll talk about this when I get back. I love you – you know that?'

'I know.'

'Good. Give me a hug.'

Liam smiled and Shepherd scooped him up and held him tight, burying his face in his son's neck. Part of him wanted to stay right where he was, with his boy, play football with him or sit in front of the television. They never spent enough time together – he was either coming in from a case, dog-tired and wanting to sleep, or on his way out, adrenaline pumping. He hardly ever hung out with his son. It hadn't been so bad when Sue had been around, but since she'd gone Shepherd's absences were all the more obvious. Katra did her best, but he was Liam's father and Liam deserved more than the occasional hug. 'I'm sorry,' whispered Shepherd.

'For what?'

'For being such a crap dad.'

'You're not crap. A lot of kids at school only see their dads once every two weeks because they're divorced. At least I live with you.'

'Once this is over I will make more time. I promise.'

'Do you really have to go?'

Shepherd closed his eyes. Another tough question. The truth was that he didn't. The Major would understand if he stayed in London. So would the rest of the guys. Shepherd truly believed that Geordie would understand, too. But that wasn't the point, he wouldn't be able to live with himself if he stayed in London and his friend died in Baghdad. He had to do what he could to save Geordie, no matter the risks. 'I'm sorry, Liam. I do.'

Shepherd switched off the ignition and sat looking at the neat semi-detached house. It wasn't the sort of place he'd expected Amar Singh to call home. A city-centre loft, maybe, or a flat near Camden Market. Somewhere young and trendy where Amar could strut his stuff in his designer sweatshirts and state-of-the-art trainers. The red-brick house with its slate roof and carefully tended rockeries looked as if it should have been home to a middle-aged, middle-class couple, as did the car that was parked in front of the wooden garage. It was a four-year-old Volvo estate with a child seat in the back. Shepherd frowned. Singh had never mentioned that he was married.

He climbed out of his car and walked towards the front gate. It opened on well-oiled hinges and the paving-stones were swept clean. The house number was above the letterbox so there was no doubt that this was the right house but, even so, as Shepherd pressed the doorbell he was convinced that the person who opened the door would never have heard of Amar Singh.

The door opened. Shepherd looked down to see a pair of large brown eyes gazing up at him. The child in Winnie the Pooh pyjamas couldn't have been much more than five. 'Who are you?' she asked.

Shepherd smiled. 'I'm a friend of your daddy's,' he said. 'Is he in?'

'Who is it, Neeta?' shouted a woman, from somewhere inside the house.

'I don't know,' she shouted back.

'My name's Dan,' said Shepherd.

'He's Dan,' shouted Neeta, 'but he's a stranger so I won't let him in.'

'That's very sensible of you,' said Shepherd.

'I'm not supposed to talk to strangers,' she said solemnly.

'And that's very good advice,' said Shepherd. 'Why don't you close the door until your daddy comes?'

'Okay,' she said, and did so.

A few seconds later the door opened again. Large brown eyes scrutinised him again, but this time they belonged to a lithe Indian woman wearing tight blue jeans and a blue sweater. She was holding a toddler and had a mobile phone pressed between chin and shoulder.

'I'm Dan,' said Shepherd, 'a friend of Amar's.'

'Come in,' she mouthed, and pulled open the door. She began speaking Hindi into the phone as Shepherd walked into the hallway. The little girl was sitting on the stairs holding a teddy bear. Shepherd winked at her.

'I'm sorry about that,' said the woman, slipping the mobile phone into the back pocket of her jeans and closing the front door. 'Everything seems to be happening at once.'

'Dan,' said Shepherd, holding out his hand. 'Dan Shepherd.'

'Pleased to meet you,' said the woman. 'I'm Mishti.' She smiled, showing gleaming white teeth. Her skin was flawless, the most amazing honey-gold, and her glossy waist-length hair was jet black.

'It means "sweet person",' said Singh, coming down the stairs. 'And she can be, sometimes.' He was wearing cargo pants and a black Armani sweatshirt.

'And my beloved's name means "immortal", but if he carries on like this, we'll try to prove otherwise,' said Mishti.

'Sorry to bother you at home, Amar,' said Shepherd, 'but something's come up.'

'Is Gita okay?' Mishti asked her husband.

'She's out of the bath and ready for bed,' said Singh. He pointed to the child on the stairs. 'Come on, bed-time.'

'I went to bed yesterday,' she said, 'and the day before.'

'And you'll be going again tomorrow,' said Singh. 'Now, up you go.' He lunged forward, threatening to tickle her, and she scampered up the stairs, giggling.

'I'll take her,' said Mishti. 'You take care of our guest.' She grinned at Shepherd. 'My husband has little in the way of social skills.'

Shepherd grinned back. 'We know,' he said, 'but we make allowances because he's so good at his job.'

Mishti kissed her husband's cheek as she headed upstairs. Singh took Shepherd along the hallway to the kitchen. 'Lager?' he said, opening the refrigerator.

'Great,' said Shepherd. Singh tossed him a can of Foster's and Shepherd caught it. 'Amar, I need your help. Big-time.'

'I guessed it wasn't a social visit.'

'I need to pick your brains,' said Shepherd. 'Can we go outside?'

'Walls have ears?' laughed Singh. 'I sweep my house every week, just for practice.'

'Force of habit,' said Shepherd. 'Humour me.'

Singh opened the kitchen door and went out into the garden. Shepherd followed him. A crazy-paving path wound across the lawn to a small copse of apple trees in front of a greenhouse packed with tomato plants. 'I didn't know you had green fingers,' said Shepherd.

'You thought I spend all my time with my head in electronics manuals?' said Singh.

'You know your stuff. I just assumed it was a full-time thing.'

Singh popped the ring top of his can and sipped. 'What about you, Dan? Are you a cop twenty-four hours a day?'

Shepherd shrugged. 'Pretty much.' He opened his lager and drank.

'What do you do for fun?'

'I run, I suppose.'

Singh chuckled. 'Running isn't for fun, it's for getting away,' he said. 'Everyone needs a hobby, something to take your mind off the crap we have to deal with day in, day out. For me it's my family and the garden.'

'I didn't even know you had a family.'

'I doubt you know three things about me that aren't work-related,' said Singh.

'True,' said Shepherd. 'We don't normally have time for small-talk.'

'You don't make time, Dan. You've got walls around you, high, thick ones,' he said. 'Sorry, I didn't mean to get all deep on you.'

'Nah, you're right,' said Shepherd. 'But don't take it personally. The unit shrink's been trying to get up close and personal for years and she's had no joy. It's what I do. I'm under cover so often that it's second nature to keep the real me under wraps.'

'Maybe.' Singh didn't sound convinced.

'I'm sorry I never asked about your family,' said Shepherd.

'It's not a problem,' said Singh. 'We work together, but no one ever said we had to be friends.'

They gazed up at the stars as they drank their lager. 'Your daughter's great,' said Shepherd.

'Yeah, they're going to cost me a fortune. Have you any idea how much an Indian wedding sets you back? An arm and a leg doesn't come close.'

'Yeah, but at least daughters take care of their parents. Boys are off as soon as they can be.'

'I still see my parents every week,' said Singh.

'Where are they?' Shepherd had assumed that they were in India.

'Ealing,' said Singh.

'You're joking,' said Shepherd. 'I live in Ealing.'

Singh raised his eyebrows. 'Small world,' he said. They clinked cans and drank again. 'You've got a boy, right?'

'Liam,' said Shepherd. 'Just coming up to ten.'

'Mine are five, three and eighteen months,' said Amar. 'Neeta,

Gita and Sita.' He nodded back at the house. 'My wife's idea. The names, I mean. Having kids was a joint decision. At least, I think it was.'

'Cute names,' said Shepherd.

'Yeah, well, you don't have to stand in the park shouting for them,' said Singh. 'What do you need, Dan?'

Shepherd wiped his mouth on the back of his hand. 'A friend of mine has been kidnapped in Iraq. He's going to be killed in a few days unless we can find out where he is.'

'We?'

'Me and a group of his friends. We'll do whatever we have to to get him back.'

'What exactly?'

'We're not sure yet. Not a hundred per cent. That's why I wanted to talk to you.'

'Okay . . .' said Singh, hesitantly.

'How easy would it be to track someone in Iraq using the same sort of gear you put in the guns?'

Singh rubbed his chin thoughtfully. 'Iraq's a war zone, near enough,' he said, 'I wouldn't know where to start.'

'Just tell me about the technology,' said Shepherd.

Singh nodded thoughtfully. 'The tracking devices we use are battery-powered and good for several days. They can be monitored up to three miles on level ground.'

'Not GPS, then?'

'We needed to keep the size down to fit them into the weapons,' said Singh.

'How about if you wanted GPS capability?'

'A bog-standard EPIRB will cost you less than a grand, and it can be tracked by satellites anywhere in the world,' said Singh.

'I'm technologically illiterate, Amar,' said Shepherd. 'Spell it out, will you?'

'EPIRB. Emergency Position Indicating Radio Beacon. They normally operate on two frequencies. A five-watt radio transmitter operating at four hundred and six megahertz and a less powerful quarter of a watt operating at a hundred and twenty-one point five megahertz. The gizmo broadcasts its unique serial number so not only can the unit be located you know who it belongs to.'

'Located how?' asked Shepherd.

Singh gestured at the sky with his can. 'Satellites,' he said. 'The EPIRB has its own GPS, which ascertains its latitude and longitude and transmits that information along with its serial number. The rescue agencies know its position to within a hundred metres or so.'

'And the satellites are, what, government-owned?'

'Private,' said Singh. 'They're operated under the Cospas-Sarsat programme, developed by Canada, France, the United States and the former Soviet Union republics. Their satellites orbit the earth about every hundred minutes, so in the worst possible scenario it'd take an hour to pick up an emergency signal. What are you planning, Dan?'

'I'm just gathering intel at the moment,' said Shepherd.

'The Western end is the Sarsat bit. Search and Rescue Satellite-aided Tracking. The Cospas bit is the Russian side. Dunno what it stands for. Basically the satellites receive the signals and relay them to ground stations where the signal is processed to work out where the beacon is. The ground stations pass the information on to the local search-and-rescue authorities.'

'And that would work anywhere in the world?'

Singh wrinkled his nose. 'The satellites cover the world, for sure, and the nearest ground station would be able to locate the beacon to within a hundred metres or so. But it depends where the beacon is as to what happens next. If it's in the English Channel they can send out a lifeboat or a helicopter. If someone's lost in the Scottish Highlands they can call out the local mountain-rescue team. But if the beacon's in a jungle in the Congo, who the hell do they call? And Iraq's a war zone.'

'What about this other frequency you mentioned?'

'Yeah, the EPIRBs also put out a signal on a hundred and twenty-one point five megahertz, the aviation distress frequency.

Planes all over the world monitor it and can take a bearing. You've heard of the Breitling Emergency watch?'

Shepherd shook his head.

'It's a watch with a hundred and twenty-one point five megahertz transmitter inside. You activate it by pulling out a wire aerial and every plane within a hundred nautical miles or so picks up the distress call. They radio in to air-traffic control and in theory a coastguard helicopter flies over to you.'

'Great way to get home if you can't find a taxi.'

Singh grinned. 'Yeah, well, it'll get you a ten grand fine if you haven't been in a plane crash,' he said.

'So, one of those transmitters can be as small as a watch?'

'Sure. The battery wouldn't last long transmitting, though. A day maybe.'

'So it's not transmitting all the time?'

Singh shook his head. 'Just when the aerial's pulled out. Same with the EPIRBs. They only send out a distress signal once they're activated. Has to be that way because they'd burn through batteries if they were on all the time.'

'How big are they?'

'They weigh a couple of pounds or so, the nautical and aviation models.'

'What about something smaller? Something that can be satellite tracked but small enough to hide?'

'We don't have anything that small. Not for satellite tracking. You'd need to talk to the spooks. Or the Yanks.'

'Could you put out some feelers? It might make fewer waves if the approach comes from you.'

'What are you planning, Dan? What's all this about?'

Shepherd shrugged. 'It's starting to look like the only way we're going to get him out is to walk into the lion's den.'

'You're crazy,' said Singh.

'You might be right,' said Shepherd. 'But keep it to yourself, yeah?'

★　　★　　★

Shepherd parked his BMW next to the Honda CRV and let himself into the house. Katra was sitting on the sofa, her legs curled up. She put down her magazine. 'Do you want a coffee?' she asked.

'I'll get it,' said Shepherd. 'How's Liam?'

'He was in bed by eight,' she said, brushing a lock of hair behind her ear.

'Homework?'

'All done.'

'Great,' said Shepherd. He went through to the kitchen. He had just made himself a mug of coffee when the phone rang. He picked up the receiver.

'It's Charlie, I hope this isn't an inconvenient time to call.'

'Something wrong?' he asked.

'I need to talk to you, Spider.'

'Now?'

'Face to face, if possible. Do you mind if I come to your house?'

Shepherd squinted at his watch. It was almost ten o'clock. And she had called on his landline, not his mobile, which meant she knew that he was home. 'Sure,' said Shepherd. 'What time?'

'Now, if that's okay. I'm outside.'

Shepherd frowned. He hadn't seen her when he'd parked the car, and he was sure he hadn't been followed to Ealing. Charlotte Button was full of hidden talents. 'The kettle's on,' he said. 'Tea or coffee?'

'Tea, please. Anything but Earl Grey.'

'It's not exactly the Ritz, and I've no cucumber sandwiches,' he said.

'Tea will be fine,' she said, and ended the call.

Shepherd put the receiver on to the cradle. That Button hadn't said why she wanted to see him was worrying. Something was wrong – and wrong enough for her to be knocking on his door at this time of night.

He switched on the kettle again, put a teabag into a cup and got a bottle of milk from the fridge. Before the kettle had boiled, the doorbell rang. Shepherd went through to the sitting room and asked Katra if she minded going to her room. 'I'm sorry, it's business,' he said.

She hurried upstairs while Shepherd went to the front door. Button was wearing a fawn raincoat with the collar up. She nodded as she stepped across the threshold, but she didn't say anything. Her eyes were cold and Shepherd knew now that something was very wrong.

'Go through to the sitting room, on the right,' said Shepherd. 'I'll get the tea.'

When he carried in the tray, she was sitting on the sofa where Katra had been. She'd taken off her coat and dropped it on the back of the sofa and was sitting with her legs crossed, the upper foot tapping the air. Shepherd placed a cup in front of her, then sat down in an armchair opposite.

He smiled at Button, but his face felt wooden. He had a sudden urge to cough and fought it. His mind was racing. Why was she in his house and why had she needed to see him at such short notice? If it was a work-related issue there would be no need for her to give him the silent treatment.

'Is there something you want to tell me, Spider?' she asked eventually. 'Something you want to get off your chest?'

His mind raced. How much did she know? And how much could he afford to tell her?

Button continued to stare at him, allowing the seconds to tick away with no sign of discomfort other than her tapping foot. It was the same technique that Kathy Gift had used, leaving long silences in the hope that Shepherd would fill them.

Shepherd shrugged. 'I'm not sure what you want me to say, Charlie.'

She arched an eyebrow. 'Really?'

'Everything's fine. Is this about my biannual review?'

She shook her head. 'No. Caroline seems to think you're perfectly fit for undercover work. I'm the one who's starting to have doubts.'

'What's the problem?' he asked.

'You are,' she said, her voice flat and emotionless. 'Did you think you could go to Dubai without me finding out? And then when you do come back, you rush straight round to Amar.'

'Have you had me followed?' said Shepherd.

Button looked at him with undisguised contempt. 'Don't flatter yourself,' she said. 'I don't have my people followed. But when one of them starts flying around the world at short notice I think I have the right to know what the hell is going on.'

'I was on holiday,' said Shepherd. 'I applied for the leave. Plus today's the weekend. It's Saturday.'

'I know what day it is,' said Button. 'So what was Dubai about? Shopping? You didn't come back with any duty-free bags.'

'So you were at the airport? Spying on me?'

Button snorted softly and didn't answer. The silence stretched into a minute. Then a second minute. This wasn't the sort of mind game Kathy Gift had played, Shepherd realised. Button was going to wait for him to speak, no matter how long it took.

'What do you think I was doing in Dubai?' he asked quietly.

'I'm not here to answer your questions,' she said.

'Then why are you here? To sack me?'

Button leaned back and folded her arms. 'Do you want me to sack you? Is that it? Do you have another job lined up?'

Shepherd frowned, confused. 'What do you mean?' he asked.

'Are you working for Richard Yokely? Is that why you went to Dubai?'

Shepherd's jaw dropped. It was the last thing he'd expected to hear.

'I know you met him in Knightsbridge last week. And you've met him before. I'm fairly sure he's offered you a job.'

'That's not why I went to Dubai.'

'But he does want you to work for him?'

Shepherd sighed. 'He offered me a job while I was still working for Hargrove. I told him no.'

'You know what he does?' said Button.

'He used to be CIA,' said Shepherd. 'Now he's something in Homeland Security.'

'He kills people, Spider. He's a government-sanctioned killer. He's worked in South America, Africa, Afghanistan, Iraq, anywhere where human rights are less accountable than they are here.'

'I sort of realised that,' said Shepherd.

'Then you should sort of realise how dangerous your life could become if you get too close to him.'

'He promised me protection, actually,' said Shepherd. 'The way I remember the conversation, if I got caught in a compromising position his president calls my prime minister and everything's hunky-dory.'

'You'd be surprised to learn how many men in British prisons claim that a smooth-talking American with tassels on his shoes told them they were committing murder in the name of national security and that at any moment a phone call from the Prime Minister's office would secure their release and a medal to boot. Conspiracy theories abound inside. Nobody listens to them. So if he's promised you a get-out-of-jail-free card, I can assure you it's not worth whatever it's printed on. So, what was the Dubai trip about?'

'Charlie, I'll swear on a stack of Bibles that I wasn't going to Dubai for Yokely. He offered me a job but I turned him down.'

'So it was a coincidence that, shortly after meeting him at the Special Forces Club, you give me some cock-and-bull story about moving house and get on a plane to the Middle East?'

'I *am* moving house,' said Shepherd, defensively.

'You've been gazumped, the sale has practically fallen through,' said Button. Shepherd opened his mouth to speak but she pointed a warning finger at him. 'And don't ask me how I know. It's my job to know what my operatives are up to. Hargrove might have kept you on a long leash but SOCA is a different set-up. If you so much as fart in the bath, I know about it.'

'I was just going to say it was a reverse gazumping. My buyer cut his offer. Anyway, it's all been sorted now and the sale's gone through. But I guess that's not the point, is it?'

'No, it's not. The point is, how many lies are you going to tell me, Spider?'

Shepherd said nothing.

'And I need you to explain why you jeopardised an ongoing operation.'

Shepherd opened his mouth to speak, but he could see that Button was in no mood to listen so he closed it again.

'Did you think that SO13 wouldn't have the Birmingham mob under surveillance? And did you seriously believe when you put the operation on hold that they wouldn't immediately call me up to find out what the hell was going on? Ali wanted explosives, and you put him on hold.' She folded her arms.

'Charlie . . .'

'What? Charlie what?'

'It's complicated,' he said.

'Quadratic equations are complicated. What you did isn't complicated. I know exactly what you did because a very angry SO13 played me the recording of your chat with Ali. And my former colleagues in Five were more than happy to track your mobile to Dubai. So I know what you did and I know where you were when you did it. What I don't know is why you've thrown away your career.' She unfolded her arms and pointed a finger at him. 'You could go to prison for what you did, Spider. You aided and abetted terrorists. What was I supposed to tell SO13?'

'I'm sorry,' he said.

'Well, "I'm sorry" doesn't cut it,' said Button. 'Leaving aside the stupidity and illegality of what you did, have you any idea of the position you've put me in? All the established law-enforcement organisations are hell-bent on proving that SOCA is unnecessary because they want to show how indispensable they are. You've just handed my head to them on a plate. I've hired a maverick who cuts deals with terrorists. Now, are you going to tell me what's going on, or do I see about transferring you to another unit?'

Shepherd could see that Button wasn't bluffing. She looked at him levelly as she waited for him to speak. She wasn't playing at giving him the silent treatment: she was giving him the chance to make a choice. He could tell her the truth, or he could lie to her. Shepherd had no doubt that he could look her in the eye and lie. It was what he did for a living. He pretended to be someone he wasn't, he lied and cheated to get close to people he would ultimately betray, and generally he did it with a clear conscience. Lying was a means to an end, a way of putting bad men behind bars, of achieving justice when conventional policing methods had failed. Lying wasn't exactly second nature to Shepherd, but he could do it well. Shepherd didn't believe that Button knew the reason for his trip to Dubai. If she did, she'd have confronted him with it. She was giving him the chance to come clean about what he was doing and why. He could tell her the truth and take the consequences, or he could lie. Either way, his relationship with Charlotte Button would never be the same again.

Button sat quietly, waiting for him to speak. Shepherd had no way of knowing if she had any idea of the struggle he was going through. He wondered if he could trust her. She was a former spook, and she had already made clear that her ultimate aim was to go back to MI5. Shepherd trusted the Major because they'd served together in the SAS. He had trusted Sam Hargrove because Hargrove was a career cop who'd proved his loyalty on numerous occasions. Shepherd wanted to trust Button, but they had virtually no history together. He'd worked for her for less than six months.

He took a deep breath and let it out slowly. If he told her the real reason he was in Dubai, he risked blowing the operation. Geordie would die in the basement, his throat ripped open as demented insurgents swore loyalty to their God. Shepherd couldn't allow that to happen. But if he lied to Button, she would find out. And then his career would be over. More than that, if she turned him in there was a good chance he'd end up in prison for what he'd done already. He'd kidnapped, threatened, abused and come close to torturing two men. Basharat and Fariq. Two innocent men. He looked deep into her eyes and wondered if he could trust her. If he dared to trust her.

Major Allan Gannon looked up at the arrivals display and frowned. The Emirates flight had landed thirty minutes earlier and Shepherd had no reason to be travelling with luggage.

'Sometimes there's a stack of VIPs going through,' said Muller. 'Anyone related to the royal family gets special treatment, and most businessmen with any clout can get met airside.'

'I hope that's all it is,' said Gannon. With Halim meeting Shepherd off the plane immigration would be a formality, but Shepherd was still bringing in electronic equipment that might attract attention if it was noticed by Customs.

Passengers continued to walk into the arrivals area. There were haughty Saudis in gleaming white *dishdasha*s, and red and white checked *ghutra*s, followed by their womenfolk, draped from head to foot in black; Western businessmen with wheeled luggage, gold frequent-flyer tags and laptop computer cases; dark-skinned labourers in cheap clothes with plastic suitcases held together by string and insulation tape; British tourists already complaining about the heat.

'There he is,' said Muller, but Gannon had already spotted Shepherd walking out of the immigration area, Halim at his side. He waved to him, and Shepherd strode towards them carrying a black holdall, Halim hurrying to keep up. Gannon realised that a woman in her late thirties with dark chestnut hair and brown eyes was walking a few feet behind him, matching his brisk pace. Her brow was furrowed and her lips formed a thin, tight line. She had no luggage, just a small leather bag on a strap over one shoulder. In her left hand she carried a fawn raincoat. She was looking in their direction and it was only when she locked eyes with Gannon that he realised who she was. He cursed under his breath.

'Who is she?' asked Muller.

'A ball-breaker,' said Gannon. 'That sound you just heard was the shit hitting the fan.'

'I'm only a stupid American. You'll have to spell it out for me,' said Muller.

'Charlotte Button,' said Gannon. 'Spider's boss.'

'Ah,' said Muller. 'I might just leave you to it.'

'I'm afraid it's a bit late for that, John,' said Gannon. 'The fact that she's here means that she probably knows all she needs to know. She used to work for MI5, but now she heads up SOCA's undercover unit.'

'Again, I'm just the stupid Yank here. You don't mean soccer, the game, I take it?'

'Sorry, John. The bloody initials become second nature after a while.' He spelled out the letters. 'Stands for the Serious Organised Crime Agency. Effectively it's a British FBI. They target drug traffickers, international fraudsters, the big criminals that local forces can't touch. Spider works for SOCA's undercover unit, and Charlotte Button there is his boss.'

'Nice legs,' said Muller, approvingly.

'You could try flattery, but from what I've heard it won't get you anywhere,' said Gannon.

He shook Shepherd's hand and clapped him on the shoulder as he welcomed him back to Dubai. Shepherd had time to whisper, 'She knows everything,' before Button joined them. She kept her hands at her sides and made no move to greet Gannon or Muller. She ignored the American and spoke directly to Gannon. 'We need to talk,' she said coldly.

'Sure,' said Gannon. He gestured at the exit. 'We've a car waiting outside. We can talk back at the hotel.'

'We can talk here,' she said. 'I'm on the next flight back to London.'

Muller held out his hand. 'Howdy,' he said. 'I'm John Muller.'

Button looked at him disdainfully. 'I know who you are, Mr Muller, and I know what you're doing here. The less you talk to me, the better. Now, would you be so good as to take Mr Shepherd back to your hotel while I talk to the Major? Thank you.' She turned away from the American and looked at Gannon again. 'There's a coffee shop over there,' she said, nodding at the far side of the arrivals area.

Muller and Shepherd headed for the exit, while Gannon walked with her to the coffee shop. She sat down at a corner table and crossed her legs. 'I'll have tea,' she said. 'Anything but Earl Grey.'

Gannon went to the counter and ordered. He carried the cups to the table and sat down opposite her, his back ramrod straight. 'Would you like something to eat?' he asked.

'I ate on the plane,' she said. She picked up her spoon and stirred her tea slowly, even though she hadn't put in any sugar. He waited for her to speak, knowing that anything he said would probably antagonise her.

'It's not often that words fail me,' she said eventually. 'I've had eight hours on the plane to think about what I was going to say to you and, frankly, I'm still at a loss. What the hell do you think you're doing?'

'Whatever it takes,' said Gannon. 'One of my men is about to be executed and I'm not prepared to let that happen without a fight.'

'But he's not one of your men, is he?' said Button. 'Mitchell is a civil contractor. He hasn't served with the Regiment for more than five years.'

'Once Sass, always Sass,' said Gannon.

'Well, that's very noble, Major, but the fact remains that Mitchell was in Iraq earning a thousand dollars a day for guarding an oil pipeline. He was in the wrong place at the wrong time for no other reason than that he was greedy. And now you're putting your career on the line in some misguided attempt to drag his nuts out of the fire.' She put the spoon back in the saucer. 'Worse, you've co-opted one of my people into your venture. You've encouraged Spider to lie to me, throw away his career and risk his life. God damn you, Gannon, he's a single parent. If anything happens to him, who's going to look after his boy?'

'It was his choice,' said Gannon. 'And the way I understand it, it was more omission than lying. He just didn't tell you what he was doing.'

'He spun me some line about needing time off to move house. That was a direct lie.'

'And if he had asked your permission to come to Dubai to help rescue Mitchell, what would your reaction have been?'

'This isn't about who said what to whom,' said Button. 'You've no right to be out here, and neither has Spider. What happened to Geordie Mitchell is a nightmare, but that doesn't give you the right to go charging in like International Rescue.'

'If we don't do something, he'll die,' said Gannon, flatly.

'What about the Regiment?' said Button.

'If they knew where he was, they'd go in,' said Gannon, 'but we've no intel. And no prospect of getting it by conventional means.'

'What you're planning is madness, you know that?'

'We've tried everything else.'

'What have you tried?'

'How much has Spider told you?'

Button flashed him a tight smile. 'There you go again, playing games. What does it matter how much he did or didn't tell me? I'm not some pretty little secretary you can treat on a need-to-know basis.'

'I don't want to bore you with details you already have.'

'No, you were planning damage limitation. Find out what I know already and do your level best not to tell me anything else. That's not how this is going to work, Major Gannon.' She held up her right index finger and thumb less than an inch apart. 'I'm this close to making a phone call that will bring your world crashing down around you.'

Gannon nodded slowly but didn't say anything. He knew she held all the cards and it was up to her how she played them. He had the feeling that anything he said then would annoy her.

'I've another axe to grind with you,' said Button.

'I've no doubt,' said Gannon, drily.

'I gather you were responsible for introducing Spider to Richard Yokely.'

Gannon nodded.

'What the hell were you thinking?' said Button. 'You know what Yokely does.'

'He's sort of CIA,' said the Major.

Button sneered at him with contempt. 'You really do think I've got my head up my backside, don't you? "Sort of CIA" is like saying that Stalin had a temper. You know he was with the Intelligence and Security Command?'

Gannon nodded. 'Yes. AKA the Tactical Concept Activity.'

'That's right, they do love to play with words, don't they?'

'The guys on the Activity tried to get it renamed the Strategic Operations Brigade so that they could call themselves SOBs.'

'I heard that,' said Button. 'I also heard that Yokely left the Activity to join Grey Fox. You do know what Grey Fox is, don't you?'

The Major sighed. 'A presidential assassination squad,' he said quietly.

'Finally I'm getting something approaching candour from you,' said Button. She sat back and folded her arms. 'Yes. Yokely worked for a black unit tasked with assassination. Now he's moved on from Grey Fox to a place that's so off the radar I don't think it even has a name. Please don't insult my intelligence by telling me that he's "sort of CIA". Richard Yokely is a very dangerous man.'

'He wanted to meet Spider after what happened down the Tube when he shot the suicide-bomber.'

'Yokely wants Spider to work for him – you know that?'

'I guessed as much,' said Gannon. 'But Yokely told me he wanted an introduction, that's all.'

'And you were happy enough to give one, were you?'

'I've known Yokely for almost ten years. And Spider's big enough to take care of himself. I'm not in the business of nannying anyone, Charlotte.'

Button's eyes narrowed. 'I hope you're not suggesting I'm nannying him because that is most definitely not what is happening here,' she said. 'Richard Yokely is a devious bastard. You know he took Spider to Baghdad on a rendition flight?'

'We needed to question someone there.'

'Yokely was perfectly capable of handling the interrogation himself. Why do you think he wanted Spider with him?'

The Major said nothing.

'You know what I think? I think Yokely wanted Spider with him because he knew I'd find out and that when I did I'd sack Spider, so he'd be looking for a job. He set Spider up.'

'I don't see it that way,' said the Major. 'We asked Yokely for help and he came through.'

'Yokely only helps people if there's a payback,' said Button. 'I'm just looking after the best interests of one of my people. One of my team.'

'Same here,' said Gannon.

'Do you have any idea how many laws you've broken so far?' said Button. 'Have you given any thought to what will happen if you're caught?'

'We won't be caught,' said Gannon. 'But if we were, we'd take whatever they throw at us.'

'Your career counts for nothing? Because if this ever gets out, you're history. No more Increment, no more Regiment. You wouldn't be able to get a job watching over a building site.'

'My career counts for nothing if my men can't depend on me,' said Gannon, 'and that's a two-way street. If it was me in that basement wearing an orange jumpsuit, I'd expect my men to come and get me. There's a loyalty in the Regiment that goes beyond Queen and country, Charlotte, and you wouldn't understand it.'

'Screw you, Gannon,' said Button, bitterly. 'I demonstrate my loyalty by never lying to my people and by watching their backs. That's why I'm here, to protect Spider. To make sure you don't burn him.'

'I'm not going to burn him,' said Gannon. 'We're here to do a job. And if it all turns to shit I'll walk away from my career without a second thought. And if you want to pull the plug on what we're doing, then go ahead. I'm sure you know who to call.'

'Damn right I know who to call,' she said. 'I might not have your famous satellite phone by my side, but the Home Secretary takes my calls and I still have a lot of friends at Five.'

'Don't threaten me, Charlotte. You do what you have to do. But if you make that call, Geordie's blood will be on your hands.'

Button glared at Gannon. 'Don't even think about laying some sort of guilt trip on me,' she said. 'I'm not the one holding him hostage.'

'No, but we're his only hope of getting out alive. The government isn't doing anything, his company has done all it can. If we don't do something, Geordie will die. And that's not going to happen on my watch.'

Button sipped her tea and grimaced.

'Not good?' asked Gannon.

'I'm not here for the tea,' she said, putting her cup on the table. 'This scheme you and Spider have cooked up, do you think you stand a chance of pulling it off?'

'It's been planned before, but never tried,' said Gannon. 'A couple of years back, a group of ex-SAS and Delta Force guys were chasing a twenty-five-million-dollar reward for al-Zarqawi. The Americans wanted him badly so they'd put the reward out. But no one knew where he was. He was as well hidden as Bin Laden. That was when one of the SAS guys came up with the idea of using a GPS-enabled chip as a tracking device, implanting it in someone and using them as bait. They already had a guy lined up to be chipped. He was to get ten million because of the risks.'

'That's apocryphal,' said Button. 'An urban myth.'

'Spider knows one of the guys,' said Gannon.

'I'm sure a group of idiots was wandering around talking about it, but I can tell you that the technology isn't there yet. It's in development, and I've no doubt that it'll come, but right now there isn't anything small enough to be implantable.'

'I bow to your superior knowledge,' said Gannon. 'I'm sure if it was available MI5 would be using it.'

'We can tag vehicles and equipment with GPS trackers,' said Button, 'but it's the battery size that precludes subcutaneous transmitters. They're small and they're getting smaller year by year, but there's still a way to go.'

'Well, you live and learn,' said Gannon.

'Supposing you do find out where they're holding Mitchell, what then? You'll need manpower.'

'Once we've got a location, we can call on the Regiment, or if time's an issue we can bring in the coalition forces. Prior to that, there's three others with me and Spider, all guys who have worked with Geordie, and John Muller. He's got a team in place in Iraq, mainly South African mercenaries they use for armed protection. Half a dozen. So, twelve in all.'

'And you think that'll be enough? The Dirty Dozen?'

'Too many and we'll stick out. This is only going to work if they think Spider's out there on his own.'

'And when do you plan to go in?'

'I guess that's up to you,' said Gannon.

'I've already told you, none of this is on my shoulders,' said Button.

'But without your acquiescence we can't go ahead.'

Button nodded thoughtfully. She picked up her teacup again, saw that a dark scum had started to form on the surface, and put it down. 'What you're planning is madness,' she said. 'I've already told Spider so. And I've also told him that his responsibilities as a father outweigh his loyalty to a former colleague.'

'There's more to it than that,' said Gannon. 'Geordie saved Spider's life in Afghanistan.'

'I know what happened in Afghanistan,' said Button, brusquely. 'That was a war zone and Mitchell did what any other soldier would have done.'

'Agreed,' said Gannon. 'But Spider's not for turning on this.'

'You're all as bad as each other,' said Button. 'You want to be bloody heroes. It's the testosterone coursing through your veins.'

'Spider reckons he owes Geordie a debt, and I can understand that.'

Button gave him a withering look. 'I'm not saying I don't understand what he's doing,' she said, 'but just because what he's doing is understandable doesn't make it any less suicidal.'

'He'll have back-up.'

'At the last count there were about a hundred and fifty thousand coalition troops in Iraq, and the death toll rises every day. Back-up counts for nothing there. What counts is not putting yourself at risk.'

'Spider's a pro. He'll be doing for me what he does for you. Playing a role. We'll be watching over him every step of the way. When they take him they'll want to keep him alive so long as he's useful to them.'

'Fourteen days.'

'You say that like it's a death sentence, but it's not. It's a window of opportunity. Nothing will happen to him during those fourteen days.'

'Other than that he'll be in the hands of men who'll think nothing of hacking off his head. I don't even know why I'm here.'

'Because you know we're doing the right thing,' said Gannon, quietly. 'Because if one of your people was out there, you'd be moving heaven and earth to get them back.'

Button put her hand up to her face and massaged the bridge of her nose as if she was trying to ward off a headache. 'If he dies . . .'

'He won't,' said Gannon.

'You can't promise that,' said Button.

'I can promise I'll do whatever it takes to keep him alive,' he said. 'Are you going to allow us to proceed? Or are you going to make that phone call?'

Button took a deep breath and exhaled slowly. 'Do what you have to do,' she said.

'What's happening about the equipment?' asked Gannon.

'I've allowed Spider to take what he needs. He has two small GPS trackers. One can be fitted into a shoe, the other is more powerful but bigger so I've no idea where you can put it that it won't be discovered. The equipment's untraceable. There's nothing that will lead back to us.'

'Thank you,' said Gannon.

Button stood up. 'Don't thank me,' she said. 'I am vehemently opposed to what you're doing, but I sympathise with your motives. I want one thing understood, though. No more going behind my back with one of my men – with any of them. If they work for me they answer to me, and if you want to start playing fast and loose with them you talk to me first.'

'Understood,' said Gannon. 'And if anything should go wrong, we never had this conversation.'

'Don't do me any favours,' she said. 'I'm a big girl, I can take care of myself.'

'I can see that,' said Gannon.

'Flattery will get you absolutely nowhere,' said Button. She walked away, heels clicking on the tiled floor.

Gannon sighed. He had the feeling he'd got off lightly.

The flight from Dubai to Baghdad was on a chartered Boeing 727 and there wasn't a single female passenger on board. Muller had a dozen of his people on the plane, most of whom were former American soldiers heading back to Iraq after a week's R&R. Shepherd sat next to him close to the front of the plane. As it taxied for take-off, Muller took a pair of reading glasses out of his jacket pocket, a sheaf of papers from a leather briefcase and began to read, occasionally making marks in the margin with a gold fountain pen.

After an hour a stewardess in a tight-fitting green uniform handed out plastic trays with finger sandwiches, followed by a colleague offering coffee or tea. Shepherd passed on the food and the drink. Muller took a cheese sandwich and put away his paperwork. 'This is your first time in Baghdad, right?' he asked.

'Yeah,' said Shepherd. The lie came easily. He doubted that Yokely would want too many people knowing that he had been a passenger on a rendition flight. 'Although I was in Afghanistan when I was with the Regiment. Another life.'

'Iraq's not dissimilar,' said Muller. 'The difference is that before Saddam Iraq was a decent enough country. He ran it into the ground.'

'The Major said you were special forces. Delta Force, yeah?'

'On the fringes,' said Muller. 'Again, it was another life. I was in Vietnam, way back when. Part of the Phoenix Program. Winning hearts and minds and throwing Viet Cong out of helicopters when that didn't work.'

'You must have been a kid,' said Shepherd.

'I was twenty when I went in, twenty-two when we ran away with our tails between our legs. But I tell you, Dan, I saw the way things went in 'Nam and I see the same things going wrong in Iraq.'

'You can't beat insurgents with brute force, you mean?'

'There's that,' agreed Muller. 'But the problem isn't so much the mootwah, it's what the hell happens after the mootwah.'

'What the hell is mootwah?'

'Military Operations Other Than War,' said Muller. He grinned. 'MOOTW. Mootwah. It's how the top brass describe what's going on over there. You see, Dan, it can't go on for ever. At some point, the coalition forces are going to have to leave. It probably won't be helicopters flying off embassy roofs, but they'll be going. When we pulled out of Vietnam in 1973, the South Vietnamese military was the fourth largest in the world. More than a million men under arms. And what happened when we left? They let the North Vietnamese walk right over them. Most of the men we trained threw away their uniforms and went to ground. Then what happened? Sixty-five thousand executions, and a quarter of a million people sent to "re-education camps" so they could be taught how to be better citizens. And two million refugees for the world to deal with.'

'And the same's going to happen in Iraq?'

'I'd bet my bottom dollar on it. It doesn't matter how much money we throw at them, how well we train them, how much we fire them up to believe in the American way, at the end of the day it's down to character and I don't think they're up to the job. The moment we leave, Iran will urge on the insurgents and you won't see the men we've trained for dust. And Europe'll be picking up the pieces. You'll have a refugee problem the like of which you've never seen before and Londonistan will be their city of choice.' He grinned. 'That's what they're calling your capital city these days, you know that?'

'Yeah, I heard that,' said Shepherd. 'So, what's the solution?'

'There is no solution. Saddam had his own insurgents to deal with, the Kurds and the Shias. His solution was to kill as many as he could, and that's not an option available to the coalition forces. We're trying to win hearts and minds, but that didn't work in Vietnam and it won't work in Iraq.'

'You're pissing in the wind, then?'

'I'll piss into any wind if I'm paid enough,' said Muller. 'I'm just a hired hand. Our company has contracts worth twenty million dollars a year in Iraq and we get paid whatever happens. They talk about the billions being spent on rebuilding the country but that's a joke because the lion's share is going to pay security firms like us. For every man doing basic reconstruction work another three are guarding him.'

'Good business to be in, I guess.'

'If you want, I could use you,' said Muller.

'Like you used Geordie?' Muller frowned and Shepherd saw he'd offended him. 'Sorry, John, I didn't mean it like that.'

'He wanted the job,' said Muller, 'and he knew the risks.'

'I know. He's a pro. I was with him in Afghanistan. But being in a place like Afghanistan or Iraq as a soldier and being there as a hired hand are two different things.'

'You'll put your life on the line out of duty, but not for money, is that it?'

Shepherd laughed. 'Doesn't make sense, does it?'

'It shows the sort of man you are,' said Muller.

'If I was just after the money, I wouldn't be a cop,' said Shepherd.

'So why do you do it?'

'You're as bad as my psychiatrist,' said Shepherd.

Muller looked surprised. 'You're in therapy?'

'No, my unit insists on regular psychological checks to make sure that its operatives are fit for duty.'

'And are you?'

'So she says. But it's a question that has to be answered. I'm an undercover cop, which means I'm putting my life on the line regularly for a civil servant's salary. That doesn't make sense to some people. There has to be another reason.'

'Because you want to be one of the good guys, right?'

Shepherd grinned. 'It's a bit more complex than that.'

'Is it? It can't just be about the adrenaline rush – you'd get more of one in Baghdad than you would on any undercover operation at home. Or you could change sides and become a criminal. That way you'd get the rush *and* the money.'

'It's not about the money, that's true,' said Shepherd. 'I wouldn't have to go to Iraq for a better pay cheque. There are plenty of opportunities in the UK.'

'So it's about being on the side of law and order?'

'It sounds corny when you put it that way.' There was a plastic bottle of water in the back of the seat in front of him. Shepherd took it, unscrewed the top and drank. 'It's something I don't quite understand myself. I get a kick out of the challenge – to go up against big-time villains, knowing it's me against them and that if I do my job right they go to prison, there's a buzz in it that's even better than combat. I mean, a bullet whizzing by your head clarifies your mind and gets your heart pumping, but it usually happens so fast that it's all about instinct. Going undercover against criminals or terrorists is more cerebral. It's like playing chess, and the player who thinks furthest ahead is the one who generally wins.'

'The thrill of the chase?'

'I suppose so. But when it works out there's also the satisfaction of knowing you've taken a bad guy off the streets. That's why I wouldn't want to work in Iraq. It's all defensive.'

'Don't tell me I'm a glorified security guard, because there's more to it than that,' said Muller, waving a finger in Shepherd's face. He smiled to show that he wasn't being too serious.

'I'm not belittling what you do,' said Shepherd. 'I'm just saying it's not what I want. There are plenty of guys who are more than happy to do the work. The SAS is losing a lot – they're getting out early so that they can work in Iraq where they can almost quadruple their salary. That's probably how Geordie saw it.'

'Geordie liked the work, too. We have a good team on the ground. The South Africans are our core and I'd put them up against any soldiers in the world. And they've trained a good group of Iraqis. There's a real camaraderie.'

'Geordie always enjoyed being part of a team.' Shepherd grimaced. He'd used the past tense. 'Shit – we're talking as if he was dead already.'

Five minutes later, the plane banked and began its corkscrew descent. Shepherd smiled as he saw Shortt and Armstrong go white. 'Bloody hell,' said Armstrong, through gritted teeth. 'What the hell's going on?

'Evasive action,' said Muller. 'Better safe than sorry.'

'Evading what?' shouted Shortt, as the plane's speed increased.

'RPGs,' said Muller.

'Lovely.' Shortt rubbed his moustache nervously.

Shepherd tried to relax as the plane spiralled down. He looked around the cabin. The majority of the passengers had clearly been through the stomach-churning descent several times and were taking it in their stride, reading or listening to iPods. Out of the window he saw the desert spinning by. A road. Sand. Palm trees. Flat-topped buildings. Then a glimpse of runway. The spinning was disorienting. Shepherd rested his head against the seat back and stared straight ahead.

Touchdown was perfect, the wheels of the airliner kissing the runway and slowing to walking pace before they turned on to a taxiway and headed for the terminal.

It took them an hour to get through Immigration. They went through together and, after showing their passport and a letter of authorisation from John Muller's company, were each given a visa. Shepherd wasn't travelling under his real name: he was using a passport he had been given for an undercover case the previous year.

The arrivals area was like the Wild West. It seemed that every Westerner there was armed to the teeth and wearing body armour. Within seconds Shepherd had seen a dozen different types of handgun, along with carbines, shotguns and rifles. There were men with bands of ammunition over their shoulders, twin holsters on their hips, huge hunting knives strapped to arms and legs, and machetes hanging from belts. There were men in baseball caps, cowboy hats or with bandanas tied round their heads.

'This is a freak show,' said Armstrong, dropping his bag on the ground and lighting a cigarette.

'Any Westerner can carry a gun,' said Muller. 'Sometimes it gets taken to extremes.'

'Who the hell are they planning to shoot?' asked Shepherd. Most of the Westerners looked as if they were about to go to war, but virtually all of the locals, other than those in police and army uniforms, were dressed casually, either in traditional *dishdasha*s or in jeans and T-shirts. There was a lot of posing going on, the heavily armed Westerners standing with their hands on their hips, scrutinising the crowds through impenetrable sunglasses.

'I wish I was hard,' said O'Brien, dropping his bag next to Armstrong's.

'Half of those guys look like they're on drugs,' said Shortt.

'They might well be,' said Muller. 'Not everyone is too selective about who they take on out here. There's a fair number of Walter Mitty types about.'

Shepherd looked at Muller. 'You're serious, are you? Any Westerner can wander around with whatever firepower he chooses?'

'I've never heard of there being any restrictions,' said Muller. 'The army might say something if you wandered around with an RPG but I've seen pretty much every hand-held weapon out here.'

'Grenades?' asked O'Brien.

'Smoke grenades, sure. And Thunderflashes. Regular grenades are probably a grey area.'

'And if they kill someone?'

'Depends who dies,' said Muller. 'Frankly, most of this shit is for show. How many guns can you fire? You need a long and a short and that's it. There's a woman we see now and then who has a samurai sword on her belt.' He grinned when he saw the astonishment on Shepherd's face. 'I'm not making that up.'

'Don't tell me your guys are dressed like Ninjas,' said the Major, walking up with his holdall. It was about the only time Shepherd had ever seen him without the metal briefcase that contained his satellite phone.

'They're a bit more restrained,' said Muller. He led them outside to where two Toyota Land Cruisers were waiting, similar to the ones they had used in Dubai, and a Mercedes SUV with gunports in the front, side and rear windows. The logo of Muller's company was on all the doors. Three large men with Uzis in nylon slings and a dark-haired woman with a shotgun, all wearing khaki fatigues and body armour, were standing by the vehicles. Muller introduced them, all South Africans. Joe Haschka was the biggest, with a shock of red hair and freckles across his broad nose and cheeks; Ronnie Markus was lanky with a crooked smile and mirrored sunglasses; Pat Jordan was the oldest, in his late forties, with a grey crew-cut and a tattoo of a leaping panther across his left forearm; Carol Bosch was in her late twenties with shoulder-length wavy black hair and charcoal grey eyes. They took it in turns to shake hands with everyone. Bosch had the tightest grip of the four, as if she enjoyed showing the men how strong she was.

There were two large duffel bags on the ground by the first Land Cruiser and Bosch knelt down to open them. 'Helmets and body armour,' she said, in a strong Afrikaans accent. 'The only time we don't wear them is when we're in the compound.' She handed out the equipment. 'You're a big one, aren't you?' she said to O'Brien. 'Biggest I've got is XXL.'

O'Brien gave her a cold smile. 'It'll be fine, right enough,' he said.

'You can loosen the straps.'

'Carol,' he said frostily, 'it'll be fine.'

Shepherd pulled on his body armour and the Kevlar helmet, then picked up his holdall. Three other men were driving the vehicles, also South African.

'No locals?' Shepherd asked Muller, who was adjusting his body armour.

'We're not going to be using any on this,' he answered. 'Our Iraqi team members have been vetted and I'd vouch for them, but in case we run into problems, a foreign passport will be a big advantage.'

'They know what we're going to be doing?' asked Shepherd.

'They know we're going to try to get Geordie,' said Muller. 'That's all they wanted to know. We'll have a full briefing at the villa.'

'Are we staying in the Green Zone?' asked Shepherd.

'Our place is a mile or so outside it,' said Muller. 'We used to have a place inside, but it was a pain getting in and out. At busy times you can be three hours getting through the checkpoint and you're more of a target standing in line there than almost any-where else in the city. We've got three villas in a compound and we control the security. We know the locals and go out of our way not to annoy them.'

Shepherd, Muller and the Major got into one of the Land Cruisers. Pat Jordan took his Uzi from its sling and climbed into the front passenger seat. He kept the gun on his lap, his finger resting on the trigger guard. He popped a piece of chewing-gum into his mouth and his jaw worked rhythmically as his head moved left and right.

O'Brien, Armstrong and Shortt got into the other Land Cruiser with Bosch, while Haschka got into the Mercedes.

The convoy started up and drove slowly through an armed checkpoint manned by American soldiers and Iraqi troops. The Americans were wearing full body armour and Kevlar helmets, but the Iraqis either had not been given armour or had decided not to wear it. The Americans stared stonily as the convoy went by, but the Iraqis smiled and one, a Saddam Hussein lookalike, gave them a thumbs-up. They drove out on to the main road. 'How's it been while I was away?' Muller asked Jordan.

'Company-wise, we've been fine,' said Jordan. 'The city's heating up. Two car bombs yesterday, three the day before. And that bloody sniper's making everyone nervous. The only good thing is that he seems to favour Americans.'

'What about hostage-taking?' asked Shepherd. 'Anything recent?'

'An American camera crew was snatched in Basra two days ago but there's been no demand yet.'

Ahead they could see two Iraqi ambulances at the side of the road, parked next to an electricity pylon. 'What happened there?' asked Shepherd.

Jordan laughed harshly. 'The electricity company's been cutting the power off at night to save money. Some of the locals realised they could climb the pylons and cut the wires to sell for scrap while the power was off. They took hundreds of metres and the power company got fed up with replacing it. So last night they cut the power off and switched it back on an hour later. They electrocuted four men, but when the army saw the bodies they were worried it might be a trap so they sealed off the area while they checked for IEDs. They're only just clearing the bodies away.'

'Poor bastards,' said Shepherd.

'Yeah, literally,' said Jordan. 'That's the biggest problem out here. Money's pouring into Iraq but there's hardly any trickle-down. The locals who get jobs with the coalition forces or the international companies do all right, but everyone else is living hand-to-mouth.'

'Not that different from South Africa, then,' said the Major.

'There's a lot of similarities,' said Jordan, 'but the murder rate here is a hell of a lot higher.'

They drove past a dusty football pitch where a group of Iraqi youngsters were kicking around an old ball between makeshift goalposts. Two Humvees were parked nearby and a half dozen soldiers in flak jackets and helmets watched the game, M16s resting on their hips.

Two horses, their ribs outlined against their hides, wandered behind one of the goalposts. Clouds of flies swarmed round them, but the animals didn't seem bothered.

Everywhere Shepherd looked he saw discarded plastic water bottles, in the road, in the gutters, on the pavements, in the central reservation of the road, and in the fields they drove past. The three vehicles powered down the main road. Shepherd could see that the driver spent as much time checking the verges as he did looking ahead. 'IEDs still the big problem here?' he asked Muller.

'It's their weapon of choice,' said Muller. 'We still have suicide-bombers but they figured out some time back that there was no point in losing an operative unless they had to. They still use suicide-bombers against the Green Zone or well-guarded buildings, but the IEDs are taking the biggest toll. They put explosives in anything – dead dogs and cats, garbage bags, drainage holes. Last month they rigged up a cow.'

'A dead one?' said Shepherd.

'No, it was still alive. They put the cow under, cut it open, pushed the IED into the body cavity and sewed it up. When it came to they tethered it by the road and blew up a police patrol, killing four Iraqi cops. The bombmakers are constantly evolving so you have to be on the alert for anything.'

'How do they detonate them?'

'Some are triggered by a sensor in the road, others by wire from a distance. Cellphones did the job until the army started using jammers.' He grinned. 'Every time an American big-shot flies into Baghdad, the cellphone system shuts down.'

'The IED that got Geordie, what was the story there?' asked Shepherd.

'It was a big one in a parked car. His vehicle was driving past and it went off. Blew his Land Cruiser across the road.'

'Why would a commercial vehicle be a target?'

'It almost certainly wasn't,' said Jordan, from the front seat. 'It was detonated by wire so they knew what they were doing. They'd parked it opposite a Sunni-run import-export business and I'd guess that was the target. When they saw Geordie's Land Cruiser they thought they'd go for two birds with one stone. That's what I think, anyway.'

'How much of a target would you be, generally?'

'Any Westerner's a target,' said Jordan, 'but there are different sorts. The insurgents generally strike at the coalition forces. They throw mortars at the Green Zone, car bombs at checkpoints and they fire RPGs at convoys. They're making a point, you know, which is lost when they blow up a commercial vehicle. The criminal gangs target any Westerner, but they tend to go for the weakest links. You never hear of them kidnapping a four-star general, do you? They take engineers, journalists and charity workers, the ones who aren't defended. Guys like us fall into the grey area between. We're not important enough to get the insurgents fired up, and we're too well armed to be kidnapped. Geordie was the first of our guys to run into a problem.'

'I saw on CNN that there are twelve hundred killings a month. They're not all coalition troops, are they?'

'Mainly locals,' said Muller. 'The insurgents keep killing police and army recruits, most of whom are Sunnis. But the Sunnis give as good as they get. There's a lot of tit-for-tat going on.'

'Do you have problems recruiting locals?' asked Shepherd.

'The problem is dealing with all the applicants,' said Muller. 'For every vacancy around three hundred men want the job. They want to feed their families. Most Iraqis are good, honest, hard-working people. I'd stack the guys working for us here against any of our employees in the States.'

'It's the insurgents that are the problem?'

'Damn right,' said Muller. 'And most are from outside Iraq. They can't afford to have democracy work here because of the domino effect around the region.'

'What John isn't telling you, though, is that every day more ordinary Iraqis are lining up with the insurgents,' said Jordan. 'They've had enough of their country being occupied and they want the coalition forces out.'

'Like I said back in London, it's a minefield,' said Muller. 'Anyway, the politics don't worry me. We're here to do a job as professionally as possible.'

They turned off the main road and drove through a pretty suburb, the pavements dotted with spreading palm trees. Most of the houses were in gated compounds.

'This is one of the more upmarket residential suburbs,' said Muller. 'In Saddam's day it was where his favoured civil servants lived. Now most of it is rented to expats.'

Several houses had armed guards in front of them, walls topped with broken glass, hi-tech barbed wire and CCTV cameras. It was a stark contrast to the peaceful suburbs Shepherd had driven through in Dubai.

Ahead there was a line of parked cars, the drivers leaning against the vehicles. 'What's going on there?' asked Shepherd.

'That's the line for the local filling station,' said Muller. 'The locals can wait up to five hours for fuel.' There were no women in the queue, and most of the men glared at the Mercedes and Land Cruisers as they went by. The filling station was surrounded by anti-blast barriers topped with razor wire, and half a dozen Iraqis with AK-47s guarded the entrance and exit.

'You'd think that with all the oil they've got petrol would be easier to buy,' said Shepherd.

'It's not that there's a shortage, it's the security,' said Muller. 'Gas stations are prime targets for insurgents.'

The convoy took a left turn, then a right, and ahead a large metal gate rattled open. Two big Iraqi men stood at attention in dark blue uniforms, pistols holstered on their waists. One was talking on a transceiver, the other saluted briskly as they drove into the compound.

'Home sweet home,' said Muller.

The three vehicles pulled up in a large concrete courtyard bordered by three two-storey houses with flat roofs. Three flags flew on angled poles that protruded over the main door of the middle building – the Stars and Stripes, the South African and Iraqi flags. The buildings were shaded by tall palm trees and terracotta pots, filled with glossy-leaved bushes, dotted the court-yard.

They climbed out of the Land Cruisers and the Mercedes as the metal gate rattled shut. Muller pointed at the central building. 'Those are offices, the communications centre and equipment store,' he said. He gestured at the house on the right, 'Most of our guys are billeted there when they're in town,' then at the third: 'We've got guest quarters over there, and the ground floor is for eating and recreation. A local cooks for us but the guys are big fans of barbecues.'

'Sounds good,' said the Major.

'We thought we'd eat first,' said Jordan. 'We've had nothing since breakfast.'

'Fine by me,' said the Major. 'The food on the plane wasn't great.'

'Pat here does the barbecuing,' said Bosch. 'He'll make someone a terrific wife one day.'

'Don't make me shoot you again, Carol,' said Jordan.

She raised her eyebrows in mock horror. 'You said that was an accident.'

Muller suggested that they shower and change first, so Shepherd, the Major, Armstrong, Shortt and O'Brien carried their bags into the guest house. Downstairs, there was a pool table and a big-screen television beside a wall lined with DVDs. A staircase led up to the bedrooms. Each had its own shower room.

Shepherd took off the bulky body armour, showered, changed into a grey polo shirt and black jeans, then went downstairs and out through a back door that led to a terraced area. Beyond, he could see a large swimming-pool, complete with diving-board. Jordan was presiding over a huge brick-built barbecue, his shirtsleeves rolled up. In front of him, hissing and spitting, were some of the biggest pieces of meat Shepherd had ever seen. O'Brien was standing next to him.

Muller had changed into a garish Hawaiian shirt, baggy shorts and flip-flops, with Ray-Bans on top of his head. He was holding a bottle of Budweiser and pointed at a blue and white cooler filled with beer and wine. 'Help yourself,' he said.

'Booze is okay here?' asked Shepherd.

'In the compound it's fine,' said Muller. 'We can't be seen from the outside.'

There was the rattle of gunfire in the distance – Kalashnikovs, half a dozen at least. The shooting went on for a full thirty seconds, which Shepherd knew meant that a fair amount of reloading was going on. 'That sounds like a waste of perfectly good rounds,' he said.

'You hear it all the time,' said Muller, laconically. 'Weddings, funerals, birthdays, any chance they get they'll let loose.'

'They understand the basic rule of gravity? Everything that goes up has to come down?' asked Shepherd, and helped himself to a Budweiser. A bottle opener was tied to the lid of the cooler and he used it to flip off the cap.

'They get so caught up in it that they forget,' said Muller. 'There's at least ten deaths a week from bullets falling out of the sky, and God alone knows how many injuries.'

'The police and the army don't do anything?'

'Most of the time it's the cops and soldiers doing the firing,' said Muller.

The sun was going down and a slight breeze blew across the swimming-pool that felt good on Shepherd's skin. Two military helicopters clattered overhead. Shepherd craned his neck and shaded his eyes. Apaches. Serious helicopters with serious firepower.

Armstrong and the Major came outside, followed by Bosch, Haschka and two of the drivers. The men were all wearing casual shirts and shorts but Bosch had changed into a green and blue rough silk dress that showed off a pair of good legs. Her hair was loose and she had put on a thin gold necklace with a jade charm. She was much more feminine without her fatigues and body armour, and had a much sexier walk now that she had swapped army boots for strappy sandals. She went to Jordan and obviously said something that riled him because he waved a spatula at her.

O'Brien walked up to them with a plate of steaks. 'Are you guys eating?' he asked.

'Is there any left?' asked Shepherd.

O'Brien grinned.

Shepherd went over to the barbecue and picked up a plate. The meat smelled good, and there was a lot of it. Jordan slapped a huge T-bone steak on to his plate, then a lamb chop and a chicken drumstick.

'Vegetables?' asked Shepherd, hopefully.

Bosch slapped him on the back. 'In South Africa, chicken is a vegetable.' She laughed. 'You need fattening up, anyway. Get some meat on your bones.' She picked up a plate and pointed at the steak she wanted, a massive T-bone that virtually covered her plate and was still dripping blood.

They walked together to a large table on the terrace, where O'Brien was already sitting. Shepherd and Bosch sat down opposite him. 'I could get used to this,' said O'Brien, through a mouthful of steak. Shepherd picked up his knife and fork. He didn't feel like eating, but he knew his body needed fuel for what lay ahead. He cut a piece of steak and forced himself to chew.

Muller's transceiver crackled. He put it to his ear and spoke into it. Then he said, 'The cavalry's here.' A minute later there was a knock on the front door. He went to open it and came back with Richard Yokely. He was wearing a blue flak jacket over a cream safari suit and was holding a Kevlar helmet.

'I just hope that Charlotte Button doesn't know you've ridden into town,' said the Major, shaking Yokely's hand. 'You're just about her least favourite person at the moment.'

Yokely grinned. 'What's upset the lovely Charlie now?' he asked.

Shepherd raised a hand. 'That would be me,' he said.

'She's on your case, is she?'

'She's not a happy bunny,' said Shepherd.

'She knows you're here?'

'She does now, yes.'

'And she's given her blessing?'

Shepherd shrugged. 'It's more that I'm here on sufferance.'

The Major put a hand on Yokely's shoulder. 'For those of you who don't already know him, this is Richard. He's going to help us keep tabs on Spider.'

Yokely raised a hand in salute, and the Major introduced the rest of the team to him. 'Have I missed much?' Yokely asked.

'We were waiting for you,' said Shepherd. 'Not everyone knows what's going to happen, so I'll run through it from the start.'

'I'm all ears,' said Yokely.

★   ★   ★

The Sniper liked shooting at night. For one thing, it was cooler. During the day, lying in wait for hours meant putting up with the interminable Baghdad heat, always in the high forties and often the fifties. Even if he was lucky enough to find a place in the shade, it was still unbearably hot and he had to keep drinking to replenish the water he lost through sweat. The nights were more comfortable: there were fewer patrols and fewer locals, which meant there was less chance of him being spotted. There were only two downsides of killing at night: fewer Americans were around to shoot at – mostly they stayed in their vehicles – and the flash from the barrel of his rifle could be seen.

The Americans had helicopters over the city all the time, and above them the unmanned planes they used for surveillance, with cameras so powerful they could look down through cloud and see everything. At night his body temperature was more visible to infrared sensors, so he shot from a concealed position whenever he could. He'd found an abandoned apartment on the fourth floor of a building that overlooked one of the city's busy inter-sections. He had a locksmith friend who had made him a key to get into it.

Tonight's kill was to be special. The Sniper was hunting a specific target. A month earlier an American Humvee had killed a four-year-old girl. It had been in the middle of the day and the child had been with her mother, walking on the pavement. The woman had stopped to cross the road. She'd seen the Humvee speeding towards them, followed by three troop-carriers, but the little girl had been looking the other way and had stepped into the path of the convoy. The Humvee hadn't even slowed and she had died immediately. Bits of her body were scattered over fifty yards.

When the Humvee stopped, the driver had stayed in his cab. A lieutenant and four soldiers had piled out of a troop-carrier but there was nothing they could do. A group of angry Iraqis had gathered and youths threw stones at the soldiers. As word of the little girl's death spread, the crowd grew and within minutes several hundred men and women were screaming at the Americans. More stones were thrown and the lieutenant had pulled his men back. The convoy had driven off, leaving the mother kneeling in the road, weeping for her dead child.

Afterwards there had been no apology from the soldier who had been driving the Humvee, no acknowledgement from the army that they had been responsible for the little girl's death. The father had queued for hours to get into the Green Zone to talk to someone about what had happened, but had been refused entry. He had phoned but no one in authority had spoken to him. He had hired a translator to write a letter in English but it was ignored. The driver of the Humvee had never been put on trial. After a month the army announced that there had been an internal investigation and the little girl's death had been 'an unfortunate accident'. The case was closed. That was when her father had approached the Sniper. He had offered to pay him a thousand dollars to kill the Humvee driver, but the money had been refused. The Sniper did not kill for money. He killed because he wanted the infidels out of his country. He killed because they were the enemy, and because he was serving Allah by doing what he did best. The Sniper was happy to kill Americans, and even happier to know that every one he killed went straight to hell. He had turned down the offer of payment but told the father that, once the soldier had been killed, he was to pay for a party for the street he lived in: he should kill a dozen lambs and distribute the meat to the poor. The father had readily agreed.

The patrol varied its route each night, but the Sniper had a dozen men around the city waiting to report on which way it would be coming that night. On the three previous nights the patrol had taken a different route and the Sniper had gone home without firing his weapon. He shifted his weight. He had padded his knees with foam rubber but, even so, it was painful kneeling on the wooden floor. The tip of the Dragunov barrel was resting on the windowsill.

As the Spotter's mobile phone burst into life the Sniper jumped. The Spotter put the phone to his ear, listened, then grinned. He nodded at the Sniper. 'He is coming,' he said. 'He will be here in five minutes, *inshallah*. There are three Humvees and he is driving the second.'

The Sniper got himself into position. Tonight's would be a difficult shot, perhaps the most difficult he had ever made. The windows of the Humvee would almost certainly be up and the glass was bullet-proof. For him to make the shot, the window had to be down.

As he waited, the Sniper recited a passage from the Koran. Reciting the Koran brought him closer to his God and relaxed him. He knew that he did what he did with God's blessing. God had given him the talent to kill Americans, so the Sniper was sure that God smiled on him with every kill he carried out. And when it came time for the Sniper to leave his life on earth, he knew that God would have a special place for him in heaven.

The mobile phone rang and the Spotter took the call. 'Two minutes,' he said. '*Inshallah*.'

The Sniper took a deep breath. In two minutes another American would be dead.

Jeff Keizer yawned and wished he'd finished his coffee before he'd got into the Humvee. He badly needed a caffeine kick – he could barely keep his eyes open. He gripped the steering-wheel with gloved hands and blinked as he tried to focus on the vehicle in front of him.

'Come on, Jeff, stay awake,' said the soldier in the front passenger seat. Lance 'Mother' Hubbard was twenty-three but looked younger and always had a comic tucked into his body armour.

'I'm double shifting,' said Keizer. 'I should be asleep.'

'Who are you covering for?'

'Buddy. His stomach's playing up again.' The Humvee ahead turned sharply to the left and Keizer swung the wheel to follow. 'Call him up and tell him we're not in a race, will you?'

'There was an IED attack along this stretch yesterday,' said Hubbard. 'Everyone's a little jumpy.'

'Yeah, but we're supposed to be patrolling,' said Keizer. 'How are we supposed to see anything at this speed?'

'Better this than we get blown to pieces,' said Hubbard.

'Yeah, well, it was driving like this that got the little girl killed,' said Keizer. 'And Buddy's been a mess ever since.'

'It wasn't his fault,' said Hubbard. 'The inquiry cleared him.'

'That was a whitewash, and you know it. What did you think they'd do? Throw him to the wolves? Have him stand trial in an Iraqi court? That was never going to happen.'

'He wanted to talk to the parents, you know that?'

'Yeah. He said.'

'The brass told him not to go near them. Didn't want him to admit liability, but all he wanted to do was to tell them he was sorry. He's got a five-year-old sister. It's fucked him up and the army's doing nothing to help him.'

'Which is why I'm doing his shift,' said Keizer.

'Nah, you don't know how fucked up he is. He's talking about killing himself.'

'Are you serious?'

'Damn right,' said Hubbard.

'That's heavy,' mused Keizer.

'Jeff!' yelled Hubbard. The Humvee ahead had braked and was skidding to the right. Keizer stamped hard on his brake and cursed. He twisted the steering-wheel to the right and the vehicle started to skid. He pumped the brake and cursed again.

The Humvee skidded to a halt just feet away from the vehicle in front. A second later Keizer and Hubbard lurched forward as the third Humvee in the convoy thudded into them. Keizer looked in his rear-view mirror. The driver behind was throwing up his hands and swearing.

'What the hell happened?' asked Hubbard. He twisted in his seat and shouted up to his machine-gunner, Jack Needham, who was still at his post. 'You okay, Jack?'

'Bit bruised, but I saw it coming,' shouted Needham.

'What happened? Why did they stop?' asked Keizer.

'A pick-up truck shed its load at the intersection,' Needham yelled back. 'Boxes everywhere. You know how they overload those things.'

'Anyone hurt?'

'Two other cars have rammed the pick-up but our guys are okay. There's a row going on between the drivers. Road's blocked.'

'I don't like the sound of this,' said Keizer.

'If it had been an ambush they'd have started shooting by now,' said Hubbard. 'Chill, Jeff.'

Keizer used his radio to call up the front Humvee. 'What's happening, Sarge?' he asked.

'Stay put,' said the sergeant. 'We'll let the locals sort it out. No reason for us to get involved. A cop car's just arrived so the road will be clear in a minute or two.'

'Roger that,' said Keizer.

'Told you,' said Hubbard. 'You worry too much.'

'It's not-worrying that gets you killed out here,' said Keizer.

A small girl in a black headscarf ran towards their Humvee, wailing and waving her hands. 'What's her problem?' said Hubbard. 'Is she hurt?'

'Doesn't look like it,' said Keizer. He picked up the radio microphone again and clicked 'transmit'. 'Sarge, are we ready to go?'

'Hold your horses, Keizer.' The sergeant's voice crackled over the radio. 'The drivers have turned on the cops now.'

'Do you want our guys out?'

'Let's see if the locals can handle it. It's no big deal, just a fender-bender. If they can't handle that then we've been wasting our time out here.'

'Lighten up, Jeff,' said Hubbard.

'I've got a bad feeling, that's all,' said Keizer.

The girl banged on his window and yelled at him in Arabic.

'What's wrong?' Keizer asked her, but she just shook her head.

She pointed at the intersection and said something in Arabic, then wiped her eyes.

'I can't understand you,' he said.

'Open the window, Jeff,' said Hubbard.

'She could be an insurgent,' said Keizer.

'She's a kid, and she doesn't have a weapon,' said Hubbard. 'Scared of a child now, are you?'

'It's not about being scared, it's about following procedure.'

Hubbard grinned and clucked like a chicken.

'Screw you, Mother,' said Keizer.

The child put her face close to the window. She was sobbing and now he could make out what she was saying: 'Please, please, please, please . . .'

She was younger than Keizer had first thought. Twelve, eleven, maybe. 'Okay, okay,' said Keizer. He pressed the button to wind down the window. 'What's wrong?' he asked her.

The girl took a step back as the window wound down. She was still making sobbing noises but Keizer saw that her cheeks weren't wet. There were no tears.

The bullet smacked into the centre of his forehead. The back of his skull exploded, splattering blood and brain matter over Hubbard. Hubbard screamed and scrambled for the window control. Keizer slumped forward, what was left of his head smacking into the steering-wheel. The girl held on to her head-scarf and ran down the road, away from the convoy, her bare feet slapping against the Tarmac.

It was almost midnight. Shepherd and Bosch were alone in the main room at the guesthouse. Yokely had left an hour earlier and the Major had gone to the kitchen with O'Brien for a late-night snack. Armstrong, Shortt and the other South Africans had turned in. The plan was that they would head out just after dawn but Shepherd didn't feel sleepy and Bosch seemed disinclined to go to her room.

She was drinking a Corona lager from the bottle with a piece of lime pushed down the neck. It was her sixth or seventh, Shepherd hadn't been counting, but they didn't seem to have had any effect on her. He was drinking Jameson's with ice and soda and wasn't trying to keep up. They were sitting together on a black sofa and had propped their feet on the low table in front of them.

'You're taking one hell of a risk,' said Bosch. 'If anything goes wrong, you'll both be dead. And the way those bastards kill isn't pretty.'

'I owe it to him to try,' said Shepherd.

'All for one and one for all, the Three Musketeers crap?'

Shepherd took a swig of whiskey. 'There's more to it than that.'

'He's your gay lover?'

'You're a funny girl, Carol.'

'Just trying to lighten the moment, you being about to ride into the valley of death and all.'

Shepherd chuckled. 'Geordie saved my life in Afghanistan ten years ago. Another century.'

'Threw himself in front of a bullet for you?'

'Dug one out of my shoulder and patched me up, then carried me to a helicopter. He was the medic in my brick.'

'Brick?'

'That's what we call our four-man units. He was the medic. A captain had just been hit by a sniper and I was holding him while he died. Big mistake on my part, I should have been looking for cover but I stayed with the captain and got hit in the shoulder probably by the same sniper.'

'Can I see the scar?'

'What?'

'Come on, you show me yours and I'll show you mine.'

'I don't want to see yours.'

'Come on,' she said. 'Please.'

'If it'll shut you up.' He unbuttoned his shirt and pulled it back to reveal the scar just below his right shoulder. 'Satisfied?'

Bosch moved closer and ran a fingertip along it. 'Nice,' she said. She put her hand on his shoulder and turned him so that she could see his back. 'No exit wound,' she said.

'Yeah,' said Shepherd. 'It hit the bone and went downwards. Just missed an artery. Geordie got it out and stopped the bleeding.'

'Tampon?'

'What?'

'Best thing to plug a bullet hole. Can't beat them.'

'I'm pretty sure he used a regular field dressing. If he'd used a tampon he'd have told me. And I'd have got stuck with a new nickname.'

Bosch ran her finger across the scar again. 'I'm guessing a 5.45mm round?'

'Good guess,' said Shepherd, admiringly.

'AK-74?'

'And you know your assault rifles. Most people assume it was an AK-47.'

'I'm a big fan of the AK-74,' said Bosch, 'but you don't want to go firing one out here. The Yanks hear it, they'll assume you're with the bad guys.'

Shepherd buttoned his shirt. 'If it wasn't for Geordie, I'd have died in the desert. Like I said, I owe him big-time.'

The Major came out of the kitchen. 'Everything okay?' he said.

'Spider was just showing me his war wound,' said Bosch.

'He does that with all the girls,' said the Major. 'I don't want to sound like anyone's father but it's getting late and we're up at five tomorrow. I'm heading up.'

'I was about to turn in too,' said Shepherd, standing up.

Bosch raised her bottle. 'I'll finish this first. Sleep well, Spider.'

'You too.'

Bosch blew him a kiss. Shepherd and the Major walked together to the stairs. 'You okay?' the Major asked.

'Fine,' said Shepherd. 'I'll be happier once we're under way, that's for sure.' They went up the stairs together.

'You've got a good team behind you,' said the Major. 'The best.'

'I know. It'll be fine.'

'I'm supposed to be the one giving the pep talk.'

'I don't need one,' said Shepherd. 'I know what the risks are, and I know what I have to do. We just roll the dice and see what happens.'

They arrived at Shepherd's room. The Major held out his right hand, clenched into a fist. Shepherd banged his own against it. 'See you tomorrow,' said the Major.

Shepherd went into his room. He had just finished showering when there was a knock at the door. He assumed it was the Major and frowned as he wrapped a towel round his waist. He opened the door.

It was Carol Bosch, with the bottle of Jameson's. 'I thought I'd come and show you my scars,' she said.

'There's no need,' he said. 'Really.'

She ran her hand down her left thigh. 'I've got a really interesting knife wound here that I think you'd find fascinating.'

'Carol . . .'

Bosch pushed the door open and slipped inside. 'Where are the glasses?' she asked.

Shepherd closed the door. 'You're impossible,' he said.

'Here they are,' she said picking two glasses off the bedside table. She poured two slugs of whiskey and handed one to him. 'Nice towel,' she said, and clinked her glass against his. 'To being shot,' she said, 'and surviving.'

Shepherd sighed, but drank to her toast.

Bosch put her glass down on the bedside table and began to undo her dress.

'What is this? A condemned man's last request?' asked Shepherd.

'This isn't about you,' she said. 'Have you any idea how difficult it is to find a half-decent man out here?'

'Surprisingly enough, no,' he said.

She stepped forward, slipped her right hand behind his neck and kissed him. For a second Shepherd resisted, but her tongue probed between his teeth and he felt himself grow hard. She ran her other hand down the towel and between his legs.

Shepherd broke away. 'Carol—'

'What?'

'There's something you should know.'

'Well, we've already decided you're not gay. And you're not wearing a wedding ring.'

'I work undercover,' said Shepherd. 'Undercover cops don't wear wedding rings.'

'If you're married, it doesn't matter,' she said. 'I'm not asking for lifelong commitment. I just want to have sex with you.'

'She died,' said Shepherd. 'Three years ago.'

Suddenly Bosch looked concerned. 'I'm sorry.'

'I loved her.'

'Okay. I loved my husband, too, right up to the point I found him in bed with our maid. But this isn't about my ex-husband or your wife, this is about you and me.' She grabbed him and kissed him again. This time Shepherd kissed her back. Bosch pushed him towards the bed.

Shepherd put his hands on her shoulders. 'Carol, wait—'

'Now what?'

'I haven't had sex for a while.'

'Shame,' she said. 'How long?'

'A while.'

'A month?'

Shepherd shook his head.

She raised her eyebrows. 'A year?'

'A bit longer.'

'How much longer?'

Shepherd swallowed. 'Since Sue died.'

'Three years?'

'Thereabouts.'

Bosch's jaw dropped. 'Wow,' she said.

'I know.'

'Three *years*?' she repeated. 'Thirty-six months?'

'Or thereabouts.'

'You must really have loved her.'

'I did. I do. I always will. Just because she died doesn't mean I stopped loving her.'

Bosch looked into his eyes, her hand still between his legs. 'Let's get one thing straight,' she said. 'This isn't about love. It's lust. That's all.'

'Got it,' said Shepherd.

'And you're okay?'

Despite himself, Shepherd laughed. 'Yes,' he said. 'I'm okay.'

Bosch kissed him, then pushed him back on to the bed, holding the towel. She tossed it aside and took off her dress. 'Three years,' she said, in wonder. 'Fasten your seat-belt. This is going to be one hell of a ride.'

Mitchell lifted up his shirt and examined his damaged ribs. It hurt if he took a deep breath but he was sure that they weren't broken. He thought a couple were cracked, but other than that he hadn't been badly hurt. He had urinated into the plastic bucket and there had been no sign of blood so at least his kidneys were unscathed.

He sat down slowly, then lay back. He took a couple of deep breaths and tried to do a sit-up. The muscles in his side burned but he forced himself up.

He didn't care about the pain. It meant nothing. For the first time since he'd been snatched he didn't feel alone. Somewhere out there his friends were on the case. Mitchell was sure that Spider Shepherd would have been behind the kidnapping, probably with Billy Armstrong, Martin O'Brien and Jimbo Shortt. And, if he'd been able to get himself away from the Increment, Major Gannon would be running the show. Mitchell grunted and lowered his shoulders back to the floor. It hurt a lot more going down than it did coming up. It had been worth the beating for Mitchell to discover that his friends were fighting to free him and, from what Kamil had said, they were fighting dirty. They had kidnapped the brother of a man who was holding him hostage.

That meant they knew the identity of at least one of his captors. And if they knew one they might be able to identify the rest and there was a chance they would locate the basement. It was an outside chance, but it was a chance. He took a deep breath and did a second sit-up, faster this time. It still hurt, but not as much.

When Shepherd woke up he was alone in the bed. He rolled over and stared at the ceiling. The last thing he remembered was curling up with Carol in his arms and kissing her shoulder. She had been right. It had been one hell of a ride. She was passionate and aggressive in a way that Sue had never been, and vocal with it, at times screaming his name, at others cursing him, alternating between kissing and biting. Afterwards, as she had lain in his arms, Shepherd was surprised at the lack of guilt he felt. As he stared up at the ceiling he realised it was because he loved Sue, and knew he always would. What had happened between him and Carol had been purely physical.

He got out of bed, shaved and showered, then dressed and went downstairs. O'Brien was in the kitchen, frying eggs. The middle-aged Iraqi woman who normally cooked for the occupants of the house was hovering at his shoulder. 'Fry-up, Spider?' asked O'Brien.

Shepherd didn't know when he'd be eating again so he nodded. 'Please.' He poured himself a large mug of coffee and added a splash of milk.

'They can't fry eggs out here,' said O'Brien. 'They just heat them from below so the yolks don't cook.' He used a spatula to splash hot fat on to them. 'It's not going to be a full fry-up. They haven't got any bacon and the sausages are lamb.'

'She's a Muslim,' said Shepherd, nodding at the cook. 'She can't touch pork.'

'She doesn't have to touch it, just cook it,' said O'Brien.

'You're missing the point,' said Shepherd. He sat at the kitchen table and sipped his coffee.

'You okay?' asked O'Brien.

'Sure,' said Shepherd.

'Sleep well?'

'Like a log.'

'Was it my imagination or did I see Carol creeping out of your room this morning?'

'Screw you, Martin.'

'Okay, I get it. None of my business. But you are one jammy bastard. She's fit.'

Shepherd took another sip of his coffee. Carol Bosch appeared at the doorway. She had changed into clean fatigues and was carrying her flak-jacket, helmet and shotgun. A holstered automatic hung on her hip, and a large hunting knife was strapped to her right leg.

'Speak of the devil,' said O'Brien.

'What's that?' asked Bosch, as she sat down at the table and winked at Shepherd.

'I just asked if Spider thought you'd want breakfast in bed,' said O'Brien.

'I'd be careful how I talked to a woman wielding a shotgun,' said Bosch.

'How do you like your eggs?' asked O'Brien, with a grin.

'As they come,' she said. She put her gun on the table. 'How's it going, Spider?'

'I'm okay.'

'Butterflies?'

Shepherd shrugged. 'With you guys watching my back, I'll be fine.'

O'Brien put plates of food in front of them. Fried eggs, tomatoes, lamb sausages and fried bread. He put his own plate on the table and sat down. 'How long have you been in Baghdad?' he asked Bosch.

'Almost two years,' she said. 'I've been with John for the past eighteen months.'

'Good money?'

Bosch grinned. 'Bloody good,' she said. 'A thousand dollars a day basic, plus overtime, plus lots of paid time off and flights home. And there's nothing to spend your money on here so everything you earn goes straight into the bank.'

'How's it going to end?' asked Shepherd. 'Everyone I talk to says we're wasting our time in Iraq.'

'Everyone's right,' said Bosch. 'You can't force these people to live together. The only guy who could do that was Saddam and now he's out of the equation.'

'You're saying democracy won't work here?' asked O'Brien, through a mouthful of egg and sausage.

'I'm saying these people don't understand democracy,' said Bosch. 'Look what happened to Yugoslavia. So long as you have a hard man forcing people to live together, they get on with it. Take away the hard man and they kill each other.' She sliced her sausage into neat sections, popped a piece into her mouth and swallowed it without chewing. 'When Saddam was in power, the Sunnis ran Iraq. They account for barely a fifth of the population. Once we have elections, power transfers to the majority Shias. Which leaves them with scores to settle.' She put down her knife and held up her index finger. 'Possible scenarios down the line,' she said. 'Number one. All-out civil war, with the Sunni, Shia and Kurdish factions fighting it out to the death.' She held up two fingers. 'Two. The Shias take over Iraq, override the wishes of the Sunnis and the Kurds and align the country with Syria, Iran and Lebanon's Hezbollah.' She grinned. 'How stable would the Middle East be then?'

'Not very,' said Shepherd.

'I was being rhetorical,' she said. She held up three fingers. 'Three. Through some miracle, democracy holds, but with the three factions infighting all the way. To keep the masses happy they're constantly picking fights with their neighbours. The Iraqi Kurds hate Turkey, the Iraqi Sunnis hate Shia-dominated Iran and the Shias in Iraq hate the Sunnis in Jordan. To make it worse, there are three factions within the Shias, all jostling for power. Saddam was a bastard, but a weak government barely holding together three warring factions would be just as destabilising to the region.'

'So it's a nightmare all round?'

'It's worse than that,' said Bosch, picking up her knife again. 'The fundamentalists are using the place as a training ground. They're coming here in their thousands. More than half the suicide-bombers in Iraq are Saudis. Less than a quarter of the insurgents killed here are Iraqi, the rest are all foreign fighters. Terrorists come here from around the world to cut their teeth and once they move on they'll be taking the *jihad* to the West, big-time. What you've had so far in Europe is just a taste of what's coming. You know your history, right? What happened in Afghanistan?'

Shepherd knew what had happened in Afghanistan, all right: he'd taken a bullet in the shoulder and almost died. 'I guess so,' he said. He put down his knife and fork. He had barely touched his breakfast.

'Back in the eighties, the Soviets were the bad guys and Uncle Sam wanted them out of Afghanistan,' continued Bosch. 'The Americans poured money into the Afghan Mujahideen, effectively funding a guerrilla campaign that was ultimately successful. After the Russians pulled out, the Mujahideen didn't lay down their weapons. Far from it. They declared a global *jihad* and went off in search of new battles. Remember the attack on the World Trade Center in 1993? The men behind it were connected to a group that collected money for the Afghan *jihad*. Talk about chickens coming home to roost. Other Mujahideen went back to Algeria to set up the Armed Islamic Group, which ended up murdering thousands of Algerian civilians in their attempt to set up an Islamist state. Another group left Afghanistan for Egypt to start a terror campaign that killed thousands of Egyptians. More Mujahideen left to set up the Abu Sayyaf group in the Philippines. And let's not forget the most successful graduate of the Afghan conflict, Osama bin Laden himself. He turned against his former masters big-time. Most of the bad shit that's happened in the world goes back to what happened in Afghanistan – the Twin Towers, the London Tube bombings, Bali.'

Shepherd sat back and stretched out his legs. 'And that's what's happening here, isn't it? It's a breeding ground for terrorists.'

'On a bigger scale than Afghanistan, in a place where the enemy is the United States, Britain, Australia and the rest of the coalition forces. The Americans have captured insurgents with British passports, French, Dutch, almost the entire EU spectrum. They're learning urban warfare, how to make improvised explosive devices, how to brainwash suicide-bombers, how to kidnap, and once they've graduated they'll take their *jihad* to the West, spreading like a virus.' The South African grinned. 'You're fucked, you just don't know it yet.'

'You paint a pretty picture,' said Shepherd, 'but you don't seem particularly worried.'

'The crazier the world gets, the more work there is for me,' she explained. 'I get paid in dollars and I spend in rand. You should visit my game farm some time. Two hundred acres and Iraq paid for it.'

'It's an ill wind,' said Shepherd.

O'Brien pointed at Shepherd's plate with his fork. 'Are you going to eat the sausages?' he asked. Shepherd shook his head. O'Brien stabbed them and transferred them to his plate.

'You should think about it,' said Bosch, 'you and Martin. Guys like you with your SAS training, you'd get work out here no problem.' She leaned over and squeezed Shepherd's forearm. 'Have to fatten you up a bit first.' She laughed.

The Major walked into the kitchen. 'Time to go,' he said. 'Are you ready?'

'As I ever will be,' said Shepherd.

'Let's go and see John, get you kitted out,' said the Major.

Shepherd stood up. Bosch smiled up at him. 'Good luck, Spider,' she said.

'It'll be fine,' he said, and wished he felt as confident as he sounded.

He walked into the courtyard with the Major. 'You sure about this?' asked Gannon.

'It's a bit late to change my mind now,' said Shepherd.

'No one would blame you if you did.'

Three helicopters flew overhead, low enough to ruffle the tops of the date palms. They were Hueys, American-made Bell UH-1Hs but with the markings of the Iraqi air force.

'It's Geordie's only chance,' said Shepherd. 'If our roles were reversed, he wouldn't hesitate.'

'Yeah, well, he was always the headstrong one.'

'He saved my life. I owe him.'

The Major clapped Shepherd on the shoulder. 'We'll be close by.'

'Not too close,' said Shepherd.

'I won't let anything happen to you.'

'Thanks, boss.'

The Major hugged Shepherd, who squeezed him in return. 'Let's not get over-emotional,' he said. 'If all goes to plan we'll be back here in a few days having a beer with Geordie and laughing about it.'

They went to the main office building and found Muller sitting behind a massive oak desk, tapping at his computer keyboard. He stood up as the two men walked in. 'Ready to go?' he asked.

'Sure,' said Shepherd.

Muller picked up a laminated card and handed it to him. 'This is a company ID card. I've used the name on the passport you gave me.' He gave Shepherd two printed letters. 'Some company correspondence. Just shove it in your pocket.' Shepherd did so, and put the card into his wallet. His passport was in the back pocket of his jeans. Muller went over to a metal gun cabinet, unlocked it and took out a Glock pistol in a nylon holster. He gave it to Shepherd, who strapped the holster to his belt. Muller handed Shepherd a company transceiver. 'The frequency is preset,' he said. 'And now the big question. Do you want something more than the Glock? An Uzi, maybe?'

Shepherd glanced at the Major. 'I'm thinking less is better.'

'The less firepower you've got, the less likely they are to start shooting,' said the Major. 'You've got to be armed because that's what they'd expect, but an Uzi might worry them.'

'That's how I read it,' said Shepherd. 'If they see the gun on my hip and that I'm not pulling it, there's no reason for them to start shooting. I send out all the right signals and they assume I'm a victim.'

'Playing a role,' said Muller.

'It's what I do,' said Shepherd.

'Is your transmitter on?' asked the Major.

'Not yet,' said Shepherd.

'Let's do it,' said the Major. 'Gives us a chance to test it.'

Shepherd sat down on a wooden chair and removed his left boot. He pulled back the insole. Nestled in a hollow below it was the small transmitter Button had given him in London. It was the size of a couple of two-pound coins, joined by a quarter-inch length of wire, encased in a slim plastic case.

'Can I see it?' asked Muller.

Shepherd gave it to him. Muller squinted at the transmitter. He could see a regular phone Sim card set into a metal disc, a battery and a tiny circuit board set into a second. 'There's not much to it,' he said.

'It's all you need,' said Shepherd. 'The battery is mercury, which gives us more power than lithium ones, and it operates on the eight hundred megahertz cellphone frequency.'

'No antenna?'

'The metal that the Sim card sits in acts as one.' He pointed at the second disc. 'This is a GPS receiver that picks up the two point four gigahertz signal from the satellites overhead. It can pick up its longitude and latitude and uses the Sim card to transmit the information as a data call.'

'It phones in?'

'That's exactly what it does. Every ten minutes it makes a ten-second call downloading its position to a computer. Yokely's going to be monitoring the signal locally but the Iraqi phone system has commercial transponder coverage across most of the country, so unless Geordie's being held in the middle of the desert you'll know where I am to a few metres.' He opened the case, flicked a tiny switch and snapped it shut. 'Do you want to tell Richard it's on?' he asked the Major. 'We ran a test yesterday but I'd rather be safe than sorry.'

'Will do.' Gannon took out his mobile phone and called Yokely. He had a brief conversation, then said, 'He'll check and get back to us.'

Shepherd put the transmitter back into his boot and the boot back on to his foot.

'You know they'll take your boots off you,' said Muller.

'But hopefully not right away,' said Shepherd.

'How long's the battery good for?' asked Muller.

'A couple of weeks, give or take,' said Shepherd. 'Should be more than enough.' He tied his shoelace.

'And you know where you're going?' asked Muller.

Shepherd grinned. 'You're worrying too much, John,' he said. 'I know what I'm doing.'

'I'm worried you might get lost, that's all. It's dangerous out there,' said Muller, gesturing with his thumb at the metal gate that led to the outside.

'You keep saying. It's a minefield.'

'I meant that it's an easy city to get lost in if you don't know the language.'

'I won't get lost. I've been looking at street maps and satellite images of the city and my memory is almost photographic,' said Shepherd. He stood up and walked up and down. The transmitter fitted perfectly into the slot in the sole of his boot and he couldn't feel it. The only way someone would find it was by taking off his boot and removing the insole. He doubted anyone would bother to do that.

'Did your American friend get clearance for the curfew?' asked Muller.

'He's passed on descriptions of all your vehicles and registration numbers and says no one will bother us,' said the Major.

'He can do that?' asked Muller.

'He carries a lot of weight,' said the Major.

'He better had because they tend to shoot first and ask questions later after dark out here.'

'Relax, John,' said Shepherd.

Muller rubbed the back of his neck. 'I just keep thinking of what Geordie's facing. And if we screw up, you'll be in the same position.'

'No one's going to screw up,' said Shepherd, coolly. He took the Glock from its holster and checked the action. Then he ejected the magazine. It was fully loaded but if everything went to plan he wouldn't even pull the gun from its holster.

'He's right, John,' said the Major. 'We'll be on him every step of the way. Let's get the vehicle ready.'

As they walked outside, the Major's mobile rang. He listened for a few seconds, then put it away. 'Yokely says the tracker's working fine,' he said, 'and he wants you to wave.'

Shepherd frowned. 'He wants what?'

'He wants us all to wave,' said the Major. He craned his neck and gazed up into the near-cloudless sky. In the far distance an airliner left a white trail as it headed west but nothing else was in the air. The Major waved, as did Shepherd.

'You're both mad,' said Muller.

'Just wave,' said Shepherd, 'and say "cheese". We want to keep our guardian angel happy.'

Shepherd drove the Toyota Land Cruiser slowly down the road. He reached for the bottle of water on the passenger seat and drank from it. He was wearing body armour, and even with the air-conditioning on full blast he was sweating. He was entering Dora, the suburb in the south of Baghdad that, according to Muller, was controlled by Sunni insurgents and was a virtual no-go area for the coalition forces. Muller had said that IED attacks took place there virtually every day and the Americans drove through at speed, rarely venturing there on foot. The population of the suburb was almost half a million, a mixture of Sunnis, Shias and Christians, with the Sunnis in the majority. The suburb opened into countryside to the south, giving the insurgents an easy escape route. There were huge farms and luxurious villas, many of which had been owned by Saddam Hussein's family and officials. Shepherd wasn't out in the farmland, though. Geordie had been taken in the built-up area of the suburb, so that was where he was driving.

Shepherd passed a group of young men wearing *dishdasha*s who all glared at him. He picked up the transceiver and pushed the transmit button. 'Okay, I'm getting ready to start the show. Are you in place?'

The transceiver crackled. 'We're here,' said the Major. 'I've just spoken to Yokely and he has you on the GPS and the eye in the sky. Whenever you're ready, Spider.'

Shepherd put the transceiver back on the dashboard. His hands were wet with sweat and he wiped them one at a time on the legs of his jeans. He glanced into his rear-view mirror. There were no vehicles behind him. The Major and the rest of the team were keeping their distance. Their plan would only work if it looked as though Shepherd was on his own. He took a right turn into a narrow street that was filled with pedestrians, all Iraqi. There were women wearing full burkhas, covered from head to foot in black, there were men in grimy *dishdasha*s, a far cry from the gleaming robes he'd seen in Dubai, and plenty more in Western clothes.

He drove past a canal, a stagnant waterway overgrown with weeds, into which bare-chested children were jumping. Two little girls yelled and waved at him as he went by.

The buildings on either side of the street were run-down, with broken windows and peeling paintwork. The cars parked at the roadside were all old and rusting; several had been broken into and stripped. Shepherd figured the road was too busy to stop but he pumped the accelerator, making the Land Cruiser lurch. Heads turned to stare. He slowed the vehicle to a crawl, then pumped the accelerator again. He looked into his rear-view mirror. There was a taxi some fifty yards behind him, white with bright orange quarter panels. Three men sat inside it, two in the front.

Shepherd saw an intersection ahead and turned right, made the car jump forward and pulled in at the side of the road. The taxi drove by, all three men looking in his direction. He took a swig of water.

He turned to put the bottle back on the passenger seat and flinched as he saw a bearded man in a grey *dishdasha* staring at him through the window. He smiled, revealing two gold front teeth. 'Hello,' he said.

'How are you doing?' said Shepherd. It was difficult to judge the man's age. His skin was dark brown and leathery, but his eyes were bright and inquisitive. He could have been anywhere between thirty and sixty.

'You have a problem?' said the man.

Shepherd opened the door and stepped out into the street. Almost everyone within a hundred feet had stopped walking and was watching him with open hostility. Shepherd heard a roar then saw two F16 bombers flying just below the cloud line.

'There is something wrong with your vehicle?' said the man.

'The transmission, I think,' said Shepherd.

'On the Land Cruiser it is usually very reliable,' said the man. 'The Japanese make excellent cars.'

'You're a mechanic?'

'Cars were a hobby when I was young,' said the man, 'but I cannot afford one now.' He gestured at the vehicle. 'May I try?'

'I don't think you'll be able to do anything,' said Shepherd.

'You never know,' said the man, 'but if I cannot find out what's wrong, I have a good friend who is a mechanic and I can call him for you.'

'Thank you,' said Shepherd, suddenly guilty at having lied to a man who was clearly a good Samaritan.

'Dora is not a safe place for you, you know that?'

'Why?'

'The people here, many do not like the Americans.'

'I'm British,' said Shepherd.

'They care more about the colour of your skin than they do about your passport,' said the man. He held out his hand. 'My name is Nouri.'

'Peter,' said Shepherd, using the name in his passport. He shook the man's hand. 'Look, let me have another go. Maybe it was just overheating.'

'The transmission should not overheat,' said Nouri.

'I'll give it a go anyway,' said Shepherd.

Another taxi drove down the road and slowed as it passed the Land Cruiser. It had the same white and orange paint as the first Shepherd had seen but two women in burkhas sat in the back, with a net bag of vegetables on the front passenger seat.

'You seem nervous, my friend,' said Nouri.

'I'm fine.'

'You're travelling alone? That is unusual for a Westerner.'

'I was on my way to pick up three of our employees,' said Shepherd. 'Then I got lost and my car started playing up.'

'Where are you going?'

Shepherd named a street two miles away.

Nouri smiled and pointed back the way Shepherd had come. 'You need to go back to the crossroads, straight on for two miles, then left. Don't you have a map?'

Shepherd shook his head.

'I shall draw you one,' said Nouri. He pulled a scrap of paper from inside his *dishdasha* and a well-chewed ballpoint pen. He put the paper on the bonnet of the car and quickly drew a rough sketch map, with all the names in Arabic and underneath an English transliteration.

'Why is your English so good?' asked Shepherd.

'I was a teacher,' said Nouri. 'My school was bombed during the war so now I do some translating for charities. It does not pay well but it is the only job I can get these days. Things will improve in time, *Inshallah*.' He gave the hand-drawn map to Shepherd.

Two men in flannel shirts and long, baggy pants were edging closer to the Land Cruiser. One reached into a pocket, pulled out a mobile phone and made a call. He stared at Shepherd as he spoke into the phone.

Nouri saw what Shepherd was looking at and put a hand on his shoulder. 'Do not worry,' he said, and walked over to the two men, stood in front of them and spoke to them in a hushed voice. Shepherd looked around. More than fifty people were now openly staring at him. Most were men and the few women were all dressed from head to foot in black burkhas. Clearly they were poor, with grubby clothing and shabby footwear. Shepherd could feel hostility pouring off them. He reached for the door handle. Nouri turned and smiled reassuringly, then made a small patting motion with his hand as if he was quietening a spooked horse. 'Everything is okay,' he said.

'I'll give the car another try,' said Shepherd. 'The transmission might have cooled down.'

Nouri walked over and stood so close to Shepherd that he could smell the garlic on the man's breath. 'They are trouble, those men,' he said.

'I think you're right, Nouri,' said Shepherd.

'If the car does not start, I will walk with you down the street. If you are with me, everything will be okay.'

Shepherd climbed into the Land Cruiser, started the engine and edged the vehicle forward. He gave Nouri a smile and a wave, then drove away. He was drenched in sweat and wiped a hand on his trousers before he picked up the transceiver. He clicked 'transmit'. 'I'm driving again,' he said. 'Continuing north.'

'What happened?' asked the Major.

'I didn't seem to be flavour of the month,' said Shepherd, 'but no one was in a rush to kidnap me.'

★   ★   ★

'That was interesting,' said Simon Nichols, leaning back in his seat to study the bank of screens in front of him. 'What do you think just happened?'

Richard Yokely sipped his coffee. 'I reckon Spider found one of the few men in Dora who likes Westerners,' he said. 'What are the odds?'

'Slim,' said Will Slater who, like Nichols, was studying the screens. 'Slim to non-existent. That's *Hajji* country down there.' That was the Arabic word for a Muslim who had made the pilgrimage to Mecca, but it had become the standard term used by the military to refer to Iraqi insurgents.

Nichols and Slater were sensor operators, responsible for studying the output from the Predator unmanned aerial vehicle that was circling Baghdad at twenty thousand feet. The drone was transmitting high-resolution real-time images of the city below from cameras so powerful they could easily pick out individual numberplates. A variable-aperture television camera gave them a live feed of what was happening on the ground and an infrared camera supplied real-time images at night or in low-light conditions. A synthetic aperture radar system capable of penetrating cloud and smoke was constantly producing still images that were transmitted to the ground-control station. As well as its hi-tech surveillance equipment, the Predator was equipped with two Hellfire missiles and a multi-spectral targeting system that combined a laser illuminator, laser desig-nator infrared and optical sensors. It could fire its own missiles or pinpoint a target far below for tanks or manned aircraft to attack.

Phillip Howell, a CIA pilot who was one of the best Predator operators in the business, was piloting the twenty-seven-foot long drone. Yokely had asked for him because he had worked with him before and he knew that the surveillance operation would be as challenging as they came. Howell seemed relaxed as he piloted the drone: he had his feet up on a table as his right hand played idly with the joystick. He scanned the screen that showed the readings, but the one he relied on most featured the output from the colour camera in the Predator's nose cone.

'How are we doing for fuel, Phil?' asked Yokely.

Howell looked at the gauge and did a calculation in his head. 'Seventeen hours, give or take,' he said. The Predator's fuel tank held a hundred gallons, enough to keep it in the air for twenty-hours if it was circling or give it a range of 450 miles at its top speed of eighty miles an hour.

It had taken off from Balad airbase, a fifteen-square-mile mini-city just forty miles north-west of Baghdad; since the coalition forces had moved into Iraq it had become the second busiest airport in the world, beaten only by London's Heathrow. It had two parallel eleven-thousand-foot runways and was surrounded by dusty, parched desert dotted with stumpy eucalyptus trees. The nearby town was a hotbed of Iraqi insurgency and every night mortars rained from the sky – the soldiers stationed there had christened the base 'Mortaritaville'. Yokely and his three companions were in one of the Predator ground-control stations, a container-sized steel capsule. After they had been launched the Predators weren't flown by Iraq-based operators but by people seven thousand miles away at Nellis Air Force Base in Las Vegas. The data transmitted by the drones could also be beamed to US commanders in Saudi Arabia, Qatar or even in the Pentagon. Yokely, however, had insisted on local control. He wanted to be at Howell's shoulder as the craft prowled over the city, keeping a watchful eye on Spider Shepherd. And the data was for their eyes only. Yokely had no intention that anyone in Washington DC should know what they were doing.

Two air-conditioning units the size of washing-machines hummed at the far end of the capsule. On the opposite wall a line of clocks displayed east-coast time, west-coast time, Iraq, Tokyo and Zulu time.

'Whose brilliant idea was this?' asked Slater.

Yokely gestured at the screen. The Land Cruiser was driving slowly down the main road, manoeuvring around two burned-out cars. 'He came up with it himself.'

Next to the screen showing the real-time video feed a smaller screen presented a computer map of the area with a blinking cursor that positioned the transmitter in Shepherd's boot. The Predator's onboard receiver was picking up a burst of GPS data every ten minutes from the transmitter, which was then downloaded to the computer in the ground-control station.

'He's mad, you know that?' said Slater.

'I expressed my reservations, but he wouldn't be dissuaded. And let's not forget it gives us a fighting chance of locating Wafeeq bin Said al-Hadi. He's high on our most-wanted list.'

'Spider's a Judas Goat,' said Nichols. 'It's how you catch a man-eating tiger – tether a goat and wait for the tiger to come a-calling. But the snag is . . .'

'The goat usually dies,' Slater finished.

'Let's lose the gloom and doom, guys,' said Yokely. 'That's why we're here, to stop that happening.'

'Are we looking to capture or kill Wafeeq?' asked Howell, using the joystick to put the Predator into a gentle roll to the right so that he kept Shepherd's Land Cruiser in the centre of the camera's vision.

'We'll take it as it comes,' said Yokely. 'I'm easy either way.'

'And your man there? Does he stand more than a snowball's chance in hell of getting close to this Wafeeq?'

'If anyone can pull it off, Spider can,' Yokely told him.

Shepherd braked to allow four young children to cross in front of him, all boys in tattered shirts and threadbare shorts. Only one was wearing sandals. They waved at him and he waved back. One ran to the passenger window. 'Chewing-gum?' he shouted. Shepherd shook his head. The three other boys joined him and chorused, 'Chewing-gum, chewing-gum.' The oldest couldn't have been more than twelve.

Shepherd was sorry he didn't have anything to give them. He thought of Liam, with his PlayStation, his football, his music lessons, the expensive trainers and his iPod. He wanted a laptop computer for Christmas and he'd probably get one. 'Sorry, guys,' said Shepherd, holding up his hands. 'I haven't got anything.' They carried on chanting for chewing-gum. Shepherd leaned forward and popped the button to open the glovebox. He fumbled inside and found a roll of mints, wound down the window and gave them to the biggest. They ran off, laughing and shouting. Shepherd couldn't imagine Liam getting so worked up about a packet of sweets.

He wound up the window and put the vehicle in gear, checking the rear-view mirror as he pulled away. There was a taxi about fifty feet behind him, with three men inside.

He picked up the transceiver. 'There's a taxi behind me, I'm pretty sure it was hanging around earlier,' he said.

'Roger that,' said the Major.

Shepherd drove slowly down the road. Few other cars were around. A rusting Vespa scooter loaded with three large Calor-gas bottles overtook him – an elderly man in a faded blue *dishdasha* was bent over the handlebars, twisting the accelerator as if he was trying to squeeze more power out of the ancient machine. Shepherd checked his mirror again. The taxi was still there, matching his speed. He pumped the accelerator, making the Land Cruiser judder, then put the gearstick into neutral and hit the accelerator again, making the engine roar. He looked in the mirror. The taxi was still there, matching his speed, which was now little more than a crawl. Shepherd took a deep breath. His heart was racing and he could hear the blood pounding in his ears. This was like no other undercover operation he'd ever been on because, for the first time, he was deliberately putting himself in harm's way.

He braked, took another swig from his water bottle, looking in the mirror as he drank. The taxi had stopped, too. Three women in headscarves and long dresses walked by the Land Cruiser carrying cloth bags filled with bread. They were gossiping and didn't look at Shepherd as he popped the bonnet and climbed out of the vehicle.

Across the road a concreted area, surrounded by a wire mesh fence, was filled with rusting car bodies, most of which had been raked by gunfire. Two young boys watched him through the fence with wide eyes.

Shepherd peered under the bonnet of the Land Cruiser. Sweat poured down his back under his shirt and body armour and he wiped his forehead with his sleeve. It was in the high forties and there wasn't a cloud in the sky. He stared at the engine. The full realisation of what he was doing hit him. He was in the most dangerous city in the world, offering himself like a lamb to the slaughter. He heard a car door open, then another and another. Three doors. Three men. A few seconds later there were three slams. Shepherd's heart went into overdrive and he took a few deep breaths, forcing himself to stay calm. His instinct was to reach for his gun but he gripped his right hand into a fist and banged it down on the radiator cap. He was unarmed so there was no reason for them to get violent. He had to play the part right. Scared, confused and not a threat. A victim. He flinched as he heard gunshots, then realised they had been distant. A Kalashnikov. It was followed by the rat-tat-tat of M16s. Then silence.

Shepherd stared at the engine with unseeing eyes. He was listening to the footsteps of the men who had left the taxi. They'd be armed, he had no doubt of that. They'd have seen the logo of Muller's security company on the Land Cruiser so they'd know he was carrying a weapon – they'd only approach him if they knew they had him outgunned. He heard the scrape of a sandal on the pavement, then a slap, which Shepherd guessed was its owner stepping into the road. That made sense. They'd come at him from both sides, catching him in a pincer movement. Probably distract him from one side, then overpower him from behind. In a perfect world they'd pull a bag over his head and drag him to the taxi, but Shepherd knew that the world was far from perfect and the odds were that they would hurt him. The adrenaline was kicking into his system, giving him the near-irresistible urge for flight or fight. But he couldn't run or fight:

he had to stand his ground, play his role and hope that what they had in mind was hostage-taking, not murder.

He heard rapid footsteps behind him and turned to see a small boy in a faded Liverpool shirt running full pelt with an apple in each hand. A bearded shopkeeper in a striped apron screamed something at him and shook his fist. Shepherd smiled. He hadn't been averse to nicking the odd apple or orange when he was a kid – until he'd realised that stealing was wrong. The kid kept running and the shopkeeper went back inside.

Shepherd turned back to the engine. A fat man in a dark brown *dishdasha* walked past briskly, his head covered with a red and white checked *shumag* scarf. He was followed by an equally overweight woman in a black *abayah* that covered her from shoulders to feet. She was frowning, clearly unhappy about something – probably that she had to carry two cheap suitcases tied up with string, Shepherd thought. She was breathing heavily and her face was bathed in sweat. The man looked over his shoulder and barked something in Arabic. She nodded and walked faster. Suddenly Shepherd remembered Fariq's wife and smiled to himself: she was from Baghdad but he couldn't imagine her covering herself and walking behind her husband. It would probably have been the other way around.

His smile vanished when two men appeared at his right shoulder. Tall, thin men with spindly arms, wearing sweatshirts, cotton trousers and plastic sandals. One had a zigzag scar that ran from his left eye to his chin. His eyes darted from left to right and he was breathing heavily. The other man was calmer and stared at Shepherd with unblinking brown eyes. He had a straggly beard and metal-framed spectacles, and his hands were low, below the wing of the Land Cruiser.

Shepherd could feel hostility pouring from them. Under other circumstances he would have gone into full-attack mode. He'd have pulled his gun and shot them both at the slightest provocation. Even if he hadn't been armed he was confident he could take them. Both were within reach: he could chop the bearded man across the throat, then step round the car and hit the second, probably a kick to the knee to disable him, then a punch to the nose. Shepherd's adrenal glands were in overdrive and his legs were trembling, not from fear but because an animal instinct was screaming that it was time to move.

'Hi,' he said, playing his role. He was an idiot, lost in a city he didn't understand, a stupid infidel who was out of his depth and didn't know it. He forced himself to smile. 'Engine trouble.'

'American?' said the man with glasses.

'British,' said Shepherd.

The man wearing glasses lifted his hand. He was holding a gun. Shepherd stared at it. The man's finger was tight on the trigger. It was a Russian-made 9mm Makarov. The body armour Shepherd was wearing would almost certainly stop a 9mm slug, even at such close range. The man had made a big mistake in pointing it at his chest. If he'd been in attack mode, Shepherd would have been able to grab the gun and pull his own, confident that even if the man's weapon fired he'd still be able to get in a killing shot. But Shepherd was in victim mode, which meant he had to stand where he was and stare at the gun as if it was the most terrifying thing he'd ever seen. 'What do you want?' he said. 'You want money?'

He heard footsteps as the third man moved along the other side of the Land Cruiser. Soft, careful steps, as if he was walking on tiptoe. Shepherd fought the urge to turn, even though he knew that the man behind him was almost certainly going to hit him – hard. He continued to stare at the gun. If they wanted to kill him they would have done it already: they could have put the gun to his head and pulled the trigger. He heard the sound of a foot scuffing along the Tarmac. Close. Very close.

'I'll give you my wallet,' said Shepherd. He slowly lifted his left hand. 'And you can have my watch.' The man said nothing. He raised the gun so that it was pointing at Shepherd's face. Shepherd stared at it, trying to block out what was happening behind him. The Makarov looked like a larger version of the German

Walther PP but internally there were many differences. Shepherd was familiar with the weapon and knew how to strip and clean it, but it wasn't a gun he liked. He heard the man behind him take a breath and knew that the blow was coming. Time seemed to stretch into infinity as he anticipated it. He had no idea if he would be hit with a gun, a cosh or even a brick, but he was sure that it would hurt. He wanted to turn and face his attacker, meet force with force. Every fibre of him fought against standing still, but that was what he had to do so he stared at the gun and pushed his tongue against the roof of his mouth so that he wouldn't bite it when he was hit. He felt his shoulders tense against the blow he knew was coming, then something hard slammed into his head just behind his ear. He felt as if he'd been struck by a bolt of lightning. His legs went weak, as if all the strength had been sucked out of them, then everything went red and, finally, black.

The Major's mobile rang and he answered it immediately. 'Yes, Richard,' he said. Balad airbase was out of range of the transceivers they were using so they'd decided that mobile phones were the best way to keep in touch. The Major didn't want to rely on the Iraqi system so he'd asked Muller to bring a satellite phone with him. It sat on the back seat of the Land Cruiser between Muller and O'Brien.

'He's been taken,' said Yokely.

'How did it happen?'

'Three Mams cold-cocked him from behind, then dragged him to a taxi. They locked him in the boot. We've got a visual on it now and the transmitter's working fine. They're heading south.'

'Mams?'

'Local jargon. Military-aged males.'

'Do you think he's okay?'

'They hit him once with something small, maybe a gun. He went down straight away. Unless he's very unlucky he'll just have a sore head.'

'Can you get a licence plate?'

'We're working on it but they're in built-up areas and the drone's high up so we can't get the angle. Tell John the Land Cruiser is being stripped as we speak. I'll text you the address but I don't think there'll be much left by the time he gets there.'

'We'll start heading their way,' said the Major.

'No rush,' said Yokely. 'I doubt they'll be going too far so we'll have a location for you soon. My bet is that they'll hold him for at least a day until they pass him on.'

The Major thanked Yokely and ended the call. He nodded at Pat Jordan who was in the driving seat, chewing gum. 'Game on,' said the Major.

Shepherd was aware of the vibration first, then the smell. He was being shaken from side to side and his head banged against the floor of the boot every time the taxi went over a bump. The smell of the exhaust was sickening and he felt more light-headed with every breath he took. Then he became aware of the noise, the roar of the tyres over Tarmac and the clunk-clunk-clunk of an engine with worn cylinders.

He was lying on his left arm. He rolled over to get his weight off it and tried to look at his watch, but his wrists were tied. He twisted round, trying to find fresher air, pushed his hooded face close to the boot lock and breathed through the gap. He hoped they didn't plan to keep him there for much longer because the carbon monoxide in the exhaust would kill him as surely as a bullet to the brain. He felt a sharp pain at the back of his head where he'd been hit, and consciousness began to slip away again. He shook his head. He didn't know if the blow to the head or the carbon monoxide was making him drowsy, but he knew that he had to stay awake. He bit down on his tongue, hard enough to taste blood, using the pain to keep himself focused.

The Major's mobile rang. It was Yokely. 'They've taken him inside a house,' said the American.

'Is he okay?' asked the Major.

'They carried him in and he wasn't moving, but if he was dead they'd have left him in the trunk.'

'That's reassuring,' said the Major, coldly.

'I'll text you the co-ordinates but you should keep your distance. He's still in Dora and Westerners stick out there.'

'We'll hang back,' said the Major.

'We're going to bring the plane in for refuelling now,' said Yokely. 'Everything seems quiet and I'd rather be up there with a full tank. We'll be down for about two hours. The transmitter's still working fine so we'll know if they move him. I'm getting our NSA guys here to monitor the tracker through the Iraqi phone service.'

'Any sign of him moving, let me know,' said the Major. He ended the call, then rang Armstrong to brief him on what the American had said. Armstrong was parked half a mile away in another Land Cruiser with Shortt, Bosch and Haschka.

'Why doesn't he have two of those things up?' asked O'Brien from the back seat when the Major finished his call. He had a KitKat, which he broke into two. He offered half to Gannon, who shook his head. Muller grabbed for it but O'Brien grinned and moved it out of his reach.

'We're lucky to have the one, Martin,' said the Major. 'They cost over four million dollars each, the ground station is another ten, and they need a ground crew of three working on it full time when it's in the air. Yokely's doing it on the quiet because the Yanks wouldn't want to put that amount of resources into one missing Brit.'

'He's a generous guy,' said O'Brien, popping the last piece of KitKat into his mouth.

'He'll want his pound of flesh at some point,' said the Major, 'but we need him. We could follow the transmitters using the regular Iraqi phone network but the Predator gives us a visual, too.'

'I hope he's okay,' said Muller.

'You and me both,' said the Major.

★   ★   ★

Shepherd tasted blood in his mouth, turned his head and spat it out, then regretted it because the result was smeared across the inside of the hood. His head was throbbing, the pain was made worse because he was lying on his back. He rolled on to his right side and felt a searing pain in his skull. He took several deep breaths, then lay still and listened. He could hear nothing, not even street noise. He was lying on hard ground, possibly concrete. His wrists were bound behind his back and he had lost all feeling in his fingers. He brought his knees up, then tried to roll over to get up. The strength had gone from his legs and he fell back.

He lay gasping for breath, then heard a door open and footsteps walking across the floor. Hands gripped his shoulders and turned him. Someone pulled up the hood and thrust a plastic bottle towards his mouth. Shepherd drank. It was lukewarm water. The man held the bottle to Shepherd's lips until he spluttered, then took it away and pulled down the hood. He turned Shepherd around, then pushed him back until he was against the wall. They'd taken off his body armour.

'Sit,' said the man.

Shepherd had the feeling he was the tall man with glasses, the one who'd pulled the gun. He slid down the wall and sat with his back to it, his knees against his chest. 'I need to urinate,' said Shepherd.

'What?' said the man.

'I need to pee. To piss.'

'Wet your pants,' said the man. 'I am not untying your hands.'

'Who are you?'

Something hit Shepherd on the side of the head, a hand maybe. The man had slapped him, hard. 'I will ask questions, not you,' said the man.

'Okay,' said Shepherd, his ears ringing. 'I'm sorry.'

'What is your name?'

'Peter Simpson,' said Shepherd. It was the name in the passport and on the credit cards in his wallet.

'Where are you from?'

'Manchester,' said Shepherd.

'What are you doing in Baghdad?'

'I work for a security company,' said Shepherd.

Shepherd heard paper rustling and realised that the man was flicking through his passport.

'How long have you been in Iraq?'

'I arrived yesterday.'

The man chuckled. 'You are in deep shit, Mr Peter Simpson,' he said. Shepherd felt the man slap his boots. 'Timberland?' asked the man.

Shepherd nodded. 'Yes.'

'What size?' asked the man.

'They're on the move,' said Nichols, nodding at the LCD screen and its real-time view of the house where Shepherd had been kept for the previous twelve hours. Yokely got up from the camp-bed he was lying on and went to stand at the other man's shoulder. It was night and they were looking at the infrared image from the Predator.

Three figures were moving from the house to the car. The one in the middle was stumbling, held by the other two. 'He's walking,' said Nichols.

Yokely nodded. 'They must be passing him up the food chain,' he said. He called the Major's mobile. 'They're moving him now,' Yokely told him.

'Is he okay?'

'He's walking. They're putting him in the car.'

'Excellent,' said the Major.

'I'll let you know which direction once they head off.' Yokely put his phone away. 'How's it going, Phillip?' he asked the pilot.

'Hunky-dory,' said Howell, who was sipping coffee from a chipped white mug. He had been piloting the Predator for more than sixteen hours and had only been able to take his eyes off the screens for the two hours when the drone was on the airfield being refuelled and serviced.

'Fuel?'

Howell flicked his eyes to the gauge and calculated in his head. 'Fifteen hours or so.'

Yokely looked at the GPS display. The cursor was blinking steadily. He smiled to himself. So far, so good.

'I can't breathe in there,' said Shepherd, as the two men pushed him into the boot of the car.

'What?' said one of the men. It wasn't the man who'd spoken to him inside – this voice was deeper and gruffer.

'The exhaust's leaking,' said Shepherd. 'The fumes will kill me.'

'Hold your breath,' said the man, and laughed. He grabbed Shepherd's shirt collar and pushed him towards the boot.

'If you kill me, I'm not worth anything,' said Shepherd, quickly. 'I kept passing out before and I could easily die in there.'

The two men talked to each other in Arabic, arguing. Shepherd heard footsteps as the third of his captors approached, then the voice of the man who'd interrogated him inside.

The man put his face close to Shepherd's head. 'What is the problem?' he said.

'The exhaust is leaking,' said Shepherd. 'The boot gets full of fumes. I kept passing out last time.'

'You want to travel first class, is that it?' The man said something to the others, who laughed.

Shepherd opened his mouth but before he could say anything something hard smashed against the side of his head.

Nichols winced. 'That's got to have hurt,' he said. 'Why did they do it?'

'Because they're tough, mean motherfuckers,' said Yokely.

'They've got him bound and hooded. Hitting him is overkill,' said Slater.

'No one said they were nice people,' said Yokely.

They watched as two of the men put the unconscious

Shepherd into the boot while the third got into the driving seat. They slammed the boot shut, then one slid into the passenger seat while the other held back to shut the gates behind them. There was no other traffic in the road.

Howell moved the joystick and put the drone into a lazy left-hand turn. Slater moved his control to keep the car in the centre of the screen. There wasn't much traffic about so he had no problem following the vehicle, but it still required his full attention.

Yokely pulled up a chair. He moved his head frequently to keep an eye on both screens – the infrared camera view and the GPS monitor.

'When are you going to move in?' asked Howell.

'That'll be Spider's call,' said Yokely.

'He'd better not leave it too late,' said Howell.

'I hear you,' said Yokely.

When Shepherd came to he was still in the boot. His head ached and he couldn't feel his hands. The car was driving fast and the road seemed smooth. His mouth was bone-dry and it hurt to swallow. The exhaust smell was overpowering and he rolled over again so that his mouth was close to the boot's lock. The combination of the hood and the fumes was making him drowsy and he fought to stay awake. 'Please, God, don't let me die like this . . .' he whispered.

Yokely watched the car on the infrared monitor. It had been driving for almost forty minutes and had now left the city, heading south towards Yusufiyah, a farming area between the rivers Euphrates and Tigris. On the monitor it moved along a road that cut through fields filled with orange and date groves. Yokely looked at the GPS screen. Yusufiyah was a Sunni stronghold, and had been ever since the coalition forces had invaded Iraq. It wasn't exactly a no-go area for the military but when they went in they went in hard and tended to stay in their vehicles.

The car made a left turn, slowed, stopped at an intersection, then made a right turn. It pulled up in front of a large L-shaped building that was surrounded by a wall. Several vans were parked outside. Two figures came out, opened a gate and the car drove in.

'Simon, see if you can ID that building,' said Yokely.

'I'm on it,' said Nichols.

'You think that's where they're holding the other guy?' asked Slater.

'Difficult to say,' said Yokely. 'We watch and wait. Softly, softly, catchy monkey.'

'See, now, I've never understood that expression,' said Howell, as he put the Predator into a slow left bank. 'Monkeys are smart and you can't creep up on one, no matter how slow you take it. You wanna take out a monkey, you shoot it with a tranquilliser gun.'

'You always were a stickler for detail, Phillip.'

'Pilots have to be,' said Howell. 'Otherwise they forget things like putting their landing gear down.'

The men got out of the car and gathered around the boot. One opened it.

'He's not moving,' said Slater.

'I see that,' said Yokely, quietly.

Two ghostly white figures on the screen pulled Shepherd out and carried him into the building. Another closed the gate and followed the others. Yokely divided his attention between the two screens. The GPS monitor continued to blink. They knew where Shepherd was, but not whether he was alive or dead.

The Major's phone rang. He put it to his ear. 'Yes, Richard?'

'It's good news, and bad news, I'm afraid,' said the American. 'We know where he is but he's not moving.'

'Shit,' said the Major.

'What's wrong?' asked O'Brien, from the back seat.

'He walked out of the building and they hit him before they put him in the trunk,' said Yokely. 'Could be he's just concussed.'

'But we've no way of knowing,' said the Major.

'We watch and wait,' said Yokely. 'He's in Yusufiyah, about thirty miles south of Baghdad. Problem is, it's not as built up as Baghdad and Westerners tend to stick out.'

'My inclination is to go in now,' said the Major.

'I understand that,' said Yokely, 'but we've got them under surveillance. They can't go anywhere without us knowing so let's give it a few more hours.'

'Okay,' said the Major, reluctantly, and put away the phone. He explained to Muller, O'Brien and Jordan what had happened.

O'Brien cursed. 'If he's dead, we go in and we go in hard, right?'

'He's not dead,' said the Major. He turned to Muller. 'What can you tell me about Yusufiyah?'

'It's full of al-Qaeda militants. They call it the Triangle of Death and it's a haven for insurgents. Is that where they've taken Spider?'

'I'm afraid so,' said the Major.

'If anything goes wrong, if he doesn't get out of this, every one of those bastards gets it,' said Muller. 'Every single one.'

Shepherd coughed and pain lanced his skull. He groaned. He could taste blood in his mouth. He was lying on his side on rough matting, which smelled of mould. He coughed again.

'Do you want water?' said a heavily accented voice behind him.

Shepherd heard footsteps, then someone pulled at his shoulder and helped him to sit up. His hands were still tied behind him. The hood was lifted and the neck of a plastic bottle was forced between his lips. Shepherd drank for several seconds, then the bottle was taken away. The hood fell back into place. 'Thank you,' he said.

'You should rest,' said the man. He helped Shepherd lie down again.

'My wrists hurt,' said Shepherd. 'Can you loosen them?'

'No,' said the man.

'I can't feel my hands,' said Shepherd.

'Shut up,' said a second voice, harsher than the first. Shepherd heard a rustle of clothing then a foot slammed into his kidney. The blow took him by surprise and he screamed at the pain.

'There's movement,' said Nichols. 'A guy's just left the house and gone to the car.' He was studying the output from the Predator's infrared sensor. It was eleven o'clock in the evening and the regular video output had shown nothing but darkness since eight.

Yokely got up off the camp-bed and walked over to stand behind him. Two more figures left the house and got into the car. Another went to the gate, pulled it back and the car eased into the street. 'They're taking a risk moving him at night,' said Yokely. 'It's well into curfew and if they come across an army patrol, they'll be shot to pieces.'

Yokely stared at the screen that showed the position of the transmitter hidden in Shepherd's boot. The cursor was still on the building, which suggested that Shepherd was inside it. It looked as if his kidnappers were returning home, which meant they had handed him over to the next link in the chain.

The figure closed the gate and went back into the building.

'What do we do?' asked Howell. 'Stick with the house or follow the car?'

'Stay put,' said Yokely. 'They've sold him to whoever's in there. The question is, is it Wafeeq or not?'

'With respect, the question is whether or not your man is still alive,' said Howell, who was keeping the drone in a gentle left-hand turn some twenty thousand feet above the building.

'Do try to be a bit more optimistic, Phillip,' said Yokely.

'They've hit him on the head twice, hard,' said the pilot.

'They're thick-skulled, the Brits,' said Yokely. 'How are we doing for fuel?'

'Thirteen hours or so,' said Howell.

'What's the plan now?' asked Slater.

'We see if they move Shepherd on or keep him there.'

'You're thinking of going in?'

'I want all my bases covered,' said Yokely.

'Richard, we've got a problem,' said Nichols. He pointed at the GPS monitor. 'Do you see that?'

'Yeah, I see it,' said Yokely. The flashing cursor that showed the position of the transmitter had moved. It was now almost a mile from the house.

'What the hell's going on?' asked Howell. 'Is one of those guys your man? And if it is, why did he get into the car willingly?'

The Major's mobile rang. It was Yokely. 'We've got a problem,' said the American. 'According to the GSM, Shepherd's on the move, back to the first place he was being held.'

'That doesn't make sense,' said the Major. 'They were passing him up the chain and there's no reason for him to go back.' He cursed quietly. 'The boots?'

'I guess so. I think the original kidnappers have gone home with their ill-gotten gains, leaving Shepherd in the house without the transmitter.'

'How's the visual?' asked the Major.

'All we have is the infrared so we've no way of knowing what's going on inside. We don't know if that's the place where Geordie Mitchell's being held or if it's another half-way house and they're planning to move Shepherd on again. The infrared doesn't work in buildings and if we've lost the transmitter we'll have to rely on the visual to see if they take him out.'

'What are you suggesting?' asked the Major.

'We need to know what's going on inside the building,' said Yokely. 'If that's where they've got Geordie, we can get ready to move in. But if it isn't and it's just another link in the chain, we have to wait and see.'

'And I'm sure you want to know if Wafeeq's in there,' said the Major.

'The two are connected, Allan. Let's not forget that. Look, the Predator can watch the building and we can track the GPS, so at the moment there's no panic. I'm going to pay the original kidnappers a visit.'

'To what end?'

'Information retrieval,' said Yokely. 'It's what I do best.'

'Are you sure that's a good idea?' said the Major.

'They can tell me what's happening inside that building. For all we know they've already put him in an orange jumpsuit,' said Yokely. 'The three guys who took him off the street are heading home. We can interrogate them and keep them in cold storage until it's over. I don't see a downside.'

'Okay,' said the Major. What the American proposed made sense, but he was starting to feel that stable doors were being locked after horses had bolted.

'I'd like to take Armstrong and Shortt with me,' said Yokely. 'I'm loath to bring in the heavy guns at this stage. If it becomes a full military operation, alarm bells'll ring.'

'Agreed,' said the Major.

'I'm about thirty miles away from them so I'll get a lift out there. Can you call and tell them to expect me?'

'Roger that,' said the Major. He ended the call and twisted around in his seat to Muller and O'Brien. 'It's got a bit more complicated,' he said. He could tell from their faces that they had gathered what the problem was.

Shepherd pushed himself backwards on the mat until his head touched a wall. He rolled over and sat up. His head was aching and his captors had given him only one drink of water since they'd taken him out of the car boot so his throat was dry. He listened but couldn't hear anyone else in the room. He had no way of knowing if they were keeping him in a basement or upstairs, or what was outside the building. 'Is anyone there?' he asked. His voice echoed round the room.

Shepherd wiggled his fingers. He couldn't tell what they had used to bind his wrists together but it was way too tight.

He pushed himself up against the wall and stood, breathing heavily. The floor was hard under his feet. Not wood, concrete maybe. That he no longer had his boots was a worry – a big one.

He moved sideways, keeping his back to the wall, trying to get a sense of how big a space he was in. His hands were so numb that he couldn't tell if it was bare plaster or wallpaper that he was touching. He rubbed his right foot along the floor. Through his sock he could feel the rough rasp of concrete. He reached a corner and started along the second wall. After half a dozen sideways steps he found a door. He groped for the handle and found it but couldn't grip. He clenched and unclenched his hands, but couldn't even feel if his fingers were moving. Three more paces took him to the next corner. The wall had been about six metres long.

He started along the next wall, rubbing it with his shoulders as he moved. It was blank and featureless. He reached the next corner in seven sideways paces. About four metres.

Midway along the fourth wall he found a window. He tapped it with the back of his head and felt the glass rattle. He'd lost all sense of time and the hood was totally lightproof so he had no way of knowing if it was day or night. He doubted they would have left him in a room with a window so he guessed that there was a shutter on it, or bars. He turned to face the window and pressed his forehead against it. Was there a shutter, he wondered, or could he be seen from outside?

The door crashed open. 'Down on the floor!' shouted a man. 'You stay down!'

Shepherd dropped to his knees. 'I need water,' he said.

A hand slapped his head and his lip split. 'You stay down or we will kill you.' The man grabbed him by the scruff of the neck, dragged him across the floor, then pushed him down on to the mat. 'You will stay here,' said the man. 'You will not move until you are told to.' Shepherd felt something hard press against his neck through the hood. 'You know what this is?' hissed the man.

'A knife,' said Shepherd.

'Yes, a knife. And I can cut your head off as easily as I can kill a chicken. You know that?'

'Yes,' said Shepherd.

The man pressed the knife harder against Shepherd's neck. 'I can kill you now.'

Shepherd said nothing. There was nothing he could say: his life was in the man's hands. The one thing he clung to as he felt the knife bite into the hood was that there was nothing to be gained from killing him there and then. If they were going to kill him they'd do it on video so the world could see.

'Maybe I will. Maybe I will kill you now,' hissed the man.

'*Inshallah*,' said Shepherd.

Shepherd felt the knife move away from his throat. 'What did you say?' asked the man.

'*Inshallah*,' said Shepherd. 'If Allah wants me dead, then you should do what you have to do.'

'You think I will not kill you?'

'I think if it's Allah's will that you kill me, you will kill me.'

'You speak Arabic?'

'No, but I've read the Koran.'

'The Koran is in Arabic,' said the man.

'I read a translation,' said Shepherd. 'It was in English.'

The man stood up and left the room. He returned two minutes later, raised Shepherd's hood and thrust a plastic bottle of water between his lips. He drank. The man allowed him to finish it, then took it away and pulled the hood down.

'Thank you,' gasped Shepherd.

'Stay on the floor,' said the man. 'If you get up again, I will kill you.' He left the room and slammed the door.

Armstrong heard the helicopter before he saw it, a sixty-four-foot-long shark-like Blackhawk, twin turbines screaming as the massive rotors kicked up a flurry of dust from the road. It loomed out of the night sky, its twin searchlights scanning the area, then bumped on the ground and a man jumped out. He was wearing body armour over camouflage fatigues and a Kevlar helmet. In his right hand he held an M16 rifle and in the left a set of industrial bolt-cutters. It was only when he ran towards them that Armstrong realised it was Yokely. The helicopter's turbines roared and it clattered into the air, then banked to the right and disappeared into the night.

Armstrong opened the back door of the Land Cruiser and moved over so that Yokely could sit next to him. 'I hope Gannon told you I was coming,' he said.

'He did,' said Shortt.

'Where are we going?' asked Bosch. She was in the front passenger seat, next to Haschka.

Yokely reached into his body armour and pulled out a map showing the location of the Land Cruiser and the route to the building where Shepherd had first been taken. He gave it to Bosch. 'Pull in just round the corner and we'll go in on foot.'

Haschka put the 4 × 4 in gear and drove off.

'Why the military outfit?' asked Armstrong. He lit a Marlboro and offered the pack to Yokely.

Yokely waved it away. 'Gives me a certain legitimacy,' he said.

'And camouflage,' said Bosch. She reached over, took one of Armstrong's cigarettes and waited while he lit it for her.

'Exactly,' said Yokely.

Haschka drove the Land Cruiser through the darkened suburbs. There was no street lighting but the 4 × 4's powerful headlights cut through the night, startling the stray dogs and cats that slept on the streets. There were few people around and those there were hurrying along with their heads down. Two military Humvees came around a corner and headed in their direction. Yokely flashed the driver of the lead vehicle a mock salute and the man waved back. Bosch kept the map on her lap and gave Haschka directions. After half an hour she told him to slow down. 'Two blocks along,' she said.

Yokely took out his mobile phone. He called Slater's number. 'Is it clear, Will?' he asked. He had told the pilot to swing the Predator over the house and check out the area.

'There's no traffic and we don't see anyone in the street,' said Slater. 'No movement around the house.'

'Thanks,' said Yokely. 'Keep a watch until we've gained entry, then tell Phillip to head on back.' Yokely put away the phone and pointed at the next intersection. 'Hang a right there, Joe, and pull in somewhere quiet.'

Haschka made the turn. Bosch saw an alleyway ahead but before she could say anything Haschka had seen it and was driving down it. He parked and switched off the engine.

They all climbed out. Yokely took out his phone again and called Slater. 'Do you see us?'

'We have you on infrared,' said Slater. 'No one else on the streets for a hundred yards or so, and that's two men walking away from you. You're clear.'

It was a cloudless night and overhead there were a million stars but no sign of the Predator twenty thousand feet above them. 'We're going in,' said Yokely. He ended the call, then nodded at Haschka and Armstrong. 'We're clear to go,' he said. He took out his Glock. 'You two, Jimbo and I will go into the house.'

'What about me?' asked Bosch.

'Stay with the vehicle,' said Yokely.

'You sexist prick,' said Bosch.

'Carol, it's nothing to do with your beautiful chestnut hair or your pert breasts, it's just that you've got a shotgun and if that goes bang every man and his dog will come running.'

'I thought the plan was not to shoot anybody,' said Armstrong.

'Yeah, well, plans change,' said Yokely. He handed the bolt-cutters to Armstrong. 'Please don't argue, Carol. I'm sure there'll be an opportunity for you to shoot someone down the line.'

Bosch nodded but didn't look happy at being told to stay behind. She glared at Yokely and climbed back into the Land Cruiser.

The four men went back down the alley, keeping close to the wall. A rat at least two feet long from nose to tail tip scurried purposefully along the opposite side.

They reached the gates and Yokely motioned for Armstrong to use the bolt-cutters on the chain. They made short work of it and Shortt pulled the gate open. Yokely and Armstrong slipped inside. Armstrong placed the bolt-cutters on the ground and pulled out his gun. They moved to the house. It was two storeys high with a flat roof. There were shutters on the windows, all closed, and no lights on inside.

Yokely motioned for Haschka and Shortt to go around to the rear. Armstrong tried the front door. The wood was rotting and the hinges were rusting, but it was locked. It looked as if it wouldn't take much to break it down but the men inside had guns so they'd have to go in quietly.

They walked around to the left and checked the shuttered windows, which were as badly maintained as the door, but, again, they were all locked. Armstrong pulled at one but it held firm. He looked at Yokely and shook his head. The American pointed to the rear of the house and they kept to the shadows as they crept around the building. Overhead two helicopters flew so close that their rotors were almost touching. The two men stayed still until they had gone, then moved to the back of the building.

Haschka and Shortt had found a loose shutter. They pulled it open and examined the window. The lock looked flimsy so Haschka took out a large hunting knife and worked away at the wood round it. As Yokely and Armstrong walked up, it splintered and Shortt eased open the window. They climbed through one by one and found themselves in a kitchen. There was a stone sink with a single dripping tap and an old refrigerator that was vibrating noisily. Yokely switched on a flashlight, pointed it at Haschka, Shortt and Armstrong, then directed it upstairs. They switched on their own flashlights and headed for the upper floor as the American went through to the sitting room.

Armstrong led the way, his Glock in his right hand. The stairs were stone and led up to a tiled hallway off which were four doors. One was open, revealing a small bathroom.

Armstrong pointed at Haschka, then at the door at the far end. He went to stand outside it. Armstrong pointed at the second door, then at Shortt. He waited until they were all in position, then held up his left hand and counted down from three to one on his fingers. As the final finger went down he twisted the handle, thrust open the door, and walked into the room, his gun arm outstretched. A middle-aged Iraqi lay on a mattress on the floor. Armstrong walked over to him and woke him with a kick to the ribs. He heard shouts from the other rooms as he pointed the gun at the man on the mattress. He had a zigzag scar across the left side of his face. 'Get up,' said Armstrong. The man said something in Arabic, then spat at him. Armstrong pistol-whipped him, hauled him to his feet and dragged him to the door.

Shortt and Haschka had the other two men in the hallway. One had a straggly beard and bloodshot eyes, the other was squat with a weightlifter's forearms. His hair was close-cropped, he had a bushy beard and he was clenching and unclenching his fists. Shortt kept his gun pointed at the man's face and raised an eyebrow, daring him to get physical.

'Downstairs,' said Armstrong.

Yokely was in the front room. There was a line of candles on the mantelpiece and he lit them one by one. There were two cheap brown plastic sofas and stained rugs on the floor and paintings of desert scenes on the walls. Two ornate hookahs stood by one of the sofas and the floor was littered with peanut shells. The American was holding a brown envelope containing US dollars. He flicked through the banknotes. 'There's about fifteen thousand.'

Armstrong shook the man he was holding. 'Fifteen thousand dollars?' he hissed. 'You sold him for fifteen thousand dollars? You stupid pricks. We'd have paid you ten times that.'

Yokely shoved the envelope into his back pocket. 'Get them on their knees,' he said. He lit several more candles by the shuttered window.

Armstrong, Shortt and Haschka forced their captives on to their knees. Yokely gestured with his gun. 'I want you to ask them if they're brothers or just fuck-buddies,' he said.

Shortt frowned. 'What?'

'You're not hard of hearing, are you, Jimbo? Just ask them if they're related or lovers?'

Shortt translated. The tallest of the three frowned and said something to him. Shortt repeated what he'd said. The three men pointed at Yokely and shouted.

'Thought that would get them riled,' said Yokely.

'They're brothers,' said Shortt.

'Good. We'll be keeping it in the family, then,' said the American. He took a bulbous silencer out of a pocket in his body armour and slowly screwed it to the barrel of his Glock. The brothers stared at it, then all three were talking at once.

'Tell them to shut up, Jimbo,' said Yokely.

Shortt barked at them in Arabic and they fell silent.

Yokely pointed at the Timberland boots on the feet of the eldest brother. 'Ask him where he got the boots,' he said to Shortt.

Shortt translated. The Iraqi sneered at Yokely and said something, his lip curled back in a snarl.

'Did he just tell me to go screw myself?' asked Yokely.

'Words to that effect,' said Shortt.

Yokely smiled. He pulled the trigger and shot the man's left leg. His trousers turned red at the knee and he fell to the floor, screaming.

'Hey!' shouted Haschka.

'Hey what?' said Yokely.

The man rolled on the floor, holding his injured leg and moaning. Blood was pumping from the wound and pooling on the floorboards where it glistened in the candlelight. His face had gone deathly white – he looked as if he'd bleed out in minutes, Armstrong thought. He undid his belt, pulled it from round his waist, then used it to bind the man's leg tightly above the knee. 'I think you hit an artery,' said Armstrong.

'Yeah, I know,' said Yokely.

The other two men stared at their injured brother in horror. The youngest was trembling with fear. Yokely walked over to him and pointed the pistol at his face. 'Tell him I want to know who he gave Spider to. I want their names. All their names.'

'Yokely, you can't do this,' said Shortt.

'I can do what the hell I want,' said Yokely. 'Now tell him.'

Shortt translated. The man seemed unable to speak and his mouth moved soundlessly. Shortt said something and pointed at Yokely.

Yokely waved his gun menacingly. The man flinched and a dark stain spread across the front of his pants. 'Tell him I'll count to five and then I'm going to shoot him too. In the balls.'

'Yokely—' said Shortt.

'Tell him I'm a pretty good shot.'

'This is madness,' said Shortt. 'We didn't come to shoot unarmed men.'

Yokely turned to Shortt. 'This is my turf,' he said. 'This is where I work. I know how the game's played here and it isn't by the Queensberry Rules. These three pieces of shit took Spider off the streets at gunpoint, knocked him unconscious, and sold him for fifteen grand to people who will happily hack off his head with a bread-knife. Let's not start feeling sorry for them. They'll kill you as soon as look at you, and think they're doing it with God's blessing. So, just do as I ask and tell them I want the names of the men they sold Spider to. If you don't, I'll shoot you in the legs.' He flashed Shortt a cold smile. 'I mean it.'

'Do it, Jimbo,' said Armstrong. He didn't believe that Yokely would shoot Shortt, but he could see they'd have to increase the pressure if they were to get the men to talk. Spider and Geordie's lives were on the line and if they didn't find out where they were they would die horribly. He lit a cigarette and watched as Shortt spoke in Arabic. The man began to wail. He put his palms together and banged his hands against his forehead.

'Five,' said Yokely. 'Four. Three.' He turned to look at Shortt. 'You did tell him, right?'

Shortt nodded.

'Right then,' said Yokely. 'Two. One.' He pulled the trigger and shot the wailing man in the groin. He screamed and fell into a foetal ball, his hands clasped between his legs. His screams turned to sobs.

'What the hell is your problem?' shouted Shortt.

Yokely ignored him and pointed his gun at the last remaining brother. 'Right, Jimbo, I want you to translate and I want to hear you do it without any bleating about human rights or unarmed innocents. This scumbag has watched me shoot both his brothers and he knows who he handed Shepherd over to. I want him to start talking or I'll put a bullet in his head, and then I'll start working on that bastard's bad leg. Tell him it's his choice.' He grinned maliciously. 'Oh, and tell him I'll slaughter a pig and I'll drench him in its blood before I bury him in the desert with the carcass on top of him. I understand that means he'll never get into heaven.'

'You're a sick fuck,' said Shortt.

'Yes, I am, Jimbo, but I get things done. Now, translate.'

Shortt spoke to the man in Arabic. As his brother before him, the man started to wail.

Shortt continued to talk to him. Armstrong stubbed out his cigarette and checked the wound of the man who had been shot in the groin. He was curled up, breathing in short gasps.

Yokely looked bored as he waited for Shortt to finish, then he aimed at the face of the Iraqi and tightened his finger on the trigger. The terrified man started to babble in Arabic. 'What's he saying, Jimbo?' asked Yokely.

'He's saying he'll talk. He'll tell you whatever you want to know.'

'Excellent,' said Yokely.

★   ★   ★

'Here they are,' said Jordan. He flashed his headlights at the Land Cruiser heading their way. The 4 × 4's lights flashed in reply and it parked on the opposite side of the road. Jordan waved at Haschka and Bosch, who waved back. Yokely climbed out of the rear and jogged across the road towards them.

'What's he doing in army gear?' asked O'Brien.

'Mr Yokely is a law unto himself,' said the Major.

'Nice shoes,' said Jordan. Though Yokely was in military desert camouflage fatigues, body armour and a Kevlar helmet, he was still wearing his brown loafers with tassels.

'Yeah, he's fussy about his footwear,' said the Major. 'He's got dropped arches.'

'He's got what?' said O'Brien.

'Dropped arches. His shoes have to have orthopaedic inserts. It's supposed to be a secret, so Mum's the word.'

The Major wound down the window as Yokely jogged up. The American was grinning. 'Spider's okay,' said Yokely. 'At least, he was when the Three Stooges handed him over.'

'And is Wafeeq there?'

'They say no, they haven't met him but they've heard of him. The guys they sold him to are middle men, known to have connections with some hard-line fundamentalists.'

'How much did they get?' asked O'Brien, from the back of the Land Cruiser.

'Fifteen thousand dollars.'

'Bastards,' said Muller.

'They're not that bright,' said Yokely.

The Major looked at the second Land Cruiser. 'Where's Billy?' he asked.

'Looking after the guys in the house. Last I saw he was blowing smoke rings at them.'

'They're still alive, then?' said the Major.

Yokely's grin widened. 'Sure. But they won't be getting any medical attention until this is over.'

'And you believe they're not connected to Wafeeq?'

'They're criminals, not fundamentalists,' said Yokely. 'And they're not the guys who took Geordie. But the guys they sold Spider to are the guys who moved Geordie on.'

'So we're on the right track,' said Muller.

'No question,' said Yokely.

'What do you think we do now?' asked the Major.

'The transmitter's gone,' said Yokely. 'They took his boots. But they didn't do a full body search on him so he still has the second transmitter.' He gestured up at the sky. 'And we still have the Predator. I think we're well ahead of the game and we can just watch and wait. The new guys have paid fifteen grand for Spider. They won't want to throw that money away so I reckon they'll get in touch with Wafeeq and sell him on.'

The Major nodded thoughtfully. 'I think you're right,' he said. 'Though I'd be happier if we were closer to where he's being held.'

'If we do that we risk showing out,' said the American. 'And it's almost certain they'll move him. Hopefully to the place they're keeping Geordie. I'd recommend we wait and see where they take him to next.'

The Major sighed. 'Okay,' he said. 'It makes sense.'

Yokely pulled a map from inside his body armour, and an aerial photograph of where Shepherd was being kept. 'The house is marked on the map,' said Yokely. 'Look, if you guys wanted to take a break, now would be a good time. Catch up with some sleep, get a bite to eat. As soon as things start to move, I'll call you.'

'We're staying put until this is over,' said the Major, emphatically.

'We're not going anywhere, right enough,' said O'Brien.

'I understand,' said Yokely. He squinted at his wristwatch. 'I'm going to talk to my NSA guys,' he said. 'I need the airwaves monitoring and I want to run a check on the names of the men who've got Spider.'

'Do you need Joe to drive you anywhere?' asked Muller.

Yokely grinned. 'I've already arranged my ride,' he said.

Date palms on the far side of the road bent to the left and a dull, thudding sound filled the air. Twin searchlight beams cut through the night and a Blackhawk helicopter dropped slowly from the sky, kicking up whirlwinds of dust in the road.

'Got to go,' said Yokely. 'Catch you later.' He ran in a half-crouch to the Blackhawk and climbed aboard.

'How does he do that?' asked O'Brien.

'Friends in high places,' said the Major.

The Blackhawk's turbines roared and the helicopter lifted off, turned through a hundred and eighty degrees, and leaped into the night sky.

Howell put the Predator into a slow left-hand turn, scanning the readings on the screen in front of him. It was cruising at fifty miles an hour at an altitude of eighteen thousand feet. There was a layer of patchy cloud at nine thousand feet but the sky above the part of the city he was circling was clear. It was early afternoon, and he was eating a cheese and tomato sandwich.

'A van's just pulled up in front of the house,' said Nichols.

Slater leaned over him. 'See if you can get the registration.'

Nichols twisted the joystick that operated the camera in the belly of the Predator, then tapped on the keyboard. The van's rear registration plate filled the screen and Nichols wrote it down. 'I'll run a check on it,' he said. He pulled the camera back to get a full view of the car. The driver opened the door, got out and stretched. Nichols pressed a button to get high-resolution snapshots of him. 'Got you,' he whispered. He transferred them to the screen in front of Slater. 'Will, run a check on this guy, too, will you?'

'Your wish is my command,' said Slater.

There was a second man in the front passenger seat and when he got out Nichols took several shots of him too. The men banged on the gate and a man in a sweatshirt and baggy trousers came out and let them in. The three walked together into the house.

★   ★   ★

Shepherd heard the door open and footsteps, then a wooden chair scraping across the ground. There were more footsteps, then hands grabbed his arms and pulled him up roughly. His feet scraped along the floor as he tried to keep his balance, then he was forced on to a chair. He heard the door close. For a few moments he thought they'd left him alone, but then his hood was pulled off.

There were three men in front of him. Shepherd recognised the one in the middle. Wafeeq bin Said al-Hadi. His heart raced. The man who was holding Geordie Mitchell hostage was standing in front of him. The man on Wafeeq's right was in his late sixties and had a withered arm, the wrist emerging stick-like from the sleeve of his sweat-stained flannel shirt. The third man was tall, standing head and shoulders above the two, with a slight stoop as if he lived in constant fear of banging his head.

'Who are you?' said Shepherd, playing his role. 'What do you want?'

'You are English?' asked Wafeeq, who was holding his passport and the letter from Muller's company.

'Yes,' he said.

'You know Colin Mitchell?'

Shepherd shook his head.

'You work for the same company,' said Wafeeq.

'I'm his replacement,' said Shepherd. 'I know of him but I never met him.'

Wafeeq stared at him coldly. Then he turned to the old man on his right and said something in Arabic. The man shook his head and Wafeeq said something else, clearly angry now. He pulled out a gun and pointed it at Shepherd, who stared at him unflinchingly. 'They should have searched you,' he said.

'They did,' said Shepherd. 'They took my boots, my gun, my wallet and my radio.' Wafeeq's two companions grabbed Shepherd's arms and pulled him up. One undid his belt and pulled his trousers to his knees. 'Are you going to rape me – is that it?' said Shepherd. 'I heard you lot were into men.'

Wafeeq stepped forward and pistol-whipped him. Shepherd

saw the blow coming and managed to move his head and avoid most of the blow, but the barrel glanced along his temple. The skin broke and blood flowed. He wanted Wafeeq angry because then he might forget about the strip-search.

'You think this is funny?' said Wafeeq. He pointed the gun at Shepherd's face. 'I could kill you now.'

'Go on, then,' said Shepherd. 'You're going to kill me anyway, aren't you?'

'That is up to you.'

'You've shown me your faces, so I can identify you.'

Wafeeq threw back his head and laughed. 'You think I care if you know what I look like? What are you going to do? Tell the police? Do you think I'm scared of them? Do you know how many policemen I've killed? How many soldiers?' He laughed again, then spoke to the two men in Arabic. The old man took a knife from his pocket and used it to cut the ropes binding Shepherd's wrists. Wafeeq took several steps back, keeping the gun pointing at his face.

The men ripped at his shirt and several buttons popped. They made him bend over, then pulled it off. One shouted and pointed at his back, and Shepherd knew that he had seen the second transmitter. They turned him around and slammed him up against the wall. The tall man ripped the piece of plaster that kept the transmitter stuck to his skin and handed it to Wafeeq.

'What is this?' asked Wafeeq.

Shepherd knew there was no point in lying. Even if Wafeeq didn't know what it was, it wouldn't take him long to find out. 'It's a transmitter,' he said. The two men turned him around again so that he was facing Wafeeq, then pushed him back so hard that his head cracked against the wall.

'Why do you have it?' asked Wafeeq.

'The company gave it to us because the other guy was kidnapped. They thought it might help.'

Wafeeq frowned as he studied the electrical circuit. 'Why did they stick it on your back?'

'That was my idea,' said Shepherd.

'Is it on now?'

'We switch them on if we get into trouble.'

Wafeeq smiled cruelly. 'Well, you are in trouble now,' he said. He dropped the transmitter on to the floor and stamped on it. It shattered into more than a dozen pieces. He said something in Arabic to the two Iraqis and they dragged Shepherd to the chair and pushed him on to it. Wafeeq said something else to the two men, then spat at Shepherd and went out, slamming the door behind him.

'I don't speak Arabic,' said Shepherd. 'What did he say?'

The man with the withered arm grinned, showing greying teeth. 'He said we are to torture you to find out what you know.'

The door opened and another man came in, stocky, with a beard and wire-framed glasses. He closed the door and stood there with his arms folded across his chest.

'I don't know anything,' said Shepherd.

'That does not matter,' said the old man. 'He said we are to torture you until you are dead, whether you know anything or not.'

Yokely raised his coffee mug in salute to the screen on the wall. 'I'd offer you one, Dean, but as you're ten thousand miles away it'd be cold by the time it got to you.'

Dean Hepburn grinned and held up a bottle of Jack Daniel's. 'I'd offer to split this with you but I don't reckon you're allowed JD in the Green Zone, right?'

'Sadly, that's true,' said Yokely. 'So, how are things in Crypto City?'

'Same old,' said Hepburn. 'You were lucky I was around. I was heading off when they told me you wanted the satellite link.' He poured himself a large slug of whiskey.

'Just wanted to run a few things by you,' said Yokely. 'I think I'm going to get my hands on Wafeeq.'

'Kudos,' said Hepburn. He raised his glass in a toast.

'Any traffic?'

'None from the man. He's too clued up to the way we operate.'

'Yeah, the CSG here says the same. He never goes near a phone these days.'

'Hardly surprising. The last al-Qaeda heavyweight to use a cellphone was al-Zarqawi and we tracked him down and blew him away.'

'Keep listening anyway. At some point the kidnappers are going to contact Wafeeq so even if they do it through a third party they might mention his name. Also, keep an ear open for anyone talking about Peter Simpson. That's the name our man is using.'

'Will do,' said Hepburn.

Yokely's mobile rang. He apologised to Hepburn and took the call. It was Nichols. 'Two men have just arrived at the house,' said Nichols. 'We have decent visuals so I'm running an ID.'

'Great,' said Yokely. 'If they move Shepherd, let me know straight away.' He ended the call and apologised again to Hepburn.

'Can't believe it, this link is costing hundreds of dollars a minute and you put me on hold,' said Hepburn. He raised his glass of Jack Daniel's. 'Still, the taxpayer pays, right?'

'For which I'm eternally grateful,' said Yokely. 'Okay, things are moving out here. I need you to run some IDs for me. Are you near a secure terminal?'

'Beside me,' said Hepburn.

'I'm going to send you eight names,' said Yokely. 'Three are guys I've already spoken to you about but I want to check whether or not they have direct links to Wafeeq.'

'Why, Richard, you don't think they'd lie to you, do you?'

Yokely smiled thinly. 'I'm fairly confident they were telling the truth, but it's always nice to have confirmation. The other five are new to me. They're the guys who are currently holding Shepherd. I need full checks and any pictures you have. Obviously I'm especially interested in connections they have with Wafeeq or any one else on the most-wanted list.'

Hepburn put down his glass and tapped on the keyboard next to him. 'Okay, I'm online. Download the names when you're ready.'

Shepherd stared at the shattered pieces of the transmitter, his last connection with the outside world.

'Who are you?' asked the man with the straggly beard.

'You know who I am,' said Shepherd. 'You have my passport.'

'Why are you in Iraq?'

'I'm here to work. Security.'

'We don't believe you.'

'It doesn't matter if you believe me or not. It's the truth.'

The old man spoke in Arabic to the tall one, who left the room.

Straggly Beard pointed at the broken transmitter. 'What is that?'

'I told your friend,' said Shepherd. 'It's a transmitter. It shows where I am. My company gave it to me. The man I replaced was kidnapped. The company was worried it might happen again.'

The man laughed, a harsh bark that echoed around the room. 'It didn't help you, did it?'

The door opened and the tall man appeared with a length of rope.

'Look, my company will pay to get me back,' said Shepherd. 'Call them. They'll offer you money.'

'We have been told what we have to do,' said Straggly Beard.

'No one will know,' said Shepherd. 'You just take the money and I'll leave Iraq.'

'Our friend will know,' said Straggly Beard. He held out his hand for the rope and the tall man gave it to him. 'He will know and his retribution will be swift.' He started to tie Shepherd to the chair. Shepherd tried to stand up but the tall man hurried over and pressed his shoulders down. The old man grabbed Shepherd's legs and together the three men wrapped the rope round him and knotted it securely. Shepherd struggled but he couldn't move.

The old man said something in Arabic and all three Iraqis laughed.

Shepherd knew there was no way he could stop what was about to happen. All he could do was hang on and hope that the Major and his men came to his rescue. It was a slim hope, but it was all he had.

Yokely walked past a coffee shop where half a dozen off-duty marines lounged on plastic chairs and sipped cappuccino. Street vendors were selling Persian rugs with Mickey Mouse motifs, T-shirts with slogans such as 'Who's Your Baghdaddy?', Operation Iraqi Freedom beach towels and coffee mugs, and framed bank-notes bearing the head of Saddam Hussein. Overhead four Apache attack helicopters rattled west. He looked at an AT&T phone centre where soldiers were lining up to call home. The temperature was climbing towards fifty degrees, and even though he had only been outside for a couple of minutes, sweat was already trickling down the small of his back.

Yokely's mobile phone rang and he pulled it out of his body armour. It was Simon Nichols. 'Richard, the two guys who went around to the house have left. They didn't take your man with them.'

'Okay,' said Yokely. 'Thanks for telling me. Have you identified the visitors?'

'Still waiting to hear,' said Nichols. 'The pictures aren't as clear as I would have liked so the tech boys are doing some enhancement. As soon as I know, you'll know. Do you want us to follow them, or stick with the house?'

'Which way are they heading?' asked Yokely.

'North towards Baghdad.'

'No reading from Spider's second transmitter?'

'Nothing.'

'And no other visitors to the house?'

'Just the one van.'

'Okay, stick with the house,' said Yokely. 'But as soon as you ID the occupants of the van let me know.' He ended the call and put away his phone. It was just before midday. He doubted they'd move Shepherd while it was light, which meant he had time for a shower, a shave and maybe a steak before he headed out to rejoin the Major.

Straggly Beard slapped Shepherd with the flat of his hand. Shepherd moved his head a fraction of a second before the blow but it still hurt like hell and he tasted blood. The man backhanded him, then punched him in the side of the head.

Shepherd slumped, feigning unconsciousness, but the tall man grabbed his hair and pulled his head back. Shepherd tried to block out what was happening. He focused on Liam, picturing himself in the park with his boy, playing football, Liam running, his hair flying in the wind, Shepherd matching his pace but not trying to catch up.

Something was pulled over his head and Shepherd opened his eyes. It was a plastic bag. He started to panic and his chest heaved, although he knew that the faster he breathed the quicker he'd use up the air. The bag tightened round his neck. He kicked out but two of the men were behind him and the old man was out of reach. The plastic sucked into his mouth and Shepherd blew out but as soon as he breathed in the plastic was back in his mouth. He shook his head from side to side but whoever was holding the bag kept it in place. His chest burned and he strained against the ropes that kept him tied to the chair but they wouldn't budge. He rocked the chair back. The pain in his chest was intensifying as if molten metal had been poured down his throat. Condensation was forming inside the bag but he could still see the old man, his lips pulled back in a snarl that showed his uneven grey teeth. He threw back his head and laughed as Shepherd lost consciousness.

The cook was a big man from New Jersey with a tattoo of Jesus on the cross on his right forearm and a floppy chef's hat. He plopped a huge sirloin steak on Yokely's plate, then shovelled on French fries and onion rings. 'Help yourself to sauce,' he said, pointing at four stainless-steel jugs. 'Red wine, Roquefort, Béarnaise or just plain gravy.'

Yokely poured some of the red-wine sauce over his steak, picked up a couple of warm wholemeal rolls and looked for an empty table. The canteen was packed. The food in the Green Zone was as good as anything the military got in the United States, and the soldiers were tucking into plates laden with steaks, ribs and pizzas.

Yokely went to a table where two female soldiers were finishing their pasta. One was a blonde sergeant in her early thirties; her companion was younger and prettier. 'Do you ladies mind if I join you?' he asked.

The sergeant smiled and waved at the free seats, then carried on talking to her friend. Just as Yokely sat down, his phone rang. It was Nichols again. 'Richard, one of the visitors was Wafeeq.'

Yokely swore, then made an apologetic gesture as the sergeant flashed him a frosty look. 'There's no doubt?'

'None at all,' said Nichols.

Yokely cursed again, under his breath this time.

'What do you want us to do?' asked Nichols.

'What can we do, Simon? I presume the van's gone?'

'No way we could find it now,' said Nichols. 'Needle in a haystack.'

'How much fuel do you have?'

Yokely heard Nichols talk to Howell, then Nichols was back on the line. 'Five hours, maybe six.'

'Stay put,' said Yokely, getting to his feet. He looked wistfully at his steak but knew he didn't have time to eat it. He phoned the Major as he walked out of the canteen into the hot sun and explained what had happened.

The Major realised the significance immediately. 'Wafeeq didn't take Spider with him? Why not?'

'Maybe he smelled a rat.'

'That's what it looks like. Which means Spider's in danger. Geordie too. Did the Predator track Wafeeq?'

'We didn't know it was him,' said Yokely. 'Look, I'm in the Green Zone. I'm going to commandeer a chopper but it'll still take time. You're going to have to go in, Allan. Now.'

'I understand.'

'I don't want to start teaching anyone to suck eggs but there's open farmland behind the house.'

'Roger that,' said the Major.

'I'll text you the number of the Predator guy and he can give you a visual before you act,' said Yokely. 'I'll be there as soon as I can. And try not to kill too many of them. They're our only link to Wafeeq.'

'And Geordie,' said the Major. 'Let's not forget him.'

'I hadn't,' said Yokely. 'But the way things stand, the only way we'll find him is if we get hold of Wafeeq.'

The Major put the phone away and twisted in his seat. 'We've got to go in now,' he said.

'What's happened?' asked Muller.

'Wafeeq came and went but he didn't take Spider with him. That means one of two things. They're going to deliver him later, or Wafeeq got spooked. We can't take the risk so we've got to get him now.' He unfolded the map Yokely had given him. 'Let's get out so we can all look at this,' he said.

They climbed out of the Land Cruiser and the Major held the map on the bonnet. 'We don't have time for surveillance. We have to go straight in,' he said. He stabbed his finger on the map and looked at Jordan. 'We're *here*,' he said. He moved his finger to the farmland behind the house. 'We can get to *here* without being seen from the house.' He put the aerial photograph on top of the map. 'That's where he is. We can come in over the wall and through the back.' Jordan nodded and slotted a stick of chewing-gum into his mouth.

'What sort of firepower do they have?' asked O'Brien.

'We don't know.'

'How many of them?'

'No idea.'

O'Brien's brow furrowed. 'Back-up?'

'Just us,' said the Major. 'We go in fast and we go in hard. But as we'll have to interrogate them to find out where Geordie is, we've got to keep casualties to a minimum.'

'Why don't we make it a real challenge and tie our hands behind our backs?' said O'Brien.

'No one said it was going to be easy, Martin,' said the Major. He folded the map. 'Let's get to it.'

They piled back into the Land Cruiser and Jordan put his foot down hard on the accelerator. The Major talked to Shortt on the transceiver and told him to get to the house as soon as possible. Shortt took down the directions and reckoned they were fifteen minutes away.

The Major's mobile phone beeped and he checked the screen. It was a text message from Yokely with a Baghdad mobile-phone number and a name. Simon Nichols. The Major called and introduced himself.

'The house is quiet on the outside,' said Nichols. 'No one has entered or left since Wafeeq.'

'We're in a white Land Cruiser, heading south,' said the Major. 'We have another unit coming from the east, also a white Land Cruiser.'

'I'll keep an eye out for you,' said Nichols, 'and I'll call you if anything happens at the house.'

The Major put the phone on the dashboard and took out his Glock.

Shepherd opened his eyes. His face was wet and when he took a breath he inhaled water. He shook his head and his eyes gradually focused. Straggly Beard was standing in front of him, holding a bucket. Shepherd had lost count of how many times they had suffocated him into unconsciousness. They kept the plastic bag on his head until he passed out, then threw water over him until he came round.

The tall man slapped him across the face. Shepherd spat to clear his mouth and bloody phlegm splattered across the floor.

'Who are you?' the man shouted.

'Peter Simpson.'

'Your real name.'

Shepherd coughed. 'That is my real name.' Shepherd knew that the questions meant nothing. The men weren't interested in his answers. There was nothing he could tell them that would stop the torture.

The tall man walked towards him, holding the plastic bag. Shepherd moaned. He had lost all sense of time. The light was on and the shutter on the windows behind him was locked so he had no way of knowing if it was day or night. He felt as if the torture had been going on for ever. The bag was dragged down over his head and instinctively he held his breath even though he knew it would do no good. His chest began to heave and burn, he took a breath and the plastic filled his mouth.

The Land Cruiser screeched to a halt and the Major undid his seat-belt. He put the transceiver to his mouth and clicked the transmit button. 'Jimbo, we've arrived.'

There was a buzz of static, then Shortt spoke: 'We're five minutes away, boss.'

'We can't wait,' said the Major. 'We'll go in the back way. When you get here, come in from the front.'

'Roger that,' said Shortt.

The Land Cruiser had stopped on a dirt road. To the left an olive orchard with stubby trees stretched half a mile to the foot of a gently rounded hill. To the right the farmland was less well tended and was mainly rocky soil dotted with date palms. A herd of wild goats looked at the Land Cruiser, then went back to grazing on a clump of brown grass.

'That's the house,' said the Major, pointing through the palms.

Two hundred metres away there was a mud-coloured wall, about six feet high, and beyond it a house with a flat roof on top of which stood a large satellite dish.

Jordan put a pair of binoculars to his eyes. 'I don't see anyone,' he said.

The Major phoned Simon Nichols, who told him that no one was outside or on the roof. The Major put away his phone. 'Okay, let's do it,' he said.

The four men ran towards the wall, bent low, guns at the ready.

Shepherd groaned and opened his eyes, blinking. The man with the withered arm spoke in Arabic. Straggly Beard replied and they both looked at Shepherd. Their attitude had changed – Shepherd could see it in their eyes. Straggly Beard put down the bucket and went out of the room.

Withered Arm muttered to the tall guy, who grunted and nodded. Shepherd pulled at his wrists. There was no give in the rope but they weren't planning to hurt him any more, he knew. They had come to the end of that phase. The two men were staring at him now. He stared back. He knew he could say nothing to stop what was about to happen. He couldn't threaten them, he couldn't intimidate them, and he knew that begging wouldn't work. His mind raced. His wrists were tied and he was in a weakened state. There were at least three of them, maybe more, and they were armed.

Shepherd moved his legs. His boots may have been taken but he could still kick – and he could kick hard. Whatever they were planning to do, he would go down fighting. His heart pounded and he consciously slowed his breathing, not wanting to appear anxious. Giving up wasn't an option. The thinking part of his brain knew it was hopeless, that he would die at their hands, but he refused to accept the inevitable. He hated the men – hated them with a vengeance – and he would do everything he could to administer as much pain and suffering to them as he could before he died.

The door opened and the tall man came back. He was holding a large knife with a wooden handle and a serrated edge. A bread-knife. He closed the door.

'My company will pay you,' said Shepherd, surprised at how calm he sounded. 'They'll pay you a lot of money.'

The tall man took a step towards him. The man with the withered arm said something to Straggly Beard, who moved to the right. Withered Arm started to mutter: '*Allahu Akbar.*' God is great. Straggly Beard repeated it, then the tall man. All three got themselves into a rhythm. '*Allahu Akbar. Allahu Akbar. Allahu Akbar.*'

The door opened and a fourth stepped into the room. Shepherd hadn't seen him before. He was stocky with a shaved head and a beard that went half-way down his chest. He was wearing a floor-length *dishdasha* and stood with his hands clasped together. He joined in the chant.

Shepherd pulled at his wrists again, even though he knew it was futile. The ropes tying him to the chair were as tight as those binding his arms. He hadn't tried to stand up but he knew that when he did the chair would force him to bend forward making his head an easy target. He stared at the bread-knife. The man was swinging it back and forth as he chanted. He pulled at his wrists again and felt the rope bite into his flesh. He welcomed the pain: it was a reminder that he was still alive, that blood was still coursing through his veins.

'*Allahu Akbar. Allahu Akbar. Allahu Akbar.*' They repeated the mantra as if somehow invoking their God legitimised what they were about to do. Shepherd knew that it was also a way of distancing themselves from it. Killing wasn't easy, and killing with a knife was just about the hardest way to take a life. Guns were easy: you pointed, pulled a trigger, and technology did the rest, but knives had to be used. You had to thrust, hack or saw and keep at it until the blood flowed and the victim died.

The man with the knife was just four feet from the chair. Shepherd could see his Adam's apple wobbling as he chanted, his right eyelid flickering, and his jaw tightening. The man was preparing himself for what he was about to do.

So was Shepherd. He grunted, bent forward to raise the legs of the chair off the ground, then turned quickly. He yelled, to get his adrenaline flowing, and to shock the men in the room. He bent further down, angling the chair legs up, then powered backwards with all his strength, screaming at full volume. He pushed hard and felt the man with the knife stagger back. Shepherd kept the momentum going and when the man hit the wall Shepherd felt the chair leg sink into his body. Shepherd pushed until he couldn't go any further, then stepped forward and whirled round. The bread-knife dropped from the man's hand and he sank to his knees, blood pouring from his stomach. Shepherd turned, bent low and lashed out with his foot. He hit the man in the throat but the kick put him off balance and he staggered forward, trying desperately to regain his footing because he knew that if he fell over he wouldn't be able to get up.

He slipped on the wet floor and went down on one knee. The man in the *dishdasha* picked up the knife. He glanced at the man with the withered arm, who nodded. Straggly Beard shouted something in Arabic and pulled a gun from under his sweatshirt. Shepherd dropped low and spun around, lashing out with his right leg. He caught the man at the ankles, tipping him backwards. The gun went off but the bullet buried itself in the ceiling. Shepherd moved backwards and kicked out again, catching him in the knee.

The man with the withered arm grabbed at the chair with his good arm and swung Shepherd round, screaming in Arabic. Shepherd staggered, still bent double – the old man had a strong grip. Shepherd saw the man in the *dishdasha* waving the knife, a manic look in his eyes, then saw Straggly Beard trying to take aim at him.

The door flew open and a man came into the room bent low with a Glock in his hand. It was the Major. The gun fired twice and Straggly Beard fell to the ground. Another man came in, this one with an Uzi. Jordan raised it but before he could fire O'Brien stepped in and slammed his handgun against the head of the man holding the knife, who went down without a sound. 'No point in wasting a bullet,' he said.

The man with the withered arm fell to his knees and began to wail. The Major kicked him in the chest and told him to shut up. He curled up into a ball and sobbed quietly.

Shepherd sighed and sat down heavily. He felt drained, physically and emotionally.

O'Brien grinned. 'Yet again we pull your nuts out of the fire, Spider.'

The Major walked over to Shepherd, picked up the bread-knife and cut the ropes that were holding him to the chair, then freed his wrists. Shepherd gasped as the blood flowed into his hands and shook them. 'Are you okay?' asked the Major.

'I am now,' said Shepherd. 'Did you follow Wafeeq?'

'No,' said the Major, 'but these guys should be able to fill us in. With the right incentive.'

'Yokely's on his way, then?'

The Major nodded. He helped Shepherd to his feet. 'Can you walk?'

'I'm fine,' said Shepherd, but he needed the Major's support to get to the door. Jordan knelt down and examined the man that Shepherd had impaled with the chair leg. Blood was pumping from the wound in his stomach, which meant that an artery had burst. He didn't have long to live.

'Get them downstairs, Martin.'

'Will do, boss.'

'This one's dead,' said Jordan. 'Or will be soon.'

The Major helped Shepherd down the stairs. At the bottom two Iraqis were lying face down on the floor, their hands clasped over the back of their necks. Muller was covering them with his gun. He grinned at Shepherd. 'Good to see you, Spider.'

'You can say that again,' said Shepherd.

'There're two alive upstairs, John,' said the Major. 'Get them all in the front room.'

The Major took Shepherd into the kitchen. Half a dozen bottles of water stood on the draining-board and Shepherd unscrewed a cap and drank. As he put the bottle down he saw a face looking in through the window and flinched, then realised it was Carol Bosch. 'Hey,' she said, and waved her shotgun.

Shepherd grinned. The kitchen door opened and Shortt came in, his gun at the ready. He relaxed when he saw Shepherd and the Major and holstered the Glock.

'Tell me, Jimbo, why are you always late?' asked Shepherd.

'Traffic was murder,' said Shortt. 'Camels, goats, all sorts of shit on the road.'

'Any excuse,' said Shepherd, 'but I'm glad you made it.'

Shortt held up a pair of boots. 'Thought you might like these,' he said. 'The guy who took them from you doesn't need them any more.' He tossed them to Shepherd.

'How did it go?' asked Haschka, following Shortt into the kitchen, Uzi in his right hand, barrel pointing at the floor.

'Two dead,' said the Major. 'Four still alive.'

'Are you okay?' asked Bosch, who was in the doorway, her shotgun at her side.

'I've had better days,' said Shepherd, wiping his mouth with the back of his hand. Blood streaked across it and he wiped it on his jeans. 'But, yeah, I'm okay. A few minutes later and it would have been a different story.' He sat down and put on his boots.

'What went wrong?' asked Bosch.

'Wafeeq found the transmitter,' said Shepherd. 'I guess he put two and two together.'

O'Brien walked into the kitchen, opened the rattling refrigerator and found a cooked leg of lamb wrapped in Cellophane. He took it out, sniffed, pulled a face and tossed it back. 'Why don't these people buy any decent food?' he growled, and slammed the door.

'What do you want, Martin?' asked Shortt. 'A kebab?'

'They probably weren't expecting guests,' said Bosch. She

went to Shepherd and put a hand on his cheek. 'Still got your rugged good looks.'

Shepherd smiled at her. 'You too.'

She patted his groin. 'They didn't hack off anything down there, did they?'

'No, it's fine.'

'Are you sure? I could check.'

'Maybe you two should get a room.' Haschka laughed.

'Yeah, and maybe you should get a life,' said Bosch.

The windows started to vibrate and seconds later they heard the rotors of an approaching helicopter.

'Five will get you ten that's Yokely,' said Muller.

'Doesn't like bullets, I guess,' said O'Brien.

'He was in the Green Zone,' said the Major.

'Convenient,' said O'Brien.

'Trust me, Richard Yokely isn't scared of a bit of rough-and-tumble,' said the Major.

Shepherd went to the kitchen door and looked out across the backyard. A Blackhawk helicopter was hovering above the farmland close to the boundary wall. The helicopter continued to hover a few feet above the ground as Yokely clambered out, holding his M16, and jogged over to let himself in through a wooden gate. He waved at Shepherd as he hurried across the courtyard. The Blackhawk lifted into the air and flew off.

'They're worried about mines,' said Yokely, as he reached them.

'And you're not?' asked Shepherd.

Yokely grinned. 'I had my palm read by a gypsy psychic a while back,' he said. 'She said I'd live to a ripe old age and I believe her.' He slapped Shepherd on the back. 'Good to see you're okay, Spider,' he said. 'You had us worried for a while.'

'What about Geordie? Do we know where he is?' asked Shepherd.

'That's why I'm here,' said Yokely. He pushed past Shepherd

and went into the kitchen. Bosch and Shortt were standing by the sink. 'Where are the Arabs?' he asked.

The Major pointed at the door that led to the hallway.

'The front room,' said Jordan.

'Anyone dead?'

'Two,' said the Major. 'They were busy giving Spider a hard time and didn't hear us coming.'

'Excellent,' said Yokely. 'Be a sweetheart and get me some rope, will you, Carol?'

'I am not your fucking sweetheart,' said Bosch.

'It's an expression,' said Yokely, unabashed.

'Yeah, well, so is "go fuck yourself". Get your own bloody rope,' said Bosch.

'I'll get it,' said Shortt.

'Thank you, sweetheart,' said Yokely. He winked at Bosch and went along the hallway to the front room, Shepherd and the Major following. The four Arabs were kneeling on the floor. Muller was covering them with his Glock and Jordan had his Uzi trained on them.

'Let's get started,' said Yokely. He reached into his body armour and brought out a handful of black plastic zip-ties. He walked behind the line of kneeling men and, one by one, bound their wrists.

In the corner of the sitting room a circular wooden table was surrounded by half a dozen small wooden stools. Yokely placed one in front of each kneeling man.

Shortt returned with a coil of rope and handed it to him. Yokely went into the kitchen and came back with a knife. He cut four long pieces of rope.

'What are you doing, Richard?' asked the Major.

'Information retrieval,' said Yokely. He made a loop at the end of a piece of rope and checked the slip-knot. 'Jimbo, tell them to stand on the stools, would you?'

Shortt glanced at the Major then barked at the men in Arabic. They looked back at him, confused and fearful.

'Tell them that if they don't stand on the stools, they'll be shot,' said Yokely. He started work on a second length of rope.

Shortt translated. O'Brien walked into the sitting room, holding his Glock. 'What's occurring?' he asked.

'Martin, help these guys on to the stools, will you?' Yokely checked the second noose and started on the third.

'Pleasure,' said O'Brien. He grabbed the first by the scruff of his flannel shirt and dragged him towards them. The old man climbed up and stood there trembling.

Muller waved his gun at the other three Iraqis, who got to their feet unsteadily and climbed on to the stools.

Bosch walked in from the hallway. 'What do you think you're doing?' she asked.

'Carol . . .' said Jordan.

'Don't "Carol" me,' said Bosch. 'You can see what he's doing, can't you?'

'Pat, will you and Joe take her outside, please?' said Yokely, as he tested the third noose. 'Secure the perimeter.'

'Screw you,' said Bosch.

Jordan put a hand on her arm but she shook it off angrily. 'He can't do this.'

'I'm afraid I can,' said Yokely. 'I can and I will.' He turned to Muller. 'John, please take your people outside.'

'I'm staying,' said Muller.

'I appreciate your enthusiasm, but you're civilians and I want all civilians out of here. It's for my own peace of mind, not yours.'

'You don't want witnesses,' said Bosch.

'Carol, sweetheart, you're beginning to piss me off,' said Yokely. 'If you're not outside within the next ten seconds, I'll make a phone call that will have you on the next plane out of this country.'

'Let's go, Carol,' said Muller.

'You can't let him treat us like this,' said Bosch.

Muller put his arm round her shoulders and led her back to the kitchen. Jordan followed, flicking the safety catch on his Uzi.

'Don't do anything I wouldn't do, guys,' said Haschka, as he closed the door.

Yokely started work on the fourth noose. 'If any of you guys don't have the stomach for this, you're welcome to go with them. Except you, Jimbo. I'll need you to translate.'

'I'm staying anyway,' said Shortt.

'Me too,' said O'Brien.

'Wouldn't miss it for the world,' said the Major.

Yokely looked at Shepherd. 'Spider?'

Shepherd knew that what was about to happen was illegal and immoral, that it went against everything he believed in. But only minutes earlier the men standing on the stools had been torturing him and planning to kill him in the most brutal way imaginable for no other reason than his nationality. What Yokely was planning to do was evil, but it was a necessary evil, because the four men were the only hope they had of finding Geordie. 'Go ahead,' said Shepherd. 'I'm not going anywhere.'

Yokely grinned. 'I think deep down you've always wanted to know what I do,' he said. 'Watch and learn.'

He tossed the loose ends of the ropes over the wooden beam that ran the length of the sitting room. The nooses dangled in front of the Iraqis as Yokely gathered up the loose ends and tied them to the bars on the window, methodically checking that each was secure.

The old man with the withered arm began to plead in his own language. 'No need to translate,' Yokely said to Shortt. 'I get the drift.' He walked along the line of Iraqis and fitted the nooses round their necks, then stood back to admire his handiwork. 'I think that'll do, don't you, Spider?'

'I guess so,' said Shepherd. 'It depends what you've got in mind.'

Yokely chuckled and pulled a bundle of papers out of his body armour, then walked up and down in front of the four men, who were trembling with fear. 'Translate, please, Jimbo,' said Yokely. He stopped in front of a man who had been caught downstairs.

He was in his thirties, with a goatee beard and a white *dishdasha*. Yokely held up a sheet of paper. There were several lines of type and a photograph of two men sitting in a car. 'Tell him this photograph shows him meeting a man called Wafeeq bin Said al-Hadi last year in Baghdad.'

Shortt translated as Yokely flicked through his printouts. When Shortt finished speaking, the man started to talk quickly.

'He says he isn't the man in the photograph and that he has never met anyone called Wafeeq,' said Shortt.

Yokely went to stand in front of the man with the withered arm. He studied one of the sheets of paper, then grinned up at him. 'Your name is Yuusof Abd al-Nuuh. You have three children and seven grandchildren. Last year you spoke to Wafeeq bin Said al-Hadi. Just chit-chat. Or code. We're not sure which. But we know you spoke to him.'

Shortt translated. The old man closed his eyes and began to mutter to himself. The man on the middle stool was the biggest of the four, with bulging forearms and a thick neck. He was staring straight ahead, eyes blank, mouth wide open. 'This guy, I don't know who he is,' said Yokely, walking over to stand in front of him. He kicked the stool away and the man fell. The rope snapped round his neck and cut deep into the flesh. The man's legs kicked and his body shuddered but the noose was so tight that not a sound escaped from his mouth.

'What the fuck?' shouted O'Brien.

The man stopped kicking and his body swung gently from the beam. A damp patch spread round the groin and drops of urine trickled down his left leg on to the tiled floor.

'Then there were three,' said Yokely. He walked to the man with the withered arm and stared up at him. 'So, Yuusof Abd al-Nuuh, what do you think? Can you bring yourself to tell me where I'll find Wafeeq?' Yokely consulted his watch. 'You see, time's running out, and the fact that Wafeeq found the transmitter means he's probably going to do something pretty terrible to a friend of ours.' Yokely put his right foot against the stool and gave it a push. The man wobbled and started to hyper-ventilate.

'Stop!' shouted the man at the far right of the group – the man with the shaved head and the *dishdqsha*. 'Leave him alone.'

Yokely smiled and took his foot off the stool. He walked over to the man who had spoken and leafed through the printouts. 'Ah, yes, of course,' he said. 'You're one of Yuusof's sons, aren't you? And you can speak English. Excellent.' He read through the information on the sheet he was holding. 'According to this, you've never met Wafeeq and there's no record of you phoning him.' He smiled sympathetically. 'So you're not much use to me, really, are you?' He rested his foot on the side of the stool and turned to the father. 'Jimbo, explain to the old man that I'm going to kill his boy unless he tells me where I can find Wafeeq.'

Jimbo translated. The father sagged and the rope tightened round his neck. Then he whispered something in Arabic.

'What did he say, Jimbo?'

'He said okay, he'll talk.'

Yokely grinned triumphantly. He pushed the stool, which shuddered. The man yelped and struggled to keep his balance. 'Tell him to be quick about it, Jimbo.'

Wafeeq parked the van and walked quickly to the house. Rahman jogged to keep up with him. Wafeeq always had Rahman with him when he left the house. He had served with Saddam Hussein's Republican Guard and Wafeeq had once seen him kill a man with his bare hands. Azeem was standing at one of the bedroom windows and waved. Wafeeq waved back. Sulaymaan opened the front door as he reached it. 'Where is the hostage?' he asked.

Wafeeq ignored him. He strode along the hallway and into the main room. Kamil was on his hands and knees on a prayer mat, his forehead on the ground.

'We have to move,' said Wafeeq. 'Abdul-Nasir is downstairs?'

'Of course.' Kamil straightened and frowned at him. 'What has happened?' he asked.

'The man they caught worked for the same company as Mitchell. He had a transmitting device. They are hunting us, my friend.'

Kamil stood and rolled up the prayer mat. 'But we knew that. We knew they would look for him. No one will find him here. *Inshallah.*'

'This is different,' said Wafeeq. 'The man was different. We kill the infidel and we leave. Now.'

'But then everything will have been for nothing.'

'No, we just bring forward the deadline. We say that the intransigence of the British government has brought about the death of their subject. We film his death and then we leave.'

The Major and O'Brien pushed the two Arabs into the back of the Land Cruiser, their hands tied behind their backs. Shortt climbed into the driving seat and O'Brien got in beside him. 'We'll be right behind you, Jimbo,' said the Major.

'Right, boss,' said Shortt. He put the 4 × 4 into gear and drove off down the road.

The Major went over to Yokely and Shepherd, who were waiting by the second Land Cruiser. 'Let's go,' he said.

'Why don't we call in a chopper?' asked Shepherd.

'We can drive in twenty minutes,' said Yokely, 'and I don't want Wafeeq any more spooked than he already is. If he hears choppers, he'll run. We need to get in place first. I've already called in troops, so we'll have the perimeter secured.'

'That doesn't help Geordie,' said Shepherd.

'We've got time, trust me,' said Yokely.

'This isn't just about capturing Wafeeq, is it?' said Shepherd.

Yokely put a hand on his shoulder. 'It's about getting Geordie out of harm's way,' he said. 'Wafeeq is the icing on the cake.'

'That had better be true,' said Shepherd.

Muller walked up with an Uzi. 'I'm coming with you,' he said.

'John, this is now becoming a military operation. Like I said before, you're a civilian.'

'Yeah? Well, I'm the civilian who has the keys to that vehicle, so without me you're going nowhere.' Muller held up the keys to the Land Cruiser and jingled them.

'We don't have time to argue,' said Yokely.

'Exactly,' said Muller. He pulled open the driver's door and climbed in. 'So shut the fuck up and get in.'

Yokely opened his mouth to argue but the Major spoke first. 'John's okay,' he said.

'It's on your head, then,' said Yokely. He got into the front passenger seat and took out his mobile. The Major and Shepherd got into the back. As Muller started the engine and drove away from the house, Yokely phoned Simon Nichols. 'Simon, do you have visual on us?' he asked.

'We have you,' said Nichols.

'Follow us and let us know if there are any roadblocks ahead.'

'I'll give you plenty of warning,' said Nichols. 'How's Shepherd?'

'All very James Bond,' said Yokely. 'Stirred but not shaken.'

'Does he know how lucky he is?'

'Oh, yes,' said Yokely. 'He knows.'

'Couldn't help but notice that you put two of the Iraqis in the first Land Cruiser,' said Nichols. 'What's that about?'

Yokely grinned. 'Watch and learn,' he said.

The Sniper watched with a growing sense of amazement. What he was seeing made no sense at all. He was lying on an inflatable bed, covered with a piece of sacking. He had chosen the vantage-point carefully. The building below him was six storeys tall and he could see for miles. There were two main roads each within six hundred metres of the building, both used regularly by American troops. There was a fire escape at the rear, which offered a quick way down to a labyrinth of alleyways. He had used the rooftop four months earlier when he had killed an officer leading a foot patrol – shot him in the small of the back as he bent down to tie a shoelace, shattering the spine just below the body armour.

Two patrols had driven along the nearest main road but they had been moving too quickly. The Sniper didn't waste bullets: he only shot when he was sure he would make a kill, and he had the patience to wait as long as it took. He had two bottles of water in the shade of a chimney-stack, and a plastic bag in case he needed to defecate. The Spotter was lying next to him on a rush mat. Like the Sniper, he was staring at the house some three hundred metres away, wondering what was going on.

They had watched the two Land Cruisers drive up together and park round the corner from the house. Ten minutes after they had arrived, an army Humvee joined them. A soldier climbed out of a Land Cruiser and went to talk to the soldiers in the Humvee. Shortly afterwards two Bradley fighting vehicles arrived with another Humvee. A dozen soldiers in full body armour climbed out and gathered round an officer.

Two helicopters had flown in from the south, then gone into a slow, banking turn that brought them in to a hover about a mile away from the military vehicles. The Sniper recognised them: they were Blackhawks, MH-60L Direct Action Penetrators. They each came equipped with two 7.62mm Miniguns, electrically driven Gatling guns that could fire up to four thousand rounds a minute, and M261 nineteen-tube rocket-launchers, capable of firing a wide range of rockets including armour and bunker penetration and anti-personnel flechette warheads that could rip apart an entire platoon, accurate up to two miles. There was also a 30mm chain gun, which could fire 625 high-explosive rounds a minute with pinpoint accuracy, and two M272 launchers each with four 100-pound Hellfire missiles that could destroy a tank five miles away at the touch of a button. The DAP Blackhawks had been equipped for special-forces operations and were just about the most deadly machines operating in Iraq.

It was what had happened next that had mystified the Sniper. Two civilians wearing body armour had pulled two Iraqis out of the back of a Land Cruiser. One of the Iraqis had been given a handgun and the other a Kalashnikov. Then a Westerner in shirt and trousers climbed out of the second Land Cruiser. He kept his hands behind his back as if his wrists had been tied, but from his vantage-point the Sniper could see a handgun tucked into his belt in the small of his back.

The two Iraqis and the Westerner walked to the house. The American soldiers fanned out, spreading round the street and taking up vantage-points. They appeared to be preparing to storm the house. The Bradley fighting vehicles kept their engines running, ready to move closer to the house, and the Blackhawks continued to hover. The Sniper knew better than to fire while the hunter-killer helicopters were in the vicinity: they were equipped with a full-range of visual, infrared and radar sensors. If they even suspected he was on the roof, they would have no hesitation in destroying the building, no matter who else was in it.

'What do you think is happening?' asked the Spotter.

'I have no idea,' said the Sniper. 'But I am sure we will find a target before too long. *Inshallah*.'

Kamil banged on the door. 'Colin, stand against the wall, please,' he shouted. He pressed his eye to the spyhole and watched as Mitchell followed his instructions. Then he unbolted the door and opened it. Behind him, Rahman and Azeem waited, their faces covered with *shemagh* scarves. Azeem was holding a Kalashnikov, the safety off.

Mitchell stared at the assault rifle. 'What's wrong?' he asked.

'Nothing. We just need to make another video,' said Kamil. He walked across the basement and handed the orange jumpsuit to Mitchell. 'Put this on, please.'

'What sort of video?' asked Mitchell.

Wafeeq walked into the basement carrying the video-camera and its tripod. 'Do as you're told or we will kill you now,' he snarled.

'It's better to keep him calm,' Kamil said in Arabic.

'You are too soft on them,' said Wafeeq, also in Arabic. 'They are the infidel. They deserve to die.'

'It is easier if they are calm,' said Kamil, patiently. 'If they struggle, it is harder.' He smiled at Mitchell. 'Everything is okay, Colin, we just need another video.'

'Why?'

'We need more publicity. We need to put more pressure on your government.'

Wafeeq glared at Mitchell as he screwed the camera on to the tripod. Mitchell slowly pulled on the jumpsuit.

'I will do this one,' said Wafeeq in Arabic.

Kamil nodded. 'It's your choice,' he said. They heard shouts from upstairs. It was Abdul-Nasir, the youngest of their group and the one most prone to panic.

'Kamil!' shouted Abdul-Nasir. 'Someone's coming. Quick! Come and see!'

'Soldiers?'

'No. Two men with a Westerner.'

'What?'

'Come and see.'

Kamil exchanged a look with Wafeeq. 'Go!' said Wafeeq, impatiently.

Kamil hurried into the kitchen, went up to the first floor and peered out of the bedroom window that overlooked the front of the house. Two Iraqis were walking down the path to the house. One was holding a pistol, the other had a Kalashnikov. Between them was a Westerner, head bowed, hands tied behind his back. He stumbled as he walked and the man with the Kalashnikov grabbed his arm. Kamil opened the window. 'What do you want?' he shouted.

'Wafeeq said we were to bring him,' shouted the man with the handgun.

'He said what?'

'He said we were to interrogate him, then bring him here.'

'What is your name?'

'I am Yuusof Abd al-Nuuh. This is my son.'

'Wait there.'

Kamil ran downstairs. A Kalashnikov was leaning against the wall in the hall and he picked it up, then hurried down to the basement. 'Did you tell them to bring the prisoner here?' he asked Wafeeq.

Wafeeq frowned. 'What are you talking about?'

'Two men, upstairs. They've brought a prisoner with them. A Westerner.'

Wafeeq looked at Mitchell. He was kneeling on the floor in the orange jumpsuit, his hands at his sides, glaring at them defiantly. The video-camera was ready to roll, and Wafeeq was ready to kill. But clearly something was wrong upstairs. He pointed at Mitchell. 'I will be back for you,' he said. 'Come with me,' he said to Kamil.

The two men hurried out of the basement. Wafeeq told Azeem to lock the door, then ran upstairs with Kamil.

'His name is Yuusof Abd al-Nuuh, he said you told him to bring the prisoner here after they had interrogated him.'

Wafeeq shook his head impatiently. 'I said interrogate him and kill him,' he snapped. 'Why would I want them to bring him here?' He shouted towards the front room: 'Azeem, Sulaymaan, Rahman, get upstairs now. Cover the front of the house.'

The three men ran out of the front room and up the stairs, carrying Kalashnikovs. 'Azeem!' shouted Wafeeq. 'Take the RPG.' Azeem scurried back to the front room, then reappeared with the weapon. He rushed upstairs after his two colleagues.

'What do you think is happening?' Kamil asked Wafeeq.

'Something smells bad,' said Wafeeq.

'Did you tell them where we were?'

'Of course not.'

There was a loud knock on the front door. Wafeeq switched off the Kalashnikov's safety catch and nodded for Kamil to open it.

Kamil kept his gun at his side as he pulled back the bolts.

Wafeeq stood with the gun on his hip, his finger on the trigger. Kamil took a deep breath and opened the door.

The two Iraqis were holding the Westerner. Yuusof's face was drenched in sweat and he looked nervous. 'What are you doing here?' asked Kamil.

Yuusof said nothing.

'Speak!' shouted Kamil, gesturing with his gun.

The Westerner lifted his head and smiled. 'Surprise,' he said.

Mitchell got to his feet. He was sure they were getting ready to execute him, and he was equally sure that Wafeeq was going to do it. Something had happened upstairs but he knew it was only a temporary reprieve. They would be back soon and when they did come back they would kill him.

He went to the paperback book, moved it aside and picked up the magnetic chess set. He opened it, took out one of the small plastic-covered metal pieces and knelt by the electric socket. The screws came out easily. He took off the cover and pulled out the wires. He wasn't sure if they were live so he touched the bare wires together. Sparks flew. He did it again and this time there were no sparks so he figured he'd blown a fuse. He gripped the wire and pulled hard. There was a ripping sound from behind the wall and several feet of wire came out of the hole. He stared at it. He would have given anything right then for a knife or a pair of scissors. He smiled to himself. If he'd had either a knife or scissors he wouldn't have been messing around with the wire. He bent over, put his head close to the wall and began gnawing at the wire with his teeth.

Shepherd pulled out the Glock and shot the man in the forehead twice in quick succession. He slumped to the ground without a sound. Wafeeq stood in the doorway, holding a Kalashnikov. Shepherd dropped into a crouch and brought the gun to bear on Wafeeq's chest but before he could fire the door slammed.

The two Iraqis who had walked him to the house dived to the

ground and lay face down with their hands over their heads. There were no rounds in their guns and they had been told to stay down until the shooting was over.

Shepherd heard shouts above his head and looked up to see two men at the upstairs windows. One was aiming an RPG, the other had a Kalashnikov. The Kalashnikov fired and bullets sprayed round the gate as one of the Blackhawk helicopters swooped down to hover above the buildings on the far side of the street.

He kicked the door, which burst open, dived inside, rolled over and got to his feet, Glock in both hands. The man with the Kalashnikov had gone, and blood was pooling round the head of the man Shepherd had shot. Outside, he heard the Blackhawk's massive chain guns burst into life. The high-explosive dual-purpose rounds ripped into the upper floor of the house for five or six seconds, then there was silence. He heard shouts outside, American voices, then M16s being fired, the thump of footsteps below him. He looked around for the door to the basement.

Mitchell had felt the shells smash into the upper floors of the building. Now he could hear the throb of helicopter blades, which meant the Americans were outside, more gunfire – M16s – and shouts and yells.

He had been standing with his back to the wall waiting for Kamil and the rest to come back, but now he knew that all bets were off. He had a length of wire wrapped round his right wrist. When he heard the thump of feet on the stairs, he moved quickly to the far side of the room and stood to the left of the door. It was all about survival now. The Americans had the technology and the manpower. It was only a matter of time before they overpowered his kidnappers. All Mitchell had to do was stay alive until that happened.

He heard the bolts slide back, then more gunfire upstairs. He let the wire swing loose from his wrist.

The door flew back and Mitchell put up a hand to stop it. One of the kidnappers stepped into the room, his Kalashnikov at waist level. Mitchell kicked out at the weapon, knocking away the barrel. It went off and bullets hammered into the far wall, the shots deafening in the confined space. He stepped forward and threw the wire round the man's neck, caught the free end and pulled it tight. The Kalashnikov went off again and two shots smacked into the ceiling. Mitchell pulled back on the wire and the man lost his balance. He looped the wire round the man's neck again, then stepped back, pulling it taut. The man twisted, trying to point the weapon at Mitchell, but the wire bit tighter into his throat.

A second figure appeared. It was Wafeeq, holding a Kalashnikov. He pointed it at Mitchell, but before he could fire Mitchell kicked at the door, which slammed shut. The man he was strangling tried to slam the butt of his Kalashnikov against Mitchell's knee but he moved backwards to avoid the blow.

The door slammed open again. Wafeeq was screaming in Arabic as he pulled the trigger.

Shepherd hurtled down the stairs. There was a doorway to the right and as he reached the bottom of the stairs he heard Wafeeq shouting. He brought up his Glock with both hands as Wafeeq's Kalashnikov fired a quick burst and the air was filled with the tang of cordite. The door to the basement room was half shut and Shepherd couldn't see inside so he ran forward and kicked the door open.

Mitchell was in a corner behind an Arab whose torso was peppered with bloody holes. As the door flew open the dead man's Kalashnikov clattered to the ground.

Wafeeq was standing in the middle of the room, still screaming.

'Wafeeq!' yelled Shepherd.

Wafeeq turned and Shepherd fired. The shot missed the back of Wafeeq's skull by an inch and thwacked into the wall. Wafeeq's finger tightened on the trigger and Shepherd dropped into a crouch and fired again, hitting him in the shoulder. Wafeeq staggered back. Mitchell dropped the man he was holding, rushed forward and kicked Wafeeq in the small of the back. Wafeeq staggered forward, Shepherd slammed the Glock against his temple and he slumped to the ground without a sound.

Mitchell stood where he was, panting. 'Bugger me, what took you so long?' he gasped.

'You weren't easy to find,' said Shepherd. 'Are you okay?'

Mitchell rubbed his hand down his face. 'I thought it was all over, Spider.'

'Yeah,' said Shepherd. 'I know how you feel.'

'The Major's outside?'

'Yeah. And the guys.'

'Thanks.'

Shepherd grinned. 'Don't get all sentimental on me, Geordie.' Mitchell gripped him in a bear hug, and Shepherd hugged him back, hard.

The Sniper pressed his eye into the scope's cup. All he saw was black until his eye was in the correct position, then through the scope he found the target. An American soldier. Superimposed on the soldier was the sight's reticule. A curved line was marked from one hundred metres to one thousand metres. All the Sniper had to do was aim his rifle so that in the scope the soldier's feet were at the bottom of the range-finder. The number closest to the target's head was the distance away in metres. The manufacturer had calibrated the sight for the average height of a Russian soldier back in the early sixties when the rifle was first manufactured, a shade under five feet eight inches. The Sniper knew that the average American soldier was substantially bigger than his Cold War Russian counterpart. Americans were brought up on full-fat milk and fast food diets and most were a good six inches taller than the height for which the scope had been calibrated. It was an easy adjustment to make.

The one-thousand metre line was optimistic, the Sniper knew. The Russians liked to claim that their snipers could hit a man with a Dragunov at a thousand metres, but the Sniper preferred never to work above five hundred. Six hundred on a windless day, perhaps.

He moved the sight slowly down the soldier's body, and frowned as he reached the man's feet. He wasn't wearing army boots: he was wearing brown shoes with tassels. The Sniper had never seen a soldier in footwear like that. He raised the sight again and focused on the man's face. It didn't matter what sort of shoes he was wearing. All that mattered was that he was an American soldier and that he would soon be dead.

He forced himself to relax as he stared through the scope. The soldier was four hundred metres away. The wind was negligible and it would be an easy shot. But he had to wait until the helicopters had left.

Yokely watched the marines pile into the house. No shots had been fired for several seconds and from inside he heard shouts of 'Clear!' as they moved through the rooms.

'I should be in there,' said the Major.

'It's a military operation. We'd be in the way,' said Yokely.

'They were happy enough for Spider to go in,' said O'Brien.

'They needed the diversion,' said Yokely. 'Anyway, all's well that ends well, yeah?'

'You can say that when Spider and Geordie are out here in one piece,' said O'Brien.

'Speak of the devil,' said Yokely. Two big marines led the pair out of the house. Yokely grinned. 'They look fine.'

The Major and Yokely went towards them. One of the marines was a captain. 'Everything okay in there?' Yokely asked.

'Four dead,' said the captain. 'No casualties on our side.'

'Excellent,' said Yokely. 'Wafeeq?'

'We've a medic working on him now.' The captain gestured at Spider. 'He shot him in the shoulder.'

'He's okay, though?'

'His injury isn't life-threatening,' said the captain.

'We're fine, too. Thanks for asking,' said Shepherd.

'I can see that,' said Yokely. He called up the lead Blackhawk helicopter on his transceiver. 'Thanks, guys, we can take it from here,' he said.

'Roger that,' said the pilot.

The two helicopters banked and flew south, turbines screaming.

'Are you okay, Geordie?' asked the Major.

'I will be after one of Martin's fry-ups and a couple of pints.'

Yokely clipped his transceiver on his belt and nodded at him. 'This is Richard Yokely,' said the Major. 'He arranged the heavy artillery for us.'

'Thanks, Richard,' said Mitchell.

'All part of the service,' said Yokely, with a grin, and saluted Mitchell.

The Sniper frowned as he saw the soldier salute the man in the orange jumpsuit, then realised the significance of what he'd seen. The man in the orange jumpsuit must be an officer. The Iraqis in the house had been keeping a high-ranking officer hostage and the Americans had rescued him.

The Sniper slowly moved the rifle until the head of the man in the orange jumpsuit was in the centre of his sights. He took a breath, slowly let out half, then squeezed the trigger.

The bullet hit the man in the side of the head. His knees buckled and he fell to the ground.

'*Allahu Akbar*,' whispered the Sniper. A perfect shot.

'What the hell just happened?' shouted Simon Nichols, sitting bolt upright. He stared at the real-time video view of the Baghdad city block. The man in the orange jumpsuit was sprawled on the ground. Richard Yokely had dropped into a crouch, scanning the buildings round him. 'Did Richard just shoot the guy? Is that what happened?'

'Get a grip,' said Will Slater. 'There's a sniper. Phillip, can you slow it down?'

'I can drop a few knots but we're close to stall speed,' said Howell.

Slater toyed with a joystick and the view on the screen swung to the left. He pulled it back so that he could see more of the city and narrowed his eyes as he stared at the screen. 'Check the infrared, Simon,' he said.

Nichols panned the sensor over the scene. He could just make out the figures in the street and hear the engines of the vehicles but the intense heat of the day made it hard to distinguish much.

'Come on, you bastard,' muttered Slater. 'Where are you hiding?'

'Got him,' said Nichols. 'West, about four hundred metres. Two figures on top of a building.'

'A sniper and his spotter,' said Slater. He moved the joystick to the left and increased the magnification, found the two figures and zoomed in. The men filled the screen. One was holding a rifle. 'We have a target confirmed,' he said.

'Let's do it,' said Howell.

Slater hit the laser illuminator button that bathed the two figures with invisible light. 'Target locked,' he said.

'Missile away,' said Howell. He pressed the button that launched one of the Predator's two Hellfire missiles. The Thiokol solid-propellant rocket motor kicked into life and the missile roared away. It had an effective range of almost eight thousand metres but the two men on the roof were much closer than that. Within seconds the five-foot-long missile had reached its maximum speed of Mach 1.3. The laser seeker in its nose locked on to the laser light illuminating the two men and the missile changed direction so that it was heading straight for them. Just behind the sensors and computer in the nose was the missile's payload, an eight-kilogram charge capable of destroying a tank.

Shepherd knelt beside Mitchell, staring in horror at the wound in his friend's skull. It was fatal, no doubt about it. Mitchell's chest was still heaving and his legs were twitching but the movements were reflex. Mitchell was dead, but his body hadn't realised it yet. The bullet had hit him in the right cheekbone and blown out a big chunk of his head. Clumps of bloody brain matter were smeared across the pavement and his left eye dangled from a blood-filled socket.

Shepherd groped for Mitchell's hand and squeezed it. 'I'm sorry, Geordie,' he whispered. The hand trembled, then went still. The legs stopped twitching. The chest rose and fell for the last time. Blood continued to ooze from the head wound but no longer pulsed. The heart had stopped.

'Spider, get to cover!' shouted the Major. He and O'Brien were behind one of the Humvees, while Shortt and two American soldiers had rolled behind the Bradley.

Yokely had stood his ground. He was scanning the surrounding buildings.

'Richard, get the hell down!' shouted the Major.

'Fuck him,' said Yokely. 'He doesn't scare me. Can you see him, Spider?'

Shepherd kept hold of Mitchell's lifeless hand. Snipers usually operated between two hundred and six hundred metres. Any closer and there was too big a chance of being spotted by the target; further, and the shot was too difficult. Mitchell had been standing with his back to the building when he'd been shot, so Shepherd concentrated on an arc away from Mitchell, his eyes darting from side to side. 'Where the hell is he?' he muttered.

'Spider, get the hell over here!' shouted the Major.

Shepherd made out a dark shape on the roof of a building. As he stared he caught a flash of light: the sun glinting off a scope. 'I see him,' he shouted, and pointed. Yokely squinted and raised his M16.

The Sniper's finger tightened on the trigger. There was virtually no wind. He took a breath, let half out, then centred his sights on the face of the man kneeling next to the one he'd shot.

'He sees us,' said the Spotter.

The Sniper ignored him. The American soldiers had M16s and they were too far away to reach him. The turrets of the Bradleys were pointed in the wrong direction and the men operating the machine-guns on the roofs of the Humvees had ducked inside their vehicles. He had plenty of time to make the kill and escape. All the time in the world. He smiled and started to pull the trigger.

He never heard the Hellfire missile because it was flying at thirty per cent faster than the speed of sound. He never felt the heat of the blast or any pain as the impact fuse detonated the eight kilograms of high explosive and blasted him and his spotter into fragments no bigger than a fingernail in a fraction of a second. One moment he was alive, about to squeeze the trigger and whisper, '*Allahu Akbar,*' the next he was dead.

Shepherd flinched at the explosion. Out of the corner of his eye he'd seen the missile streak through the azure sky, leaving behind a thin white trail, but hadn't realised what it was until the top of the building had exploded in a ball of flame. The noise was deafening and his ears were ringing as the thick plume of smoke spiralled up into the sky.

The Major and O'Brien came out from behind the Humvee. 'What the hell was that?' asked Armstrong.

'A Hellfire missile,' said Yokely. 'Courtesy of my guardian angels.'

Shepherd gazed at Geordie. The Sniper was dead. There was no question of that. But so was Geordie Mitchell, and he had been worth a hundred Iraqi snipers.

Three days later

Shepherd checked himself in the hall mirror. Black suit, white shirt, black tie. His funeral outfit. 'You look very smart, Daniel,' said Moira, behind him. 'You should wear a suit more often.'

'The job doesn't always call for it, Moira.'

She adjusted his tie. 'Maybe you should look for a job where a suit is the usual attire.' She took a step back and flicked a speck off his shoulder. 'The last time you wore it . . .'

'I know,' he said quickly. Sue's funeral.

Liam came out of the sitting room. 'Why can't I come?' he asked.

'It's a memorial service, not a party,' said Shepherd. 'And you didn't know him. He was someone I knew at work.'

'How did he die?' asked Liam.

'Liam!' said Moira, shocked. 'That's not a polite question to ask.'

'That's okay, Moira,' said Shepherd, and put a hand on his son's shoulder. 'He was killed in Iraq.'

'What happened?'

'He was shot.'

'It's a terrible place,' said Moira. 'I don't understand why our troops are there. That Mr Blair has a lot to answer for.'

'Was he a soldier, Dad,' asked Liam, 'like you?'

'Yeah. He was in the SAS with me. He helped me when I was shot in Afghanistan.'

'So that's why you're going to his funeral?'

'It's not a funeral, Liam. He was cremated in Iraq. This is a memorial service where we all get together and say goodbye to him.'

'Just be thankful your father isn't a soldier any more,' said Moira. 'He doesn't have to go to terrible places like Iraq.'

Shepherd's mobile rang and he took it out of his jacket pocket.

'I hope that's not work,' said Moira, disapprovingly.

'So do I,' said Shepherd, and looked at the screen. It was Jimmy Sharpe. He took the call and walked into the sitting room.

'Have you seen the news?' asked Sharpe.

'About you threatening the guy who bought my house?'

'What?'

'You know what, Razor. You threatened the guy who bought my house. Threatened to have his company turned over.'

'It wasn't like that,' said Sharpe. 'We just had a chat.'

'Razor, aren't you in enough trouble already? If Charlie finds out, she'll hit the roof.'

'Charlotte Button is going to have a hell of a lot more to worry about than me,' said Sharpe. 'It's on Sky News now but it'll be all over the media within the next few hours.'

'What the hell are you talking about?'

'The Birmingham cops have just shot the wannabe terrorists.'

'You're joking.'

'Yeah, I called you up to make you laugh. The armed cops went in on the back of local intelligence, something about anthrax or a chemical bomb. The guys had the Ingrams we sold them and it all went tits up. Three dead, one's in intensive care.'

'And did they find the bomb?'

'My guys says no they didn't. Just the guns.'

'Shit.'

'Yeah, deep, deep shit. But I guess we're in the clear. It was an Anti-Terrorist Branch case, so it's their fault for not liaising with the local cops. Just thought you'd like to know. Button said you were taking some time off. When are you back in harness?'

'Next week.' A car horn blared outside. 'Razor, I've got to go.' He put his phone away as he went back into the hallway. He pointed at Liam. 'Is your bedroom tidy? It was a pit this morning.'

'I tidied it already.'

'Okay. I'll be back before it gets dark so we can play football.' He smiled at Moira. 'Thanks,' he said, and kissed her cheek.

She looked at him, surprised. 'Thank you for what?' she asked.

'For everything,' he said. He had a sudden urge to hug her, but instead he smiled and left the house. He walked over to the Major's black Range Rover – Armstrong was standing by the front passenger door, finishing a cigarette. He flicked away the butt and climbed into the front. The rear door opened and Shepherd got into the back next to O'Brien and Shortt.

The Major twisted around in the driving seat. 'Everything okay?' he asked.

'Fine,' said Shepherd. 'Anyone else going?'

'John Muller's over with some of his people.' He grinned. 'I gather Carol Bosch has come too.'

O'Brien nudged Shepherd in the ribs.

'A fair few lads from the Regiment have promised to be there, so we should have a good turnout,' said the Major. He put the car in gear and pulled away from the kerb.

'Yokely's not going, then?' said O'Brien.

'He's not big on funerals,' said the Major.

'Neither am I,' said Shepherd.

It was a fifteen-minute drive to St Martin's, the grey stone church where the SAS honoured its dead. As Shepherd climbed out of the Range Rover he saw a woman in a long black coat standing at the gate to the churchyard. It was Charlotte Button.

'She's not after giving you another bollocking, I hope,' muttered the Major.

'She's dressed for a funeral,' said Shepherd.

'Yeah, well, I hope it's not yours,' said the Major.

Shepherd walked over to her. 'I didn't expect to see you here,' he said.

'He was a friend of yours so I thought I'd pay my respects,' she said. She was holding a small black leather Prada bag.

'Thank you,' said Shepherd.

'And I needed a chat,' she said. 'Did you hear the news?'

'Razor phoned me. What's the story?'

'It's a bloody mess. The local cops went in without talking to the Anti-Terrorist Branch. They'd received a tip-off from a well-meaning mullah in one of the local mosques. He'd overheard Asim and Salman talking about anthrax. They went in with armed support and someone grabbed a gun. Details are still a bit sketchy as to who fired first but three of the Asians died and another's only just hanging on.'

'What about the informant?'

'You were right. It was Ali. He's the one in intensive care. The brothers died, and so did Asim. Fazal was in the bathroom when the cops went in and threw himself into the bath. He's okay and singing like the proverbial canary. But it looks as if they were enthusiastic amateurs rather than an al-Qaeda cell.'

'And no anthrax?'

Button shook her head. 'But there were downloads from the Internet about chemical and biological warfare and homemade explosives.'

'Any schoolkid has access to that sort of information, these days,' said Shepherd.

'It shows intent,' said Button.

'They were shot because they had guns, and they had guns because we sold them guns.'

'Well, like I said, it's a bloody mess.'

'Any of that mess heading our way?' asked Shepherd.

'It'll stop at my desk, whatever happens,' said Button. 'I don't think there's anything we have to worry about, though. It was an SO13 operation, through and through.' She sighed. 'Anyway, I've got some good news for you.'

'That'll make a nice change,' said Shepherd. She flashed him an icy look, and he grinned. 'Sorry.'

She wagged a gloved finger at him. 'I've a good mind to cancel your promotion, except that it's out of my hands.'

'Promotion?'

'Detective sergeant, as of today. Nothing to do with me. Sam Hargrove put it through before he left. You were due, I gather. Congratulations.'

'Thanks,' said Shepherd.

'Yeah, well, like I said, it's nothing do with what's happened over the past week. If you ever lie to me again, Spider, we're through. You, more than anyone, know how important it is that we trust each other.'

'It won't happen again,' said Shepherd.

'It had better not,' she said. She straightened her shoulders. 'Right. I suppose I'd better go and say hello to the galloping Major. I just hope he doesn't give me one of his famous bone-crushing handshakes. You men do like to prove yourselves, don't you?'

'It's the hormones,' said Shepherd.

Button smiled. 'Isn't it just,' she said, and went to the black Range Rover, her high heels clicking on the pavement.

At about the same time as Shepherd and his colleagues were standing in the pews in St Martin's Church in Hereford, a Gulfstream jet with an American registration was landing at a military airfield in the north of Ukraine, some eight miles from the nearest population centre.

It was a cold day and flecks of snow were falling when the door opened. A single Russian Jeep, with two soldiers wrapped up in thick green overcoats, was waiting to meet it.

Only two people got off the plane. One was an Arab, blindfolded, shackled and wearing an orange jumpsuit. He moved unsteadily, as if he'd been drugged or badly beaten. His right arm was in a sling. The other man was wearing a brown leather bomber jacket and brown loafers with tassels.